The Tale of the Merchant and the Prince

Neither here nor there, but not so long ago...

There lived a merchant named Loulie al-Nazari who was as legendary as she was elusive. Garbed in midnight-blue robes, she was known as the Midnight Merchant, a magic-peddler who sold enchanted jinn relics in hidden souks. For years, she remained an enigma, evading the notice of the sultan, who would have hanged her for her illegal sales. But even the most slippery thieves are sure to be found should they overtempt fate, and so it was with Loulie as well.

One day, as she was wandering the souk, she came upon a man possessed by a shadow jinn and saved his life. Unbeknownst to her, this man was none other than Prince Mazen bin Malik, the youngest of the sultan's sons. The disguised prince thanked her profusely: "A thousand blessings upon you!" he cried. "Had you not come to investigate, I would have lost my soul to the Sandsea."

But though a fortuitous encounter for the prince, this rescue marked the beginning of a series of unfortunate events for

Loulie, who upon saving Mazen's life was repaid by his father with blackmail. For years, the sultan had been searching for a lamp that contained a jinn so powerful it was said to have the ability to grant any wish. None had ever located this lamp, but Loulie was renowned for her ability to track magic.

The formidable man had Loulie captured and brought to him in his palace, where he offered her an impossible choice: "Will you find the relic and become a hero? Or will you flee like a criminal and perish in the desert, with no one there to mourn you?"

It was no true choice at all, but Loulie was forced to accept. She would go on the sultan's quest with his son Omar, high prince and King of the Forty Thieves, as her escort. But little did she know that Prince Mazen had also been blackmailed. Not by his father, but by Omar, who threatened to tell the sultan of Mazen's forbidden excursions if he did not take his place.

"I have kept your secrets, akhi," the high prince warned. "You owe me this."

Terrified he would be trapped in the palace if his secrets came to light, Mazen agreed to his brother's scheme, using a jinn-enchanted bangle to switch appearances with him.

And so it was that Loulie al-Nazari embarked on her journey with the wrong prince; one of Omar's infamous forty thieves, Aisha; and Loulie's bodyguard, Qadir, a jinn hiding in plain sight. The group traveled far, through hidden ruins where they unearthed a collar belonging to a powerful jinn queen, and across sunlit dunes haunted by ghouls. They passed through thriving cities made vibrant by jinn blood and rested in oases lit by starlight.

It was not an easy journey. On the way, they weathered nightmares both real and immaterial, surviving a sandstorm, a

THE
ASHFIRE
KING

By Chelsea Abdullah

The Sandsea Trilogy

The Stardust Thief

The Ashfire King

THE
ASHFIRE
KING

THE SANDSEA TRILOGY:
BOOK TWO

CHELSEA
ABDULLAH

orbit

orbit-books.co.uk

ORBIT

First published in Great Britain in 2025 by Orbit

1 3 5 7 9 10 8 6 4 2

Copyright © 2025 by Chelsea Abdullah

Map by Tim Paul

The moral right of the author has been asserted.

A CIP catalogue record for this book
is available from the British Library.

HB ISBN 978-0-356-51746-9
C format 978-0-356-51747-6

Printed and bound in Great Britain by Clays Ltd, Elcograf, S.p.A.

Papers used by Orbit are from well-managed forests
and other responsible sources.

Orbit
An imprint of
Little, Brown Book Group
Carmelite House
50 Victoria Embankment
London EC4Y 0DZ

The authorised representative
in the EEA is
Hachette Ireland
8 Castlecourt Centre
Dublin 15, D15 XTP3, Ireland
(email: info@hbgi.ie)

An Hachette UK Company
www.hachette.co.uk

orbit-books.co.uk

For the storytellers.
Never doubt that your words can move hearts.

The Jinn Realm

Eastern Marid City

Khanjem

Ziyad's dhow

al-Malath

Nabila's dhow

Dhahab

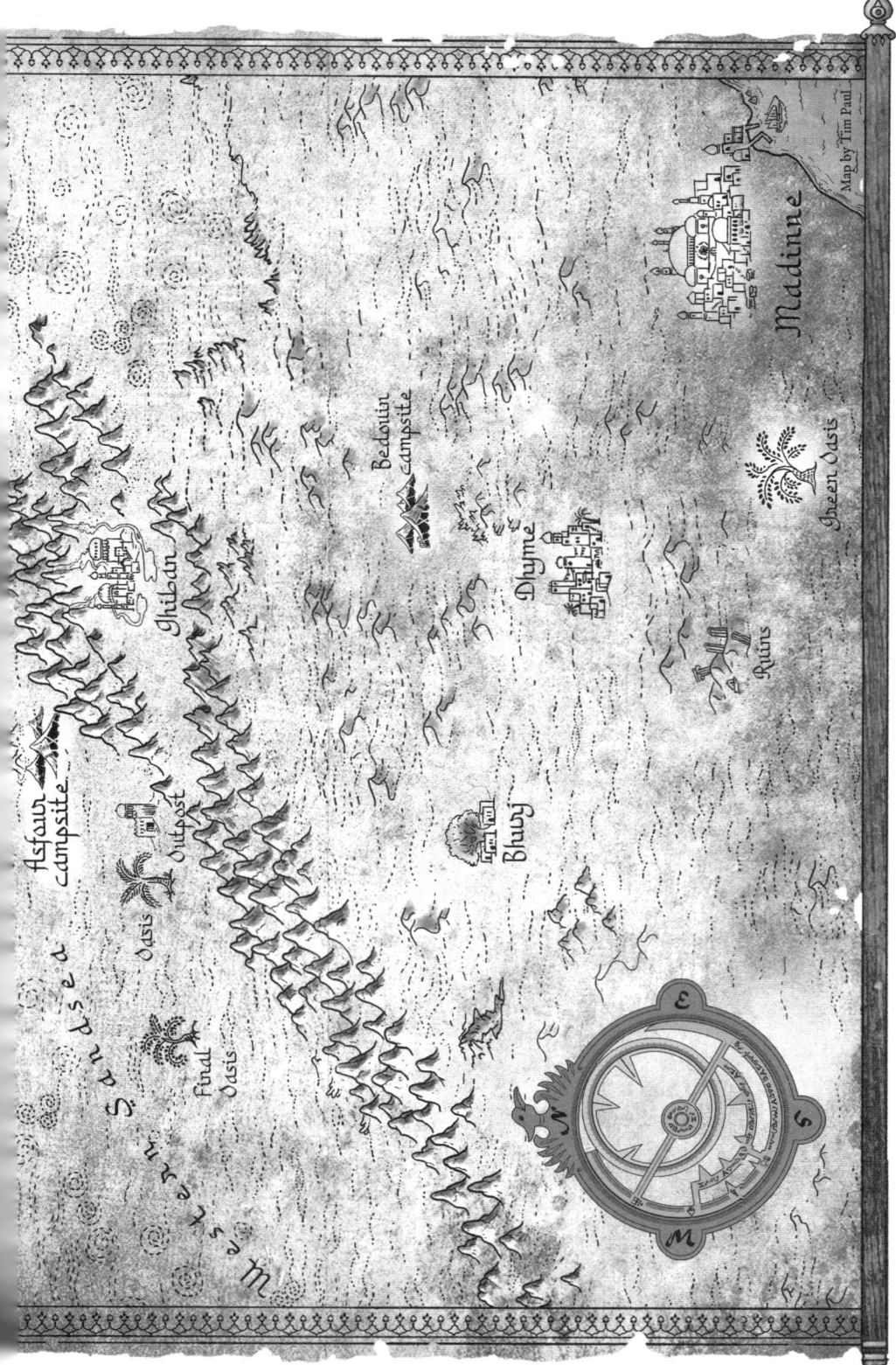

Map by Tim Paul

Madinne

Sheen Oasis

Bedouin campsite

Dhyme

Jhilan

Ruins

Asfaun campsite

Oasis

Outpost

Bluzj

Final Oasis

Westernm Sandsea

horde of ghouls, and the nefarious queen trapped in the collar. They fought the wali of Dhyme, whom she had possessed, and in doing so, they learned the true nature of relics as objects that housed a jinn's departed soul.

The revelation was an omen of things to come, for when they returned to the desert, they rode headfirst into another peril: a trap set by a reclusive villain known as the Hunter in Black. This man was one of the sultan's original forty thieves, Imad. Years ago, on Omar's orders, he had massacred a Bedouin tribe to steal a jinn king's relic, but the thieves had met their demise at the hands of the jinn they were seeking. The only survivors had been Imad, the jinn king... and the young tribesgirl the king had saved, none other than Loulie al-Nazari.

At first, it appeared Imad had succeeded in capturing the group. His iron trap had killed Qadir, and he locked the three humans in a prison at the heart of the Eastern Sand-sea. But Imad had not stolen all their magics. The prince had his shadow, enchanted by the jinn who had possessed him in Madinne, and when he saw it on the wall, he said to himself, *If no one is coming to help me, I have no choice but to save myself.*

And, so saying, he peeled the shadow from the wall and used it to escape his prison. With it, he freed Aisha, and together the two of them tracked Loulie to the hunter's treasure chamber, where she lay debilitated by a severe injury. With the help of their relics, the three of them broke free, using the chaos caused by Imad's rampaging ghouls to cover their escape.

Mazen rushed through the corridors with Loulie in his arms, but their flight was short lived. Turns later, Imad cornered them and killed Aisha, leaving the merchant and the prince to face him alone, helpless and terrified.

But then: a miracle! The ruins around them began to shake and crumble, and Loulie and Mazen realized they were sinking into the Sandsea. The two fell through a chasm until they reached the bottom, where whom did they meet but Qadir, miraculously revived. Injured and unable to hold his physical form, the jinn guided them through the sinking ruins as a smoky apparition. When Imad appeared again to thwart them, Loulie finally took her revenge, plunging her dagger through his heart until nothing remained of him but ash.

Loulie and Mazen barely had time to mourn before another twisted miracle appeared before them: Aisha, alive but transformed by the death magic of the jinn queen in the collar. Beyond all doubts, the group had survived, but they were irrevocably changed. A shroud of distrust hung above them as it became apparent they were all keeping secrets.

It was Qadir who broke the silence first. "Fine," he said. "Let us speak of lies and truths, and of the story hidden between them." And he sat before the fire and began to tell them a story.

He revealed that he was not just a jinn, but one of the seven mighty kings who had sunk the jinn cities beneath the Sandsea. Ifrit, they were called in his country. Years ago, he had lost a compass in the desert, and while tracking it, he had unintentionally led Omar's thieves to Loulie's tribe. This truth was an unexpected and awful epiphany, and it cleaved a divide between the merchant and her bodyguard. They traveled to the final city, Ghiban, in somber silence.

But the greatest healer of wounds is time, and the group's stay in Ghiban mended the rift between them. Mazen told stories in the souk to gather coin for their travels, Loulie searched the cliffs with Qadir for a relic to sell, and Aisha opened the door to a lucrative opportunity: the den of one of the forty thieves, which contained enough relics to sell for a small fortune.

Before they left the city, the group enjoyed a night of merry-making on a ship, where they danced beneath smoke and glowing lanterns. The next, they returned to the desert with hope in their hearts. It was not long, however, before fate tested their bonds again. At the final oasis, Mazen stumbled into his greatest horror yet—a wanted poster of his face, proclaiming him the sultan's murderer. This had been Omar's plan all along: to wear Mazen's face and to blame his father's murder on Mazen in his absence.

Aisha, who had known his scheme, had already fled, leaving Mazen to escape the pursuing mercenaries with Loulie and Qadir. Later, as the broken group sat upon a plateau in the cold desert, the merchant turned to the prince and made him a promise: "We'll make your brother regret this," she said. "I swear it."

With vengeance burning in their hearts, Loulie and Mazen followed the compass and Qadir's magic beneath the sand, where they found the lamp and the King of the Forty Thieves. Omar stole the lamp from Mazen and, using the invocation of his ancestor, commanded the ifrit in the lamp: "Jinn king! You are bound to me and you will *serve* me."

The mighty jinn might have destroyed them then had one last secret not been revealed. Aisha, who had followed her king beneath the Sandsea, had discovered some of her fellow thieves were jinn. Enraged that she had been forced to work with the creatures she despised, she turned on her king, and Loulie and Mazen used the distraction to steal the lamp and free the jinn king, Rijah, from Omar's command. After Rijah had regained their freedom, there was an epic battle between Omar's force and their small group.

But though the merchant and her companions fought valiantly, they were unprepared for the King of the Forty Thieves' illusions. Besides that, they were fighting against a cause they did not understand, for none of them knew what Omar hoped to accomplish in working with jinn and collecting ifrit relics. Still, they managed to steal the relic that gave him his greatest advantage: the crescent earring that had once belonged to his mother, a jinn king named Aliyah.

The prince and the merchant escaped the Sandsea on the back of Rijah, who had transformed into a legendary rukh. Qadir remained on the surface to buy them time, and Aisha—the thief who had betrayed, then saved them—stayed behind to carry out her revenge against the king who had lied to her.

Loulie, Mazen, and Rijah plummeted down a hole so deep it seemed to lead to the center of the world. And then, eventually, they arrived at an end.

Or, perhaps, a beginning.

For now they found themselves in the sunken jinn realm, a legendary place no human had ever set foot in. It was a place of stories and mysteries and danger. An escape. A sanctuary.

Or so they hope.

1

LOULIE

There were two reasons Loulie al-Nazari was in a foul mood.

The first was that she was trapped in a foreign land with a temperamental being made of fire and a starry-eyed storyteller who was recounting their journey in painstaking detail. The second was that they were physically *stuck* between a large rock and an ever-shifting, ever-sinking ocean of sand.

In the distance, on an island in the middle of the Sandsea, lay their destination: the legendary jinn city of Dhahab. Even from here, Loulie could see the domes and towers glowing gold beneath the sunlight. *Beacons of hope*, the temperamental being of fire—Rijah—had called them. But standing at the edge of the sea, Loulie was not hopeful at all.

"I hate this place already," she said.

Rijah, shapeshifter and self-proclaimed mightiest of jinn, glowered at her from beneath the shade of the date tree they were reclining under. "It hates you too."

Mazen, who looked significantly less starry-eyed as he concluded his story, cut an irritated glance at Rijah. "Were you listening to anything I just said?"

Rijah lifted a shoulder in a half shrug. "Why would I when I do not care?"

Loulie sighed as the two of them bickered. She turned her gaze to the sky. Or at least, it was a sky in theory. But it was hard to think of it as such when the clouds had been replaced with swarms of fish and the sun wavered, faint and fractured like light on water. Since their arrival, the expanse had shifted multiple times, one hour filled with marine life, the next speckled with strange birds. According to Rijah, it was a jinn-made illusion, an unreliable fabrication of reality.

Looking at the strange sky, Loulie had the odd impression she was sinking. That feeling only intensified when she looked at the shifting sand around them. On the surface, the Sandsea was rumored to be all that was left of the fallen land where the jinn cities had once stood. But if that was the case, why did the Sandsea also exist here, in this realm *under* the sand?

Earlier, when she had asked Rijah, they had not had an answer for her. The ifrit had been just as unsettled by the sight of the Sandsea and the islands scattered across it.

A pointed cough pulled Loulie from her musings. She looked up to see Mazen standing on the shoreline, gazing out at Dhahab. "We could fly there," he said.

The prince-turned-criminal looked as if he'd trudged through a particularly vicious sandstorm. His wavy hair was wild and unkempt, his tunic and trousers rumpled and torn. But the injury he had sustained during their last battle was healed, and despite the ordeal they had faced, his golden eyes were bright. Though Mazen's title had been stolen from him, he was still the softhearted prince Loulie had been conned into traveling with. He was still Mazen bin Malik, the youngest son of a now-dead sultan.

Rijah scowled. "You mean *I* could fly, and you could ride on my back."

Mazen looked at them uncertainly. "Yes?"

"No," Rijah said flatly.

Loulie bit her tongue. Rijah had been tasked with watching over them, but so far all the ifrit had done was begrudgingly stomp after them and complain about it.

Though it was impossible to measure time in this world, with its odd sky, Loulie suspected they had been traveling a long time, meandering through terrain both rough and tortuous. And now here they were, marooned on a beach with a small cliff behind them and the Sandsea before them. To begin with, the land they'd traversed had been splintered with cracks and scars but whole. It was only here at the edge of the Sandsea that Loulie realized they were on an isle.

Rijah, who had surveyed the area from on high as a bird, claimed the Sandsea had eroded not just the immediate area but the entire landscape. Cities that had once been on the same plain had now become displaced and distant, accessible only over stretches of the Sandsea. According to them, there was no way around it, but Loulie did not believe that.

She planted herself in front of the ifrit. "Don't you *want* to go back to your home?"

Rijah crossed their arms. A dent appeared briefly between their brows but smoothed away just as quickly. Loulie recognized a tell, fleeting as it was.

Mazen seemed to pick up on it as well. "You're nervous to return?"

Loulie balked. She had been so busy worrying about her own safety in this realm that she had not stopped to ponder Rijah's history within it. She had forgotten they'd been named an ifrit because it was a title for the powerful jinn kings who had sunk these cities.

Rijah scowled. "Would *you* be eager to return to the city that has a price on your head?"

"But you're ancient," Mazen said. "Surely no one will remember—"

A sharp, mocking laugh burst from Rijah's lips. "Jinn hold their grudges for centuries. Human resentment is evanescent by comparison."

Looking at the fierce glower on their face, Loulie could not help but wonder if they were referring to their *own* grudge. Before she and Mazen had met them, Rijah had been trapped for hundreds of years beneath the Sandsea in what was rumored to be the most powerful relic in the desert—a small, unremarkable oil lamp. And now Mazen, a descendant of the man who had trapped Rijah and forced them to do his bidding, was carrying that lamp in a satchel at his belt.

Though Mazen had promised never to abuse the lamp's power, Rijah was clearly cynical. Loulie did not imagine the ifrit's demeanor toward them would warm anytime soon.

She returned to searching for a land crossing they could use to traverse the small stretch of Sandsea between them and the city and was surprised when she spotted a silhouette on the shifting sand that had most certainly not been there before. She squinted until the shadow resolved into a shape. Until she realized she was looking at...

"A ship?"

Mazen came to stand beside her. He shielded his eyes with a hand. "It's...a boum?"

It was indeed a boum, moderately sized, with three sails. It was very likely there were jinn on the vessel. The realization made Loulie's stomach knot. How did one conduct themselves in a world where humans were an anomaly?

Mazen made a "hmm" sound under his breath. "You think they're explorers? Travelers?"

Loulie shook her head. "It doesn't matter. Whatever their purpose, they're headed to the city. The better question is how to grab their attention."

There was a thoughtful pause. And then, in unison, they looked at Rijah.

Unsurprisingly, the ifrit was displeased. "Imagine, for a moment, that I draw this ship here. What will you do when the sailors find out you are humans? Will you spin your long-winded tales and pray their curiosity outweighs their animosity?" Rijah scoffed. "And what if they capture you? Will you wave your pathetic dagger at them?"

Impulsively, Loulie pulled her *pathetic* dagger from a hidden pocket in her robe and pointed it at Rijah. "I know how to lie." She angled the knife at Mazen, who cringed. "*He* knows how to lie. What was it you told us when we first came here? That you would not baby us?"

Rijah opened their mouth to level a retort at her but then paused, suddenly captivated by her blade. Loulie knew immediately what they were looking at: the golden qaf on the obsidian hilt, the first letter of Qadir's name.

Qadir. Bodyguard to her, King of Jinn to Rijah.

She tamped down the surge of emotion that swept through her when she thought of her partner in crime. Qadir, who had told them to flee. Qadir, who had stayed behind to cover their escape. Qadir, who had still not caught up with them, despite his promise. Had Rijah been able to take them back through the Sandsea, Loulie would have already returned for him.

The ire vanished from Rijah's expression when they beheld the engraving. "Fine. I will bring the ship here, but you must deal with the consequences." With that cryptic declaration, they faced the vessel, cracked their knuckles—and sighed loudly. The sharp exhalation strengthened into a gust of wind, rippling through the air with enough force to tear at their clothing.

Loulie watched in amazement as the squall arced over the Sandsea. Between one breath and the next, it had overwhelmed the boum and was steering it toward their little island.

Mazen was visibly gaping. "Incredible," he whispered.

Rijah smirked. "This is nothing." They turned toward him, and midmotion their body quivered and blurred. When Loulie blinked, Rijah was no longer standing before them in a human shape but flying above their heads as a bird, a hawk with startling turquoise-blue eyes.

Mazen made a sound of distress as Rijah alighted on his shoulder.

"Let me guess." Loulie crossed her arms. "You don't want to reveal yourself to other jinn?"

When Rijah did not deign to respond, Loulie returned her attention to the ship with a grumble. With the tempest clearing, they had mere moments to catch the sailors' attention before they resumed their course. She straightened, donning her false bravado like a cloak as she wound her scarves around her face. Mazen mimicked the motion, concealing everything but his eyes. She was surprised when he took the initiative to call out to the ship, waving his arms for added effect. He stopped only when it turned toward them.

"I hope this does not end badly," he mumbled as he lowered his hands.

Loulie forced herself to shrug. "Don't think too hard on it. What will be will be."

Mazen glanced at her over his shoulder. There was a spark of recognition in his eyes—a memory, hovering between them, of Qadir sharing that advice before they'd all plunged into the Sandsea to find the lamp. But Loulie had heard it from him countless times before and had parroted it without thinking.

She turned away from Mazen's pitying look. She did not want to remember Qadir. Not now, when thinking of him and the people she had left behind made her feel helpless. Loulie did not know Dahlia's fate, but Ahmed's...

Unbidden, her thoughts returned to the ever-smiling wali of Dhyme: Ahmed bin Walid, the jinn hunter who had always welcomed her to the city with cheer. The man who had asked for her heart and then died in Omar's raid before she could give him an answer.

Loulie swallowed a knot in her throat as she focused again on the ship, which was near enough she could make out a figure standing on the edge. The figure gestured toward a rope ladder hanging off the hull.

"After you," Mazen said softly beside her.

Loulie hesitated for one heartbeat. Two. And then she ran at the ship, leaping over the small gap between the sea and the hull. She began to ascend the ladder, Mazen following less gracefully behind her, with Rijah still perched on his shoulder.

It was a short climb. The first thing Loulie noted when she regained her footing was that the wood beneath her was surprisingly stable. And then she realized—this ship did not bob on the sea so much as slide across it.

Magic?

Her curiosity was quickly snuffed out, replaced with alarm as she took in the man before her. No, not a man. A jinn. For though he was human shaped, his eyes were a solid, edge-to-edge ink black, and his skin glittered oddly with what looked like swaths of scales. The hems of his clothing wavered like smoke, blurring even the golden trinkets pinned to his flowing velvet coat.

Loulie's stomach dropped. Covering her features wouldn't fool anyone; she clearly did not belong here. But the jinn was looking at them expectantly, and she had to say *something*—

Abruptly, Rijah let out an earsplitting cry that made them all cringe. It was a strangely judgmental sound, made worse by the ifrit's bird-eyed glare.

The sailor looked at the hawk, perplexed. "You have . . . a very vocal bird."

Relief crashed through Loulie at the sound of his voice. His accent was more clipped, the syllables more pronounced, but—he spoke her language. She laughed, soft and breathless. "Yes, I apologize for the creature." She ducked into a bow. "You have our deepest gratitude for saving us. Me and my"—she hesitated as she glanced at Mazen—"companion."

Mazen immediately swept in to offer his own gratitude and to enlighten the sailor about their fictional history. It was a simple story, one that painted them as explorers who had lost their way. They'd apparently been searching for a mysterious treasure and consequently found themselves in rigorous territory. This, Mazen claimed, was a most serendipitous rescue.

There was a thoughtful pause after the story. The sailor considered them quietly, his dark eyes unreadable. And then, remarkably, he thanked them for their explanation. Loulie was nonplussed when he asked them only one question: "The area you came from—is it still afloat?"

She scrutinized the sailor's expression, taking in the skepticism of his furrowed brow and the downturn of his lips. She had spent years studying customers—the way their eyes wandered over merchandise, the way they fidgeted when indecisive. Though she never knew what brought them to her stall, the success of her business depended on her being able to read their tells.

She did not know what the sailor was referring to, but she knew the answer he was expecting. So she let sorrow seep into her voice when she said, "I'm afraid not."

The jinn sighed as he gazed past them to the broken land they'd minutes ago been marooned on. "Yet another isle lost to the bindings," he mumbled. "I expected as much, but that does not make it any less a tragedy. Perhaps it is the gods' mercy that brought us together."

Or an ifrit's magic. Loulie cut a glance at Rijah, but the ifrit was staring at the beach they had come from. Loulie wondered if that word—*binding*—had any meaning to them.

"Normally I would ask for payment," the sailor continued. "But I am not so heartless as to demand coin from those in need." He began to lead them across the deck.

It was then, as they were walking, that Loulie noticed the other jinn on the ship. Though they moved with the same ease and grace as human sailors, they, unlike humans, did not sway with the movements of the boum. Rather, *they* were shifting the sand upon which it traveled, manipulating it with hand motions that parted the sediment in waves.

Too late, Loulie realized she was staring, her expression mirroring Mazen's own wide-eyed wonder. She forced herself to turn away, only to notice the sailor in the coat looking at her. "Your story is a mysterious one, ya sayyida. It is unfortunate we have no time for the rest of it." He inclined his chin toward the city wall, lips curled into an amused smile.

The moment Loulie paused to observe the city, all thoughts of their threadbare story vanished from her mind. She was rendered speechless by the sight of the architecture. From a distance, the buildings had been a haze of gold. This close, she could discern the details that had been invisible to her from the shoreline.

She beheld the diaphanous enclosure rising before them: a barrier surrounding the city that at once seemed immaterial as smoke and solid as ice. Though everything behind it was distorted, the architecture looming above the massive walls inside was radiant. Loulie saw alabaster towers sparkling with shards of gold and domes made up of effervescent stained glass. She saw jade-green terraces dripping with ivy and enormous ebony doorways lined with jewels.

The city was stacked as high as it was stretched wide, the layered tiers so cluttered with buildings it seemed a miracle they had not yet collapsed on each other. Rising above the decadent chaos was a palace, a vision so impressive it warped Loulie's senses. The towers were so tall their tops were lost to the clouds, and the golden domes were simultaneously vivid and faded, like a relief that lost its depth when viewed in shadow.

She recognized this place. When they had been searching for the lamp in the Sandsea, they had navigated this city's labyrinthine pathways. It had been a mirage then, an illusion crafted by an ifrit, meant to ensnare them. But this was no illusion.

She glanced at Mazen, who had gone to stand at the bow. He was staring with unabashed marvel at the buildings as they circled the perimeter of the strange wall. Eventually, they came to a gateway made of gold that stood between two deity statues. As far as Loulie could tell, it was the only usable entrance into the city.

No sooner had they arrived than the gate began to open. Loulie swallowed her nerves as the ship pressed forward into the city.

"A word of advice, ya sayyida."

She looked up at the sound of the jinn's voice. Her heart crawled into her throat when she saw the disarmingly mischievous smile on his face.

"Yes?" Panic pulsed in her veins as the city walls closed in around them.

"You may want to prepare a better lie before we dock." He tapped his knuckle and gave her a meaningful look.

Frowning, Loulie glanced down at the back of her hand. She stared as lines, red and dark as her own blood, materialized on her skin and connected to form an oval. And then the shape *opened* to reveal a slit at its center.

Not an oval. Terror dug claws into her mind. *An eye.*

The city gate slammed shut behind them.

2

MAZEN

His whole life, Mazen had assumed he knew his fate. All he'd ever yearned for was a break from that destiny, an escape from the mundanity of court life. He had thought himself unimportant. He was, after all, a third son with no political sway or physical prowess.

How wrong he had been.

In his mind he saw his father lying atop bloody sheets, a black blade jutting from his chest. And he saw Omar standing above him, smirking with Mazen's face. The thought made his heart shudder, his lungs tighten.

With an effort, he pulled himself back into the present, forcing his attention to the city of Dhahab as it unfolded around them. The Sandsea disappeared, replaced with a canal of bright crystal blue water that buoyed a floating deck. Sailors balanced on gangplanks between ships while passengers in elegant clothing strolled across the deck. Mazen saw cloaks embroidered with shifting patterns, shawls that floated without a breeze, and sandals that glittered with gemstones. It was not just the clothing the passengers wore that was extravagant, but the luggage they carried with them—cages containing vibrant-colored birds, carts stacked with living paintings, bags filled with impossibly enormous piles of jewelry...

Mazen did not realize he had drawn close to the edge of the ship until Rijah squawked a warning in his ear. He staggered back and, in doing so, became aware of a smear on his hand.

A bruise?

His breath caught when he held up his hand and saw that it was very much *not* a bruise. At some point, red lines had carved themselves into his skin, forming an oval. Nothing happened when Mazen scratched at the strange shape. There was no injury, no torn skin. Just the mark, which looked as if it had been inked onto his flesh.

And then the oval *blinked* at him.

Mazen swallowed a gasp as he whirled, only to find Loulie already marching toward him. "It seems this city has eyes," she murmured.

She glanced at Rijah, but the ifrit just clicked their beak at her disdainfully. "Do not look at me. I know nothing about this vile magic."

Loulie sighed. "We have another problem on our hands. Our rescuer knows we're lying." She glanced at the sailor who had saved them. Though he was helping one of his fellows steer the ship toward the dock, Mazen had the distinct impression he was watching them.

He frowned. "If he cared, wouldn't he have..." *Tied us up? Taken us prisoner?* He did not want to tempt fate by putting a voice to his confusion.

Loulie merely shook her head in response, eyes flicking between the ship and the port. It was clear she was already focused on their next goal: escape. Mazen followed her gaze to the port filled with passengers and seafarers alike. Those headed into the city had to pass through a gate built into a wall surrounding the area. As far as Mazen could tell, it was unguarded.

Loulie glanced at Rijah. "Can you guide us somewhere safe once we're inside?"

Somewhere safe. They had come here seeking shelter, perhaps answers, if there were any to be found about Omar's plans. But now that they were here, they lacked a destination.

Rijah absently picked at one of their wings. "Perhaps. It has been...a long time since I was here. The city has likely changed in my absence."

Centuries was a longer absence than Mazen could comprehend. Still, while Rijah's words were hardly a reassurance, escaping the ship was better than waiting around to be interrogated.

Mazen steadied himself as the boum came to an abrupt stop, the deck swaying as an anchor was dropped overboard. Sailors began to skirt around them as they secured the vessel. One of them passed Mazen with a grumble, yelling something over his shoulder at their rescuer, who was now securing the gangplank.

Rijah dug their talons into Mazen's shoulder. "What are you waiting for, foolish human? *Move.* Or do you plan on loitering until someone takes you away in chains?"

Mazen swallowed his nerves. Rijah was right. Confidence was key.

It was unfortunate he had so little of it.

He straightened as he strode down the gangplank. Loulie kept pace with him, her steps sure and steady. Relief swept through him when she decisively pushed ahead, leading them off the ship and into the port with enviable poise. Mazen trailed her, hesitating only when he spotted their rescuer speaking with what appeared to be a dockworker. The sailor had *saved* them. The least Mazen could do was thank him—

Loulie grabbed his sleeve and tugged him after her. "Safety takes priority over gratitude."

Rijah grumbled their agreement from Mazen's shoulder. "Yes, and I can assure you that a marid does not *deserve* your appreciation."

Mazen startled at the word. "Marid?"

He recognized the name of the fabled wish-granting tribe that had once inhabited Ghiban, the city of waterfalls. Was the sailor truly one of those beings? Before he could ask, Loulie hissed under her breath, "Stop talking to the bird. You'll draw attention."

She was right, of course. Mazen distracted himself by turning his attention to the crowds. Though some of the passengers could have passed as human, most had features that would have given a human a heart attack. Some had what appeared to be scales running down their arms and necks. Others had eyes that flickered and burned like lit braziers, or skin that glowed and blurred, mirage-like. Instinctively, Mazen drew his scarf closer around his face.

At first, he was overwhelmed by the push and pull of the crowds. His nerves built up to a suffocating pressure, tightening in his chest as the crowd bottlenecked through the gateway. But then he remembered how, back when he'd escaped the palace in Madinne, he'd yearned to lose himself in such chaos, and a familiar calm washed over him. It became easier to follow Loulie after that; all he had to do was keep his eyes on the midnight color of her robes, easily distinguishable in the vibrant crowds.

He followed her through the gate and into an alley, where she stopped to assess their surroundings. It was only then, as Mazen paused to catch his breath, that he noticed the depth of the shadows between the buildings. He looked up and, sure enough, saw that the sky had dimmed since they'd entered the city, the blue expanse darkening to a deep violet. Where the stars would have normally been, there was a strange darkness that felt portentously empty.

"What now?" Loulie said. She too was frowning up at the ominous sky.

Rijah flitted from Mazen's shoulder, shifting in midair to stand before them in their jinn shape: wiry body, sharp cheekbones, aquiline nose, black hair pulled into a tail, the familiar turquoise eyes... and now, the strange tattoo on their hand. Mazen grimaced as he beheld the mark. What did it mean that the ifrit was susceptible to this strange magic as well?

Rijah saw him looking and curled their fingers into a fist. "Now, you let me lead. I have a location in mind." They turned sharply on their heel, promptly guiding Mazen and Loulie from one thoroughfare into another. This area was cramped, an obstacle course with crates and debris littering the ground. The view of the sky was obscured, barely visible above a tangle of crisscrossing clotheslines. A myna bird watched them intently from one of the wires.

A few turns later, they reemerged in a more spacious plaza. Or at least, that was Mazen's initial perception. But if this was a square, it was unlike any he'd ever seen, more closely resembling lived-in ruins than a thriving city. He was surprised to see jinn ducking through half-crumpled archways and wandering between dilapidated buildings. In the center of the square, a circle of children stood clapping and laughing around a run-down well. He startled when one of them surged out from the water with a grin, revealing a mouth of razor-sharp teeth.

"*Focus,*" Loulie said.

When he looked up, he saw that she had already gone on ahead, quickening her pace to catch up with Rijah's increasingly frantic strides. Mazen hurried after her, his unease growing as they chased the ifrit past cramped buildings with splintered doors and smashed roofs.

Rijah's gaze had become unfocused, their attention flicking rapidly across the landscape. Out of the corner of his eye, Mazen saw shadows stretch across the alleys, but every time he looked up, the streets were empty. His disquiet only grew as the buildings collapsed into structures so gutted and hollow it became impossible to make out their original shape.

"I have a bad feeling about this," Loulie mumbled.

Unable to offer reassurances, all Mazen could do was nod in nervous agreement.

The two of them followed Rijah up a sloping dirt path into a clearing. When the ifrit abruptly stopped, Mazen nearly fell right into them. Hesitantly, he stepped back to survey the sight that had given them pause, and inhaled sharply when he beheld the destruction before them.

Like the plaza they'd passed through, this area was filled with ruins. But unlike the plaza, it was devoid of life. The ground here wasn't just barren but *scorched*, the wreckage spotted with odd tar-black smudges. This was not a place that had fallen into decay; it had been decimated.

"*No.*" Rijah's voice caught. They staggered forward, each of their steps slow and weighted. And then, like a puppet with its strings cut, they fell to their knees with a pained keening sound.

A shudder traveled up Mazen's spine. "What is this place?"

"A place burned so deeply it's been scarred." It was Loulie who responded, her voice so soft it was nearly a whisper. Her hand hovered over her neck, where a shackle had once encircled her throat—a relic put on her by Imad, one of the villains who had burned her home to ashes.

Mazen brushed the memory of the hunter and his fiery death aside as he glanced at Rijah. The ifrit was staring up at the ruins with raw anguish on their face. "There was a settlement here before. It should have been safe. It should have..." The words broke into a choked exhale.

Mazen hesitated. He knew how it felt to have the world shatter beneath his feet. Reluctant to intrude on a misery he was clearly not meant to witness, he let his attention stray back to Loulie, who was inspecting the surrounding wreckage. He followed her to a broken pillar, where she stood frowning at an object cupped in her palms.

Mazen recognized her compass. He did not know how its magic worked, only that it could lead her to specific locations and objects. On multiple occasions, it had also guided them out of danger. He glanced at it over her shoulder. "What did you ask it to locate?"

"Sanctuary." She watched the arrow for a few moments before wandering deeper into the ruins. Mazen spared a brief glance at Rijah, then followed her through an archway into a broken enclosure where granite walls jutted from the ground and towered like crooked gravestones. It was in the shadow of those looming ruins that Loulie abruptly paused to pat at her robes. Without explanation, she turned and shoved the compass at him.

Before Mazen could question her, she pulled Qadir's dagger from one of the inner pockets of her robe and raised it to her eyes. "Qadir?" Her voice quavered—with hope? Or was it fear? Mazen did not know what she was looking for, but there was clearly something about the blade that was making her anxious.

He moved toward her cautiously. "Is something wrong with the dagger?"

Loulie was staring into the steel with a concentration that unnerved him. "I don't know. It's...humming?" A dent appeared between her brows. "I think it's reacting to something."

Mazen's fingers curled over the compass. He remembered the last time its magic had hummed through his blood, the way the wood had warmed beneath his touch and the magic had poured through him with such intensity it had fogged his mind. He could see that same cloudiness descending on Loulie now as she searched their surroundings.

Mazen reached out a hand—to gently shake her, anchor her—when he saw movement above them and froze. He craned his neck to see a *creature* descending on them.

He pulled Loulie back so quickly she yelped in surprise and stomped on his foot. Mazen flinched, but the pain was forgotten when he saw the creature they had avoided by mere inches. It was a snake. Or at least, it looked like one. But it was the most bizarre reptile Mazen had ever seen, its body a line of misshapen knots. It reminded him of . . .

A rope?

He and Loulie watched the creature slither away, up one of the ruined walls, to a figure sitting cross-legged at the top. The reptile latched on to the stranger's outstretched arm and hissed at them with an invisible mouth.

They stared at the jinn. The jinn stared back. And then she smiled.

It was a disarmingly innocent smile, very much at odds with the mischief in her slit-pupil, catlike eyes and the knife she twirled in her fingers. Mazen spotted more knives strapped to her arms and a curved scabbard at her hip. The weapons glittered eerily beneath the black cloak she wore—a garment that roiled around her like smoke.

"Salaam." Her tone was light, conversational. "You forgot to declare your goods at the port." The dagger stilled between her fingers. "Also, yourselves."

Mazen had just realized she must have been following them, before she threw the rope-snake at them again. This time, he was too slow to avoid it. Desperate, he stomped on it, but the snake didn't just look like a rope. It *was* a rope, and it did not seem to feel pain beneath his boot. It wrapped itself around his foot, then his ankles, binding them together. The world blurred as Mazen pitched forward. He hit the ground with a wheeze.

In the periphery of his vision, he saw Loulie back away, still clutching Qadir's knife. The cloaked assailant jumped down from the wall and landed with unnatural grace before her. She straightened to her full height—a remarkably intimidating five feet—and lunged at Loulie.

The merchant reacted sluggishly, her knife sailing over their assailant's head without precision. The jinn easily caught her wrist. Loulie retaliated by trying to knee her in the stomach, but her opponent easily circled her and pulled her arm above her head.

Panic beat a frenzied crescendo in Mazen's head, but every time he tried to move, the rope grew tighter around his ankles, cutting off his circulation. As his body quaked with pain, he shaped his whimper into a plea for help.

"Rijah!"

The Shapeshifter must have heard the skirmish, because they were already approaching, the murky anguish in their eyes cut through with blue lightning. "Unhand my companions."

The stranger tilted her head as Loulie struggled. As the jinn's grip tightened, her nails sharpened into claws that punctured the merchant's skin. Loulie threw herself backward with a yell. She managed to catch the jinn off guard, but by the time Loulie staggered away, the damage was already done. A thin stream of red blood trickled down her wrist.

The jinn stared from the crimson tipping her strange claws to Rijah. "Care to explain why your companion's blood is red?"

Rijah looked imperiously down their nose at her. "No."

At first, the jinn looked taken aback. But then, as she stared at Rijah, her surprise mellowed into something like awe. "Your eyes..."

"Captivating, I know. Captivating even on *your* face, I suspect."

Rijah's form wavered as they stepped forward. The effect was not unlike watching ripples distort a reflection on the surface of a lake. Only, after the reflection had settled, Rijah stood before them in a completely different shape. Five feet tall, rotund figure, a sharp face with jagged, stonelike features, and a mane of riotous black curls. Except for their eyes, which remained the telltale turquoise, they were a mirror image of the jinn standing before them.

As the stranger stepped back in surprise, Mazen saw his opening. He reached out, grabbed her ankle, and pulled. It was enough to unbalance her, and Rijah used the opportunity to lean down and burn the rope off his legs. The Shapeshifter hauled him roughly to his feet. "What are you waiting for? Both of you, *go*."

Mazen did not have to be told twice. He tucked the compass into his satchel and spun to grab Loulie. But the merchant was no longer beside him. She had withdrawn to the edge of the fight, putting a broken wall between her and the jinn. When Mazen called to her, she didn't react, just stood there with her knife raised. It was only then he noticed her unnatural stillness.

And then he saw a flicker of light. Blue fire, dancing across the edge of her dagger.

The ground lurched. Mazen's breath snagged when he saw thin lines of flame spiral into existence beneath his feet. The lines flared and spread, shooting inward like the threads of a spiderweb. A spiderweb with *Loulie* at its center.

The force of the mysterious magic threw Mazen off his feet. By the time he'd regained his balance, the fire had risen into walls, forming a maze of smoke and heat.

And Loulie, much to his horror, had vanished into the heart of it.

3

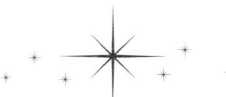

AISHA

Aisha bint Louas was dying.

Or she would have been, had she not already been undead.

I did not know undead things had still-beating hearts, said a soft voice in the recesses of her mind. Though Aisha was loath to admit it, she was grateful for its flippant reassurances. The ifrit sharing her mind was not good company, but she was company all the same, and Aisha preferred her voice to the haunting lament of the dead souls buried beneath the desert sand.

Making a deal with death is not the same as cheating it, Aisha thought as she pressed a hand to her eyelids. The afternoon sun filled her vision with red shadows as she dragged her exhausted body past yet another godsdamned sand dune.

She could feel the smile in the Resurrectionist's words as she responded, *Indeed. But our deal did not bring you back from the dead; it saved you from it. There is a difference.*

Aisha scoffed. Dying might have been easier than this aimless, torturous misadventure.

It had been three days since she'd crawled her way out of a sinking hellhole. Three days since she'd fled from the man she'd sworn revenge against. Every time she closed her eyes, she could see him: Omar bin Malik, smirking at her. She could remember the exact moment the King of the Forty Thieves—now the sultan of this country—had defeated her beneath the Sandsea.

She had not been the only one overwhelmed. The last time she'd seen Qadir, who had remained in the ruins with her, he'd been reduced to a faint, smoky figure with Omar's blade pressed to his neck. While Aisha had been able to use the Resurrectionist's magic to escape, Qadir had not been so lucky. And as for the other people she'd been traveling with . . .

Aisha shook off her concern for the missing prince and merchant to refocus on her current predicament. She had made it out of the underground ruins and onto solid ground, but now she was lost in an unfamiliar part of the desert and her exhaustion was catching up to her, blurring the strange white-colored dunes into pale smudges.

She ignored her thirst and pressed on, concentrating on the weight of her boots in the sand, the whistle of the wind in her ears—and then, horrifyingly, the burn in her legs as her knees buckled. She would have collapsed if not for her blade, which she thrust into the sand to keep herself balanced. When she stumbled, it was the desert, not the ifrit, that mocked her. The whispers of the dead were nonsense, and yet she could discern their tone.

Cold, laughing, mocking.

Aisha was too tired to block them out. She deeply regretted her decision to fight Omar's thieves with magic borrowed from the Resurrectionist. That cursed power had kept her alive, but it had also drained her. Now she felt bereft, reduced to a mere shell of herself.

She did not know how long she stood there, eyes shut against the glaring sun, before she recognized the crunch of hooves in the sand and looked up to see a cloaked stranger riding toward her on a stallion.

The man paused feet away, sliding off his saddle and venturing forward to peer at her through his scarves. "Are you a human?" His eyes narrowed. "Or jinn?"

"Human," she snapped in a voice raspy with disuse. She straightened—or tried to.

When she staggered, the stranger reached for her. Unthinkingly, Aisha grabbed for his hand. It was only after he'd steadied her that she realized her body had gone numb. No, that her limbs had suddenly *tightened*, like they'd been wound through with string.

Aisha's body moved, but she was not the one moving it.

Such a simple thing, the ifrit mused, *to push a human past their breaking point.*

Aisha's stomach sank as she tried and failed to dig her heels into the sand. When they'd made their deal to share a body, Aisha had made the Resurrectionist promise never to make her do anything against her will. She ought to have known better than to trust her.

This is *your will*, the Resurrectionist insisted. *I am merely helping you realize it.*

The stranger, unaware of Aisha's internal struggle, released his hold on her and stepped away. He unwound his scarves to reveal a youthful, bearded face, then assessed her disheveled condition with a flinty expression. "You are traveling alone?"

If only. Moments ago, she'd been grateful for the ifrit's presence. What a fleeting sentiment *that* had been.

Something softened in the stranger's face at her sullen silence. Perhaps she was so pathetic a sight he felt sorry for her. "The gods must have led me to you, then." He gestured skyward with a gloved hand. "Perhaps they were acting through Samira."

Aisha glanced up. A blur of motion caught her eye: a falcon drifting above their heads.

"Samira and I were out hunting," the stranger continued. "When she saw you from a distance, I thought you were a jinn." His bushy brows scrunched. "And yet you—"

The falcon released a shrill cry that made them both freeze. Aisha immediately spotted the movement on the horizon that had disturbed the bird. At first, she did not know what she was looking at. Then she heard the distant whinnying of horses.

Omar? Her heart gave an involuntary lurch at the thought of facing his army again.

She relaxed only when she realized the approaching riders were not the jinn she'd fled from—not Omar's mysterious soldiers. They were simply men, bearing crude weapons.

The hunter turned and, with a muttered prayer, reached across his saddle for a bow and quiver. "Stay here," he said. "Whatever the dispute, I will resolve it." He strapped on his quiver and trudged ahead, calling Samira to his leather glove with a whistle.

A palpable tension hung in the air as the hunter paused before the four riders. One of the strangers—a tall, muscled man whose features were hidden beneath his hood—spurred his horse forward. "You are of the Asfour tribe, no? We have come seeking recompense. Last night, one of your tribesmen hunted on our land without permission and shot two of our livestock. He fled before we could pursue him." He lifted his chin. "Your tribe owes us compensation for the loss."

The Asfour hunter stood with his back to her, but Aisha could hear the disbelief in his voice when he replied, "We know better than to disturb the peace for such a thing. Besides that, I oversaw last night's hunt. We did not travel beyond our lands." He inhaled slowly, calmly. "I will excuse your lies if you leave us in peace, ya sayyid. We do not want any trouble."

Silence.

Aisha shuddered as the rider glanced toward her. A slow smile curved his lips. "Fine. Give us the woman and we will be on our way."

Hmm, the Resurrectionist said as Aisha bristled. *So, they think us a prize?*

The Asfour hunter sputtered as the horseman rode past. When the villain paid no heed to his pleas, he nocked an arrow. A painfully slow moment passed as the hunter hesitated. Aisha was not foolish enough to think he would risk his life to protect her, a stranger.

She tensed as the leering rider approached. As he drew closer, something in his face changed. "You look..." *Familiar* was the unspoken word. Aisha saw the spark of recognition in his narrowed eyes. It dawned on her that she had a reputation—*Omar's* reputation—hanging over her head and that it was possible this man had caught word of her betrayal.

But before the rider could condemn her, an arrow stopped his words. Aisha stared at the shaft protruding from his throat, at the red bubbling from his lips. The man toppled from his horse with a bloody cough. His comrades gaped in shock. The Asfour hunter looked on in horror, as if stunned by his own actions.

And then: chaos.

The second rider charged forward with a scream, blade drawn. The hunter barely managed to dive out of the way in time to avoid being skewered. His falcon took to the sky in the same moment, diving toward the third rider, who was rushing toward his dying companion.

Come. The ifrit's voice was a hum in Aisha's bones. *Let us show them our worth.*

The creature's cursed magic overwhelmed Aisha before she could steel herself against it. It rushed through her body in a heady wave, seeping into her weakened senses until all she could hear—all she could *feel*—was the fading soul of the downed rider. The Resurrectionist's magic shot out like a tether, connecting Aisha's mind to the body. When her resolve wavered, the ifrit was there to fan the flames of her determination against Aisha's will.

Obey me, she—they—commanded.

The third rider was too busy warding off the falcon to see the corpse shift. By the time he'd noticed, it was too late. His gasp pitched into a scream as the dead man lunged.

Bleary-eyed, Aisha searched for the fourth rider. She was too numb to feel anything but relief when she saw him fleeing back toward the dunes. *Coward*, she and the ifrit thought.

And then she did not have the energy to think at all. Aisha felt distinctly as if every second of the corpse's unnatural life shaved off one of her own.

This was how it had been in the ruins when she'd fallen to Omar. She would never forget the sight of him looming above her, eyes twinkling with triumph as she struggled to breathe. At that point all the corpses she'd raised had fallen back into death, and the well of magic inside of her had run dry, leaving behind nothing but a bone-deep fatigue.

I never thought you would fight me with the magic you so despised, Aisha, Omar had said. *And here I thought you were too proud to rely on a jinn's power.*

Back in the present, Aisha's world dissolved into a blur of colors and sound. The battle blinked in and out. She saw the corpse stab his companion. The remaining rider, in his shock, left himself open to attack. By the next blink, the hunter had felled him with a barrage of arrows.

The cursed jinn magic faded to a dull throb in Aisha's limbs. Her eyelids drooped as she sank to her knees. She was vaguely aware of the smell of iron. Blood. *Her* blood, on her lips.

"Ya sayyida?"

She looked up to see the nameless hunter standing above her. When their gazes locked, the concern on his face morphed into open-mouthed horror. Aisha did not have the strength to wonder why before exhaustion dimmed her senses to oblivion.

When Aisha woke, she had control of her body.

The first thing she realized was that she was lying on a bedroll. She surmised, based on the dark cloth walls surrounding her, that she was in a tent. Beside her, sitting on a low table, were a ewer and a small, chipped cup. A platter of dates rested beside it.

"You're finally awake."

Aisha sat up so quickly black spots burst before her eyes. She had to squint through them to make out the middle-aged woman sitting cross-legged on a cushion beside her. The stranger had a stern face and graying hair dyed brown red with henna.

"At ease," she said. "You saved my son, and for that I owe you a debt. You are safe here." Her gaze drifted languidly to the collar at Aisha's throat.

Unthinkingly, Aisha set a hand to it. The band of grimacing skulls was a relic—a vessel containing a jinn's soul and their magic. This one contained the soul of the Resurrectionist. The general populace did not realize relics were living heirlooms; they simply thought them jinn-enchanted tools. Most would not have been able to discern she possessed such an object, but her fight in the desert would have been evidence enough.

Which was why she was unsurprised when the stranger said, "You possess jinn magic." Her voice was soft, though with caution or wonder Aisha could not tell. "There is a story we tell in these dunes. A tale about a jinn queen who can raise the dead. They say she has eyes as black as midnight and that you can see stars in them if you look closely."

She frowned at Aisha. "My son says *your* eyes looked like that after the slaughter."

Aisha flinched but said nothing. She and the stranger stared at each other for a long moment, neither of them blinking.

In the end, it was the woman who turned away first. She filled a cup and proffered it to Aisha with a sigh. "As I said before, you have nothing to fear from me."

Aisha was too desperate to be cautious. She gulped down one cupful of water and then another and another until the ewer was empty. Before her caretaker could rise to collect more, the tent flap opened, and a man entered. Aisha recognized the hunter who had found her.

"You're awake." He stepped forward, and Aisha saw that he'd brought a bucket of water with him. He spoke softly as he set it down in front of her. "I've been wanting to thank you. Your, ah, magic saved my life."

The collar warmed against her throat. *How does it feel to be someone's savior rather than their executioner?*

Aisha ignored the twinge in her chest. "A life for a life. You saved mine first." She frowned. "You haven't told me who you are. Or where I am."

The woman sighed. "You ought to introduce yourself first, Aisha bint Louas."

Aisha's mind went blank. Instinctively, she reached for her blade, but there was nothing for her to wield, because, of course, they had confiscated her weapons. How did they know who she was? Was it the collar? Or were there already rumors? If Omar found out she was here—

"Please, uma. The least we can do is offer names." The hunter smiled. "My name is Jaber Asfour al-Fakhoury. I—"

"Enough, Jaber," his mother snapped. "We are obliged to be hospitable, but the least we deserve from our guest is the truth." She settled her pointed gaze on Aisha. "My son says you helped defeat fiends that twisted the tribal honor code. He says you used magic from afar, magic that brought dead men back to life. When he came to your aid, your eyes were black.

"He brought you back, thinking you were possessed by a jinn. But someone from our tribe recognized you as Aisha bint Louas, one of the forty thieves."

Aisha's heart hammered in her chest. "Who? Who recognized me?"

Jaber and his mother exchanged a look. But before either of them could speak, the tent entrance opened again, revealing another figure. Aisha blinked, but the phantom did not disappear.

The last time she'd seen this man, it had been as she and Mazen departed Madinne on the sultan's orders. She remembered how somber he had looked, his hazel eyes downcast. Like the softhearted prince Aisha had betrayed, he'd been an obstacle standing in Omar's path to the throne.

And yet here he now stood, alive. Hakim, the bastard prince of Madinne.

His splendid robes were gone, replaced with a beige tunic and trousers, but he looked more regal than he ever had before, with his head held high and shoulders squared. The only royal ornaments he still wore were the possession-resisting iron rings the sultan had given him.

"Salaam, bint Louas," he said.

Aisha could not stop herself from staring. "You're alive."

"And so are you." Hakim glanced between Jaber and his mother, a faint smile crinkling his eyes. "Would you mind if I spoke with her alone?"

Umm Jaber's knees cracked as she stood. She slapped Hakim on the back, hard enough to make him stagger, and said, "Jaber will be outside if you need him." With a brisk nod, she grabbed her wide-eyed son by the arm and pulled him out of the tent.

In their absence, Aisha eyed Hakim warily. She had never formally spoken to the second prince before. She knew only that he was a talented mapmaker who drew impossibly accurate maps of a desert he had not traveled for years.

She cleared her still-parched throat. "So, you escaped from the palace."

Hakim settled himself on Umm Jaber's cushion. "Indeed. Thanks to the wali of Dhyme."

Aisha said nothing. She knew Loulie al-Nazari had possessed some affection for Ahmed bin Walid and that Mazen had been jealous of him. But to her, the wali had been just another jinn hunter. An obstacle for Omar and, ultimately, one of the fatalities of his takeover.

"You escaped too." Hakim's brow furrowed. "But Mazen is not with you."

Aisha thought of the smiling, naive prince she'd been journeying with. Omar had tasked her with leading him away from Madinne and then to his demise. She had not cared for Mazen. At least, not at first. But she would never forget the way he'd reached out to her beneath the Sandsea. He was the first person who had ever tried to understand her.

She took solace in the knowledge that he was safer than she was, hidden away in some sunken realm Omar would hopefully not be able to chase him into. When she told Hakim this, his gaze became contemplative. He frowned down at his lap and said nothing.

Aisha narrowed her eyes. "What happened in Madinne? Why did you come *here*?" She needed to know what her once king had done to take the city. The city he was dragging Qadir to. The city she would need to chase him to if she wanted her vengeance.

Hakim regarded her coolly. "Here is home. The Asfour tribe is my mother's family."

Aisha paused to consider this information. It was well known that Hakim had been taken from his mother's tribe at a young age by the sultan. It made sense, she supposed, that his first instinct upon escaping Madinne had been to seek out the people least likely to betray him.

The mapmaker continued: "I propose a story for a story. I will tell you what transpired in Madinne if you tell me what happened to my brother."

"Deal. On one condition." Hakim's eyes flashed with suspicion, but Aisha just waved a hand at him and said, "I am famished and need refreshment. Am I not a guest?"

A shadow passed over Hakim's face, but he conceded, rising to fulfill her request. Aisha leaned back against her bedroll as he left the tent. For the first time in days, she was clearheaded enough to discern a way forward. But before she could craft a plan, she would need to tell Hakim about their journey.

She would start at the beginning, with the merchant and her bodyguard.

4

LOULIE

"You didn't tell me it would burst into fire!" Layla pointed at the dagger accusingly.

Qadir looked up from where he sat cross-legged on the floor of their shared rooms, brows lifted in faint amusement. "I thought it was obvious."

"You told me it would protect me, not that it was enchanted." Her glare flickered between the knife she'd set on the floor—far away from her—and the jinn who had unceremoniously relinquished it to her that morning. He had shown her how to angle the knife into a stab or a slash and told her that if she was ever in danger during one of her deliveries and he was not there to protect her, the knife would do so in his stead.

Today, Layla had used it to threaten a pickpocket. He'd been undeterred by her knife-waving until the blade caught fire, at which point he'd been too stunned by the magic to chase after her. He, unlike Layla, had not witnessed the other enchantments: Qadir's eyes on the blade and his voice pounding through her mind, telling her to run while the man was distracted.

Qadir leaned forward to grab the dagger off the floor. "How do you expect me to assist you from a distance without a weapon?" He sighed at her wary look before beckoning her to join him on the floor. Layla planted herself on a cushion beside him and, when he bade her to do *so, cautiously held out her palm. She flinched when he pressed the hilt between her fingers.*

"It is a simple enchantment," he said. "Think of the dagger as a thread, linking us together."

Layla flipped the dagger in her hand and thought of the way the jinn sometimes watched her through fire. When she asked him if this was similar, he nodded. "In a way. But if the fire is a spyglass, the dagger is a conduit. With it, you may call on me and my magic."

Layla hummed, thoughtful, as she ran her fingers over the golden qaf on the hilt. "Why use this blade as a conduit?" She had only ever seen him use this knife for mundane tasks like breaking a seal or skinning prey. It seemed more a tool than a weapon.

Qadir arched a brow. "Are you skilled enough to wield a shamshir? A kilij?"

Layla blushed at that, wrapped her fingers around the hilt defensively. But she smiled despite herself, recognizing the knife for what it was: a gift. Or, perhaps, a show of trust. Qadir would never admit to either, but she had learned enough of his silent language in the year they'd been together to know his intent. So Layla accepted the dagger with gratitude.

The questions, she buried in the back of her mind with all the others. She had long ago discovered prying was a futile endeavor with Qadir.

—⁂—

Looking back, Loulie wondered if she had given in too easily to Qadir's silences. Perhaps if she had pressed him harder, she might have guilted him into unveiling his history and magics much sooner. Perhaps if she had learned to ask the right questions, she might have avoided her current predicament of being engulfed in an *inferno*.

Loulie did not remember being swallowed by the blaze. The only thing she recalled was Qadir's knife humming with magic as she'd entered the clearing and fought the mysterious jinn assailant. And then she'd stepped away, and the humming had become a sudden burning, a fire that submerged her mind in smoke. She'd heard a familiar voice in that fog calling her name.

LOULIE?

The sound of Qadir's voice in her mind, laced with so much pain and desperation, hit her like a physical blow. When the inferno surged to life in its wake, Loulie barely noticed she'd been consumed by it. One moment she was retreating from the fight. The next, the ground was on *fire*, and she was in a burning labyrinth. But the magic did not harm her, only brushed harmlessly against her arms, like...like Qadir's magic.

"Qadir?" Her voice broke as she held up the dagger, searching for any sign of his presence. She thought she saw something on the surface—a shadow, or perhaps a flicker of movement. But when she peered closer, the blade had grown dull and dark. *Impossibly* dark, as if it was repelling light rather than reflecting it.

Where Qadir's voice would normally have filled her mind, there was instead a sensation. *Pain*, excruciating and sharp, stabbing through her body. Loulie staggered beneath the sudden force of it with a gasp. Her ears rang, her nerves screamed in agony...

And then, suddenly, it stopped. She swayed on the spot, body numb, and realized that the inferno was receding with the pain. It was not her pain, she realized, but Qadir's. She glanced blearily at the blade. The dullness remained, but there, in the faint reflection—

"*Qadir.*" His name was a whisper on her lips. "Where are you? What's happening?"

His phantom eyes, round with panic, locked onto hers. For a moment, a heartbeat.

And then the humming, the burning, the eyes—it all vanished, leaving Loulie feeling bereft and empty. Only the echo of pain remained, pulsing from the dagger like a heartbeat. Loulie couldn't make sense of it. Qadir had only ever spoken to her through the blade; she had never *felt* him through it. What did the shock wave of discomfort mean? Had she caused it? Was he in danger?

The world rematerialized in blurry fragments. As her vision cleared, Loulie saw that the fire that had moments ago encircled her was gone. The landscape of scorched ruins once again stretched before her, the ground glowing dimly where the flames had been.

Mazen and Rijah stood on the other side of the clearing, staring at her in shock.

They weren't the only ones. While Loulie had been trapped behind the fire, a small group of jinn had amassed. One glance at their crimson uniforms and blades made it clear they were soldiers. Before she could speak, the dagger was snatched from her grasp. She felt the burn of rope against her wrists as she was pulled back from the outskirts of the flaming threads.

"You survived ifrit magic." The voice came from directly behind her, laced with suspicion. It sounded like the jinn who had attacked them.

Loulie startled at the accusation but quickly smothered her surprise. "Ifrit? I've never heard that word before." She spoke the lie with as much conviction as she could muster.

Her eyes darted to the glowing marks on the ground. Loulie recognized them as the labyrinth she had minutes ago been trapped in, only the walls had vanished, the maze flattening into a complicated pattern that was dimming beneath her feet. She was reminded, bizarrely, of the tattoos on Qadir's arms.

The thought fled from her mind as she was forcibly turned toward her captor. Though the jinn was shorter than she was, the fire in her narrowed eyes was a living thing, and even Loulie balked at the heat in her glare. Belatedly, it occurred to her that she had further condemned herself. *Ifrit* was a foreign word on the surface, but not here.

"So you *are* a human," the jinn said.

Loulie's dread sat heavy as a stone in her chest. She forced herself to breathe—slowly, calmly. With secrecy no longer a strategy, she had to pivot. She could do that; she'd done so many times before. As a human, she could rely on ignorance as a shield.

"I am." Despite the feigned nonchalance of her tone, her voice cracked beneath the pressure of the jinn's gaze. "Is this how you greet visitors in your city?"

"It is when we find them skulking through ruins and interfering with forbidden magic." She lifted the dagger. There was no fire, no spark, nothing. But when she set the point of the knife between

Loulie's collarbones, its silence did not matter, not when the edge was still deadly.

"Did Nabila send you?" The question was sharp as the knife she pressed into her skin. "Did she give you this blade? Speak, and perhaps Her Majesty will be merciful."

Loulie swallowed. "I have no idea who that is. No one sent me here."

"Then how did you make it into the city? And the binding—how did *you*, a human, ignite and survive its magic? Not even jinn can withstand that fire."

Loulie's mind whirred but offered no excuses. She had no idea who Nabila was. The captain of their ship had mentioned bindings, but she knew nothing about them either. And how could she possibly answer the jinn's first question without explaining that she was here because of two ifrit this city might resent for sinking their lands?

"Hayat!" one of the soldiers yelled in warning. Loulie's captor— Hayat—looked up at the call to see Rijah charging toward her, blue eyes blazing on their borrowed face. They paid no mind to the four soldiers pointing their weapons at them.

"That human is my charge," Rijah snapped. "You will release her."

Hayat sneered. "Shapeshifter. You *dare* command me in my own body?"

One look at the defiance on Rijah's face and Loulie had a sudden premonition of what they would share about their identity. She stepped away from the knife, drawing Hayat's attention. "They are a refugee. We all are." It was true she knew little about this city and its magics, but even if she could not yet buy herself answers, she could buy herself time.

The trick is to fake it until you make yourself believe it, Qadir had always said. So she would keep bluffing until she could take charge of the situation.

She was grateful when Mazen added, "We have a story to tell, but it would be easier to tell it once, to whomever it is you serve."

There was a brief silence as Hayat considered them. Then, with a gesture, she ordered a soldier to pat them down. Loulie's heart fell when they took Mazen's satchel—along with the compass and the lamp inside of it. She herself was left with nothing but the crescent earring and the two-faced coin, which remained unnoticed in the hidden pockets of her robe.

After, Hayat turned to Rijah. "What about you, shapeshifter? Will you come quietly?"

Loulie stared hard at the ifrit. *Play along*, she thought fiercely. The sanctuary the ifrit had been guiding them toward was destroyed, which meant there was little point in fleeing. They had nowhere to run, nowhere to hide.

To her immense relief, Rijah did not resist. With a sigh, they held out their wrists, surrendering to the enchanted ropes. The only sign of their discomfort was the shudder that traveled through their shoulders as their body rippled back into its previous shape.

While one soldier ran ahead to deliver the satchel, the rest gathered around them in a phalanx to usher them deeper into the city. Though Loulie was accustomed to winding streets and hidden alleys, it was more difficult than usual for her to map their route. Now that the immediate danger had passed, her mind returned to the dagger and the magic it reacted to. A binding, the soldier had called it. Had Qadir's pain been in response to that magic? At a loss, she turned to Mazen, who was already watching her with concern.

"I'm glad you're unharmed," he whispered.

"So it seems," she muttered back. "What happened back there?"

He blinked at her. "I was hoping you would tell me. You were staring at your knife, and then the blaze appeared and...and you were inside of it. Did you call it forth?"

Mazen frowned when she shrugged. He stopped talking when he noticed the soldiers around them eavesdropping.

Eventually, they came to a deserted square surrounded by stone buildings and canopied stalls and wagons. Lanterns swayed between the structures, filled with an eerie blue-white glow that illuminated the darkening city in rich shades of indigo. But more ominous than the fire was the sky. If it had reminded Loulie of the surface of the ocean earlier, it now resembled what she thought the depths might look like: deep and dark and endless—a shimmering, watery void.

Mazen put a voice to her question first. "What's happened to the sky?"

In answer, Hayat raised her hand and pointed to a mark on her skin. Loulie startled at the sight of the familiar eye tattoo, though she noticed its shape had changed slightly, the eye narrowed to a slit. A quick glance at her own hand revealed the tattoo had altered there as well.

"Curfew is nearly upon us," Hayat explained. She said nothing else, leaving them to wonder about the connection between the tattoo and the quickly darkening sky.

Loulie's attention drifted uneasily back to the soldiers. Stone-faced as they were, they appeared more tense in the open space. She could not help but notice the way they avoided the shadows, gravitating toward the lanterns as if they were guideposts. Once, when the firelight flickered so intensely Loulie thought it was in danger of burning out, a soldier froze in place and murmured something about unstable magic. The comment had an odd effect on Rijah, whose gaze lingered on the fire long after they had continued.

The streets were conspicuously empty as they traveled north. The few loiterers Loulie saw were rushing through the alleys, their attention torn between the sky and their eye tattoos.

She smothered her apprehension to focus on the architecture, which had become increasingly extravagant. Rather than ruins, she saw manors—beautiful edifices constructed from gold and marble and, in one peculiar case, a sparkling, multifaceted glass. Each had multiple floors and balconies, along with a gated courtyard. She was reminded of the lavish mansions in Madinne's noble quarter, though even those buildings seemed colorless by comparison.

Eventually, they came to a solid-gold bridge that led to the palace grounds. Though the bridge was a marvel, the palace was even more so. Up close, its golden towers and domes were more imposing, glowing so vividly in the dark they seared Loulie's eyes.

By the time they arrived at the entrance, Loulie was unprepared for the dimness of the interior. The same blue firelight she'd seen outside illuminated corridors patterned with geometric stars. Turquoise gems studded the center of the stars, their surfaces green and murky with age, and dust caked the crevices between the gold tiles on the floor.

As they navigated the eerily empty corridors, the soldiers around them began to peel off, taking up sentry positions by the walls as Hayat ushered them onward. Loulie was mystified. Though it was impossible to discern a jinn's age with certainty, she had gotten the impression Hayat was younger than these soldiers, perhaps even closer in age to her and Mazen. Who was she, to command the others so easily?

Hayat led them through a maze of corridors to a spiral staircase, where they ascended to a landing marked by a pair of grandiose doors. Intricate engravings stretched across the wood, portraying the city as it must have existed in the past: whole, unbroken, and vibrant. More remarkably, the depiction *moved* as Loulie peered at it, the figures roaming the streets so lifelike she could believe they were a memory. Loulie was still staring when the doors opened from the inside, revealing two lines of guards on either side of a long corridor.

Hayat turned to face them. "Her Majesty suffers no insolence from her guests. Remember to show her the utmost respect and speak only when granted permission."

Inside, Loulie was immediately taken aback by how cold and cavernous the space was, unadorned except for the sconces and weapons on the walls. There must have been hundreds of them: knives, bows, spears, maces, and other deadly tools she had never seen before. Most were made from bronze and steel, but even the more unconventional armaments looked deadly. Loulie shuddered as she passed a razor-sharp spear that shimmered like sea glass.

She wondered, *Is this an audience hall or a torture chamber?*

Mazen was studying the weapons with a similar nervousness. When he caught her eye, he attempted a smile. Strained as the look was, it settled Loulie's nerves. If Mazen could smile in the face of such adversity, then she could muster her own mettle.

They walked the hall for what felt like an immeasurable time before the darkness peeled away, illuminated by the same lantern light as the corridors. The halo of light revealed an alcove containing a throne made of solid gold. Two large braziers, inexplicably filled with water, framed the seat on either side. A figure sat between them, garbed in deep blue and wearing knives at her waist and a circlet atop her thick, inky hair. Loulie found herself spellbound by her eyes, which had rings of bright, glowing silver around the pupils.

Behind the ruler, barely perceptible in the shadows of the alcove, stood another jinn. A third figure knelt before the throne, back turned to them. "That is the end of my report, Your Majesty." His voice was strikingly familiar. "In summary, the zaeem of Kharjem refuses to fall into line until we can assure him of the stability of his lands."

The queen clicked sharpened nails against the arm of her throne. "He knows I cannot guarantee such a thing when the bindings are unstable." Her lips curled in a sneer. "A miracle or a war—quite an ultimatum."

"With all due respect, Your Majesty, nothing short of a miracle would appease him. I am sure he will proclaim as much upon his arrival. The sinking sands took his last home. If the zaeem's kin had not been rescued by Nabila, then—"

"Do not speak that foul pirate's *name*."

As the jinn ducked his head in apology, the queen at last looked up to acknowledge them. "Ah, so the stowaways finally arrive." She leaned into her throne, rested a cheek against her fist. With her other hand, she twirled a knife—*Qadir's* knife. When she noticed Loulie staring, her colorless lips stretched into a smile that did not touch her eerie eyes.

"I hear you have a story for me. Let us pray it is a good one."

5

MAZEN

Once, when Mazen had been a child, he'd asked his mother if the stories she told were truth or fiction. Many years later, he still remembered her answer.

Every story is a memory, she had once said. *A tale that happened neither here nor there, but in another time and place. Our job as story-tellers is to describe that reality as we understand it. It is the listener who must determine what is and is not.* He remembered the way her voice had fallen to a whisper as she spoke, as if she were sharing some precious secret with him. *Remember, Mazen, there is no such thing as a single truth. There are just the stories we tell others, and the ones we tell ourselves.*

Mazen knew how powerful stories were. It had been stories that had swayed the sultan's heart after the wife killings and, only recently, stories that had painted Mazen as the murderer who had stolen his father's life. But down here, Mazen was not yet shackled to that lie.

Down here, the narrative was still his to control.

Remembering Hayat's words, Mazen lowered himself to his knees and pressed his forehead to the floor. "I cannot promise it will be a good story, but it *will* be the truth."

He kept his head lowered until the queen bade him to rise. Back on his feet, he noted the other jinn in the hall. His eyes fell first on the figure behind the throne. *Wraith* was the first word that came to mind when Mazen looked at him—at his form, which was blurry and indeterminate, and his clothing, which was smoky and floating around him. The willow-thin jinn was wrapped in so many layers his body was all but lost beneath them. But his eyes were a different story; they were arresting pinpricks of bright red fire, boring into Mazen with such a hateful intensity it made him shudder.

He quickly averted his eyes to the second guest—and startled. Mazen recognized him by his coat first: a rich, long-sleeved velvet garment trimmed in gold. And then he noticed his eyes, pitch black and bright with mischief. He was, unmistakably, the sailor who had brought them to Dhahab. A *marid*, Rijah had called him, though Mazen did not know what that meant here.

The sailor winked when Mazen caught his gaze, lips parting to reveal unnervingly sharp teeth. "I thought you would end up here sooner rather than later."

The jinn with the smoky visage scowled. "*These* are the passengers you brought into the city? And you let them walk free even after realizing they were human?"

The captain's grin never faltered. "I was curious to see how far they would get. As you can see, Hayat brought them here before curfew-fall, so no harm was done."

The queen waved a dismissive hand. "If Ziyad had not let them walk into Dhahab, we may never have learned they possessed ifrit magic." She angled her gaze toward him. "We will finish our discussion later, Ziyad. For now, I would speak with the stowaways myself."

Ziyad acknowledged her dismissal with a graceful flourish. The fanged smile remained on his face as he exited, leaving Mazen to wonder about the conversation they had interrupted.

The queen tapped the dagger against one of the arms of her throne, drawing Mazen's attention back to her. "Tell me: How is it humans possess a key to the bindings?"

Bindings. There was that word again. Mazen glanced at Rijah, but the ifrit remained stubbornly standing a distance away, lips sealed.

The jinn behind the throne spoke: "Clearly, they are working with Nabila. How else would they come upon such powerful magics?"

Hayat cleared her throat. "Esteemed wazir, they claim they are unfamiliar with the ifrit."

"And you would take their word for it? All humans do is *lie*—"

The queen hissed through her teeth. "Let him speak, Firas." Silence cleaved the conversation like a blade, stopping Mazen's breath. He swallowed when the queen looked at him. "Well? You said you would tell me the truth. So speak. Who are you, and what are you doing in my city?"

Mazen felt the attention of the entire room fall on him. He forced himself to stand tall, gathering the loose threads of his make-shift story until they were a tapestry in his mind. Then he imagined himself reworking the embroidery at its seams, tearing out threads and replacing them with a pattern that was similar—but different—to their reality.

Slowly, he began to weave a fiction from the truth.

"It is as you say. We are stowaways in a world that is not our own." He felt the reality of those words settle on his shoulders, and let himself sag beneath the weight of them. "I am but a wanderer, a storyteller who shares stories in souks. I am known as Yousef."

The name stirred his heart and loosened his tongue. He didn't dare look at Loulie or Rijah when their surprise might unravel his lie. *No*, he reminded himself. *Not a lie. Just a different version of the truth.* He had been Yousef before—he could be Yousef again. He *wanted* to be Yousef here, in this world where he could escape the reality of his shattered life.

"Some would say my occupation is a simple one, but those people do not understand the power of stories. I have been sought out by sheikhs to provide counsel." He let out a grievous sigh. "But alas, my reputation is what landed me in this unfortunate predicament, for it was the reason I was called upon by the most powerful man in the country—the sultan's eldest son."

In his mind, he saw his brother. Omar, who had been the one to send him on this perilous journey. Omar, who had worn Mazen's face when he plunged a blade into the sultan's heart.

Mazen's vision darkened at the edges. He was vaguely aware of his increasingly erratic heartbeat. Of his breathing, which was beginning to come in fast, uneven gasps. He knew the jinn were still watching him, waiting. But he could no longer find the words to continue. His mind was empty of everything but those vicious visions. What must his father have thought seeing Mazen standing above him with a knife? Had he feared him? Hated him?

Mazen would never know. His father was dead now, and he had perished thinking Mazen was his murderer.

He could see Firas speaking pointed words at the queen, but when Mazen tried to focus, their conversation fell to pieces in his mind. The words were nothing but too-loud sounds, pressing in on him like dark walls. Mazen breathed in, in, in—

And then he felt a hand, firm but gentle, on his arm. "Forgive my companion. He is sometimes swept away by the very emotion he hopes to inspire in his audience." He recognized Loulie's voice, a whisper beneath his thudding heart. "It is that empathy, I think, that makes him such a compelling storyteller."

The words were so unexpected they startled Mazen from his stupor. The shaking in his hands subsided as Loulie spoke, tugging the story thread loose from his fingers. "Yousef and I have worked together for many years, trading rumors for wares. He told me in advance he was returning to the city. It was how I knew something had gone amiss." Her eyes cut back to him, and she gave him a brief nod as if to say, *Go on.*

A merchant. A storyteller. All that was missing...

"The prince sought me out for the rumors I had gathered. Without my consent, I became embroiled in his uprising." He swallowed around a lump in his throat. "I fled to safety, chased by my client's men. Had it not been for..." His voice faded as he looked at Loulie, uncertain.

A memory surfaced. In it, he was crouched beside Loulie in the sultan's courtyard, trying to piece together the two parts of her—the woman he'd met in the souk and the merchant he had only ever known as legend. He remembered asking her, *What should I call you?*

And her wry response: *Loulie. Layla is another identity for another time.*

What was this if not another, more desperate time?

"Layla—" he said, and the merchant cringed only slightly at the name. "I would never have escaped. She is a merchant and aware of escape routes that I am not." He glanced at Rijah. "And we both would have perished if not for our acquaintance, who was unjustly imprisoned by the prince. They lent us these magics to aid our escape, and now here we are."

It was a frayed story. A shallow, redecorated truth. He could only hope it was enough, that the jinn ruler despised embellishment as much as his own father had.

"I know the history between us is a complicated one," he pressed. "But I appeal to you not as a human but as a refugee. We are fleeing for our lives, and we descended into your realm by accident. We know nothing about your bindings or the ifrit you speak of."

A heavy silence hung in the air after he had spoken. The queen and her wazir exchanged a glance, her expression carefully guarded, while Firas's remained distrustful. It was Hayat who spoke first, eyeing them with suspicion all the while. "If you came here seeking sanctuary, why did I find you sneaking through the city like criminals?"

Firas scowled. "It is a fantastical tale, to be sure. Tell us, ya sayyid: How did humans such as yourself survive the Sandsea to make it into our city?"

Mazen thought of the illusory city beneath the Sandsea and of Qadir burning a hole through the sand. But before he could think of a way to explain, the queen spoke over him: "There is no need to pretend at ignorance, Firas. You said it yourself; the only way the humans could make it here is with ifrit magic." Her gaze slid to Rijah. "Is that not right, Shapeshifter?"

Mazen's heart froze in his chest. When he dared a glance over his shoulder, he saw that Rijah had gone abruptly still. But they did not refute the claim, only glared determinedly at the queen. "On what grounds do you make this assumption?"

The queen wordlessly held out a hand to Firas, who reached into the pockets of his smoky attire to withdraw an object. Mazen knew what it was even before he saw the glimmer of copper. Even so, his breath stopped when Firas relinquished the lamp to her.

"When the messenger brought your magics, I knew this one was different. I did not know how at first. And then..." She rubbed at the copper body. At first, nothing happened. There was no thrum of power, no outpour of magic like when he and Omar had used the lamp.

But then something *did* happen. The lamp glowed with a dull light as a series of marks flashed across the surface. Mazen was astonished; the patterns reminded him of the markings they had seen in the ruins, but he had certainly never spotted them on the lamp before.

"Well, Shapeshifter? Look familiar?" The queen's eyes narrowed, cutting the halos of silver around her pupils into crescents. "Roll up your sleeves."

The ifrit dithered only briefly. One look at the encroaching soldiers and they folded, pulling up a sleeve and baring the underside of their arm. Instead of veins, scorching red marks ran up their skin. Even from a distance, Mazen recognized the same symbols burning on the lamp. As they dimmed on the object, so too did they fade on Rijah's skin. Recognition flitted across Loulie's face, but whatever the realization was, she kept it to herself.

"I knew it." The queen set the lamp on her lap. "You did not just enchant this object; you cast a binding on it. Only an ifrit would have the power to bind a still-living soul to an object."

A beat of silence. And then Rijah said, "Everything I did, I did to save this city."

"So says every revolutionary who leaves behind a legacy of destruction."

A sharp exhale tore from Rijah's lungs as they snapped, "*I* did not decimate this city beyond recognition. *I* was not the one to raze it to the ground."

Mazen thought of the barren square Rijah had led them to. He remembered the distress on their face as they'd beheld the devastated landscape. How long ago had that destruction been wrought? How old were the scars maiming this city?

"You ifrit left these lands to decay beneath the sands," the queen said. "And in the ensuing pandemonium, *I* fought to restore the peace." She rubbed at the lamp until the invisible symbols flared back to life. "But tell me, *Rijah*, mighty Shapeshifter." The name was a barb on her tongue. "Why did you bind your soul to this relic when you are still alive? Surely you, an all-powerful ifrit, know what would happen to you if the lamp was destroyed?"

Mazen stared at the lamp. It was only recently he had learned relics were vessels for their owners' souls. Rijah had divulged little about the lamp and its connection to Mazen's family, but looking at the markings on it now, he could not help but wonder, What *was* this magic that bound Rijah to the lamp?

Rijah did not answer. The queen was unfazed by their defiance. "Fine. If you will not tell me about your magic, then I will extract the answers myself."

When she set her hands once more on the lamp, the markings flashed bright and hot beneath her fingers, blazing like fire. There was a ripple in the air, a beat of pressure, and then Rijah collapsed with a gasp. Mazen's body reacted before his mind did. He ran toward the ifrit.

The moment his fingers brushed Rijah's skin, a scorching heat shot through his hand. He pulled it away with a yelp, horrified to see that his palm had been burned red. When he looked at Rijah, he realized that was exactly what was happening: the ifrit was *burning*, their skin flaking away to reveal a shadowed, smoldering figure with blazing turquoise eyes.

Mazen hovered helplessly as Loulie rushed to Rijah's other side. She knelt beside the ifrit, then whirled on the queen. "What are you doing to them?"

The queen's fingers tightened on the lamp, which glowed in her hands. "It was the ifrit's bindings that doomed these lands; so too shall it be the magic that dooms *them*."

Disparate pieces of a puzzle snapped together in Mazen's mind. He remembered the talk with Ziyad on the ship and the conversation they had just overheard in the throne room. The ifrit had been the ones to sink the world, but it seemed their magic—these bindings the ruler kept mentioning—had resulted in unintended consequences.

"Your lands are sinking," Mazen said quietly. When the queen looked at him, her expression grim, he knew he was correct.

Firas's eyes burned with wrath as he emerged from the darkness of the alcove. "You witnessed it yourself when you traveled the sinking sands. This is the truth of our world. Do you regret your *accidental* descent into it now?"

Mazen glanced urgently back at Rijah. Ash beaded the ifrit's crackling skin, and their breathing had grown labored, each exhale a rattle. Mazen could barely make out the blue of their slitted eyes, which were narrowed in agony.

No one should have been able to command Rijah through the lamp except for Mazen's family, but as far as he could tell, the queen was not directing Rijah so much as using the relic to injure them. Perhaps this was what it meant for a still-living jinn to be bound to an object.

"Behold." The queen spoke to the soldiers watching the spectacle with open-mouthed awe. "*This* is how you subdue an ifrit. With their own warped, unnatural magic."

Mazen could do nothing but watch helplessly. The only magic he still possessed was his shadow, and this was not a situation he could run nor hide from. Short of that, all he had was his frayed story, but the queen did not want a story. She wanted magic. A *solution* to her problems.

He surged to his feet. "Your Majesty. You saw the influence Layla had over the binding. Tell us how we can help, and we shall do so with Rijah's guidance."

Firas glanced at the queen. "Who needs them when we have a key to the binding?"

Hayat shook her head. "The dagger was cold in my hands, sayyidi. It seemed only the human could use it. Unless..." She faltered. "Has the weapon spoken to you, Your Majesty?"

Spoken? Mazen turned to face the queen, who had stiffened in her throne. Though her nails still pressed into the lamp, her hands were shaking. For the first time since they'd entered, Mazen remembered the weapons on the wall, the deadly tools that were now quivering like the queen's hands, looking, for all the world, like an enraptured audience.

Watching them rattle on the walls, Mazen had the peculiar impression they were *alive*.

It was only when the queen released her trembling hold on the lamp that they stilled, the room quieting as the fire coating the lamp vanished. Rijah gasped into the silence, drawing in ragged gulps of air. Hesitantly, Loulie reached out to set a hand on their back. Mazen was relieved when the ifrit's ashy skin did not burn her.

The queen handed the lamp back to Firas, who took it from her, looking baffled.

"No," she admitted.

The wazir gaped at the admission, then glared at Mazen as if it was *his* fault. Everyone else stared in shock as the queen continued, "The dagger keeps its secrets close. If what you say is true and only the human can use it to access the binding, then I must reassess my strategy. For now, the ifrit remains alive. But now you know, Shapeshifter, what happens if you defy me."

With Loulie's prodding, Rijah gave a nearly imperceptible nod.

The queen turned to Mazen. "Tell me, Yousef. What do you know of our sunken cities?"

Mazen hesitated. "I know nothing about them beyond the human stories."

"And what do your stories say?"

"They tell of faceless kings who doomed the world with dangerous magic, and of the ocean of sinking sand that was created in the wake of their destruction."

Firas scowled. "Tattered stories born from human ignorance."

The queen held up a hand for silence, waiting until Firas had stopped seething before she said, "The faceless kings of which you speak are indeed criminals." She turned a pointed frown on Rijah. "We call them ifrit. They are jinn who have overstepped the boundaries of their gods-given power. As for the dangerous magic in your stories..." A dry smile touched her lips. "It is no simple chaos. We refer to them as bindings, seals that trap our lands beneath the Sandsea. They are volatile; if tampered with, they can destroy that which they sustain."

Loulie glanced at the queen warily. "And the reason your bindings are failing now?"

One name had cropped up many times since their arrival. "Nabila?" Mazen ventured. Too late, he remembered the way the queen had reacted when the captain spoke the name aloud.

But she did not reprimand him. "Yes. She alone knows where these bindings are, and so we have been unable to stop her from meddling with them. If you are so eager to prove your worth, you and the Shapeshifter will help us find and repair them. But..." Her eyes darkened. "If you are lying to me and are allied with Nabila, I will make you suffer a torture so terrible you will beg for the release of death. Do you understand?"

Mazen looked at Rijah, who was still heaving in breaths through deteriorated lungs. He nodded and was glad when Loulie did the same, though her gaze flashed with determination as she stood to face the queen. "It is as Yousef said: We came here to escape, and have no reason to defy you. But if I may be so bold, I would make a request."

A ripple of shock went through the throne room. Mazen tensed as Firas stepped forward. "Entitled creature! You are in no position to make demands."

Loulie turned her frown on him. "A *request*," she corrected.

The queen's colorless lips lifted into what Mazen thought might be a smirk, though it was difficult to tell with her strange eyes. "Speak your mind."

The merchant stood tall beneath the wazir's withering glare. "I propose a trade. I will repair your bindings if you return us to the surface with magic to defeat the usurper."

Loulie framed it as a bargain, but it was less an exchange than a demand. Mazen was amazed that even now, without her magics, she had the confidence to barter as the Midnight Merchant.

The queen surprised them both by acquiescing. "Why not?" She looked amused. "A world for a single human life is an easy trade. I shall give you the means to destroy your sultan. In exchange, starting tomorrow, you will assist us." She turned to Firas. "Tell the zuama'a that the summit will proceed as planned in a week's time. I have a strategy to propose to them..."

The deal having been struck, the queen commanded Hayat to guide Loulie and Mazen to the guest quarters, where they would be joined by Rijah after they recovered. A chill settled on Mazen's skin as they were led outside. It dawned on him that by offering their assistance, he had placed them all on some political battlefield he did not understand.

All he could do now was hope he'd allied them with the correct side.

6

LOULIE

As the Midnight Merchant, Loulie was accustomed to being the center of attention.

What she *wasn't* accustomed to was being stared at like some many-headed oddity. Here, she was not some mysterious celebrity. She was simply a human with a gossamer-thin lie for a history, and it was clear the jinn did not know what to make of her. Everywhere she went they stared at her—soldiers and servants, gaping at her with equal parts scrutiny and surprise.

If Qadir was here, he would know how to speak with them.

She had been turning the sullen thought over in her mind since they'd been dismissed from the audience hall. Losing the dagger and compass had left her feeling unmoored, but worse still was Qadir's unknown fate. Even with the queen's threat hanging over their heads, she could not stop thinking of the agony that had speared through her in the binding.

Never mind the queen and her demands—she had to get back to Qadir. But how?

She tamped down her panic as Hayat led them through a shadow-shrouded garden and into a walled-in compound. Inside was an expansive courtyard interlaced with flower patches and streams. To the west, in the shadow of the palace walls, stood a cluster of buildings with slanted gold-tiled roofs. Loulie's gaze caught on a bright blur floating between them. At first, she thought it was a trick of the light, but as the object hovered closer, she became certain. The woolen surface, the intricate embroidery, the tassels wavering in the wind—

Mazen gasped beside her. "A flying carpet?"

Hayat arched a brow at them. "Is it so strange a sight? We use them here for maintenance. And, when necessary, travel across the city."

Loulie stared at the rug as it passed above them. "They seem..." She searched for a word that was not *magical*. "Convenient."

Hayat snorted. "They are better than climbing, yes." She turned to face the courtyard. "This is where you will be staying." She swept a hand toward the buildings, and in the same moment, a jinn stepped forward from the shadows, appearing so suddenly it was as if she had materialized out of thin air. The figure was a hazy impression in the night, her only discernable feature the shards of blue that were her eyes. The jinn introduced herself as the servant who would attend them during their stay, though she offered no name.

Hayat grabbed Loulie's arm before she could follow her. "Her Majesty has commanded baths be drawn for both of you. Layla, I will show you to the hammam first."

Loulie could feel Mazen staring at her, uncertainty plain on his face. For once, she shared his anxieties of being separated. After what had happened to Rijah, she shuddered to think of herself holed up in a room alone and defenseless.

Still, she shot Mazen a reassuring smile before trailing Hayat east through the compound. The jinn led her to an unassuming building that sat at the intersection of crystal blue canals. Trees surrounded it, the leaves shining like diamonds in the dark and glinting with every rustle of the wind. Beneath the canopies, tendrils of steam wafted out from the gated hammam windows, giving the trees a misty, mirage-like quality.

Hayat pushed open the large entrance doors and led her inside. The moment Loulie entered, she was enveloped in a suffocating mist. Her alarm heightened when she saw four jinn waiting inside for her. At first, she thought her mind was playing tricks on her. But then the jinn moved in unison to surround her, and she was unable to deny the magic staring her in the face. The figures were barely shadows, as insubstantial as the steam surrounding them, but there was no mistaking the icy eyes. Somehow, she was looking at mimics of the servant from outside.

"You...you were just in the courtyard. How are you here? How are there so many of you?" Her eyes darted between them, searching for some trick.

"Her Majesty has put you in my care, sayyidati. It is an honor to serve you." The words were spoken in unsettling unison.

Hayat sighed. "This is a part of her magic."

One reflection stepped forward and held out her hands. "Your robes, please."

"Your attire will be returned to you after it is inspected and cleaned," another said.

Too late, Loulie remembered that the earring and the two-faced coin were still tucked in her pockets. She stepped back, fingers instinctively falling to her sides.

The attendants pressed closer. Staring between them was like looking into a broken mirror. It reminded Loulie of the illusion magic Omar had used to create duplicates of himself. But this was no illusion.

Dread weighed her limbs as she slipped out of her robes. The servants stole the clothing from her before she could think how to smuggle the magics out of her pockets. Then they handed the garments to Hayat, who promptly folded them under her arm. "I will be back to collect you when you are done." Without another word, she left Loulie to stand amidst the reflections in nothing but her undergarments.

The servants led her from the vestibule into a small, branching corridor with two bathing chambers. Loulie was taken to the right-hand room, a chamber filled with thick incense that curled through the air in pungent whorls. Two more shadows crouched at the far end of a bath carved into the tile, sorting through a basket filled with bottles and ointments.

At first, Loulie was wary of the attendants who hovered at the edges of the bath, handing her soaps and oils as they scrubbed her hair and body clean of sand. But as time passed, her discomfort washed away with the grime, replaced with a peaceful drowsiness. Relaxed, she was emboldened to attempt conversation.

"How is it possible for anyone to tamper with bindings in the first place?" Loulie asked. "I thought the magic harmed anyone who came close."

The shadow behind her answered, "Yes, but Nabila is an ifrit, able to command the wind itself. If anyone can interfere with the bindings, it is someone with her magic."

The thought of some mad ifrit traveling the Sandsea, ripping apart bindings, confounded her. "But why? Why would she damage them if..." She struggled to hold the question in her mind as her thoughts blurred with exhaustion. "If they keep the world from collapsing?"

The servant smoothed more ointment onto her scalp. "Her Majesty believes Nabila's goal is to wreak havoc upon the surface. After all, the magic not only keeps this land beneath the Sandsea, but also separates our two realms."

The words gave Loulie pause. The queen had accused Nabila of sinking *this* realm, not infiltrating the surface. When she asked the attendant to clarify, she said "It is mere speculation" and dropped the conversation. But Loulie's mind continued to whir. She remembered what her mother had told her long ago—that the reason jinn were able to break through the Sandsea was because they had magic. But if what the servant was saying was true, then perhaps it was a *specific* magic. An ifrit's magic.

Was it possible Nabila was the reason jinn were making it to the surface?

The musing evaporated as she sank into the bath. She did not know if it was the water, the incense, or some other invisible magic, but she suddenly found herself too tired to care. Her anxieties had become as formless as the steam, wafting through her fingers when she tried to hold on to them. She was only distantly aware of the shadows combing their hands through her hair. She allowed herself to close her eyes, to rest her head against the lip of the bath...

She did not realize, at first, that she had sunk low enough for the water to close over her head. Did not realize she was falling asleep beneath the surface until she opened her mouth to breathe and gasped in a lungful of water. Loulie crashed back to the surface, coughing water as her heart thudded in her throat. She looked up, half expecting one of the shadows to shove her back under, but they were all staring at her with indecipherable expressions.

"What…" Loulie clung to the lip of the bath, breathing ragged. "What just happened?"

"You ought to be more careful, sayyidati," one of the reflections said. "It is one thing to allow yourself the luxury of relaxation, another entirely to let the magic put you to sleep."

Loulie trembled as they eased her out of the water and rubbed lotion on her legs and doused her in perfumes. Despite her best efforts to keep a clear head, it was not long before the strange haze descended on her again. By the time the attendants had draped her in layers of silk and slid slippers onto her feet, Loulie could barely feel her body.

When she finally emerged, Hayat was waiting at the entrance as she'd promised. At first, Loulie did not recognize her—she had traded her ominous cloak for a long-sleeved dara'a with beaded sleeves and looked more approachable without a hood drawn over her face. Loulie was relieved to see her own robes tucked beneath Hayat's arm, apparently cleaned.

"You look…" Hayat considered. "Less dusty."

"And you look less murderous," Loulie mumbled.

Hayat grumbled as she turned toward the doors. "Come. I will lead you to your chambers, and then we can be done with each other for the night."

Loulie had never been more eager to obey an order. The first thing she did when the attendants were out of earshot was ask Hayat if the incense in the bath was enchanted.

The jinn gave her a strange look. "Everything in this city is touched by magic. So much so that we do not give its existence a thought. But you…Are you humans truly so weak that you—" She cut herself off abruptly, expression shuttering as she turned away. "Forget it."

Loulie recognized the jinn's curiosity as an opening for

conversation. "We aren't weak, only unprepared. We know nothing about this court and its magics. We don't even know what *you* do. Are you a soldier or an errand runner?"

The words had their intended effect. The jinn bristled as she snapped, "I am no *errand runner*. I am a soldier, and Her Majesty trusts me to perform very special tasks for her."

A glorified errand runner, then, Loulie thought. She asked, "What kind of tasks?"

But Hayat had already turned pointedly away, making it clear she was no longer willing to speak with her. Though Loulie was frustrated by the sudden end to the conversation, she was grateful, at least, that no other magical surprises presented themselves on the way to the guest quarters, a large, three-story building just off a branching path.

Inside, Hayat led Loulie up a stairwell, bypassing the second-story landing she claimed was for Rijah and making her way toward the third. The staircase connecting the landings was dark and musty, the area dim save for the torches on the wall, which flickered with the same strange blue-white fire Loulie had seen in the city.

Loulie glanced at the flame in passing. "That fire—is it magic?"

She was not expecting Hayat to answer and so was surprised when the jinn nodded. "We call it ashfire. It is an immortal flame, crafted by a banished king to burn even in his absence."

Loulie nearly tripped on a step. She caught herself against the wall. "Banished king?"

But Hayat had already gone on ahead and did not answer her. Loulie quickly gave chase.

A banished king... Qadir? She glanced again at the fire. Qadir had watched her from a distance before but... an immortal flame? *Ashfire?* She had never heard of such a thing.

Eventually, they came to a door on the third-floor landing that Hayat opened with a simple key. Beyond the entrance, Loulie was surprised to see not just a room, but an entire *floor* waiting for her. Though it was sparsely decorated, the furniture was more than lavish enough to make up for the barrenness. The bedroom Hayat showed her to contained a canopied bed, a gold-encrusted table with gilded legs, and a beautiful metal chest inlaid with gems. A closet wedged into the corner of the room contained an absurd assortment of outfits and shoes, each so ostentatious Loulie could not help but glower at them.

As Hayat set her robes down on the table, the click of a door sounded in the sitting room. When Loulie went to investigate, she was just as surprised to see Mazen as he was to see her. The storyteller hovered uncertainly by another door. A second bedroom, Loulie realized, when she saw a replica of her canopied bed in the space beyond.

Hayat trailed her outside. "I have never seen two guests look so shocked by a courtesy." She glanced between them with a quirked brow. "You could share a room, if you prefer."

Loulie must have made a face, because Mazen immediately swept in with his brightest smile to thank Hayat. Loulie was torn between mortification and relief. Space had always been a difficult thing for her to share, but here in this strange place she found herself glad for Mazen's company. The thought surprised her. When had she gone from tolerating the storyteller to feeling reassured by his presence?

Her eyes swept across the chamber until they fell on a pair of glass doors leading out to a balcony. This high up, she could see over the wall surrounding the palace. Her breath caught when she beheld the city steeped in shadow. It looked as if every light in Dhahab had been burned out, the moon forcibly concealed behind clouds.

"It's dark as sin out there," she muttered.

The conversation paused as Hayat looked at her. "The unnatural darkness is a consequence of the weakened bindings. It is a malicious magic. Any who get caught in it lose their senses. Sometimes, their lives.

"For the citizens' safety, Her Majesty has issued a curfew." The jinn tapped the now fully closed eye on the back of her hand. "Watch the tattoo; it is the only magic that can predict curfew-fall."

Mazen looked torn between horror and fascination. "The curfew falls at different times?"

"You think we would need the wazir's magic if it did not? The sky is unpredictable here."

Loulie grimaced. Given his behavior in the throne room, she

had marked the wazir as an adversary, but unpleasant as he was, it seemed his magic was at least not malevolent.

She glanced at Mazen, who was staring out the glass doors with a perplexed look on his face. "What happens if you don't make it back inside in time?"

Hayat jutted a thumb back toward the stairwell. "Layla asked earlier about the ashfire. If you look closely, you'll see it burning faintly in the city, even now. If ever you find yourself stranded during curfew-fall, seek out the fire. It will lead you down the main roads." She nodded toward the courtyard, which was aglow with the blue light. "We keep the courtyard and indoor areas well lit; you need not be concerned on palace grounds."

The explanation inspired more questions than answers, but Loulie was given no time to ask them. As if she'd just become aware of overstaying her welcome, Hayat abruptly cleared her throat and reached for the doorknob. "You can ask more of your insipid questions tomorrow when the Shapeshifter returns. For now, I've been ordered to show you to the hammam, Yousef."

The room quieted after they left. Alone, Loulie drifted into her room. Though she knew she ought to check the area for traps or magics, she made it only as far as her desk before she slumped into a chair. It was here, in the isolation of her own chamber, that her exhaustion gave way to grief. Qadir's absence hit her again, suddenly and with the intensity of a wave.

Gods, she missed his company. She missed the way he listened to her and the patient way he helped her untangle her thoughts. She missed his quiet, reassuring composure.

She missed *him*.

Loulie reached for her robes, the only piece of her old life she had been allowed to hold on to, and buried her fingers in the fabric as tears stung her eyes. She relished its familiarity—

Her palm brushed against something with sharp edges.

Wary, she reached into one of the pockets. Her breath caught as she slid an object out and held it between pinched fingers.

Omar's crescent earring winked at her in the firelight.

7

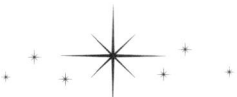

MAZEN

Mazen woke to a pitch-black sky.

At first, he struggled to make sense of the sight. There were no clouds, no stars, no moon. But then he remembered where they were. The memory sank his already-low spirits. His despair was tenacious; it had lingered since the nightmares started earlier that night.

In one of them, he'd plunged a dagger into his father's heart and smiled at the shocked anguish in his eyes. In another, he'd banged his fists against the locked doors of his burning bedroom and begged to be let out as Hakim screamed on the other side. Every time he'd woken, it had been with a single question beating through his head: *What if? What if?*

What if he had stayed in Madinne? What if he had been honest with his father?

He remembered the way Omar had smirked at him beneath the Sandsea. The words he had spoken: *It is because you are a coward that I could pin this crime on you.*

The memories pressed down on Mazen with such suffocating force they made him tremble. His legs were quivering as he slid from his bed and made his way out of his room. He needed fresh air. He needed to get *out* of this place filled with shadows and nightmares.

No one was there to stop him when he stumbled through the

sitting room and out into the stairwell. By the time he emerged into the courtyard, there was a sheen of sweat on his forehead, and his body was trembling so badly he had to lean against the entryway to keep himself upright.

Breathe. He pressed his back to the wall.

Breathe. Closed his eyes.

Mazen forced himself to take deep breaths and count his heart-beats until they were steady. Then he concentrated on the things outside of his mind: the kiss of the grass against his ankles and the buzz of the insects beneath his bare feet. He noted the absence of the wind and the clamminess of the air, which stuck oddly to his skin.

It was only when his mind quieted that he opened his eyes. Though the sky was still unnaturally dark, the courtyard was coated in the soft blue light of a dozen ashfire-lit lanterns. The first time Mazen had seen the strange fire in the city, he'd thought it unsettling. Now, against the backdrop of the ink-black sky, it was a comforting sight.

Curiosity drew him toward the nearest source: a large brazier in the center of the courtyard. Mazen shuddered as he approached it. The air was stagnant but cold, and it sank through the fabric of his sleeves to his arms. Instinctively, he held his hands out above the ashfire to warm them.

And that was when the flame, calm up until that moment, *snapped* at his fingers.

Mazen staggered back, hands tucked beneath his elbows. Even from a distance, the fire roiled, spitting wild sparks onto the grass. Mazen stared at it, aghast. Of course *he* had somehow managed to anger an immortal flame. If there was anyone capable of ruining magic, it was—

"Yousef."

Mazen jumped at the sound of his alias. He turned, eyes search-ing, until he spotted a shadow emerging from the other side of the brazier. A...black cat? The situation became increasingly more bizarre when the creature settled on its haunches, looked him dead in the eye, and said, "Is it your habit to meddle with magics that could kill you?"

All thoughts left Mazen's mind when the feline spoke. He recognized the haughty tenor of its voice. *Her* voice. Even now, he saw her slit-pupil eyes in his mind. *"Hayat?"*

She sighed as she stepped forward, her body changing between strides. When she stood before him again, she was wrapped in her smoky cloak, and her golden eyes peered at him from a jinn's face rather than a cat's. "What are you doing out here, human? Scheming?"

"I was just getting some fresh air."

"Your apartments have a balcony," she said flatly.

He managed a sheepish smile as he ran his fingers through his hair. "Sorry. I just had to ..." *Get out.* With him, it had always been about getting out, getting away.

His lungs tightened as Hayat continued watching him. Nothing about her expression inspired sympathy. But still, he found himself fumbling for an excuse. "I apologize. I'm prone to restless pacing, and I just thought—"

"You can pace on the balcony."

Mazen sighed, defeated. He glanced at the ashfire over Hayat's shoulder. Though it had stopped sputtering, it still wavered, oddly animated. When Hayat shot him another suspicious look, he quickly redirected the conversation. "What are *you* doing out here? Patrolling?"

She lifted her chin, somehow managing to look down at him despite her height. "Hunting."

"Hunting... intruders?"

"Birds," she said.

At first, Mazen was unsure of how to respond to this declaration. He eventually surmised, based on her smug smile, that these hunts were boastworthy. So he smiled through his confusion and said, "You've certainly chosen the right form for it. I didn't realize you were a shapeshifter."

Hayat shrugged, but he could tell by the slant of her lips that the comment had pleased her. "Yes. It is a fine shape, is it not? Much easier for hunting birds."

She looked to be in a better mood as she led him back to the apartments. Mazen easily matched her footsteps on the walk back. When they moved side by side like this, it seemed especially appalling that she had been able to overwhelm them in the city.

"Do you conduct these hunts often?" he asked.

Hayat nodded. "Every day. Every night. I am always on the lookout for the birds."

"Are they . . . ah, dangerous?"

She stared at him, blank-faced. "Why would I hunt them if they were not? Her Majesty gave me this responsibility *because* it is important."

Mazen was nonplussed. Was she a soldier or an exterminator?

"The hunts are a special assignment," she continued as her gaze wandered to the black sky. "My brother used to lead them. Now I carry them out in his stead."

He blinked, surprised. "You have a brother?"

"*Had.* He was—" She paused suddenly as they came to the entrance, and her eyes narrowed. "My history is not your business."

Her animosity caught him off guard. "I'm sorry. I was just trying to make conversation."

But Hayat was no longer in the mood for chatter. With an unnecessarily hard yank, she pulled the door open. "Talk to Layla if you are so restless. I have more important things to do."

She left before Mazen could say anything else, transforming once more into a cat with a sweep of her cloak. Mazen watched her until she disappeared, then retraced his steps to the sitting room. Unenthused by the idea of pacing on the balcony, he returned to his room.

He was surprised to find the door open.

Cautiously, he peered inside. In his absence, another lantern had appeared on his desk. And seated beside it, haloed in dim firelight, was Loulie al-Nazari.

Mazen jumped at her sudden appearance. "Lou—Layla?"

Harsh shadows contoured the merchant's face, rendering her usual scowl in a stark light. But the severity of her frown was softened somewhat by the many shawls she had wrapped herself in. With her knees tucked up to her chest, she looked less like a person than a bundle of clothing. Mazen swallowed a startled laugh at the sight of her before remembering that he himself was barefoot and dressed in an evening robe.

The merchant looked unamused. She sighed, and he could not tell if it was for him or the name. "I need to talk to you." She gestured to the chair on the other side of the table. "Where were you? I knocked for a long time, thinking you were sleeping like the dead."

"And then you . . . came into my room regardless?"

"I wanted to make sure you weren't *actually* dead." She made another sharp, exasperated motion toward the chair, then repeated her question after he'd seated himself.

Mazen thought for a few moments about what to tell her. Even though she had helped him in the throne room, he did not want to keep worrying her unnecessarily. He settled on "You know how restless I get behind locked doors."

Her brow shot up. "What, so you decided to wander? In *this* darkness?"

He briefly considered telling Loulie about the nightmares. But the thought sent a wave of shame through him, and he only muttered, "The courtyard is filled with ashfire—I think it's safe."

He told her about the flickering fire and the run-in with Hayat. Her skepticism mellowed to amusement when she heard about the hunts. "You think the queen has a vendetta against them? She seems the type to hold grudges."

"A vendetta against *birds*?"

Loulie shrugged. "I don't trust anything or anyone in this place, including the birds." She paused, frowning. "The ashfire, though . . . I wonder if it's still connected to Qadir."

It was strange to imagine Loulie's stoic bodyguard as a king. Strange to think of him sitting on a throne, like Mazen's own father. Like Omar now. Mazen pushed aside the grim imagining before it could settle.

"Have you managed to reach him since we came here?" he asked her.

"No. But I know he's in danger." Her words hung heavy in the air, her expression falling with them. "I don't know how or why, but I felt his pain through the dagger. I need to get back to him. If Rijah can't return us to the surface, then maybe this queen can."

Mazen was at a loss for words. But before he could think of some way to reassure her, she waved the subject away. "I didn't come here to talk about Qadir." She bade him to hold out his hand so she could set something in his palm. Mazen recognized its shape immediately. Still, he was shocked to see Omar's earring.

"I found it in my robes," she said.

Mazen's eyes flickered up to hers in surprise. "And your other magics?"

"Stolen. Hayat even took the two-faced coin." She leaned back in her chair with a glower. "I thought she might have left the earring on purpose, but I can't think of a reason for it."

Mazen pinched the relic between his fingers, thoughtful. "Maybe the ifrit kept herself hidden during Hayat's inspection?" At Loulie's doubtful expression, he added, "She could make Omar vanish with her illusions. Maybe she did the same for her relic."

Loulie still looked unconvinced. "But why would she hide away in *my* pocket?"

Mazen could think of little reason the ifrit would want to remain with them after they had stolen her from her son. Unless...

She prefers to be in our possession rather than the queen's?

Mazen considered the earring with a frown. "Has Aliyah done anything to you?"

"No." Loulie grimaced. "I almost wish she would. At least then I would have some idea of what she's trying to accomplish."

In the Sandsea, Aliyah's magic had been powerful enough to craft an entire city. But when Loulie had stolen the earring from Omar, she'd had no success using it. She was a merchant who had experience with magic; what could *he* possibly do with it?

He addressed the earring: "For what reason did you hide yourself, ifrit?"

It was hard not to feel self-conscious when the earring did not respond to him. Mazen felt no flicker of life from the relic. It did not warm nor hum against his skin. It simply . . . existed.

Loulie raised a brow. "You think I haven't tried talking to her already?"

"Maybe we're not asking the right questions." He held the earring up to the light from the lantern. "What do you want from us?"

Still no answer.

Loulie looked exasperated. "Of all the magic to be stuck with, it had to be *this* one. Even the two-faced coin would have given me a clearer answer." She fell back in her chair with a sigh. "Did they leave you with anything?"

In answer, Mazen pointed to the wall, where his shadow remained a barely perceptible smudge. He wrapped his other hand reflexively over the earring. "Let me try speaking with Aliyah. I know Omar; perhaps I can find a way to unravel his magics."

In truth, Mazen could not stand the thought of Loulie falling prey to the ifrit's nefarious magic. Omar had already stolen everything from him—and from *her*. He did not want her to suffer any more losses because of his family.

Besides that, perhaps the ifrit in the earring would be able to answer some of Mazen's questions. Even Aisha had not known why Omar was working with jinn; perhaps Aliyah would.

Loulie rose from her chair with a shrug. "Fine. But when Rijah returns, we're seeing if they have some means of communicating with Aliyah." She watched as Mazen walked to his bed and slid the earring beneath his pillow. She was still there, lingering, when he turned back.

"I know what it's like," she said haltingly. "To lose family. And the helplessness that comes afterward . . . I understand that too. Whenever the grief became overwhelming, I would speak to Qadir." She hesitated. "You could . . ."

You could speak to me. Mazen heard the unspoken words in her silence. He remembered the last time she had tried to console him on the surface, the bluntness with which she had spoken. He had a feeling she did not do this often. That she was trying meant everything to him.

He was smiling when she abruptly excused herself, muttering that she needed to check on something. After she had left, Mazen settled on the edge of his bed and closed his eyes.

So long as he was still alive, there was a chance he might survive whatever lay ahead of them. Though the world above may have forsaken him, no one knew who he was in this place. Here, he *was* inconsequential—but perhaps there was a freedom in that.

At the very least, he wasn't alone, and that was enough for now.

8

LOULIE

"Finally, the dead has awakened."

Loulie groggily blinked sunlight out of her eyes as she sat up. Sleep crusted her eyelids, and her mind was still foggy but . . .

Qadir?

She looked up and saw him standing before her, limned in light. Qadir, his lips quirked into the familiar exasperated half smile. Qadir, who was alive and *here*.

Loulie threw off her sheets with a gasp. "You're not an illusion, are you?"

"Of course I am not an illusion."

Loulie froze at the voice, both familiar and not. When she blinked, Qadir was gone, and the shadow attendant stood in front of her. The jinn's form was hazy, her features indecipherable even in daylight. Two of her mimics stood watching Loulie from the doorway with the same clouded expression.

An illusion after all. Loulie dolefully rubbed sleep from her eyes.

The attendant was unimpressed by her misery. "I am to prepare you for a meeting with Her Majesty this morning." She beckoned her out of bed.

Loulie grumbled as she stood. The last thing she wanted was to be dressed up and paraded around in needlessly extravagant clothing.

She had played this game before with the sultan and hated every moment of it. But what choice did she have?

Begrudgingly, she consented to being fussed over, frowning out her window as the shadows stuffed her in excessively bright and shimmering layers. With the unnatural curfew darkness lifted, she could at last make out the palace grounds.

She saw buildings that spread across a field so filled with flora it grew through and over broken walls, and massive fruit trees that towered over destroyed pavilions, their thick roots winding beneath the ground like cracked veins. She saw crumbling pillars that had become home to a strange, shimmering ivy, and tiled paths half hidden beneath clusters of arfaj.

And then she saw a myna perched on her windowsill and jerked back at the sight of its beady eyes on her. When the attendant turned to follow Loulie's gaze out the glass, the bird had already flown off. Evidently, Hayat had not caught all her quarry last night.

The attendant regarded Loulie coolly. "Is something the matter, sayyidati?"

Loulie hesitated. She imagined what Qadir would say if he were here. The way his lips would twitch upward at her scowl. He would say, *What did that bird ever do to you?*

And she would respond *Nothing* and try to explain to him that while birds had never done anything to her, she could not help but be distrustful of them. Their constant head twitching and beady eyes were unnerving and unreadable, and Loulie had never liked things she could not predict. Qadir would raise an amused brow at her, and Loulie...

She would have welcomed his teasing, if only he'd been here.

Her shoulders sagged with her sigh. "Nothing," she muttered, and the attendant returned to her work without further comment. After she was done, she and her shadows ushered Loulie into the sitting room, where Mazen already sat waiting.

Loulie was briefly taken aback by his appearance. The storyteller had been traveling in plain, dusty attire for so long that she had forgotten what he looked like in fine clothing. Dressed in a rich embroidered vest and sirwal trousers, he looked more a prince now than he had at any point during their long journey. He smiled at her when she entered, but it was a wan look, a subdued curve of his lips that did little to hide the sleepless shadows beneath his eyes.

Recalling their conversation from last night, Loulie felt a pang of sympathy. She still remembered the long, restless nights she had suffered after her tribe's passing. She understood Mazen's grief, but she was at a loss for how to comfort him. She was accustomed to using words to deflect, not console. Besides that, what kind of advice did you offer a man who had not only lost his family but also been betrayed by them?

She settled on an awkward greeting before turning to the shadow attendant, who waited for them by the door. "Where will we be meeting the queen?" she asked. "And what of Rijah?" She thought of their decomposing form and swallowed. "Are they recovered?"

Much to her relief, the attendant confirmed that Rijah was revived and would be waiting with the queen at their designated location. As for the place they would be meeting—

"You will meet with Her Majesty in the archive. It is an old building, cursed by an ifrit."

Mazen shot upright on the divan, suddenly alert. "Archive?"

Loulie fixated on a different part of the explanation. "What do you mean *cursed*?"

Not more than a quarter hour later, they received their answer in person. The archive was a tall, square tower that loomed above a courtyard on the palace grounds. From a distance, it appeared a beautiful structure, shrouded with flowers and leaves that sprawled in thick patterns up the walls and windows. But up close, Loulie saw that the flowers were gray and withered, and the vines growing over the windows were replete with thorns. A mournful silence clung to the decaying walls and radiated outward, suffocating the conversations of patrolling soldiers. Loulie spotted Hayat among them, though she pointedly ignored them.

The servant took them as far as the front doors, where three jinn waited. The first was the queen, who stood with her back to them. Even from behind, Loulie could make out the absurd number of weapons strapped to her body. The second jinn was her wazir, Firas, who stood threateningly holding Rijah's lamp. The third guest Loulie knew for their turquoise-blue eyes.

Mazen inhaled sharply beside her. *"Rijah?"*

As far as Loulie could tell, the ifrit was in one piece. No scars, no burns...and none of the markings that had flashed across their skin in the throne room, though it was impossible to tell when their arms were covered with the sleeves of a midnight-blue kaftan. It was a beautiful robe, woven with whorls of rippling silver. They looked a distinguished guest in it.

Loulie's shoulders sagged with relief. "You're unharmed."

The ifrit bristled as if she'd insulted them. "You think I am so easily defeated?"

Firas scoffed. "Is everything that comes out of your mouth bluster?"

Had Rijah been able to burn someone with their gaze, Loulie was certain they would have scorched a hole through the wazir. But the queen interceded before either of them could pick a fight. "We are not here to waste breath on petty arguments," she said.

Loulie eyed her, suspicious. "Then why *are* we here?"

The queen looked down at Loulie as if she were an insect she would have liked to crush beneath her foot. "We are here on the rec-ommendation of the Shapeshifter. They claim information on the bindings' whereabouts is locked inside." She gestured to the omi-nously looming tower. "We call this place the archive. Before the war, it was home to the city's greatest collection of memories. Now it is a tomb locked with the magic of the ifrit who created it."

"His name was Jubayr," Rijah said sharply. "Though many called him the Wanderer."

Loulie vaguely recalled the title from Qadir's story of the seven ifrit. She remembered the shape Qadir had drawn of the ifrit in fire—a figure with plants sprouting beneath his feet. Looking at the walls of flora, it was easy to make that connection.

Mazen was scrutinizing the walls too, but with less dread than she'd expected. In fact, there was an almost reverent look in his eyes as he said, "Is this place...a library?"

Loulie felt a laugh bubble up in her throat and coughed to clear it. It never failed to amaze her, how easily this man could lose himself in wonder. She should have expected he would be drawn to a library, story obsessed as he was.

"It is nothing so mundane as a human library," Rijah said. "Jubayr's knowledge was more intimate than words in a dusty tome. That is why I have brought us here. Though the land has shifted too much for me to remember the binding locations with certainty, the archive will contain that information. Jubayr did not only know things as they were, but also as they will be."

Mazen blinked, clearly mystified, but Loulie was unsurprised. Jinn rarely spoke straightforward truths. She sighed. "How do you plan on getting inside? Burning the foliage?"

The queen crossed her arms. "You cannot *burn* away a curse, foolish human."

Loulie frowned at the flowers, unimpressed. She wondered, dimly, what would happen if she tried to cut at them with Qadir's dagger. The thought made her heart hitch. Part of her wanted nothing more than to reclaim the blade from the queen's clutches. Another part dreaded that the edge would still be dull and dark and that Qadir would be silent.

She was still stewing in her thoughts when Rijah came to stand beside her. The ifrit surveyed the rabid undergrowth with raised brows, looking, for all the world, as if they were facing down some trivial pest rather than a curse.

They said, "Watch."

And then, with a grin, they thrust their palms through the foliage to the wall. The magic's response was immediate. The dead greenery shot outward, vines, leaves, thorns, and gods knew what other undead plants climbing up Rijah's arms and traveling across their shoulders to their neck. The outburst was quickly chased by a hissing beneath their feet. When Loulie looked down and saw the withered grass reaching toward her ankles, she fell back with a swear.

She made it only a few steps before the queen grabbed her by the shoulder, rooting her and Mazen in place on either side of her as her retinue of soldiers drew warily closer.

They all watched as Rijah's shape began to change, the contours of their form shifting into a new body that was smaller, lither, with twiglike limbs. There was a moment when the ifrit was blotted completely from sight, their body lost beneath the vicious bramble. Then, abruptly, the foliage began to shrink back toward the wooden walls. And as it receded, it *bloomed*.

Ashen buds unfurled into vibrant nuwair flowers, leaves regained their shimmer, and the wall of foliage grew as verdant as fresh undergrowth. Through the transformation, Rijah remained statue still, palms pressed against the wall.

When it was over, the foliage around the building had withdrawn enough for Loulie to make out a set of doors. Rijah faced them with a familiar grin on a different face. It was a wizened, chiseled face, one that looked as if it had been crafted from stone. Silver hair twined with roots and leaves dusted their cheeks and chin, bright against the rich brown hue of their skin. Only the color of Rijah's eyes, now half-lidded, remained unchanged.

A collective murmur went up at the ifrit's changed appearance. Loulie saw various reactions on the soldiers' faces. Fear, shock—and awe, though they tried their best to conceal it. Hayat hovered at the outskirts of the group, expression torn between surprise and wonder.

Rijah was clearly delighted by the stunned reception. They smirked, and when they spoke, the timbre of their voice had altered, becoming deeper and more sonorous. "You think I would bring you here without knowing how to get inside?"

The queen held up a hand for silence, and the soldiers quieted around her. "That magic was Jubayr's; how did *you* unravel it?"

The ifrit crossed their arms and shrugged. "The answer is plain before your eyes. The magic responds to Jubayr, so I became Jubayr."

The wazir scowled. "Impossible! You are nothing but a facsimile."

Rijah's grin was more a threatening baring of teeth than a smile. "On the contrary, I am not some pretender who relies on imagination. Every form I take is true, inside and out."

It seemed an impossible proclamation to make, but how would Loulie know? Besides Qadir, she had never seen the other ifrit in person. It struck her then, as it had many times since their arrival, that she had fallen into this country with little knowledge of its histories and magics. The thought unsettled her. As a merchant of the Night Market, she knew the value of knowledge; people would trade more than coin for it. They would barter treasure, lives.

Loulie cautiously approached the doors. This close, she could make out a figure carved into the bronze. Though their face and body were shrouded with smoke, Loulie felt an unexpected twinge of familiarity. She recognized the broad shoulders, the physique toned with muscle... and when she saw the flame-shaped markings carved onto his arms, she knew for certain.

Still, she made herself ask, "Who is this?"

Firas answered scornfully behind her, "That is the banished king."

Qadir.

She had known, but even so her chest tightened as she set a hand to the center of the door, to Qadir's chest. She wished she could see his face. She wished he were *here*, beside her.

Rijah came to stand beside her. "You dishonor him with that title," they growled. "We knew him as the Ashfire King, named for his magic."

The Ashfire King.

It was a grandiose title, one suited to legends and myths. And yet all Loulie could see in her mind was the ifrit *she* knew. Qadir, reclining casually on a tavern rooftop, watching the stars as she vented to him about her day. Qadir, curled up on her shoulder in the unassuming form of a lizard. She could not reconcile those memories with the enigmatic depiction on these doors.

Even more so because Qadir had never shared this name with her. The one and only time he had confessed to being an ifrit, he had called himself the Inferno. She wondered now if that title had been a deflection—one more half-truth to conceal his past.

The queen sighed. "A king who forgets his kingdom does not deserve to be remembered." She ignored Rijah's sharp look to address Loulie: "Open the doors, human."

Loulie hesitated only briefly before heeding her command.

9

MAZEN

Much like everything else in the city, the archive had the appearance of a grand ruin. The memory of opulence still clung to its surface, in the faded cursive script stretching across the walls and in the intricate, ivy-warped latticework on the windows. Shattered tiles lined alcoves and doorways, and the carpets scattered throughout the space were frayed and dulled by time.

And yet despite its clear age, it was still a marvel. The doors that blocked off the rooms were decorated with murky but precious-looking stones, and pearl-shaped lanterns hung from high, vaulted ceilings. And then there were the shelves—hundreds of them—stretching up so high Mazen could barely see the tops. Each was packed tight with scrolls, tomes, and on occasion, objects. Things like glass vases and dishes, topaz figurines and jewel-studded daggers.

At first glance, it had the look of a library, but Mazen knew it was something else, something *more*. As they entered, his attention was drawn to a phrase carved into the top of the doorframe: *Everything I have seen once, I know in perpetuity.*

He was still staring at those words, trying to puzzle them out, as the queen entered with her soldiers. With a wave of her hand, she bade them to secure the area. Only Firas remained by her side, frowning distrustfully at the paraphernalia on the shelves.

Mazen hovered by the doorway, uncertain. "You said this place contains memories?"

"Every archive contains memories of some kind," Loulie said. She wandered toward the nearest bookcase, eyes narrowed as she searched the shelves. "These objects—relics?"

Mazen flinched. So they were not just objects, then, but vessels containing jinn souls.

"It is as I said," the queen said dryly. "This place is a crypt."

Rijah's voice echoed from the entrance: "Such a thoughtless sentiment. Are relics not the most precious memories we can pass on?" The tenor of their new voice dulled the edges of their usual bitterness into a gentler, more chiding tone.

Looking at Rijah in this form, Mazen could believe their shapeshifting was flawless. After all, it was easy to tell from the soft crinkles at their eyes and mouth that this was a face meant for a smile that was not Rijah's. It was kind, patient—not at all what one would associate with the vicious jinn kings in the human stories.

Jubayr. Mazen committed the name to memory for when he next told the tale.

The queen approached the shelves. "Perhaps to you they are memories. But *I* can hear the voices of the dead trapped within them."

She dragged her fingers across the wood, and though Mazen heard no voices, he *saw* the relics shudder at her proximity. He was suddenly reminded of the walls of weapons in her throne room and of the question Hayat had asked: *Has the weapon spoken to you, Your Majesty?*

Now he understood; the queen possessed the ability to hear the dead, like Aisha.

His hand drifted absently to the chest pocket of his vest—to the place where he had hidden Omar's earring that morning. Not wanting to risk the shadow attendant finding such a precious relic in his room, he had decided to take it with him every time he left, but it had not occurred to him that the queen might have the ability to *hear* the voices in relics.

But if she sensed anything amiss, she gave no indication as she idly surveyed the shelves. Beside her, Loulie reached for one of the scrolls. The parchment was so caked with dust it looked like a second skin. "Well, I, a magicless mortal, cannot hear anything." She eyed the parchment with clear skepticism. "What was it you were saying about this place having *more* than dusty tomes and scrolls?" She blew on it.

Mazen startled as the parchment crackled and then *collapsed* in her fingers, bursting into a rabble of gray-winged moths. The merchant fell back with a gasp, shielding her face. Before Mazen's mind had even processed the sight, the queen reached out to crumple the paper insects in her hand. When she unclenched her fist, only dust drifted to the floor.

The merchant stared, wide-eyed, at the pile of sand. "What in nine hells was that?"

Rijah looked exasperated by them. "It is as I said: Jubayr's knowledge was more extensive than any human's. He created this place to store the information from his travels, but..." They gestured at the shelves surrounding them. "He did not store it in the way humans do. Instead, he breathed his memories into parchment and maps."

There must have been thousands of scrolls on the shelves—did they all contain some living memory? The thought made Mazen's breath catch.

"I am uninterested in investigating the memories of a criminal," the queen said starkly. "I have granted you permission to come here so that you may show me the bindings."

Rijah grumbled something about being unappreciated before leading them all through the main corridor and into a clearing littered with tables. Bookcases rose on either side and stretched to a windowless wall, the surface of which was covered with maps—land maps and nautical charts, diagrams of countries and drawings of cities.

It is like Hakim's room, Mazen thought.

It was more an atrium than a study, but the scrolls and equipment cluttered on the tables so reminded Mazen of his brother it left him breathless. A memory descended on him then: Hakim, hunched over his desk and working meticulously on his map while Mazen watched over his shoulder, amazed by the sites his brother was sketching into existence.

Once, Mazen had thought he and Hakim were the same, that they were both prisoners living vicariously through fictions. Hakim had possessed his maps, and Mazen had lived through his stories. It was only now he realized how foolish the comparison was. Hakim had been trapped by the sultan; Mazen had been *protected*. But such realizations would save no one now.

Dread struck suddenly, with the force of a blade between his ribs. Mazen steadied himself against one of the tables as he drew breath into suddenly tight lungs. Rijah shot him a curious look in passing but thankfully made no comment as they paused before the display of maps. After some consideration, they pulled down a piece of parchment pinned to the center, then returned to the table to unroll it across the surface.

As the parchment unfurled, it stretched and flattened into the wood, the lines of the map bleeding into the table until they had become imprinted upon its surface. Then, with a casual flick of their fingers, Rijah made the engraved geography *rise*. Flat mountain ranges transformed into tall wooden spires, the Sandsea smoothed into a wide, sunken crevice, and cracks splintered the table where scattered islands began to materialize. When it was over, it was not a map that lay before them, but the entire realm of jinn carved in miniature.

Mazen stood gaping at the towers that represented Dhahab, his misery sluiced away by awe. Loulie came to stand beside him. "Show-off," she mumbled.

Rijah was clearly preening, but the queen was unimpressed. "Bindings?" she prompted.

With a shrug, the ifrit swept their hand across the surface. Magic flared on the map beneath their fingers in concentrated bursts. One flame ignited in the miniature city of Dhahab, glowing red across its clustered buildings. Another kindled in the east, above the Sandsea. A third, in what appeared to be a small hole in that same sea. And the fourth was not a fire at all, but a glow—a dim light that faded in and out, constantly reappearing in a new location.

"This," Rijah said grandly, "is a map of the bindings."

Firas arched a brow. "How are we to know it is accurate?"

Rijah mirrored his glower. "Jubayr's maps are always accurate. His magic allowed him to render this land in its past, present, and future forms. You can use his maps to find anything."

Mazen recalled the phrase engraved above the entryway: *Everything I have seen once, I know in perpetuity.* He now understood the meaning of those words.

Loulie was squinting at the flare in Dhahab, brow furrowed. "This is the binding we saw when we first came into the city, isn't it? Why does it look so much bigger here?"

In response, Rijah pressed their palms flat to the table's surface, compressing the miniature until the buildings were small enough for them all to make out the magic glowing in the roads. There were the intricate markings he and Loulie had seen in the scorched clearing, now stretched across the city. Mazen surveyed the pattern with awe. "It looks like a maze," he observed.

The ifrit gave him an appraising look. "Sah. At its simplest, a binding can trap magic in an object. But bigger, more intricate bindings like these are a living, breathing magic." Rijah traced the lines through the streets. "Every binding has a center—a place where the magic unfolds. That is the only place it can be influenced. Or in this case, repaired."

Mazen leaned closer to the miniature, trying to locate the scarred plaza and the magic Loulie had ignited within it. "The magic that we ran into—was it the center?"

Rijah shook their head. "No, merely an extension of the magic."

"How can you be so certain?"

"Because"—Rijah raised a sharp brow—"I helped my king craft this binding."

Mazen remembered the markings on Rijah's lamp, so much like the ones they had stumbled into in the city. His eyes darted to the ifrit's sleeved arms, where he had seen similar markings glowing on their skin. "The patterns on your body…"

Rijah nodded. "They are the same as the ones you saw in the city. A binding of this magnitude requires a source to draw its energy from. Each of us ifrit is anchored to one."

With a start, Mazen remembered the markings on Qadir's arms—tattoos he had first noticed when they were fleeing ghouls in the desert. At the time, he had been surprised because they were glowing with magic. Now he wondered if those markings were related to the bindings.

Loulie was squinting at the map, tracing the lines of magic with a careful finger. "So the center of this binding would be...here?" She paused at the highest tier of the city, where the palace sat.

"It is on the palace grounds," Rijah confirmed.

Mazen thought of Qadir's dagger, which had sparked to life at the magic's proximity. A question sat on the tip of his tongue, but the queen voiced it first. "What of Nabila's ability to interfere with the bindings?" Her suspicious gaze landed on Loulie. "And Layla's?"

Rijah shrugged. "Nabila is not influencing; she is tampering. It is like eroding a stone with water. With enough perseverance, she can weaken the magic from the outside."

"And the dagger?" Loulie's voice was sharp, but in the serrated way of broken glass.

"The dagger is the instrument that connects the magics across the land. It was by our king's hand—his blade—that the bindings were carved, and through his instruction that each of us contained our magic within them. And so it is the single key to manipulating them."

It was difficult for Mazen to picture the dagger being used to carve such an expansive mark. How could such a small weapon cut so deep? So far? He had seen the knife burn before, had even felt its heat on his face and seen the way Qadir's eyes flashed across the surface, but...

He glanced at Loulie, whose hand had absently risen to her neck. It was a familiar motion, one that reminded him of Imad and the shackle he had clasped around her throat. He remembered, suddenly, the way Loulie had used the blade not only to end the man's life but to burn his body to cinders. He shuddered. Perhaps the knife *was* that powerful.

The queen's eyes narrowed. "And why is it that only Layla can use this knife?"

Mazen tensed at the question, but Loulie looked unperturbed.

She shrugged, an admirably calm motion. "How should I know? *I* can't hear voices in relics. The knife started burning in proximity to the binding; that is all I know."

It was a nonanswer, but perhaps the queen trusted Loulie's frankness. Though she and her wazir exchanged a skeptical look, she did not probe further as Rijah launched into an explanation of the other bindings. The second was tied to the ifrit known as the Tide Bringer. According to the table, it was . . . in a hole in the Sandsea?

"The Eastern Marid City," the queen explained.

Mazen peered at the gaping hole, curious. On the surface, the marid had once had a city as well—Ghiban. They had lived there, for a time, until they had been overwhelmed by the humans invading their land and had perished trying to protect it. He wondered how many settlements they had in this country.

Rijah had paused to look at the hole too, but there was no wonder in their expression. "The privateer who brought us into the city is a marid," they said flatly.

The queen inclined her head. "That is Ziyad, my most trusted envoy."

Mazen awkwardly cleared his throat. "Who are the marid? We have few stories of them on the surface."

"The marid are a tribe of traitors," Rijah spat. "When my king called on them during the war, they hid in their oceans. Instead of sinking the ships of the invading humans, they helped guide them across the waves."

The ifrit's anger was palpable—Mazen could see the scorch marks on the table from where they were clutching it. The queen saw the markings too; her lips lifted into a faint smile as she said, "No, they simply refused to die for *your* king when he asked. But Ziyad has proven his loyalty to me time and again since I took the throne." She gave them a pointed look. "Unlike a certain wrathful ifrit, he is not trying to sink these lands."

Rijah scowled. "Nabila has the temperament of a storm and is as unpredictable as the winds she controls. Her actions do not speak for the rest of us."

Firas looked unimpressed. "And yet your king trusted her."

"He trusted *all* of us. Would you blame the victim over the traitor?"

The queen laughed. It was a sharp, venomous sound. "Your king is hardly a victim. He left this realm to decay beneath the Sandsea, after all. Left *you* to fix his mistakes."

The gibe landed. Rijah's cheeks flushed with humiliation as they glared at the queen. One glance at the glowing lamp in Firas's hands, however, and they brusquely turned their attention to the third binding, another magic lying at the center of the Sandsea. "This one was crafted on the moving island Nabila calls home."

Now it was Loulie who leaned forward, resting her arms on the table as she peered at the island on the Sandsea. "How is it moving?"

The wazir scoffed. "If we knew, we would have captured Nabila long ago."

In his youth, Mazen had heard many tales of magical islands. Sailors liked to gossip, but more than that, they liked to embellish, and Mazen had always appreciated the stories they shared when visiting his father's court. There were tales of lost magics and treasures, of course, but there were also stories of ancient creatures and civilizations that had hidden themselves from the world. He wondered, What was the story behind *this* island?

The last binding was more of a mystery than Nabila's. Even Rijah hesitated as they watched the light vanish and reappear at different corners of the map. "The final binding is my king's. It is tied in some way to the ashfire, but I know nothing of its nature."

Mazen watched Loulie out of the corner of his eye. Though she did not react to the veiled mention of Qadir, her gaze remained intently fixed on the shifting magic.

The queen regarded the markings thoughtfully. "There were seven of you, and yet there are only four bindings. Why?"

Rijah stepped away from the table, a consternated look on their face. "They are gone. By Nabila's hand or someone else's, I cannot tell you. But that is everything I know."

So there were four bindings and four locations. Mazen glanced at Loulie, whose expression had frozen into a guarded scowl. He recognized that look, this tension. Not even one month ago, she had looked at his father that way when he ordered her to find a magic lamp in the desert. What was this but another impossible magic to find? Another impossible quest?

The last time she had been forced into such a hunt, she had fought. This time, she looked her blackmailer in the eye and said, "You're looking for this magic to fix it?"

The queen's lips pulled into a wry smile. "It is the only way to keep this country safe. We have tried many times to capture Nabila herself, but she always slips through our fingers."

Firas shook his head. "Hayat has had some success capturing her spies, but it is an empty victory if we cannot get the birds to speak."

Mazen stared at him. He and Loulie both said in unison, "*Birds?*"

The queen crossed her arms. "Nabila employs birds as her messengers and spies."

Mazen's mind reeled with the revelation. He recalled the bizarre conversation he'd had with Hayat last night. He saw the realization dawn on Loulie in the same moment, the soft dent between her brows betraying her unease.

The queen continued speaking, unaware of their befuddlement. "So now you see, Layla: this is a righteous expedition."

Do you see, al-Nazari? This is a just quest. The memory of his father's words hit Mazen like a slap. He felt as if he were reliving a memory. Or, perhaps, a nightmare.

But Loulie al-Nazari did not flinch. "I used the compass and the knife to find the binding the first time. I'll need them both back."

Seeing her resolve, Mazen felt a stab of shame. Loulie would clearly do anything for Qadir. And yet even when Hakim's fate was unknown to him, the thought of returning to the surface—of having to face Omar as a wrongfully convicted man—made his limbs lock with fear. Mazen *should* have been trying to unravel his brother's plans and clear his name. But the fury that had initially motived him had vanished, replaced with a craven emptiness.

Mazen could feel his nightmares encroaching at the edges of his mind. Even in daylight, there was no escaping them. After all, they were the truth he had run from. A truth he was *still* running from as Loulie and the queen discussed what came next.

It was a straightforward arrangement. Loulie would again become a magic tracker. With the assistance of the queen's envoy, Ziyad, and her governors—zuama'a, they were called here—they would sail the Sandsea, locate the bindings, and repair them. In exchange, the queen would use the magic to return them to the surface and give them a weapon against Omar. For the sake of this quest, she would also return Loulie's magics to her before the summit.

"The zuama'a will be arriving in five days' time. I shall present you to them during our summit, and once we have their cooperation, you shall set sail with Ziyad." The queen paused, considering Rijah. "I cannot predict how they will react to your appearance, ifrit, so for now I would keep your involvement in this a secret."

Rijah bristled. "You would have me hide away?"

"I would have you prove yourself an ally before anyone jumps to conclusions."

The Shapeshifter, clearly disgruntled by this decision, nonetheless assented. Perhaps they had realized what Mazen and Loulie had: that whatever sanctuary this world had been meant to provide, it was a broken place now.

Mazen was quiet as he trailed the sullen group back through the archive. His eyes wandered the shelves, seeking—well, he wasn't sure. Did he expect to find some relic that would heal his ailing heart? A map that would show him how to outwit one brother and find the other?

As they exited, his eyes caught once more on the phrase above the doorway: *Everything I have seen once, I know in perpetuity.*

Mazen wished, suddenly and with great desperation, that he could predict the trajectory of his own life with such certainty. That, like Jubayr, he could map out not just the present, but whatever fate awaited him. Perhaps then he might be able to trust Qadir's final promise.

The bodyguard had sent them to this realm to protect them.

Now he wondered more and more if this place would be their grave.

10

AISHA

The sky had darkened to an ashy gray by the time Aisha let loose her seventh arrow. Like the previous six, the projectile went off mark, flying past the straw dummy to land in the dirt a distance away.

Mabrook, the Resurrectionist said. *You missed. Again.*

Aisha wasn't sure which was worse: the ifrit's sarcastic praise or the pandering encouragement her audience was lobbing at her. At first, it had just been she and Jaber out here. She had convinced the tribesman—her *savior*, the Resurrectionist mockingly called him—to let her accompany him to the shooting range on the outskirts of the camp where he practiced. She'd needed the fresh air after being sequestered in a tent for five days.

It had been good to be out in the sun again, to enjoy the breeze on her face and the sand beneath her feet, and to hear the voices beyond the muted whispers of the dead that now seemed to always muddy her mind. But then Jaber's friends—Hakim among them—had arrived to watch them practice, and she'd become acutely aware of how pathetic her archery was. She'd missed seven shots thus far, and with every miss, the men's applause grew more boisterous. Only Hakim did not cheer, just assessed her movements quietly.

Aisha could confess to being many things: a thief, a liar, a killer—

but she refused to be a failure. There was nothing she hated more than receiving pity from men.

I could help you aim. The Resurrectionist's suggestion was infuriatingly tempting.

No. Aisha's fingers tightened on her borrowed bow as Jaber shuffled up beside her. She already knew what he would say: that it was exhaustion marring her aim, not lack of skill. But gods, she really did not want to suffer his insincerity right now.

Let us show them. The ifrit's restlessness reverberated in Aisha's limbs, but she held firm. She would not let the ifrit take control of her body again. She would not—

"That one nearly hit." Jaber flashed a sympathetic smile as he gestured toward her fallen arrow, which was nowhere near its intended target. "And your posture is perfect. I suspect it was the wind that set the arrow off course."

There was no godsdamned wind.

Let us show *them.* The refrain had the calming cadence of a lullaby, fogging Aisha's mind as she reached for her quiver. She nocked another arrow. Jaber said something, but she couldn't hear him. There were just the Resurrectionist's words, which beat like a war drum in her mind. Aisha turned toward the target. She raised her chin, pulled back the string, lined up the arrow.

And shot.

The arrow hit the dummy square in the center of the chest.

Something dangerously close to triumph flared in her chest, but it was a foreign pride, one that quickly burned away to shame when she recognized the feeling did not belong entirely to her. Her hands trembled on the bow. Was she truly so desperate to prove herself that she would accept help from one of the creatures she had spent so much of her life despising?

But you shot the arrow. *It was your hands and eyes that perfected the aim.*

Aisha shuddered. The night suddenly seemed too cold, her arms too bare. She forced herself to look away from the patchwork of scars running down her skin. Scars that, not long ago, had been painted over with henna. But now the paste was fading, and she could see the unnatural blue her scars had become when she'd made her deal with the Resurrectionist.

Aisha knew they were still her scars, but they did not *look* like her scars anymore.

The men were applauding in earnest now, but Aisha could not hear them over the storm in her mind. She had always striven to keep a clear, calm head. But that was no longer so easy with the damned ifrit plaguing her thoughts.

"Bint Louas?" Jaber stood in front of her, brow furrowed. "Are you well?"

Aisha shoved the bow at him. "Fine. Excuse me."

She walked off, ignoring the murmurs from Jaber's companions as she made her way toward the encampment. Some of the tension eased from her body when she saw the fence delineating the tribe's land from the rolling dunes.

The fenced-off pasture she'd passed on her way to the shooting range was emptier than it had been before. The shepherd had retired to the shed at the outskirts of the field for his break, and the animals he'd fed stood sleepily in the area, watching her with lazy disinterest.

She had just reached the outer circle of tents when a familiar voice called her name. She turned to see Hakim walking toward her. With his leisurely pace, one might have thought he'd chanced upon her rather than chased after her.

Aisha could feel the beginnings of a headache building behind her eyes. She turned with a groan, fingers pressed to her temple. "Did Jaber tell you to follow me?" The tribesman was a gracious but overbearing host. Aisha much preferred his mother, who gave her space.

"No. I came to speak with you but did not want to interrupt your practice." He fell into step beside her. "Do you often rely on your jinn when you are at a disadvantage?"

Aisha's blood simmered at the insinuation. "She is not *my* jinn." The ifrit forced her to add, "There is no such divide or ownership between us. We are one and the same."

The mapmaker stroked at the stubble on his chin. "Is that so?"

"*No*," Aisha gritted out before the Resurrectionist could make her say anything else. "And you are mistaken. I rely on this demon for nothing."

She pointedly turned away before he could follow up with another question, annoyed by his perceptiveness. And, even more than that, annoyed at herself for allowing the ifrit to slip through the cracks of her control. The Resurrectionist, foul creature, only laughed at her frustration. *Someday you will see the folly of your ways and stop denying me.*

I will die before that happens, Aisha snapped back.

The ifrit thankfully quieted as they stepped into the heart of the encampment. In one tent, Aisha spotted a group of girls sitting cross-legged on the ground, watching a weaver pull threads through a loom. In another, a visitor spoke bashfully to a woman whose face was concealed beneath a veil. A meeting between a prospective bride and groom, most likely. Two boys fake-battled around the campfire, waving sticks in the air and proclaiming themselves warriors. When they caught sight of Aisha looking at them, they turned on their heels and fled.

"It seems your fame is intimidating." Hakim stopped beside her, a fond expression on his face as he watched the children whisper and point at them from a distance.

"Fame for *what*? I've been trapped in a tent all week."

His eyes danced with mirth. "That has only deepened the mystery, I'm afraid. You may as well be a hero out of a story to them. You possess the power of a jinn, after all."

The words were a stone in Aisha's lungs, difficult to breathe around. The *power* he was referring to had drained her body and eroded the walls of her mind. If anything, it was a curse.

Aisha chose to ignore the comment entirely. "What did you wish to speak to me about?" She darted a look at him. "Are we finally continuing our conversation from the other day?"

A few days ago, she and Hakim had traded stories. She had told him about their journey through the desert, and he had told her about the invasion of Madinne, enlightening her about the wali of Dhyme's investigation and explaining how Ahmed's suspicions of Mazen—Omar in disguise—had driven him to unravel Omar's plans. After Ahmed had discerned that Hakim was keeping Mazen's secret, he'd sought Hakim out, and together, they had tried to out-smart Omar.

They had failed. But though Ahmed had been unable to save the sultan, he'd sacrificed himself to protect Hakim, who had managed to escape the city through its underground tunnels.

Hakim's account had ended there. Because he'd spoken of the whole event haltingly and offered only the barest details, Aisha had avoided pushing him for fear he would shut her out. But now she had been here for nearly a week, and her patience was wearing thin.

She was relieved when the mapmaker acquiesced, pointing her beyond the line of tents to an oasis where they could speak more privately. The crystalline body of water was surrounded by scraggly yellow grasses and date trees plucked clean of their fruit. When they arrived, Hakim seated himself in the shade of one of those trees and pulled a rolled-up piece of parchment from his robes. He stretched it out on the ground.

Aisha crouched before the parchment with a frown. "What's this?"

Hakim regarded her somberly. "A map."

Aisha observed the twisting paths. To her, the mess of lines looked more like a spiderweb than a map. If she were to attempt tracing it, she would lose her trajectory within seconds. The sight worsened her headache. "Well, it's a shit map, then," she said. "It looks like a trap."

A faint smile touched his lips. "That is the idea, yes. The sultan's council knows some of these paths but not all of them. If they did, the tunnels would be rendered useless." He ran his fingers over the nexus of lines. "You wanted to know how I escaped the city so you could break into it, yes? This is the map I made to lead me through Madinne's underground tunnels."

"If these tunnels are so secret, how could *you* have mapped them?" It was a question she'd had ever since using one of Hakim's maps to cross the desert. How could a man who had seen so little of the world depict it so accurately?

Hakim lifted a shoulder in what Aisha assumed was a shrug. "I have a contact in Madinne."

She looked at him, dubious, but was too tired to pester him when he remained tight-lipped. Instead, she asked, "Why keep the map if only you can read it?"

"For security." Hakim raised a pointed brow at her. "And because you never know when your brother's old traveling companion might try to barter it off you." Though his words were devoid of malice, there was clear expectation in his eyes.

Aisha rose, crossed her arms. "You want something from me in exchange for the map?"

"A favor. I will guide you into Madinne if you help me find Mazen."

Aisha frowned. She had figured from the way Mazen spoke of his brother that the two of them were close, but still—it was strange to witness firsthand the bond Mazen had with Hakim, so different from his relationship with Omar.

"You've only just escaped, and now you want to go back? There's a price on your head."

"That fact remains unchanged no matter where I am. But there is one fortunate shift in my circumstances: I have an accomplished hunter to protect me."

Aisha nearly laughed aloud. "Your wish to find your brother is not enough. You need a plan, and *I* do not have the power to burn a hole into the jinn realm. I cannot help you."

"No, but you know a jinn who can."

Aisha was disquieted by the intensity of his gaze. "Your price is awfully steep. It seems to me it would be easier to take my chances breaking into the city on my own."

It was more difficult than she thought to dismiss the proposal outright. She did not regret turning away from Mazen when he'd reached out to her beneath the Sandsea; she had unfinished business here, after all. But Qadir—she could not so easily shake the guilt that gnawed at her when she thought of leaving him in Omar's hands.

She knew Omar; he never killed his prey immediately. He tortured them first.

Are you concerned for a jinn? The Resurrectionist's laughter was a mocking chuckle. *And here I thought you despised us with your entire being.*

The creature was right. This pity did not suit her. Aisha was relieved when the call for asha'a came, breaking her from her thoughts. There was a flurry of movement as the tribe abandoned their work to gather for the evening meal. Aisha could smell the spices of the food even from here—turmeric and garlic, onion and cardamom.

"Ah." Hakim smiled wistfully. "Machboos."

Aisha's stomach twisted. The last time she'd shared the chicken-and-rice dish with anyone, it had been her family. She could still remember following the aroma of spices into her mother's matbakh, where she and Aisha's aunts had worked to prepare the chicken and the fragrant bed of rice it was served with. On the occasion Aisha's mother saw her sneaking clumps of rice into her mouth, she would guilt Aisha into helping them cook.

The memory dissipated when Hakim spoke up. "Consider my offer, bint Louas. That is all I ask." A half smile tugged at his lips as he rolled up the map and stood. "I will let you have the night to think on it. Clearly, your mind has already turned to the food."

Aisha walked away with a grumble, ignoring his smile as she retraced her steps toward the crowd that had assembled before the large trays of food. While most of the hunters and scouts ate around the fire, the women preferred to eat their meals separately, recounting the day's events in their own private spaces.

Aisha had been able to escape those gatherings thus far because she'd been sequestered in Umm Jaber's tent. But devoid of that excuse tonight, she was immediately whisked away by an excitable tribeswoman. By the time she'd been hauled into the women's tent, she was regretting leaving Hakim behind. The only relief was that she was seated beside Umm Jaber, who was just as disinclined to gossip as she was. And, small mercy, her headache had vanished.

At first, Aisha was content to tune out the women's voices as she helped herself to the food. The spices were immaculate, the chicken tender and easy to peel off the bone. But then she accidentally caught the eye of the tribeswoman who had pulled her into the tent, and the woman seized the chance to renew her quest for information. This time, she had a crowd to encourage her.

The gathered women asked Aisha all manner of questions. Did she know what Omar meant to accomplish in Madinne? Did she know how his politics would differ from his father's? When Aisha declined to answer those questions, they tried more personal ones.

They pointed at the golden collar around her neck and asked her about the jinn magic humming beneath her skin. Then they asked about her journey and her companions. The longer Aisha suffered through the barrage of questions, the more exasperated she became. As one of Omar's forty thieves, she had often been treated as one of his accessories and thus disregarded. She was not accustomed to this kind of torturous attention.

The women were still trying to coax her into joining the conversation when Umm Jaber served the after-meal chai. The warm beverage did little to cool Aisha's irritation, which only grew as the interrogation changed course. The final question—the one that nearly had her hurling her cup at a wall—was whether she fancied any of Jaber's friends.

It was at that point Umm Jaber interceded, setting her fingers on Aisha's wrist as she addressed her companions. "I'm afraid our guest is ill prepared for such titillating conversation."

Aisha drank her too-hot chai and ignored the Resurrectionist as she cackled in her mind.

Thankfully, Aisha was able to finish her chai in peace after that. When it came time to excuse herself, however, Umm Jaber rose with her, insisting on accompanying her back. Aisha did not protest; it was clear from her commanding look that this was not an offer.

The campsite had quieted by the time they exited the tent, filled with the songs of mothers coaxing their children to sleep and tribespeople tending to the calmer evening chores. Aisha was surprised to see Hakim and Jaber seated by the fire, engaged in conversation. At some point, the hunter must have left to bring Samira, for the falcon now sat close to him on her perch. Whether she was awake or asleep, Aisha could not tell; her face was covered with a hood.

Based on the men's hushed voices and solemn faces, their talk looked to be a serious one.

"But you've just arrived—and now you're going *back*?" Jaber sounded aggrieved.

Hakim fiddled idly with one of the rings on his hand. His response was soft but defensive. "You know it is for my brother, ya sayyid."

Their conversation faded as Aisha trailed Umm Jaber to their tent. The first thing the woman did upon their entrance was turn on her with a scowl. "You could at least *pretend* to enjoy the conversation."

Aisha frowned. "I never asked to be a part of—"

"You have been here longer than the customary three days; you are more than just a guest now."

Aisha opened her mouth—then closed it. She *had* been here longer than the traditional three-day stay offered to most visitors. Just as there were rules of etiquette within the cities, so too were there rules of hospitality within the tribes.

Umm Jaber crossed her arms. "Do you find most conversation intolerable?"

Aisha hated that she felt like a scolded child. "I simply prefer my own company."

Her hostess regarded her cynically, one brow cocked. Aisha was beginning to realize this was Umm Jaber's most neutral expression—that skepticism had naturally etched itself into the harsh lines of her face over the years.

Eventually, Umm Jaber turned away, brushing past Aisha to root for something in a chest. "Hakim told us you did not speak to anyone in the palace, that you were like some vengeful wraith."

"No more a wraith than he was."

"There is a difference between choosing silence and being silenced." When Umm Jaber turned back to her, she was holding a small jar and a paintbrush. Aisha knew from the earthy smell that it was henna, most likely mixed for Umm Jaber's hair. Before she could help it, she glanced at her scars—at the awful visibility of them, and the terrible dead color they'd become.

Umm Jaber settled herself on a cushion and dipped her brush into the paste. "Do you want me to redraw the henna on your arms?" The offer was nonchalant; Umm Jaber did not even look up. She must have read Aisha's surprise from the quiet, however, because she added, almost as an afterthought, "Your eyes stray to the scars when your mind is occupied."

"Why would you offer me such a thing?"

Umm Jaber mixed the henna with careful precision. "I owe you for saving my son's life." It was the only thing she said before she gestured to the cushion opposite her.

After a moment of hesitation, Aisha sat and gave Umm Jaber her arm. The woman's hands were worn and calloused but firm. She settled Aisha's arm on her lap and began to paint. For a time, the tent was quiet, and there was only the sound of the brush against Aisha's skin as Umm Jaber drew. Rather than the jagged leaves and flowers Aisha usually painted, the matriarch drew interlaced lines thatched through with embroidery-like patterns.

Aisha saw the full extent of the design only when Umm Jaber released her arm. She was surprised to see words tucked between the lines. "What is this? A prayer?"

"Poetry." Umm Jaber's lips quirked. "But it can be a prayer if you wish it."

Aisha stared at the lines. She had not prayed to the gods in a long time. She was not in the habit of asking anyone—human or deity—for assistance. But these words did not feel like a plea. They felt like armor.

"Shukran," she managed to say through an irksome knot in her throat.

Umm Jaber just made an impatient sound and held out her hand for Aisha's other arm. This time, she spoke as she worked. "The last time I did henna for someone, it was for a bride."

Aisha thought of the veiled woman she'd seen speaking with the foreign tribesman. Had Aisha lived out her life in Sameesh with her family, she would have been expected to become someone's bride too. She had never thought too deeply on that future, always imagining she would run off to live on her own before she was forced to rely on a man for things she could very well do herself.

She glanced up at Umm Jaber. "Family?"

"My daughter." The matriarch swept the paintbrush carefully across Aisha's skin. "I am lucky if I see her every other season since she moved to be with her husband's tribe."

"Do you miss her?"

Umm Jaber smiled—a melancholy smile. "I have missed her every day and night since she left." She tilted Aisha's arm so that she could continue the pattern on the underside of her wrist. "And you, bint Louas? Do you miss your family?"

Aisha startled. No one had ever asked her that question before. At a loss for what to say, she simply nodded. It occurred to her only afterward that she had not told Umm Jaber about her family's passing.

For the remainder of the hour, Aisha let Umm Jaber talk. She found she did not mind this type of idle conversation where she was not expected to respond. She could relax as Umm Jaber spoke about the weather, the herds, and the sister tribes. But then the conversation shifted to the sultan's political dealings and to the taxes and trade routes that would now be under Omar's control. The moment his name came up, Aisha remembered her restlessness. She remembered her mission to kill him, and she realized Umm Jaber was right: she *had* overstayed her welcome. She needed to leave.

After the design was done, Umm Jaber set her brush down and regarded Aisha with her familiar aloof expression. "May I ask another favor of you, bint Louas?"

"So this henna *is* for a favor."

Umm Jaber shrugged, unscathed. "I have heard Hakim say he

plans to accompany you to Madinne." Her eyes narrowed. "I want you to leave without him. We could not stop the sultan from stealing him away before. But now this is the least I ask to keep him safe."

"You think I *want* to steal him away?" Aisha draped her drying arms carefully over her knees. Now, when her eyes wandered to her scars, she did not feel repulsed. They *almost* looked as if they had gone back to their normal color.

"You, a woman who prefers her own company? I think not." There was a harsh dip between the woman's brows. "But Hakim is stubborn when it comes to his brother."

"So I am learning."

Hakim had told her to consider his proposal, but here was Aisha's answer, offered to her by someone who wanted to protect him. It was easier this way. Just her, the desert, and her blades. Hakim would be a liability, likely to get himself killed before they made it to the city.

"Fine." Aisha sighed. "I shall leave once I obtain his map."

"Oh? And how do you plan on acquiring this map?"

"I'm a thief, remember? It will be a simple task."

It had *always* been a simple task. And yet Aisha had lingered. Even though she ought to have been eager to move on, she'd hesitated to leave this place for some reason.

The ifrit's voice sounded in her mind, unwanted. *Ah, sentimentality, that mortal foible.*

"Tomorrow," Aisha said roughly. "I will leave tomorrow, so long as I can steal a horse."

Umm Jaber's eyes shone with amusement. "*That* I can help you steal. Better a horse than a man." The glimmer softened as she smiled. This time, it was an honest smile, suffused with a warmth that made Aisha's heart burn. "Shukran," the woman said.

Aisha's lips curved as she tapped her wrist. "Consider it payment for the armor."

11

Mazen

The night before the queen's summit, Mazen dreamed he was stab-bing his father to death. He was in the sultan's chambers, and the bedroom was empty of people save for his father, who lay dying beneath white muslin sheets stained red. The sultan held up his hands. He begged. He screamed. But Mazen did not have control of his body. Tears streamed down his face as he stabbed his father. In the throat. The chest. Again and again and again...

Mazen woke in a panic, heart tight and body trembling. Blue lantern light streamed into his vision, illuminating his bedroom in Dhahab. Shadows shifted in the light of the flame, so bloated on the walls they all but swallowed them.

It was a dream, he told himself. *Just a dream.*

But he had to blink back tears even as he thought the words, because they were a bald-faced lie. He had not been there to witness it, but his father *was* dead. That was no fantasy.

He turned his attention out his window. Through his sheer cur-tains, he could make out the unnatural darkness of the curfew. Though he'd had time to grow accustomed to the unstable magic in the seven days they had been here, the sight always filled him with dread. Like most of the other magics they had encountered, it was incomprehensible.

A sinking country, broken bindings, a rioting ifrit... The reality of Dhahab was far more depressing than the adventure stories Mazen had grown up with. Even Rijah, who had once lived here, seemed discomfited by what the city had become. But, like the silent ifrit in the earring, Rijah seemed uninterested in speaking with them about the past.

As was his habit, Mazen reached beneath his pillow to check on the earring. But it was cold and unresponsive as always. Even Rijah had been unable to coax Aliyah into a conversation.

Mazen stood with a sigh, skin prickling with unease as he shuffled through the darkness to his closets, where he found a simple cloak to wrap around his shoulders. The fabric brought to mind his mother's shawl, which he had left in Hakim's care. His heart twisted at the memory. What if something had happened to his brother? What if Omar had captured him after all? What if he had been hurt?

What if, what if, what if?

Mazen fumbled with the doorknob until he escaped out into the sitting room. Only a single lantern was lit, and the ashfire barely brightened the space. In the dimness, Mazen noted a shawl discarded on the sofa and pearl-encrusted slippers by the open balcony doors.

Loulie al-Nazari stood barefoot on the terrace in a gown of blue gossamer, her gaze trained on the black sky and her elbows resting on the balustrade. Mazen was struck by the serenity of her profile, which looked softer still limned in firelight. She was humming— that mournful melody the Queen of Dunes had sung about a sheikh searching for his lost love.

When Loulie turned, his thoughts scattered. There was just the present—just the weight of her eyes and the heat in his chest as her gaze burned through him. Belatedly, he noticed the glassiness of her pupils and realized there were tears in her eyes.

"Salaam," he managed to say. The single word came out hoarse, paper thin. He felt as if he had intruded on some private moment.

Loulie rubbed at her eyes. "What are you doing here?"

"Nightmare," he said. And then, reflexively: "You?"

At first, he didn't think she would answer. Her attention seemed fractured as she tilted her face up to the sky. But then she echoed softly, "Nightmare."

Relief washed over him when she stepped aside in invitation. "I don't know why I thought I'd feel better out in this godsforsaken darkness," she said. "I miss the stars."

Mazen stepped onto the balcony. From the railings, he had a better vantage of the palace grounds. When they had first arrived, those gardens had been empty of visitors. Now Mazen saw movement in the courtyard as the shadow attendant guided the newly arrived jinn leaders across a field illuminated by ashfire. His and Loulie's glimpses of the zuama'a were fleeting; the queen insisted she make their introductions at the summit tomorrow night.

He turned to Loulie with a weak smile. "My brother Hakim used to tell me that it is impossible to understand a thing's value until it is gone."

Loulie grew suddenly still. "And yet there are those who would easily destroy something—*someone*—even knowing that value."

Mazen flinched. He thought of his father, who had determined that the only worth of the jinn was in their magical blood. And his brother... Suddenly, he was back in his nightmare, but it was not Mazen standing before the sultan but Omar, face streaked with blood. He did not realize he was shaking until Loulie asked him if he was okay.

"I'm sorry." Her grip tightened on the rails. "I did not mean to make you think of Omar."

Mazen resisted the urge to loosen her fingers and press them between his own. He opened his mouth to say something—anything—to assuage her worries, but Loulie spoke first.

"I know what it's like to keep living after losing everything," she said softly. "It's like sinking in the Sandsea. You don't know when the end will come or if it will. And either way, it doesn't matter, because there is no reprieve. You just sink and sink..." Her breathing hitched. "Until someone pulls you out and gives you a new purpose.

But even then, the hole remains. You can build a new life around it, but it never fills. You continue living, but you never stop sinking."

The words settled on Mazen's skin like frost, chilling him to his bones. The pain he had been trying to forget—the chasm that grew larger and deeper by the day—once more yawned open inside of him. Loulie al-Nazari was one of the strongest people he knew. If she could not escape the throes of grief, then what hope did *he* have?

His gaze wandered helplessly to the unnatural sky. It was only then, when he saw the dark veil between the realms, that Mazen was struck by the impossibility of his situation. It was true his future had been stolen from him. But against all odds, he and Loulie had made it to *another world* and survived. So long as he still breathed, there was a chance he might take his future back. He had to believe Hakim had survived. That he could return to him.

He breathed out softly. "I imagine what you say is the truth. But both of us are still here, alive. Surely it would be a shame to waste that miracle."

Loulie paused to look at him, an odd expression on her face. Was it surprise or concern written across her features? Mazen didn't know, but in the next moment, she was smiling. It was nothing but a faint curve of her lips, but it was a smile nonetheless. "True. And we did manage to survive sinking in the *real* Sandsea, which is a miracle in and of itself."

No sooner had she spoken than her smile faltered. Mazen assumed her mind had returned to Qadir, the "miracle" who had rescued them. The ifrit had saved them—and now he was suffering someplace neither of them could reach. Even now, after the queen had returned her relics, Loulie was unable to contact her bodyguard.

Mazen wished he could comfort her, but he knew her well enough to understand that she would not appreciate empty assurances. At a loss, he instead searched the courtyard for a distraction. The moment he looked up, he noticed that the air was…shimmering? No, there were *lights* in the sky. Not ashfire, but glowing orbs that bobbed gently in the air.

Mazen squinted until he could make out a blur of motion between the lights. He was surprised to see a floating carpet. A jinn stood atop the undulating surface, threading cords of light through the air that separated into the glowing orbs.

Even Loulie had paused to stare. "It's beautiful," she muttered.

Mazen felt a soft smile pull at his lips. "They look like stars."

For a time, the two of them stood there watching the jinn-made constellations scatter in the breeze. Loulie hypothesized that the lights were a display for the visiting zuama'a. Mazen was too hypnotized to speculate at all. He was so focused on the lights, in fact, that he forgot there was an enchanter until the rug drew up to their balcony.

The moment Mazen saw the jinn—*ifrit*—on the rug, he startled. "*Rijah?* What are you doing here?"

The ifrit wore a different shape tonight, a petite, curvaceous figure. Their hair, previously black, was now a pale, sandy brown that they had wrapped above their ears in a braided crown. They looked at him flatly with eyes that were, as always, turquoise blue. "My rooms are here."

Loulie peered at them over the rails. "And the light show?"

Rijah shrugged. "I was bored." In one fluid motion, they stepped from the rug onto the balcony, where they seated themself upon the rail. An irritated yowl revealed that they were not alone. A small, writhing mass of black fur struggled beneath Rijah's arm, hopping away with a hiss when they released it. Hayat crouched on the balustrade in her cat shape, fur bristling.

Loulie's brows shot up. "You've acquired a pet."

"I am not a *pet*," Hayat spat. "I was out hunting when I caught the ifrit fiddling with one of the servants' rugs. I was *surveilling* them to make sure they did not use it to escape."

Ever since witnessing Rijah's shapeshifting at the archive, Mazen had noticed Hayat "surveilling" Rijah frequently. As far as he could tell, it was not a malicious investigation. He wondered if Rijah knew she was enamored of them. If, perhaps, they were showing off on purpose.

Regardless of the intent, the display *was* breathtaking. Rijah smiled smugly when Mazen complimented them. "Ifrit magic is powerful enough to carve out an entire realm beneath the Sandsea," they said. "And yet you are surprised by magic like this?"

Hayat objected, "But your magic is false. The sky, the Sandsea, the scattered islands—all of it is a mockery of the gods' work. This realm is a trap, not a sanctuary."

Rijah waved away the protest with a flap of their hand. "We are not so haughty to think we could replicate the gods' work. Our work is not nature; it is *magic*. There is a difference." For as confident as the words were, Mazen caught a waver of regret in their tone.

He cut a glance at Loulie, whose attention had fallen to the rug floating in front of the balcony. She was frowning at it with a distinctly distrustful look.

Suddenly, he had an idea.

"Rijah." He turned to face the ifrit. "I have a favor to ask of you."

They eyed him suspiciously. "I am not in the habit of granting wishes."

"I swear it's a simple thing. We just want a moment on the rug to look at your stars."

Loulie looked up sharply. "We do?"

It was the shock in her eyes—the spark of emotion he had been looking for—that cemented the decision for him. He could not bring Qadir to her, but he *could* bring her closer to the stars. "We do. Is there a way to keep the magic contained in the palace walls?"

The ifrit regarded him, thoughtful. "I can control it from a distance." They cut a glance at Hayat. "So long as this one finds no issue with it."

Hayat looked equal parts irritated and gratified to have been addressed as *this one*. After a few moments of careful consideration, she said, "I shall allow it."

When Mazen turned to Loulie, she was glaring at the carpet over the balcony. The sight made him chuckle. Loulie scowled at him. "What are you laughing at? Must I remind you we are very magicless, very *mortal* beings? Earlier this week, we were attacked by a curse. And now you're trying to convince me to fly around on a dusty old rug?"

"Sah. It will be a good time."

"A good time until we *plummet to our deaths.*"

Looking at her flushed expression, Mazen couldn't help but smile. He remembered the last time she had looked like this—when they had danced together on a ship in Ghiban. He recalled that it was not an invitation that had motivated her, but a challenge.

"Are you scared, Layla?"

Loulie went still. Her glare became icy with determination. *"Never."*

Without preamble, she hefted herself over the balustrade. Mazen rushed forward, but Loulie was down and off the balcony before he could stop her. She dropped, landing gracelessly on the rug. A moment passed. Two. When the rug remained steady beneath her, Loulie released a breath and looked up at him expectantly.

Mazen managed to keep the smile on his face despite his nerves. Before he could think too hard on it, he pulled himself up over the rails and carefully stepped onto the rug. When his foot came down, there was a moment when it felt as if the surface might give beneath his weight. Loulie must have felt it too. She floundered, hands searching for purchase until her palm came to rest on Mazen's shoulder.

They both stood frozen for a few moments, holding their breath until the rug steadied.

On the balcony, Rijah was cackling. "I recommend you sit, unless you *want* to fall off?"

Loulie seated herself with a grumble. As Mazen lowered himself beside her, it occurred to him that though the rug was big, it was significantly smaller with *two* people on it. There was barely enough room for him and Loulie to sit side by side, and still she gave him a pointed look when their knees brushed.

Mazen was beginning to wonder if this *had* been a good idea when Rijah leaned over the balcony. "I've enchanted the rug to fly a set route. Long enough for you to take in the sights."

Loulie craned her neck to look up at them. "Wait, how fast—"

The rug lurched forward.

Mazen's breath caught in his throat as the carpet shot north on an invisible current. Loulie muttered a string of curses beside him. When the rug rippled beneath them, she grabbed for his arm, eyes darting wildly across the sky as if searching for some exit. But of course there was no escape. They were suspended in midair, with only the breeze and lights for company—

And they were *flying*.

The wonder sank in slowly, a warmth that burned Mazen's nerves away until he felt nothing but exhilaration. He didn't realize he was laughing until Loulie spoke up beside him. "You're *enjoying* this?"

"How can I not be? Look." He raised a hand and pointed.

Loulie looked. The moment her gaze fell on the web of shifting constellations around them, her grimace slackened into awe. The carpet flew them past waves of bobbing lights up to the palace walls, where large, ashfire-lit braziers illuminated a view of the city beyond.

Mazen saw their apartment wedged close to the palace's outer wall. On the other side, what he assumed were sentry towers had been built across the palace's moat. Mazen glanced beyond that moat to the city, where bursts of ashfire lit the roads and canals between the manors. As Hayat had said, the fire was scarce, the streets shifting with more darkness than light. And yet there was still a striking symmetry to the sight amidst the chaos of the ruins.

"So this is what the city looks like from up high," Loulie said softly.

Mazen marveled at the unbridled astonishment on her face. Her eyes glowed in the jinn-light, so bright and hopeful it brought the smile back to his face.

The rug turned them away from the wall, flying them back across the better-lit courtyard and above the servants walking through it. From above, the space seemed more verdant. Mazen's eyes fell on the archive, which, like the rest of the architecture, seemed smaller from up high. He wondered, Was this the way a bird saw the world? It seemed a much more welcoming place.

No sooner had he thought this than a shadow streaked across the sky beneath them. Mazen could just barely make out the flash of a yellow beak before the bird darted out of sight. It moved so quickly he could not have tracked it for Hayat even if he wanted to.

"That damned myna," Loulie muttered beside him. She frowned at his startled look. "It's been tailing us since we've arrived. Have you not noticed it?"

Mazen shook his head, perturbed. How could he possibly miss *any* bird after what the queen had said about them being Nabila's spies? When he asked Loulie why she had not told Hayat, she shrugged and said, "I assume it's what she's been hunting."

Mazen wondered at her calm but did not push the subject. They had come up here to escape prying eyes; he did not want to belabor the point.

As they passed the upper windows of the archive, his mind wandered to Hakim, who would have loved this place filled with tomes and—

Maps.

He straightened. It was an abrupt motion, one that made the rug ripple. Loulie whirled on him, a complaint on her tongue, but stopped when she saw his face. "What's that look for?"

"You said you could not reach Qadir through the dagger," he said. "But didn't Rijah say Jubayr's maps could help you find anything? And maybe...anyone?"

Understanding dawned on her face. He could tell from her sudden silence that she was thinking. *Scheming.* "You still have your shadow?"

"Yes. Why?"

"I'd like to borrow it." Gods help him, now she was grinning. "You've used the magic multiple times to avoid being murdered. *I'll* just use it to sneak around for a bit."

It was true. Mazen had used the shadow to hide from all manner of creatures, ghouls included. But even then, it was an imperfect strategy. Though Mazen was fairly certain it could trick most human eyes, ghouls were still able to smell him. What if jinn could sense the magic too? What if one of them noticed the conspicuous absence of Mazen's shadow? Of Loulie?

But Loulie would not hear his concerns. She was already planning for contingencies. She reasoned that if he could just cover for her briefly during tomorrow's summit, she could sneak in and out of the archive fast enough to locate Qadir before they all left the city. If she could not go to him, she at least wanted to know where he was, and this would be her only opportunity to avoid the queen's stifling supervision in the archive.

"This is a bad idea," Mazen protested weakly.

"It's only a bad idea if we fail."

Mazen knew he would regret this, but he did not have the heart to deny Loulie. So he told her, haltingly, about his plan. Whom it involved.

Afterward, she looked at him thoughtfully. "And you think Rijah will cooperate?"

Mazen couldn't know for certain, but he was optimistic. Rijah had been fiercely loyal to their king; surely they would want to know his fate too. Mazen just needed to convince them.

His worry must have been apparent, however, because Loulie nudged him. "So morose. Was it not you who said we shouldn't waste a miracle?"

Mazen smiled despite himself. "You're right," he said, and found himself believing it—believing in *her*.

The rest of their flight was quiet. Despite knowing what the future had in store, Mazen was hopeful. He carried that hope with him long after they had returned to the balcony and to bed, and for the first time in a long time, he did not dream.

12

LOULIE

The strangest thing about wearing Mazen's shadow was that Loulie barely felt it. The magic was featherlight when she donned it the next night, resting so loose on her shoulders she had to constantly check to make sure it had not fallen off. Skulking through the palace grounds filled with patrolling guards, she could take no chances.

Thankfully, the heightened summit security around the palace had cleared up surveillance by the archive. The few guards who had been left to circuit the area neither saw nor heard her. Loulie was relieved. By the time she ducked quietly in through the building's front doors, the weather had taken an odd turn, and the wind rippled Mazen's shadow so fiercely she worried it would fly from her shoulders.

She had just made it inside and unlatched an ashfire-lit lantern from the wall when a sudden rumble made her jump. She whirled, but there were no jinn pursuing her. Instead, she was met with the unsettling sight of lightning in the sky. The storm seemed to be progressing quickly; she hated to think how much worse it would become while she was in here.

The sooner I can find this map, the better.

For her sake, and for Mazen's and Rijah's.

With one final glance at the ominous sky, she shut the doors behind her and turned to the task at hand. Illuminated by nothing but dim firelight, the archive seemed larger than it had before, its walls and corridors intimidatingly infinite. It would be easy to get lost in a space like this without a map. But Loulie did not need a map—not when she had Khalilah's compass.

She withdrew the instrument from her bag and whispered, "Show me how to find Qadir."

The compass arrow obeyed, pointing her west through a dark corridor. Curiosity warred with caution as she wandered past shelves stacked high with scrolls and relics. She remembered the gray-winged moths she had freed the last time she was here. Was the thing the compass was leading her toward another of the Wanderer's living memories, or a true map?

The instrument led her to a bookcase, where a brief examination of the scrolls revealed that each contained a unique enchantment. One reflected the colors of a sunset when she unrolled it from a specific angle. Another contained cursive script that slithered across the page too quickly for her to decipher. But it was the last document she found that the compass arrow reacted to, shuddering visibly as she unrolled the parchment to read the single instruction written on the otherwise blank surface: *Ihraqne.*

Loulie paused. It seemed an ill-conceived idea to set fire to a piece of parchment in a library, but . . . well, she had always preferred leaping to overthinking. And she did, very conveniently, have a source of fire on hand.

She pried the lock on the lantern door open with Qadir's dagger and carefully held the parchment to the ashfire. It caught fire immediately. Less expected: the parchment began to fold in on itself as it burned, creasing into some new shape.

By the time the fire had burned out, a paper lizard sat in Loulie's palms. It was intricately formed, its body fragile but well shaped. And its eyes—they were the only thing still burning with fire as it craned its neck to look at her.

A terrible pressure built in Loulie's chest as she caught the creature's piercing gaze. How could it possibly be a memory, she thought, when there was such intention in those eyes?

"Qadir?" His name left her lips, a stunned whisper.

The memory lizard held her gaze a few moments longer before scurrying down her arm. Even the feel of its tiny claws on her skin was familiar. Only, instead of climbing up to her shoulder, where he often stood sentinel, the lizard ran *away* from her. As he moved, a pattern sparked across his back. A map, Loulie realized, though she could not read it in motion.

With a curse, she scrambled after the lizard and had nearly gotten close enough to trap it between her hands when a sudden motion caught her eye. She drew back with a gasp, fear muddying her mind as she searched for the intruder. But when the light of her lantern finally found its target, it was not a jinn she saw.

It was a bird, roosting on one of the high shelves. Loulie recognized the myna that had been watching her for the last week.

For a few moments, she stood baffled, wondering how it had followed her inside. Then she saw the squirming lizard in its talons and shot forward. "Foul menace," she snapped. "What do you want with me?"

The bird met her frown with a blank stare, its head tilted so that only one beady eye bore into her. To Loulie, that look was a dare.

"Give him *back*." She reached for the bird, but it was no use. Even on the tips of her toes, she was too short to reach the shelf. When it did not respond to her commands, she shook the bookcase, hoping to startle it into action. Unfortunately, the bird flew in the opposite direction.

Loulie chased after it, rushing through the corridors and past shelves stuffed with relics and tomes until the bird began to *ascend*, drifting out of sight to land somewhere on a second-floor walkway. Loulie paused just long enough to glance at her compass. Even knowing what she would see, she was disgruntled to witness the arrow pointing at the bird. It knew what she already did—that it had stolen her only clue.

Loulie had little choice but to backtrack and search for a staircase. It was a futile effort; there were no stairwells in the atrium that she could see. But there were ladders. Thin, rickety things she had not noticed before, because they were on the other sides of the bookcases.

She hesitated only briefly. She would not be thwarted by a *ladder*.

"Don't think too hard on it," she muttered to herself as she grasped the rungs. "What will be will be." If she tried hard enough, she could imagine it was Qadir speaking the words, that he was at her back, waiting patiently for her to climb so that he could follow.

Thankfully, the ancient object withstood her weight long enough for her to make it to the second floor, where she paused momentarily to catch her breath. It was only when she resumed her search that she realized Mazen's shadow had slipped from her shoulders during the climb. When she glanced down, she could make out the now very visible star-dusted hem of her robes.

Well, she thought grimly. *I'll deal with that later.*

The peculiar chase for the myna led her up three more floors, through four hidden doors, and into a dark passageway that would have been untraversable without the ashfire. By the time she had reached the fifth floor, she was out of breath. But she was in luck: the bird had paused to roost on the sill of a stained-glass window. This time, when Loulie approached it, it did not flee.

Instead, as she drew nearer, it began to peck agitatedly at the window.

She glowered at it. "I am *not* letting you outside."

The bird continued to tap at the glass, all the while staring at her with a disturbing intentness. Loulie considered her options. If she rushed the creature, it would likely take to the air again. She could try to bait it, but thus far she had been unsuccessful trying to coax it.

Her eyes flitted to the paper lizard still struggling feebly in the bird's talons. The sight made her heart hitch. *It is just a memory*, she told herself. *It is* not *Qadir.*

And yet, with only the dull dagger in her pocket, a memory was the closest thing she had to the reality. If Jubayr's maps changed to reflect the present, who was to say his memory magic did not work in a similar way? What if that lizard was, in some way, tied to Qadir? What if...

Her thoughts drifted as she became aware of a soft, melodic trilling that was coming from the bird. It was haunting enough that the bird had begun to sing in the silence, but even more troubling was that Loulie recognized the melody.

An old song, Qadir had called it. A song for the jinn who called Dhahab home. How many times had she heard him hum it under his breath during their travels? Just last night, she had sung it on the balcony.

> *The stars, they burn the night*
> *And guide the sheikh's way.*
> *Go to her, go to her, they say,*
> *The star of your eye.*

The world narrowed to the song and to the creature singing it. Loulie stepped forward cautiously, her eyes pinned to the bird. Was it mimicking what it had heard last night, or was it singing the song because it knew it had some meaning to her?

"Where did you learn that song?"

The melody died as the bird shuffled to hold her gaze. It gave her a meaningful look, but Loulie was at a loss for how to decipher it. Uncertainly, she approached the window.

As she had expected, the storm outside had worsened. Even through the glass, she could hear the howl of the wind and the rumble of thunder. Curiously, there was no rain, no sand. This was a dry storm.

When the bird renewed its persistent pecking, Loulie focused again on the window, searching until she found a latch on the bottom of the sill. With a few forceful yanks, the window gave and the bird—*cursed creature*—shot out into the sky.

Loulie lunged for it, but too late. It slid through her fingers, leaving her leaning precariously out a window hundreds of feet from the ground. She quickly pulled herself away from the drop, heart hammering in her throat.

The bird circled just outside, waiting for her. Where could the damned thing possibly be leading her? This was the last floor of the archive. She could go no higher than ...

The roof.

She scowled out the window. "Are you *trying* to kill me?"

The winged nuisance responded with an awful, high-pitched squawk she assumed was either a confirmation or an insult. With a growl, she tucked the compass into her pocket and carefully leaned out the window to glance at the walls. From the sill, she could make out the ivy-wrapped latticework caging the top of the building. It was broken in some places, but as far as she could tell, the latticework *did* extend to the rooftop.

Her mind spun. If Qadir were here, he would chide her for her foolishness. But he wasn't, and that was the whole reason she *was* here. So Loulie forced herself up and out the window. She eased her way out through a hole in the latticework and hooked her fingers into the structure. Ancient as the building was, the framework did not yield when she tugged on it.

This is the worst idea I have ever had.

She would have given anything to have Qadir say that to her face right now. Exasperated or not, he had always been there for her. Even distance had never been a deterrent, as he could protect her through the dagger. But now the dagger was dull and Qadir was silent. If she fell off these walls, no one would be there to catch her.

Loulie tested one of the footholds and then, when she had determined it was secure, slid in her other foot. Her whole body trembled as she flattened herself to the wall. She forced herself to take deep, calming breaths as she counted down in her head.

Thalathah. She steadied herself against the wall.

Ithnan. Took another deep breath.

Wahid.

Loulie set her sights on the dark sky and began to climb.

13

MAZEN

Mazen was no stranger to long nights, but this was the longest night of his life.

He had been restless ever since Loulie left for the archive, pacing his room and raking his fingers through his hair as he circled the fine-patterned rug. He had *known* helping her sneak into the archive was a bad idea. How had he convinced himself it was not?

Rijah watched him pace from the window alcove with a bored expression on their face. They had barely spoken since agreeing to his plan, which was maddening. Mazen had never done well under pressure, and this silence was filled with it.

He paused abruptly to look down at the rug and grimaced at the absence of his shadow. He had allowed Loulie to use the magic to conceal herself, but what if one of the visiting leaders noticed he did not cast a shadow tonight?

Rijah released a beleaguered sigh. "Can you stop moving? Watching you is exhausting."

Mazen looked at them. "Are you not afraid we might be caught?"

"I am never afraid," the ifrit said with enviable nonchalance.

Mazen could not imagine navigating the world with such brazen confidence. His father had told him many times that decisiveness was necessary to be a competent leader, but if that was the case, how had he ever trusted Mazen to rule?

"Human." Rijah was frowning at him now. "*You* were the one to come up with this plan. If you do not calm yourself, you will be the one to give it away."

Mazen knew they were right, but the knowledge did little to quash his anxiety. There seemed a thousand ways this plan could go wrong and only one way it would succeed.

When Mazen didn't say anything, the ifrit sat up and cracked their knuckles. "The merchant is not concerned for her safety, so neither should you be. We must focus."

It was the only warning they gave Mazen before their visage shuddered and re-formed, their features shifting and softening until their face was a mirror of someone else's. Mazen nearly fainted at the sight of Loulie al-Nazari sitting before him, a characteristically crooked grin on her lips. But then he saw her eyes—*Rijah's* bright turquoise eyes—and the illusion shattered. The resemblance was uncanny but incomplete.

"So?" Rijah spoke, disconcertingly, in Loulie's voice. "Are you calmer now?"

Mazen stared at them in horror. "What?"

"You are surer of yourself in her presence."

Mazen glanced toward the window. Defenestration suddenly seemed an incredibly appealing way to exit this conversation. What was he supposed to say? He *did* feel surer of himself in Loulie's presence. He must have been making a face, because Rijah's smile turned smug. Seeing the look on Not-Loulie's face made Mazen even more embarrassed.

"What?" Rijah said in Loulie's voice. "You act as if this is not a part of your plan."

Mazen rubbed his hands over his face with a groan. "It's just... you need to change your eyes. The queen will not be convinced if you don't get them right. They're a distinct color." He could see that color very clearly in his mind. They were an arresting visual, easy to call forth. "They're the shade of smothered flame," he said. "A rusted brown—no, an earthy, ember color."

Rijah raised a brow. "Is that it?"

"It's more than that. They're..." *Beautiful*, he wanted to say. Even when the rest of her face was covered, those eyes burned into his soul. "It's just, your eyes are very striking and..."

He drifted off as something occurred to him. In all the shapes Rijah had taken, they had always kept their eye color. Was it by choice, or was that the one part of their appearance they could not change?

"What?" Not-Loulie said sharply.

"You *can* change them, right? Your eyes?"

The ifrit looked moments away from punching him. Mazen tensed as they stalked toward him, stopping mere inches away. Normally, at such close proximity, they would have loomed. Now, at Loulie's height, they had to crane their neck to glare into his eyes. This close, there was no mistaking the rust-brown color they had become. "Satisfied?"

Mazen nodded hurriedly, with great relief. Not-Loulie strode back to the window alcove with a scowl. Even the way they sat, with their knees tucked up to their chin, so reminded Mazen of Loulie that he had to convince himself—again—that *she* was not the one seated before him.

As he settled himself on the edge of the bed, it struck him that this was the first time Rijah had worn a shape he recognized. He was stunned by its accuracy. In the stories he'd grown up with of the Shapeshifter, they had always taken a monstrous form. In those tales, the ifrit *was* a monster, a creature who had been buried in the Sandsea as punishment for killing the first sultan's wife. But the ifrit sitting before him now was a different being entirely.

"Will you tell me a story?" Mazen asked. "To pass the time?"

Not-Loulie eyed him suspiciously. "You want to hear a story from *me*?"

"I am curious to know how you became the Shapeshifter," Mazen said.

The ifrit's expression shuttered with suspicion at the question. It was uncanny, how quickly Rijah had mastered Loulie's faces. The irritable twist of her lips, the indignant tilt of her head, the dent between her brows Mazen so often wished he could smooth over...

He was relieved when the ifrit spoke, pulling him from the musing. "Surely you already know my story. You are a descendent of the villain who abused my power, after all."

Mazen felt a pang of shame at the words. Never mind that his ancestors' actions were not his own. If the stories were true, then his family had built their entire legacy on the back of an enslaved ifrit. He shook his head. "The story we tell is Amir's tale. It is not *your* story."

"And what image did your wicked sultan paint of me? Am I a villain? A monster?"

Yes. Again, there was that surge of indignity. It did not matter that the story had never been his. After all, Mazen had shared it before too, had even told it to Loulie al-Nazari.

Rijah must have read the answer from his face. Mazen would not have faulted them for ignoring him. Instead, the ifrit surprised him by humoring his request. "Long ago..." Rijah gave him a significant look. "*Long* ago, before your ancestor walked this world, I was a renowned hunter. No, I was the best, for I did not just capture my prey; I learned from them. Every creature I defeated, I studied inside and out so that I could mimic its shape."

Mazen cringed at the thought of Rijah opening up some creature to examine its bones. "You couldn't just understand that from looking at it?"

Rijah scoffed. "To replicate a thing's appearance is nothing but an illusion. Shapeshifting goes deeper than that, to the bones. That is why most jinn can only master one shape, if any. But *I* am not most jinn. I am the mightiest, and such a feat was not beyond my ability."

They went on to tell Mazen about their escapades, describing how they had used the shapes of other creatures to overtake their prey. But though these hunts had garnered them quite the reputation, it was one particular expedition that had connected them to Qadir. A competition that their king had hosted to test the might and cunning of hunters across the kingdom. Rijah had, of course, chosen to pursue a legendary creature.

"You hunted a *rukh*?" Mazen repeated. He remembered the shape of the large bird Rijah had taken when they'd fled Omar. They had been in that form when they fell into this realm.

Rijah smiled smugly. "A rukh the king's own soldiers could not defeat. It was a harrowing battle, but I triumphed. Of course, my king asked for evidence of the kill. I brought back more than a quill; I wore the rukh's body back into the city.

"In recognition of my skill, the king honored me with an invitation to serve at his side. That is how I came to command his armies."

"You must have been mighty indeed, to have been trusted with his army."

Rijah straightened. "I am still mighty. Mighty enough to be respected, to be *feared*—" They choked on the last word, the implication sinking in belatedly. They shook their head, dismayed. "No, that is wrong. We were not meant to be villains. My king promised us power, but only with peace. That is why we followed him. That is why we...sunk this country..."

Mazen experienced a disconcerting dissonance watching the ifrit break down in front of him. There was Loulie, expression twisted with pain, and there was Rijah, panicking in her skin. He wanted to kick himself. He had meant for the story to brighten Rijah's mood, not dampen it.

But before he could think up a way to apologize, the door burst open so violently it made them both jump. Mazen turned, expecting the shadow attendant, but it was Hayat who stood in the doorway. The jinn looked as if she had rushed here; her smoky cloak was lopsided on her shoulders, and her hair was a mess of tangled curls.

She did not bother with greetings. "Your attendant has already been called to serve the zuama'a. I am here on the wazir's orders to bring you to the diwan."

Rijah stood with a sigh. "It's about time." Their grief had abruptly vanished, replaced with a long-suffering, very Loulie-like scowl.

Hayat ushered them down the staircase and out into the

courtyard. After making sure the crescent earring was tucked in his vest pocket, Mazen followed. He made it as far as the entryway before he stopped, surprised by the sudden change in the weather. Inside, all he had seen of the sky was the darkness of the curfew.

But outside, he could *feel* the shift in the air. The wind was sharper, the cold more biting.

A storm?

A crack of lightning illuminated the sky. The sight made Mazen gape. It was as beautiful as it was eerie, a gold so stark against the blackness it looked like a tear in the fabric of the world. Not long after, thunder rumbled through the air.

Even Rijah looked disturbed by the lightning. "This realm has storms now?"

"No," Hayat said flatly. It was only then, seeing the way she grimaced at the sky, that Mazen realized the hunter was *afraid*.

"Come," she said as she strode ahead. "The zuama'a are expecting us."

14

LOULIE

The climb up the archive was never-ending.

Step by painstaking step, Loulie made her way up the wall, testing every foothold on the latticework to make certain it was secure before she hauled herself up. With every step, she told herself she was closer to the top, that an end must be in sight.

The bird—her target—circled higher and higher as if to mock her, always remaining tauntingly out of reach. It was a miracle Loulie's legs did not turn to liquid while following it. Even more of a miracle that the storm did not thwart her progress.

Smallest of mercies, the wind had changed direction during her climb. Rather than pulling at her, it *pushed* her against the wall. During one terrible moment when her foot slipped, it was powerful enough to pin her to the latticework until she regained her balance.

By the time she finally made it to the rooftop, Loulie was too weak to stand. She was thankful for the flat surface, which allowed her to collapse without fear of falling. She could barely hear her thoughts over the wind, which now pulled at her as an upward draft.

Look up, it seemed to insist.

Loulie craned her neck to look at the bird as it coasted downward, flying in lower and lower circles until she could make out its beady eyes. Carefully, she inched her way toward it—only to fall back with a gasp when the ground in front of her erupted with fire.

It was a familiar flame, made up of etchings that glowed beneath her feet. Another part of the binding, she realized with shock. But unlike the markings in the scorched city clearing, these lines tangled together at the center of the roof to create a complicated knot.

She glanced across the markings, searching for the myna, but it had vanished.

"The bird was merely a guide and is of little consequence to you. Approach the binding."

Loulie froze. The howl of the wind was no longer just a scream in her ears. It was a *voice*, goading her forward. She reached for Qadir's dagger as she rose, holding it before her as she turned in place, searching for the source.

The wind—*was* it the wind?—snapped at her arms peevishly. *"Careful, human. You will hurt yourself with that blade."*

Wherever the voice was, it was being carried to her from all directions. Loulie was still searching for its owner when a blur of motion caught her eye. She spun, half expecting the spy to have reappeared, but the figure approaching the rooftop was no bird.

"I see you have found the center of the binding."

Loulie's heart stuttered at the sight of the queen. The jinn stepped from the sky—off a floating carpet—and onto the opposite edge of the rooftop. Her silver eyes narrowed, glowing with accusation. "I knew you were working with Nabila. Where is she?"

Loulie struggled to make sense of the queen's sudden appearance. What did it mean that she was here during the summit? Had she discovered Mazen and Rijah's plan?

"What are you doing here?" She backed away. "How did you know where I was?"

"I asked my question first." When the queen stepped forward, Loulie saw blades glimmering on her back, her hips.

The jinn began to circle the binding. "Answer me, human. *Where is Nabila?*"

It was then the pieces clicked in Loulie's mind. The storm, the wind, the voice—the tempest that had spoken to her was no tempest at all. It was the infamous ifrit.

"Show yourself, Nabila!" the queen called to the wind. "Or shall I kill your servant?" Her eyes fell on Loulie at those last words, and there was the promise of death in them.

"*The human means nothing to me.*" This time, the words reached them both. The queen froze, canting her head toward the sound. The invisible ifrit continued, "*I am here for the dagger, which is mine by right. It belonged to the Ashfire King. In his absence, it belongs to me.*"

Two things happened then.

First: the queen saw the dagger in Loulie's hands and charged toward her.

Second: the howling wind pulled at Loulie's body, dragging her toward the binding. "*Give me the knife,*" it commanded. Loulie struggled helplessly against the ifrit, but the gale was a wall she could not surmount.

Rage scorched through her at the pull of the magic, burning brighter than her confusion. She knew then that she had been used—that the bird and the wind had guided her here to deliver the dagger to this ifrit, who would use it on the binding. But Loulie refused to hand it over.

The knife was *hers* by right.

"No!" In one final act of defiance, she dropped to her knees. She scrambled to hold on to something—anything—that would stop the storm from pulling at her, but there was just the binding burning warm beneath her fingers.

But she had the dagger. With a yell, she thrust the weapon into the floor.

There was a terrible howl. The queen's scream, magnified by the wind. And then: a soft rumbling, as if the ground itself was quaking. Loulie braced herself as the world went white.

15

MAZEN

Much to Mazen's relief, the queen's summit was being held not in her weapon-filled throne room, but in a much less intimidating diwan. Or at least, he assumed it would have been a less threatening space without the wide windows, which were currently flooding the room with storm light. The garish brightness illuminated a chamber filled with beautifully dressed jinn. The zuama'a, Mazen assumed, seated on cushions around a low-rising table.

The scene was hazy, clouded by the smoke emanating from a lit mubkhar at the room's entrance. Mazen recognized the scent of bakhoor, pungent and sharp. It was a nostalgic smell, one that reminded him of the incense his mother had burned for her guests. As a child, it had made him feel warm and drowsy. Now it put him on edge. The amount of smoke coming from the mubkhar seemed unnatural. Was it? Or was his paranoid mind playing tricks on him?

He and Rijah entered the chamber to heated conversation.

"And where is Her Majesty now?" one of the jinn leaders demanded. "Did she not organize this meeting with the intention of solving this very problem?"

The wazir curtly responded, "As I earlier explained, Her Majesty is responding to a matter of great urgency and will return as soon as she has resolved it."

"A matter more urgent than *that*?" Another jinn jutted a finger at the flashing sky.

The question remained unanswered as Hayat led them into the chamber. The moment the visiting jinn saw them, the conversation dwindled into silence. Hayat faltered briefly as their eyes fell on her. She promptly cleared her throat, announced "the two human guests," and then sidled away to a more discreet corner of the chamber.

Mazen felt stripped bare by the leaders' scrutiny. Amongst the patricians seated before him, he recognized only two. The queen's envoy, Ziyad, who sat close to the entrance, casually leaning back on the palms of his hands, and the wazir, Firas, who sat at the end of the table.

It looked as if they had interrupted not just a conversation but a meal. Mazen saw dishes piled high with kabda. Other guests had decided to fill their plates with murabyan rather than liver, topping their cooked shrimp with onions and dried loomi. There was even a plate of malfoof on the table; Mazen was surprised to see the stuffed cabbage rolls at a formal gathering.

"Humans." Firas's voice seethed with annoyance. "Please, have a seat."

He gestured to two cushions on either side of the table and waited until they were both settled before turning back to the zuama'a. "And there you have it. The rumors confirmed. I am pleased to introduce you to the *living*, breathing humans the queen has taken in as guests."

One of the visitors—a jinn whose coal-black eyes smoldered a disconcerting red—leaned forward to peer at him. "They look dull," she declared. "Weak."

Firas shrugged. "I assure you they are only weak-bodied, not weak-minded."

"I assure you we are neither," Not-Loulie said with an edge of defensiveness. "We would not have made it through the desert if we were incapable of protecting ourselves."

Another guest, a large, barrel-chested jinn who wore jeweled chains in his belt, released a laugh loud enough to shake the platters on the table. "*Your* desert is tame. How long will you last wading through sinking sand?" He cut a sharp look at the wazir. "Surely these are not the creatures Her Majesty has put her faith in. What skills could they possibly possess that would help us? My tribe has already fled one home—I must be able to promise them safety."

Mazen dimly remembered the conversation he had overheard in the throne room between Ziyad and the queen. They had mentioned a jinn—the zaeem of Kharjem—petitioning the queen for help. *A miracle or a war*, he had threatened. Mazen assumed this was him.

Ziyad spoke up from the other side of the table: "They are good liars," he offered. And then, after a moment of consideration: "They are *confident* liars. But more importantly, they possess valuable ifrit magic and have reason to assist us. Is that not enough?"

The zaeem of Kharjem scoffed. "It was the ifrit who trapped us here to begin with. And it is an ifrit who would destroy the country. What reason do we have to trust their magic?"

Not-Loulie bristled. "Their magic is the only thing stopping this place from collapsing."

The zaeem with the coal-black eyes smiled flatly. "Had the ifrit not sunk this country in the first place, we would not have needed their protection at all."

The comment sent up a flurry of heated conversation as the jinn began to argue about who was at fault for their stagnant world. Mazen did not know what to do with himself. He did not want to say anything that might make either the zuama'a or the queen condemn them. But...

His attention shifted to the wazir, who was attempting the impossible task of placating every guest. He was clearly filling in for the queen, but why? Where had she gone? The thought of her wandering the palace while Loulie was unaccounted for made Mazen nervous. Was it possible to ask after the queen's disappearance without drawing suspicion?

As the jinn argued, attendants—their attendant, split into various shadows—swept soundlessly through the chamber, pouring chai. She set a steaming cup in front of Mazen without so much as acknowledging him. He gaped at the liquid inside, which was so hot it was *boiling.*

"Too hot for you, Yousef?" Mazen turned to see Ziyad grinning at him. "You are awfully quiet tonight. The storytellers I know are more verbose."

Mazen plastered what he hoped was a confident smile on his face. "A good storyteller waits for the opportune time to make his introduction." He glanced at Ziyad's cup. Unlike the others, this one was not steaming. As far as he could tell, it was filled with water.

"Not one for chai?" he asked.

"This is not for drinking; it is for seeing." Ziyad presented the cup to Mazen. "With my magic, water is a mirror, and I can see any reflection in it." He gestured to the water's surface, which reflected a chamber filled wall-to-wall with weapons—the throne room.

Mazen gaped. "You can see through any surface of water?"

"Any water that is marid enchanted." Ziyad inclined his head toward the bickering jinn. "How do you think Her Majesty summoned the zuama'a here so quickly? There is a reason she named me her messenger."

Mazen was amazed despite himself. He had witnessed many magics since his arrival, but the marid remained as mysterious here as they had on the surface. "Do all in your tribe possess this magic? Can you speak through the water as well?"

Ziyad's brows lifted as he took the cup back. "You are full of questions, ya sayyid. Are there no stories to share of my tribe on the surface?"

Mazen fought a flinch. Most of the stories *he* knew of the marid were tragedies. But he could not confess that, so he said, "I am afraid not. The marid are an enigma to us."

Ziyad looked amused by this answer. He twirled the cup in his fingers. "You must understand, Yousef, that water is our life. It is how we travel, how we communicate, and how we live. The war may have scattered us across the country, but the water connects us."

Mazen was awed. As he glanced at the reflection, he recalled the water-filled braziers by the queen's throne. It made sense she would use the magic to speak with her envoy, but the chamber was currently empty. Who was Ziyad speaking to? Before Mazen could ask, a deafening howl rattled the windows, scattering his thoughts. The conversation paused as everyone in the diwan stopped to stare outside.

The tempest had worsened, the wind tearing so viciously at the trees they looked in danger of being ripped from the ground. Strangely, there was no rain. No sand. There was just the wind, pitched into an angry shriek.

It was the wazir who broke the nervous silence first. "I assure you Her Majesty is no fool. She has summoned you here tonight because we are all working toward the same goal. The humans' appearance in the city is serendipitous."

"Serendipitous like *ifrit* magic," the zaeem of Kharjem spat. He gestured out the window with a scowl. "Am I right in assuming that is what this storm is? The only reason Her Majesty would not be here is if she had finally caught her prey."

Mazen stared out the window. Hayat had earlier confirmed that storms were unusual here, but he had not given thought to what that meant. Now his chest tightened with dread at the thought of an ifrit stalking Loulie's steps.

He had to find a way to warn her. But how?

The jinn had gone back to arguing about the storm. One of them said, "How could Nabila have possibly gotten past the barrier around the city? You said it barred all magic."

Firas had apparently given up on any pretense of keeping the peace. He grimaced as he spooned sugar into his chai. "Her Majesty believes she entered through the gate."

One of the zuama'a, a jinn with an impressively long, knotted beard, said, "The single gate into the city, which is *guarded*, sayyidi? You said only we would be allowed to pass through it in the coming days."

"I know what I said," the wazir snapped. He raised his cup with a glower and drank the scalding liquid without flinching.

Mazen shot a look at Rijah, but the ifrit was thankfully not partaking in the too-hot chai. Their attention was fixed intently on the jinn. "Then . . . Nabila is here? One of you let her in?"

Firas set his cup down on his platter hard enough to crack the porcelain. "*Khalas.* We will speak no more of conspiracies until Her Majesty returns." He flicked his wrist, a subtle motion that moved the guards around the room like shatranj pieces. They stepped in front of the windows and the door, indiscreetly blocking off the exits. The message was clear: none of them would be leaving this chamber until the queen returned.

Mazen swallowed. *Please let Loulie be safe. Please.*

"I suggest," the wazir said coolly, "that we find some other topic of conversation."

The leaders were notably tense as they stared around the table at each other. Only Ziyad looked untroubled as he swirled a finger through the water in his cup. Behind the glass, Mazen could just barely make out the shimmering scales that had appeared on his skin.

He must have been staring, because the marid winked at him, once more revealing the sharp teeth in his mouth. "I have a suggestion, sayyidi," he said.

The wazir nodded at him to continue.

Ziyad angled his head toward Mazen. "We have a storyteller in our midst. A *famous* one, if he spoke the truth. Does this not seem the perfect time to put his skills to the test?"

All eyes turned to Mazen. He fought the urge to shrivel beneath the sudden attention. What kind of story could he possibly tell to entertain a group of jinn that lived and *breathed* magic? He thought back to the tales he had shared in the Ghiban souk. Most of them had been his own adventures—"The Tales of Yousef," he had dubbed them. But it seemed unwise to share those stories here. Perhaps the zuama'a would enjoy the story of some mythical creature?

He thought of the birds Hayat had been hunting. He knew a good many bird stories—tales of birds who possessed infinite wisdom and birds who were big as mountains. He knew stories about birds who granted wishes and birds who were jinn in disguise. But in all those stories, the heroes used the mythical birds' magic to defeat jinn.

He thought of the other magics he had experienced. The shadows, the curfew, the—

Ashfire.

His eyes flitted to the torches on the walls. There were many stories of magic fire in the human realm, but one came to mind immediately. This story too he had shared in the Ghiban souk. It was different from the others, a lesser-told tale because it did not have a happy ending. Not for a human, at least.

As the memory of the story filled his mind, Mazen felt reinvigorated. He sat up, pulling the story around him like a shield. "It would be my honor to share a tale with you all." He glanced around the table, taking in the sight of the suspicious jinn. Even Rijah looked exasperated. The attention, which would have moments ago unnerved him, now emboldened him. A grin stretched on his face as he spoke. "This is a tale powerful enough to cross worlds. A story of a creature lost to time but never to memory.

"This," he said grandly, "is the tale of the bird with the flaming feathers."

The Tale of the Bird with the Flaming Feathers

Neither here nor there, but long ago...

There once lived a human king who ruled a prosperous desert kingdom. The great man was known far and wide for his generous spirit and for providing succor to all who petitioned him, citizens and foreigners alike. His reputation drew all manner of visitors to him, including, one day, a sheikh who arrived at the start of the Storm Season.

As he had with all the guests before him, the king bade the sheikh to kneel before his throne and share his woes. The man humbly recounted his story thus: "As you know, Your Majesty, the season has turned and, with it, the weather. But this year has been worse than the others, for these storms have brought with them an adversary like no other."

He went on to tell the king that a fearsome beast had begun to appear during the storms: a bird made of fire whose feathers streaked an inferno through the landscape. Already the sheikh had lost countless of his people to the catastrophes.

"We have tried time and again to destroy the creature, but

with no success," the sheikh said. "Its body burns every arrow we shoot at it, and it flies too high for any of our hunters to capture. I beseech you, Your Majesty: please help us capture this foe before it decimates our lands. The bird has flown west, where it makes its nest in a giant hole."

Upon hearing this sad tale, the king was filled with great sympathy. After promising the sheikh he would capture the bird, he called his three sons to the throne room and relayed the sheikh's story. "You all are competent hunters. Now, I should like to see which of you is the finest. Whoever finds a way to capture this bird shall earn my favor and the throne."

And so the three brothers made ready for their trip. The eldest, Ghassan, packed hunting equipment. The middle brother, Hussein, packed provisions. And the youngest, Fayez, packed the cage they would use to capture the bird. Knowing the nights would be long and the journey demanding, he also packed his riqq so that he might play his instrument to lift their spirits.

For a time, the brothers traveled in each other's company. The eldest brother, Ghassan, hunted for them every night. The middle brother, Hussein, tracked the creature's most likely path on a map. And what of the youngest brother, Fayez? Like his brothers, he was dedicated to his task, and he spent every daylit hour searching the horizon for the flaming bird. The nights, he spent playing his riqq for his brothers, who were grateful for the respite.

The three brothers traveled a great distance until they reached a hole so wide it took one whole day to circle it. By night's end, they knew that it must be the hole where the flaming bird made its nest, for it was both unnaturally deep and hot. Crevices such as these were where jinn made their home, and Ghassan and Hussein were understandably wary. Only Fayez peered determinedly over the edge and insisted they investigate.

When it became clear he would not be deterred, Ghassan held the rope, and Hussein helped him navigate. Fayez climbed a long time, but the dark was endless and the heat hot enough to blister his skin. Sensing his exhaustion, Hussein begged Ghassan to pull him up.

But an idea had occurred to Ghassan. He had realized his brother's life was in his hands and that all it would take to eliminate him from his father's consideration was a simple slip of the rope. His mind made up, Ghassan feigned fatigue. He pretended to pull and tug at the rope, and then, when Fayez was nearly to the top, he dropped it. With nothing to anchor him to the surface, Fayez plunged into the depths with a scream.

But rest easy, gentle friends, for the gods watch over those with just hearts! Though Fayez fell for a long time, he eventually reached the bottom of the hole, whereupon he landed on a field of clouds, uninjured. Just as he had suspected, the hole was a gateway into a hidden realm. Thanking the gods for their mercy, he descended the layers of clouds to a tower where a dozen birds circled. No sooner had his foot touched the structure than the creatures opened their beaks and screamed in unison, "An intruder! An intruder! A human intruder!"

In a heartbeat, Fayez was captured and brought before the master of the palace, a fearsome jinn warrior with burning eyes and blazing skin. The warrior sat upon a grand throne, but more brilliant still was the bird made of fire perched behind him on a large brazier.

When the jinn commanded Fayez to speak his business, Fayez pointed to the fearsome creature and said, "That creature is my only business. I am the son of a king, and his order is to capture the bird that has been terrorizing our people."

The jinn released a rumbling laugh that shook the foundations of his palace. "Would you condemn a creature for its nature? Fire is made to burn, foolish human."

Fayez shook his head. "Even fire must be contained, else it will spread relentlessly."

The jinn tapped his nails against the arm of his throne and thought. After some consideration, he offered Fayez a deal: he would give him the bird if he found a way to trap it. Fayez had until the end of the day, and if he was unsuccessful, *he* would become the jinn's prisoner instead. There was nothing to be done for it. Fayez agreed, and the moment he made his promise, the palace unfolded around him, the small chamber stretching into wide corridors filled with traps. The warrior and his throne vanished, as did the flaming bird.

And so the prince began his hunt. He wandered the enchanted corridors until day darkened to night and only shadows remained to keep him company, and still he saw no sign of the bird. It was only then, in his panic, he remembered the burning brazier in the throne room.

Back through the corridors he rushed, sprinting until he had returned to the chamber. Inside, he pulled two objects from his hunting satchel: a bow and a manacle. He wielded the bow first, loosing an arrow into the faint embers. Just as he had hoped, the bird had been hiding in the fire, and it rose from the brazier with a scream. Fayez immediately moved to set the manacle on its talon, but the bird's fire was so intense it burned through the metal immediately.

The jinn's laughter echoed in the chamber as the creature fled. "Foolish human, you cannot trap fire in chains! Continue like this until midnight and your life will be mine."

With only hours remaining, Fayez returned to his task. He

attempted to catch the bird with weapons, with steel, even with water, but all his tools were ineffective. As the day neared its end, he combed frantically through the sheikh's story in search of another solution.

It was then he recalled the bird's fascination with storms. Acting on a premonition, Fayez returned to his bag of supplies. This time, he withdrew his treasured riqq. Instead of a song, he shook and beat a rattling disharmony upon its surface, replicating the chaos of a storm.

Just as he had hoped, the bird mistook the sound for rainfall and rushed into the chamber. It rode Fayez's music with the grace of a bird riding the winds, and when Fayez walked it to the cage, the bird was enamored enough to follow him.

The moment Fayez trapped the creature inside, the jinn materialized before him in a shower of angry sparks. "What trickery is this, human?"

Fayez lowered his riqq and looked the jinn in the eye. "You told me my task was to capture the bird, and so I have. I may not have the power to conjure a storm, but I can emulate the sound with my riqq. Do you intend to break your promise?"

The jinn drew himself up at the accusation. "I gave you my word, and my word you shall have. But remember, foolish human: fire is made to burn."

Having repeated his ominous warning, the jinn returned Fayez to the surface with a snap of his fingers. A blink, and Fayez was standing before his city with the flaming bird in its cage. When the king saw the youngest son he had thought dead returned, he was filled with euphoria. True to his word, he declared Fayez would have his throne, and the decision was celebrated by everyone but Ghassan, who cursed his brother's miraculous return.

For one week, the eldest brother locked himself away and refused any guests. Until, one day, his isolation was interrupted by the very sheikh who had begged for their help. When Ghassan asked his business, the man bowed his head and said, "Your family was kind enough to offer assistance when I was in need. Now I would repay the favor with advice."

Clouded as his heart was with malice, Ghassan thought nothing of this strange visitation. He beckoned the man to go on, and the sheikh continued, "Your brother has proven himself superior because he captured the bird. If you would hope to best him, you must do more than keep the bird in its cage. You must tame its fire."

Perhaps, had Ghassan not been consumed by his greed, he might have noticed the sheikh's conniving smile. But his heart was stained deep with jealousy, so he made his way through the palace until he came to the vault where the bird was housed. There, as the sheikh had advised, he tried to command it. But the bird was not so simple a creature. It was made of magic and fire, neither of which would obey a human, and it was uncompelled by Ghassan's voice.

With a cry, it took to the air, fleeing its cage and escaping into the corridors. The servants watched, helpless, as it trailed fire through the halls and then into the city, where an unnatural storm had begun to brew.

As the city burned, a single man approached the tempest. It was Fayez, attempting to call the bird back to him with his riqq. But the instrument was no match for the wail of a true storm.

A single figure strode toward him from the heart of the tempest. Fayez was shocked to see the jinn warrior, now wearing a sheikh's robes. All at once he understood that the sheikh and the jinn were one and the same. "Why have you done this?" he demanded. "Why would you trick us into trapping your own creature so that you could unleash it upon us?"

The warrior's smile was fearsome in the burning light. "It was your brother who doomed you. I have approached many humans with my story. Always, they are the cause of their own demise. You cannot condemn fire for its nature, but you can condemn a human for his greed."

Fayez saw then that the hunt was a test they had been destined to fail. It was never the fire he ought to have feared, but the ambitions of his brother. Knowing he had already lost, he lowered himself to the ground. "Please. Call off your creature and I will give you anything."

The warrior smiled. "Surrender your lands to me and I will spare your citizens."

Fayez was filled with despair. In naught but a week, he had won, then lost his throne, but he had no choice. Even without his land, he was still a king, and he could not bear to see his people suffer. So he lowered his head and said, "My land for their safety."

The jinn smiled. "I gave you my word, and my word you shall have." He snapped his fingers, and as if they had been nothing more than a dream, the bird and the city vanished.

Fayez found himself in the desert, a king of refugees. It is said he and his people still wander to this day, though the name of their tribe and city has been lost to time. But though the city may be forgotten, the inferno that claimed it lives forever in our memories. The firebird, we call it, a creature that can be neither contained nor chained.

Remember this, gentle friends: what might today be a flame will tomorrow be ashes. We cannot condemn fire for its nature, but if we attempt to master it, we are doomed to burn with it.

16

MAZEN

The last time Mazen had shared a story with an audience, he had spun a fiction from his family history. This tale was different. *This* story was not a confession but an escape, and Mazen lost himself in its telling. Just as he had become Yousef, he was now Fayez, and he shouldered the young man's grief as everything he loved collapsed into sand between his fingers.

It did not occur to Mazen until the story had ended that for as much as the tale had sunk into him, he had also sunk *himself* into the story. Beneath the fiction lay an echo of his own truth. The quest for magic, the stolen kingdom, the betrayal of a brother... It was as if Mazen were seeing himself in a shattered mirror of his own creation.

Had his mother always told the story this way, or had he given it a new shape in his grief?

The question gnawed at him as the tale ended and silence washed over the chamber. There was no applause, no commentary, but the ensuing quiet was a thoughtful one, interrupted only by the faint shriek of the storm beyond the windows. Even the glow of the ash-fire seemed more subdued than before, burning low on the torches.

The bearded zaeem was the first to break the silence. "Is this a true story?"

Mazen was gratified by his curiosity. "All stories contain a sem-blance of truth."

Ziyad flashed a grin from the other side of the table. "So, what is the truth of this story? That power-hungry humans are easily deceived? That they ought not to play with fire? Or…" His eyes glinted with mischief. "Is this a history? The truth of a king who escaped to the surface?"

The implication settled slowly. One of the jinn muttered, "The banished king?"

The title sent a ripple of disquiet through the chamber. The Ash-fire King had escaped to the surface long ago—what if this story explained his absence?

The zaeem of Kharjem hummed under his breath. "If anything, the firebird reminds me of one of Nabila's spies. *She* is the harbinger of storms, after all." He shot Mazen a wary look.

Mazen watched, nonplussed, as this possibility was discussed in earnest.

"Silence!" the wazir barked. "We are done with the subject of the ifrit."

The ashfire wavered with Firas's command, and even the storm seemed to grow more turbulent, but now that Nabila's name had come up again, the jinn were restless. Mazen suddenly felt claustro-phobic. The questions, the darkness, the storm—it all rang too loud in his mind.

He had just opened his mouth—to say what, he was uncertain—when the ground shuddered beneath them. The conversation halted as the ashfire flickered so aggressively on the torches it threw a parade of menacing shadows across the walls. Even the wazir froze as he tried to pinpoint the disturbance.

When the shaking came again, the whole *building* shuddered, and the ground beneath them gave an ominous moan. The tremor could not possibly be a consequence of the tumultuous winds.

Mazen's panicked mind offered only one suggestion: "An earth-quake?"

"No," Rijah said faintly. "Something is happening to the binding."

They were looking at their wrists—at the exposed skin above their sleeves where the binding marks had materialized on their skin.

His mind immediately went to the only person he knew who could enter those bindings.

Loulie.

The diwan erupted into pandemonium as the leaders drew to their feet. The floor was not the only thing shaking. The ashfire too quivered erratically on the torches. Mazen watched in horror as, one by one, the flames around them guttered out.

Without the ashfire, the room was plunged into a void-like darkness. *Curfew magic*, Mazen thought, but there was no making sense of the blackness that had suddenly engulfed the space. This was more than darkness; it was *emptiness*, a blankness so heavy it carved out Mazen's senses.

Suddenly, it was impossible to breathe. Impossible to *move*. His body felt like it was encased in stone, his limbs heavy and useless, as if he were underwater. A strange coldness began to creep into his skin, making him shudder.

And then, as abruptly as the darkness had fallen, it shattered.

Mazen gasped as one of the torches surged to life behind him, the fire rising with a shriek. As his vision slowly returned, he saw that the ashfire had not just grown larger—it had taken on a defined shape. He saw wings, a beak, and hollow eyes.

A bird.

No, not just any bird. This was the creature he had moments ago described in his story.

The ashfire burned bright above his head, so hot and fierce he found himself sluggishly ducking to the ground to avoid it. He saw the jinn do the same, their eyes round with fear as the bird soared above them.

It's . . . real? Mazen stared incomprehensibly at the creature.

Someone grabbed his arm—Rijah. "Human," they whispered. "What have you done?"

Mazen helplessly shook his head. He had no idea what was happening—how the firebird he had just described was *here*, circling the chamber. He and the zuama'a watched the bird until it crashed through one of the windows and out into the night. In the wake of its absence, there was only the wind, which howled angrily through the room.

The moment the bird vanished, the ashfire in the diwan shuddered back to life, revealing the shattered remains of plates and silverware that had been on the table. But no one was looking at the broken porcelain. They were looking at *him*.

The wazir's flaming eyes bore into him with such intensity it made Mazen's skin crawl. "You summoned one of her spies," he said. "I *knew* you were working with Nabila."

Firas raised his hand. Mazen flinched back, thinking the wazir would strike him. Instead, he felt a sudden burning under his skin. He gasped as the feeling scorched through his blood, his veins and...into his hand? He realized it was coming from the tattoo on his skin. When he glanced down at it, he saw the eye's iris, normally a stenciled oval, was beginning to fill. Mazen's vision expanded with it, the world around him dissolving until he was...

On a rooftop?

He could not be sure, but the way the sky was angled above him, he felt closer to the darkness than he had before. The strange perspective, the constant motion—he realized he was watching this scene through a tattoo on someone else's hand. A moment later, the vision stabilized enough for him to see the ground flash with bright blue fire. A part of the binding, he realized, just like the one in the scorched clearing. And standing in the center of the magic, staring at him with terrified rust-brown eyes—

Loulie al-Nazari.

Even as the diwan unfurled once more around him, he could still see Loulie staring at him with horror in her eyes. He came back to himself slowly, noticing that the leaders had a similarly foggy look in their eyes. They must have all been held captive by the same magic.

It was then Mazen realized the wazir's magic could do more than predict the fall of the curfew. It could see everything—*everyone*—in the city. They had been fools to underestimate it.

Firas regarded him coldly. "Now you see the urgent matter the queen is attending to."

Too late, Mazen realized what he had seen—what they had *all* seen—was Loulie standing in the center of a broken binding. And that same person was also, impossibly, here.

"*Human.*" The wazir snapped as he looked at Not-Loulie. "How are you here?"

Rijah did not bother responding. Not with words, anyway. In one fluid motion, they claimed a blade from one of the surrounding soldiers. On their command, the weapon began to burn, the flames licking at hands that should not have been able to withstand their heat.

"She has a flaming sword!" one of the zuama'a cried.

"*She* is no human at all," the wazir snapped. "Capture them!"

Perhaps, had they not all been reeling from the chaos, the soldiers might have succeeded. But Rijah had the element of surprise, and they easily cut through the jinn barring the doors, yanking Mazen after them.

The two of them made it as far as the courtyard before they ran into another blockade of soldiers. Rijah shed their disguise as easily as if it were a cloak, shifting from Loulie's petite form into a more muscular body. They tackled one soldier as another came after Mazen.

Mazen, weaponless, had no choice but to flee. But the storm pushed at him as he moved. Against that terrible force, he was helpless. When he toppled backward, the pursuing soldier was unprepared to catch him. The two of them collapsed in a heap on the ground.

"Human!" Rijah's voice was a roar above the storm.

Mazen looked up just in time to see the ifrit, now in the form of a panther, lunge at a still-standing soldier. When the soldier's blade fell, Mazen scrambled toward it on his knees. He picked up the blade just in time to deflect the strike of the soldier chasing after *him*.

His arms burned as he held the sword up. Out of the corner of his eye, he saw that they had been surrounded. The zuama'a stood dazed outside the diwan, watching from a distance as the soldiers drew closer. Mazen could make out Hayat in the crowd, staring with wide eyes. And then his attention was caught by the wazir. Firas, who strode confidently past the guards with an object cradled in his hands. Mazen froze at the sight of the lamp.

"I *told* Her Majesty you were not to be trusted. Now we know for certain you are working with Nabila." Firas's lips pulled into a cruel smile. "I am afraid to say that by the time my queen is done with your friend, she will be nothing but a corpse. She will not let Nabila escape."

Mazen was not the only one who had noticed the lamp. Rijah turned, shooting toward the wazir with a desperate shout.

Firas clutched the lamp in his hands. "You will desist *at once*."

Fire flared across the lamp, burning the binding across its surface. When Rijah fell, Mazen rushed toward them. The blade fell from his fingers as he crouched at their side.

"Rijah!" Mazen reached for them, only to hiss when their skin burned his palm.

"Go," the ifrit whispered.

Mazen felt the burn of the tattoo on his skin as the wazir approached. Again, he found himself torn between realities. He was on his knees in the courtyard before Rijah. He was on the rooftop watching Loulie flee as the queen pulled a blade on her.

She was in danger. She was—

"Listen to me, human." Rijah's voice was a pained murmur at the edge of his consciousness. "My king commanded I protect you. So *go*. Find the merchant."

Mazen shook his head. He saw the queen's soldiers approaching. The moment they surrounded them, there would be no escape. But Mazen could not leave Rijah. He searched frantically for the blade that had fallen from his hands, but it was too far for him to reach.

His eyes landed on his shadow. His shadow, which, at some point, had returned. The sight filled him with despair. He had not noticed its reappearance in the dimly lit chamber.

The soldiers were nearly on them now. Mazen's fingers found the edge of his shadow. His eyes darted helplessly to Rijah. "But you—"

"*I* will help myself," the ifrit said. "Have you forgotten what I said in your room?"

I am never afraid.

Watching the ifrit's body crumble, Mazen struggled to believe it. But he was running out of time. With a mumbled prayer, he swept his shadow over his body and ran into the storm, charging past the startled soldiers and toward the heart of the cyclone on the archive rooftop. The rooftop where he knew Nabila would be.

The rooftop where Loulie was.

17

LOULIE

Loulie sat in the center of a cyclone, unharmed.

The world shifted beneath her feet. *Earthquake*, her rattled mind supplied. She had only meant to anchor herself against the wind, not disrupt the binding. But there was no mistaking its source, not when an inferno raged around her.

She drew slowly to her feet and eyed the threads of magic that had snapped beneath her dagger. Even as she watched, the center of the binding was beginning to unravel. She remembered what Rijah had said about manipulating it at its center. Had . . . had she broken it?

Loulie braced herself as another tremor shook the building. Though she herself was unhurt, another deeper pain welled inside of her chest. She recognized the phantom ache she had felt in the scorched clearing. It was not her agony at all.

Qadir? She searched for his presence in the dagger.

The surface of the blade remained dull and dark, but though the weapon was silent, Qadir's anguish was loud enough to fill her mind. She felt another stab of pain, a tremor in her limbs. When she concentrated on the ache, she could make out something cold around her body.

Iron? She felt its suffocating embrace on her limbs, tomb-like.

And then she heard the warning snap of Qadir's voice. *Loulie, in front of you!*

His presence faded as Loulie looked up. A translucent figure stood before her in the fading light of the fractured binding, arms outstretched to hold up the cyclone.

The ifrit—*Nabila*—was crafted from wind, her body barely corporeal. Her hair was a tangled zephyr, her skin near translucent. And her eyes—when she glanced over her shoulder, Loulie saw that her eyes were like mirrors, silver white beneath pale blue lashes. But even those details, as striking as they were, faded in and out. The ifrit may as well have been a phantom, her face a reflection on a rippling lake.

It occurred to Loulie that this ifrit had just manipulated her. But the accusation caught in her throat; the visceral hatred in Nabila's gaze rendered her speechless.

She and the ifrit stared at each other for a long moment.

And then Nabila collapsed, her body smudging at the edges. Loulie flinched away, barely managing to land on her hands as the building shuddered again beneath her feet.

The queen watched them beyond the stormy barrier, her eyes wide with anger—or was it fear? "Despicable human," she whispered. "What have you *done*?"

Loulie crawled toward Nabila, meaning to shake the ifrit out of her stupor. But the moment her hand touched Nabila's shoulder, she withdrew with a curse. The ifrit's misty form was as hostile as the storm she had trapped them in. Loulie felt as if she had suffered a lash across her skin.

The queen toed the edges of the cyclone, a predator waiting out its prey. "The moment you are too weak to hold this barrier up, I will kill you."

Though the jinn only had eyes for Nabila, Loulie knew the promise was meant for both of them. There would be no bargaining her way out of this, not after what she had involuntarily done to the binding. Loulie turned her anger on the fading ifrit. The criminal who had gotten her into this mess was now her only means of escaping it. She would not let Nabila flee without her.

Loulie knelt closer to the ifrit. Close enough to whisper, "I'm not dying because of your folly. Tell me what you mean to do when the wind dies down."

Nabila's icy-eyed glare slid up toward her. A shudder ran through Loulie at the coldness of the expression. Something shifted in the air as their eyes connected. A small, minute thing.

In Nabila's eyes, Loulie saw her own defiance reflected. She—*they*—would not die here. Not over some misunderstanding. Not for some nameless queen. Not when Qadir was in peril.

Loulie's vision swam as she rose. Her legs were leaden, her muscles sore. A dense fog filled her mind, making it difficult to grasp her thoughts. But a spark of anger flared within it, persistent. *Help me, king*, she thought. The voice in her mind was not her own.

When the dagger did not respond, Loulie felt a surge of foreign wrath. The voice that was not hers said, *Fine. If you will not help me, then help your human.*

The weapon burst into flame. Qadir's fire, which had always wrapped around Loulie's fingers in comfort, now surged up her arm like a viper, bright and hot. Confusion battled with fear as Loulie swayed on the spot, struggling to breathe. She felt strange—oddly detached from her body. And yet her rage remained, burning a path of heat through her.

No. She shuddered. *This is not my anger.*

The heat was magic, crashing through her veins and burning away any command she had over her body. Her breath froze in her lungs as she—the ifrit—curled her fingers adamantly around the hilt of the dagger and braced her feet.

Belatedly, Loulie realized Nabila and the cyclone had vanished from the rooftop. Instead, Loulie felt Nabila's presence crawling beneath her skin and bleeding into her mind.

The jinn queen stared at Loulie, face ashen. "You fool."

Loulie grinned. It was not her grin. And the words that came from her mouth—those were not hers either. "You are the fool," the ifrit said with Loulie's voice. "How many times have you tried and failed to capture me? Even if you killed me, my corpse would come back to haunt you."

Loulie's body surged forward, but she herself was a phantom cut loose. Unable to resist, all she could do was focus on the battle.

Though the queen's shock had initially given them the upper hand, she clearly knew how to use the blades she wore, and her skill far outstripped Loulie's as their steel clashed.

Why are you doing this? Loulie beat her hands against her own mind. *Get* out *of my head!*

She recoiled when the ifrit snapped back, *You think I want to command your frail human body? Your only use to me is your ability to control the Ashfire King's dagger.*

The jinn ruler slammed her blade against the dagger with enough force to bend Loulie's knees. She—Nabila—grunted with frustration. It did not matter how skilled the ifrit was; neither the knife nor Loulie were made for a battle like this. They could not win with steel.

"*Qadir.*" His name came out a pained gasp, a breach in the ifrit's control.

The fire on the blade flashed, the ashfire growing bright enough to encompass the area in a bright white light. Loulie heard the queen fall back with a curse. For a moment, Loulie's heart beat tremulously with hope—both hers and Nabila's—as the jinn dropped her weapon.

But then: a flash of iron as the queen threw a hidden blade. It cut through the curtain of ashy whiteness. Loulie felt pain in her stomach. The warmth of her own blood seeping through her robes. Her vision darkened as she stumbled back, agony tearing through her body.

The ifrit's shock mirrored her own. *Fragile creature! Why must you bleed so easily?*

Loulie's breath rattled in her lungs as she keeled over, hands pressed to her stomach. She felt tears on her cheeks, blood on her hands, and Nabila's panic, pulsing frantically in her bones.

The queen stood feet away, teeth bared in a vicious, triumphant smile as she recovered the dagger off the floor. The edge of the blade shone crimson. That same blood—*Loulie's* blood—splattered the floor beneath her.

Panic crashed through Loulie in a dull wave. She straightened— or tried to, but pain shot through her body so violently it seared her vision black. She cried out—a sound that barely made it between her pressed lungs—as she fought for control.

Get out of my body! she screamed in her mind. *Get out, get out!*

But Nabila was no longer responding to her.

As Loulie's body weakened, so too did the boundary between her and Nabila's mind. Loulie could feel the pain tearing it away, tearing *her* away from the present until she was *standing on a battlefield, drenched in her own blood. It was a foreign and unsettling feeling, to see the silver on her lucent skin. She did not like it. It was like ants in her veins. An anchor, sinking her into the waves. A grave.*

Graves.

She glanced around and saw them—the graves. The relics, marking the places where her comrades had fallen. Standing amidst the field of bloodied weapons was her king. He was burning, but not with his usual radiance. No, this was the flicker of a dying flame. His shoulders were bent inward, his head bowed in defeat.

She knew, then, that he was giving up. That their sacrifice had been for nothing.

*"Sayyidi." Her voice was faint—*she was growing faint. But she was not dead, not yet. She could fight. *"We can still win. They are only humans. We are stronger, we have* magic—*"*

"There are no victors in war." His voice was heavy with resignation. When he angled his head to look at her, his profile was shadowed, his features eclipsed by the sinking sun. But she could still see the grief in his eyes when he said, "Nabila. Do you trust me?"

The memory shifted. Loulie was on a different battlefield beneath the sand. They were losing, again. But this time, Qadir faced her with more certainty. His ruby-red eyes glowed with determination as he pressed a hand to her cheek. "Loulie," he said. "Do you trust me?"

His face blurred. The memory changed.

"The humans have stolen everything from us," she insisted. "If we do not destroy them, then we will be left with no future." Even now, she could not stop the anger from clouding her heart. That anger was all she had. In this war, her heart had room for nothing else.

The vision split. There was Qadir her king, and Qadir her bodyguard. Loulie could feel his hand on her cheek. "There is no future *here*," he said.

The Ashfire King turned to her as the world began to sink. He had never looked so exhausted, so weary. "If you cannot live in this world," he said, *"then hide in another."*

The memories dimmed into pain, flaring red hot through Loulie's veins. She felt Nabila's magic carving a path toward her injury. It was a familiar feeling; Loulie recognized this sensation from when Qadir used his blood to heal her.

When she removed her hands from her stomach, she found her wound had been sealed. The ifrit was powerful enough to heal her in her own body—but perhaps not powerful enough to leave it, because Loulie could still feel her magic thrumming beneath her skin.

She forced Loulie to look up at the approaching queen, who was moving faster now that she had noticed the sealed injury.

Distantly, Loulie was aware of Nabila commanding her feet. She forced Loulie backward, toward the edge of the roof. *Trust me*, she said. *You are too valuable to kill.*

Loulie felt the cool kiss of the wind at her back as she turned. She was vaguely aware of Nabila lifting one of her feet over the roof as the queen rushed forward, screaming Nabila's name.

There was a single moment when Loulie felt anchored in her own body. When she could stare down at the city with her own eyes. The curfew darkness had lifted during the battle, and the red sky cast ominous twilit shadows between the buildings. Loulie's gaze caught on a shadow in the courtyard. A man, screaming her name. The wind carried his voice to her.

"Layla." He called her name in a panic. "*Layla, Layla, Layla.*"

She dimly recognized Mazen's voice.

It was then the realization of what she was about to do sank in, along with the fear. She tried to say his name, tried to scream for help, but the plea was trapped in her throat.

Jump, Nabila said.

And Loulie, puppeteered by a mad ifrit and her violent wind, had no choice.

She stepped off the roof.

18

MAZEN

Everything Mazen witnessed, he saw through a haze of panic.

Through Firas's tattoo, he saw Loulie step to the edge of the roof. He saw the blood on her robes, seeping through her fingers. He screamed her name from the courtyard, but she gave no indication of hearing him. One moment she was on the ledge. The next, she had fallen.

The world tilted beneath his feet as he rushed forward. He forgot about the soldiers pursuing him. All he could think about was Loulie, falling toward the ground. He had just screamed her name again when a shadow flashed through the air above him. A flying carpet.

Relief crashed through him when she fell onto the rug. But then the wind—that strange, sentient magic—was carrying her away, across the city. No, *away* from the city.

No.

Mazen ran. Away from the archive, across the still-rumbling courtyard, and out the palace gate. But Loulie was out of sight before he had even made it into the city. Mazen did not know where she had gone, but when he realized he'd lost her, a yawning emptiness opened inside of him. Loulie had been stolen away. Their plan had failed.

And Mazen was alone.

19

AISHA

It was raining the night Aisha prepared to leave the Asfour campsite. Dusky gray clouds obscured the constellations, and water dampened the earth, weighing each of her footfalls. Back when she'd lived in Sameesh, rain had meant puddles to play in and the refreshing smell of petrichor in the air. It had meant meals by the hearth and breaks from working in the field. And, most excitingly, it had meant stories from her aunts, who had liked to share haunting tales about the marid with the rain rapping ominously against the windowpanes.

That had been then. Now the rain was a nuisance.

Aisha glared into the gloom as she drew the hood of her cloak up over her head. It was just her luck that the weather had taken a turn for the worse the night she planned to set out, but she could not second-guess her departure now, not when Umm Jaber had already gone out to retrieve a horse for her. She would ride out tonight, and then, when she was a good distance from this place, she would seek shelter.

And then it will be just the two of us, the Resurrectionist said. Intangible as the ifrit was, Aisha could hear the smirk in her words. *Do not worry, jinn killer—we can pass the time trading stories. I will tell you about my beloved Munaqid, and you can tell me about your family, hmm?*

I would rather be struck by lightning, Aisha snapped back.

She ignored the ifrit's laughter as she navigated the muddy pathways. Though the storm had made her footfalls heavier, the sound was thankfully drowned out by the rainfall. The weather had also done her the convenience of burning out the torches around the campsite, making it easier for her to sneak around. Now all she had to do was locate Hakim's tent.

She focused on lightening her footsteps as she wound her way around one line of tents to another. It was not difficult to find the place she was looking for. Devoid of any family to share his space with, Hakim was one of the only members of the tribe who slept alone. But just as Aisha approached his tent, the entrance opened. She quickly ducked behind a nearby tree before she paused, realizing it was not Hakim who had exited.

It was Jaber, standing outside with a rolled-up piece of parchment in his hands. With most of his profile carved in shadow, Aisha could not read his expression, but she could spot the tension in his posture. She had known Umm Jaber would be helping her tonight; she had not expected her son would assist her as well. But then, the man *had* seemed unhappy about Hakim's imminent departure.

When she stepped out of the shadows, Jaber looked unbothered by her sudden appearance. In fact, from the way his gaze caught hers, it looked as if he had expected her to be there. He held Hakim's map out to her. "Take it. My mother said you would need it."

Aisha slid the map into the satchel hidden beneath her cloak. She did not ask questions; the last thing she needed was to become involved in affairs that were not her business. When she thanked him, Jaber merely nodded. He looked stricken, standing in the dark with rain streaming down his cheeks. She wondered, briefly, how long he would carry this guilt with him.

The hunter insisted on seeing her off and followed her to the gate where Umm Jaber had promised to bring the horse. Sure enough, there was a mare tied to the fence, and huddled beside it, trembling in a cloak, was Umm Jaber. She straightened at the sight of Aisha and her son. "You took longer than you said you would."

Jaber smiled apologetically. "Sorry, uma."

The woman simply grunted as she handed Aisha the reins. At first, the mare resisted when Aisha threw herself over its back. But with a few calming words from Umm Jaber, the horse settled enough for Aisha to situate herself in the saddle.

"And so we come to the end." Though Umm Jaber's arms were crossed and her gaze steely, her shoulders had begun to shake.

Aisha decided she would make this quick. For the woman's sake, and for hers. "Shukran." She glanced between Jaber and his mother. "For saving me in the desert and for your hospitality." She tapped her painted wrist. "And for the henna."

Umm Jaber's lips quirked. "I never leave a debt unrepaid."

Jaber's laughter was so soft Aisha barely heard it over the patter of the rain. "In case you're wondering, that means she's fond of you," he said. The woman simply shrugged. Though she was not smiling, there was a fond glimmer in the crinkle of her eyes.

"For what it's worth, I did not find my stay to be unpleasant," Aisha said.

Umm Jaber *did* smile fully then, chuckling as she said, "Then I expect we shall see you again soon. When next you visit, I'll repaint your arms."

Aisha found herself reflecting the smile back at her as she nodded. For the first time in a long time, her resolve wavered. She wondered, *What would happen if I stayed just one more day?* The thought filled her with longing. And then with loathing.

This is not my home.

No, her home had been destroyed by jinn. The creatures had ruined her life, so she had made it her mission to destroy them, and now to destroy the man working with them. She had made herself into a weapon so that she would not falter. And she would not. Never again.

With a decisive tug of the reins, Aisha guided her horse toward the gate. She looked past the fence to the cliffs where she would seek shelter, but found it hard to concentrate with Umm Jaber's eyes on her back. One last time, Aisha turned around—

And tensed as a scream shattered the quiet.

She spun in her saddle, searching for the source, but the rain muddied the sound. Jaber's hearing must have been sharper than hers, because he was already moving toward one of the paths, reaching for the bow on his back. He glanced over his shoulder. "Bint Louas, you—"

"I'll come with you."

Another scream cut through the air, followed by the soft rumble of thunder. Aisha glanced urgently at Umm Jaber, but the matriarch was already retreating toward the tents. She waved a curt hand at them. "What are you waiting for? Go! I will gather the women."

She fled before either of them could call her back. The moment she was gone, Aisha turned to Jaber and patted her saddle impatiently. "Horseback will be faster."

The man did not hesitate to throw himself onto the saddle behind her.

As they shot down the dirt pathways, the wail of the wind was replaced with human screams. By the time she and Jaber reached the encampment, the area had become a cramped battlefield, packed tight with bloodied bodies and flying projectiles. Aisha searched for the enemy as she cut through the stampede of fleeing tribespeople.

"Bint Louas, in front of you!"

She looked up at Jaber's warning and saw two men rushing her on horses in a pincer movement. Jaber jumped from the saddle. Aisha followed, landing hard on the muddy ground to avoid the blades slicing through the air. Her horse snorted in fright before bolting.

Aisha put its disappearance from her mind immediately. Another man had spotted her on the ground and was approaching with a knife. She had just enough time to take in his blood-spattered attire before she brought up her blade to block his strike.

The mysterious assailant smiled at her. "I thought my eyes were playing tricks on me, but it *is* you. Aisha bint Louas, in the flesh." His smile widened as he threw more weight into his assault, pushing her back. "When the sheikh told us you'd left, we feared ourselves deprived of a prize. The sultan has put quite a price on your head—worth this bloodshed and more."

Aisha remembered, suddenly and with great clarity, the raiders she and Jaber had slain in the desert. One of those men had recognized her, and the last she had let escape. Which meant—

This is my fault.

The ground tilted beneath her with the realization. Too late, she realized the shock had cost her. When the raider surged forward, Aisha took a slash to her arm. But the pain, the blood—she could barely feel it beneath the sudden numbness that had taken hold of her.

She'd let a single man escape, and it had led to this slaughter. This chaos and death and—

No. Her grip tightened on her blade. *This is* Omar's *doing.*

Aisha's vision seared red as her opponent came at her again. This time, she feinted, sidestepping him as he stumbled. Without hesitation, she plunged the blade into the back of his neck. Blood splashed her face as he fell. It ran down her cheeks with the rainwater as she turned on her next assailant, a man who came at her with two blades.

The fool practically threw himself at her. Aisha let him fall into her reach before ducking around him to land a kick to his kneecaps. But before she could end his life, another man came at her on a horse. He had an arrow pointed at her chest.

Aisha froze.

Move, fool! The Resurrectionist's voice cut through the haze of her hesitation. Aisha shifted. Or at least, she tried to. But the raider on the ground had grasped her leg and pulled her down, sending her toppling into the mud.

Aisha kicked at him and felt something break beneath her boot—his nose?—but he was slow to release her leg. She had to get away. She had to—

There came a loud, ear-piercing scream. Aisha looked up to see the archer slump on his horse, an arrow protruding from his throat. Jaber stood shaking behind him, face streaked with dirt and blood. His eyes were wild and unseeing; he had the look of a man possessed.

When another attacker rushed him from behind, Aisha knew he would be too slow to react. She saw Jaber's death, and she knew she would not prevent it.

Why do you hesitate, jinn killer? the Resurrectionist snapped. *You bargained for my power. Use it.*

Suddenly, Aisha's blade felt heavy and unwieldy in her hands. Why would she use it when she had other weapons at her disposal? The Resurrectionist's magic pulsed beneath her skin like a second heartbeat. She pulled on it, let it bleed into her will and into a single command.

"Rise."

The corpse Jaber had felled released a howl through broken lungs. Everyone in the vicinity froze as the dead man shuddered to life. He would not be fast enough to disarm Aisha's target, but she had only meant to use the corpse as a distraction.

Aisha lurched to her feet, leapt over the reanimated corpse, and in the beat of hesitation the terror had earned her, slashed her blade across the second man's throat. She then whirled on the raider who had grabbed her leg. Though he had regained his footing, he was clearly hesitant to attack her. Aisha smiled at the fear in his eyes. She would never tire of seeing terrible men cower.

She waited as he readied his strike. Aisha looked past the angle of his blade to his body, as Omar had taught her. She knocked the weapon from his hands, kicked his legs out from beneath him, and buried her sword in his chest. A quick survey of the area revealed another casualty, a corpse punctured with arrows. Jaber stood quivering over the body. "Bint Louas?" His lips moved soundlessly for a moment. And then he said, "My mother—I saw Hakim guiding her to the pasture. Please..."

Aisha delved back into the mayhem. With her blade, she cleaved a path through the onslaught. With the Resurrectionist's magic, she turned them against each other. While the humans saw corpses, she saw an army. *Her* army, which she let tear itself apart.

Against the dead men, strategy was useless. Unhindered by pain, they threw themselves at their living comrades with abandon, their bodies as much weapons as their blades. They bit and clawed and howled, and it was all the raiders could do to fend them off. Only Aisha passed easily through the tangle of bodies, her clothing soaked through with water and blood.

When she came to the pasture, the fence had been destroyed. People ran screaming across the flooding fields. Aisha's gaze snagged on two figures rushing through the turmoil: a woman hobbled with age and a man dragging an injured leg. Even from a distance, Aisha recognized Umm Jaber and Hakim. The mapmaker was leading the woman to the shed at the corner of the field, the last remaining sanctuary in the area.

But they were moving too damn *slow*.

A third blur shot across the field—a raider, giving chase on a horse. Static roared in Aisha's ears as she threw a dagger from her belt. She released a breath only when the hunter tumbled from his injured horse.

Hakim turned. Surprise, then gratitude flashed across his face as he ushered Umm Jaber toward the door. The old woman paused briefly to glance at Aisha but had no time to say anything before the door opened, revealing a small crowd urging her inward. Without a word, Umm Jaber stepped inside. Hakim followed her through and secured the door behind him.

Reassured, Aisha fell on her next assailant with vigor. As the Resurrectionist's memories poured into her mind, she was no longer on this battlefield, but on another *at the edge of Dhahab. Fire roared beneath her feet as the humans came. She snapped their bones and tore their flesh, and even when she'd bled them out on the sand, she thought,* This is not enough.

A terrible cracking sound drew Aisha from the memory—the sound of splintered wood. She blinked water from her lashes as she turned just in time to see one of the raiders hack the shed door down with a triumphant yell. Inside, women and children screamed.

No.

When Aisha tried to move, another man stood in her way. She lashed out, but her panic made her careless, and her opponent easily avoided her attack. Aisha swerved, but too late. The man's weapon tore into her arm, spraying the air with her blood.

Focus, the Resurrectionist hissed.

This time, when the raider came at her, it was the Resurrectionist who moved Aisha's body. She ducked his strike and then launched *herself* at him, tackling him to the ground. With a curse, Aisha drove her blade through his chest, stealing his life.

The world shuddered as she drew slowly to her feet. She realized that the screaming had stopped, replaced with the rumble of thunder. Much to her relief, the shed had been secured by tribesmen. Which meant the people inside had to be safe...right?

Her concentration slipped as she stumbled forward. At some point, the dead had fallen back to the ground as corpses. It was only now, walking past their bodies, that Aisha saw the formidable size of the army she had raised.

She made her way very slowly toward the shed. It was difficult to ignore her injuries—the knee that was oddly bent, the gashes in her arms and legs. When she moved, it was with a limp, each step pained and heavy.

I can fix you, the Resurrectionist said. *As I fixed you before.*

Revulsion swept through her. What kind of human was she, that she could be so easily mended? *An abomination*, her mind supplied, but she quickly shook off the thought as she entered the shed.

The first thing she became aware of was the smell of blood. Then she noticed the women huddled together at the back of the shed, leaning over a collapsed figure.

Aisha stared at Umm Jaber.

The matriarch's clothes were drenched in red, and her head lolled strangely on her neck, angled so that her glazed eyes bore into Aisha as she entered. Jaber sat behind her, shaking with sobs as he cradled her body in his lap. Beside him knelt Hakim, face ashen and blood weeping from a gash on his arm. It was only then the truth of the situation sank in.

Aisha swayed on her feet. "How did this happen?"

It was Hakim who looked up first. He responded in a tight voice,

"When the raider broke down the door, she threw herself at him." His throat bobbed. "She pushed me out of the way, saying...that we were all too young to die."

It was easy to imagine the fierce matriarch planting herself in the doorway as a shield, a look of defiance on her face. If Aisha had been faster, if she had just *reached the door* in time...

Jaber glanced up, a sudden desperation in his eyes. "You have magic," he said hoarsely.

All attention fixed on her. Aisha flinched at the hope in the tribespeople's eyes. No one had ever looked at her like that before—like she could save them. Her throat was painfully dry when she swallowed. "Cursed magic."

"I don't care what kind of magic it is! You revived the raiders. You can bring her back."

Aisha stared at the fallen matriarch. At the gash of red across her neck. She could imagine the way the blade would have cut her flesh—could imagine the woman's eyes rolling up, her scream cut short as her body slumped to the ground.

"Please, bint Louas." Jaber's voice broke. "Please, help her."

Aisha thought of the mindless corpses she had brought back to life. Dead things, with empty soulless eyes. She thought of Umm Jaber's eyes, which had always glimmered with such vivaciousness. No magic could return that light.

"I'm sorry." Her words were a whisper, but they were loud as a crier's call in the quiet shed. When Jaber's expression crumpled, Aisha felt as if she had been punched in the stomach. She couldn't bring herself to linger. What right did she have to bear witness to this grief?

She turned and hobbled away. The numbness had returned, but now it felt less like she had shoved aside her emotions and more like they had been drained from her.

It is no fault of yours, the Resurrectionist said softly. *Blame the killer, not the target.*

"Leave me alone." Try as Aisha did, she was unable to summon her usual anger at the ifrit. She wandered back through the now-ruined campsite, heedless of the pain shooting through her body with every step. Her only desire was to get as far away as possible from the shed. To forget the wrong, wrong sight of Umm Jaber's dead eyes staring blankly at her.

The raid was Omar's fault, but *she* had been unable to save Umm Jaber.

As Aisha wandered, she received looks from the tribespeople. Crying children who watched her with red-rimmed eyes and women and men who stared at her in fear—or anger.

She had just made it to the shattered fence when she heard footsteps behind her and turned to see Hakim. There was something imposing about the sight of him standing statue still in the rain, composed amidst the tragedy. But his voice quavered as he said, "This time, you will not leave me behind, bint Louas. You take my map, you take me as well."

Aisha stared at him. "You still insist on accompanying me? Even after all this?"

"*Especially* after all this. I will not let Omar steal anyone from me again." He gave her one last warning glance before turning to the wreckage and to the people who needed him.

In his absence, Aisha rolled up one of her sleeves and touched the thatched henna pattern Umm Jaber had drawn on her arm. Armor, Aisha had called it. She only wished she could wear it over her heart. She clutched her arm and glanced up at the weeping sky.

Aisha was envious; she had forgotten how to cry long ago.

20

LOULIE

Before tonight, Loulie had traveled by air two times in her life. First on the back of a legendary rukh, then atop a flimsy enchanted rug. It had been two times too many. Yet despite her determination to never fly again, she somehow found herself in the air a *third* time.

With Mazen, flying on a carpet had been tolerable—enjoyable, even. Buffeted by Nabila's urgent wind, it was anything but. Loulie did not sail through the sky so much as shoot through it, the world moving so quickly it blurred across her vision. Though she had regained control of her body, she could not control the rug, which darted between and above the buildings, faster than any bird. Then, abruptly, the carpet swept toward land, unceremoniously dumping her onto a hard wooden surface. The deck of a ship, she realized.

Before she could examine her surroundings, the floor slanted beneath her and the vessel shot forward. Loulie threw herself at the rails and held on for dear life.

Nabila's ship was not flying exactly, but it may as well have been for the way it sped away from the city, never once disturbing the surface of the Sandsea. The last time Loulie had sailed across this expanse, Ziyad's sailors had been guiding the ship forward by moving the sand. But this ship was itself cushioned on a fast-moving gale that kept it hovering above the Sandsea.

As the city shrank into the distance, it occurred to Loulie that she had been kidnapped.

Terror mixed with shock as she knelt at the ship's edge, clinging desperately to the rails as Nabila's squall pulled at her scarves. A single haunting image hung suspended behind her eyelids: Mazen bin Malik, a look of despair on his face as she left him behind.

She glanced ahead, past the sailors frantically rushing about on deck and to the ifrit who had kidnapped her. Nabila stood at the ship's prow, watching the city vanish into the distance. Outside of the eye of the storm, her body seemed more defined. Loulie could make out the faint outline of clothing: a long coat, the snap of a scarf across broad shoulders, and thigh-high boots. Even now, however, it was Nabila's eyes that stood out most: a vivid silver that contemplated Loulie coldly as she inched forward.

"Take me back," Loulie said through clenched teeth.

There was no indication from the ifrit's expression that she was frowning, yet Loulie had the distinct impression she was glowering at her. "If you have a death wish, it would be easy to push you off my ship. The Sandsea can be your tomb."

"My companions are still in the city. We need to go back for them." It was becoming harder for Loulie to speak—the ifrit's gale stole the breath from her lungs with every word.

Nabila lifted her chin. "You dare make a request of me after I saved your life?"

"You used me to break a binding," Loulie snapped. "And then you kidnapped me!"

"Do not complain, human. It is unsightly."

Loulie glanced at the shadow of the city, no more than a speck on the horizon now. She thought again of Mazen, screaming her name from the courtyard. "Please," she whispered.

But Nabila had already turned her attention to calming the winds. As the ship slowed, Loulie attempted to rise on shaking legs. She startled when a sailor stepped in front of her and offered a hand. A jinn—*marid?*—with pitch-black eyes grinned down at her. Loulie was struck by the elegance of her features: the razor-sharp cheekbones, the smooth forehead, the aquiline nose—and the scales that cut across her face, streaks of gold that glimmered in the moonlight.

The sailor's dark eyes shone with amusement as she tugged Loulie to her feet. "You are so *small*." She sounded delighted. "I could crush your ribs with a single embrace!"

"Duha." Nabila sighed. "Leave the human alone."

"My *name* is Loulie al-Nazari." She saw little point in aliases now.

Nabila merely waved a hand as if Loulie's name was a formality she did not care for. "Leave the human to me and see to the ship, Duha."

"As you command, nokhitha." With a playful bow and a wink, Duha walked off to join the rest of the sailors, who were shamelessly eavesdropping on the conversation. Nabila paid them no mind. She approached Loulie with a single-minded determination, eyes flashing.

Loulie retreated, her grip tightening on the dagger. "I don't know what your plans are, but I want nothing to do with them. Take me back to the city."

Nabila's expression twisted—a motion Loulie read as an eyebrow raise. "Oh? I had heard you wished to return to the surface and reunite with your bodyguard."

Loulie's mind went blank. How could the ifrit have possibly known that? Unless...

That damned bird. She remembered the myna on the windowsill. In the archive. How many of their conversations had it overheard? She searched for the spy in the sky, but the bird was nowhere to be seen.

Nabila continued, "It is lucky for you that you have some use to me." With a flick of her wrist, she summoned a gust of wind that snatched the dagger from Loulie's hand. When Loulie lunged for it, Nabila held it out of her grasp. "You possess the Ashfire King's dagger, which must mean you know where he is. Tell me."

Loulie glared at her. "We were separated. He saved me from a criminal on the surface, and I have been trying to return to him ever since."

"The king *I* know would not sacrifice himself for others. It is more likely he was trying to escape you, not protect you."

"Qadir is my bodyguard," Loulie said icily. "He would never willingly leave me behind."

But even as she spoke, a different truth occurred to her. A truth Qadir himself had confessed: that he was a coward. That, this whole time, he had been running from his mistakes. What if he *had* decided to flee?

The ifrit must have realized the impact of her words. She scoffed. "Ask yourself this, human: Has he helped you, or has he simply made you dependent on him?"

In that moment, Loulie would have done anything to run from this conversation, perhaps even thrown herself into the Sandsea. Nabila spoke aloud all the fears she had harbored in her heart. How could she deny her words when Nabila was *living* evidence of his betrayal?

No. She remembered when she and Qadir had spoken on the cliffs in Ghiban. When he'd said they were a team. She had believed him—she would never stop believing in him.

"Khalas." The word came out a gasp; she didn't realize she'd been holding her breath. "I do not owe you our history. Tell me what you want with me."

Loulie already *knew* what Nabila wanted. She had puppeteered Loulie's body to make it happen. Still, she shivered as the ifrit said, "You want to return to the surface with your companions? Then help me sever the bindings."

"Why do you need my help? You've been damaging them just fine without me."

"Even with my power, all I can do is chip away at the magic from the outside. But *you* can access them with the dagger. You alone can break them."

"And then what? I help you destroy this land?"

"And then I am one step closer to saving this country you humans doomed. The bindings hold this realm in place. To destroy them is to return the cities to the surface."

Loulie stared at her. "Destroying the bindings is making the cities *sink*."

The ifrit shook her head. "That is the curse of the bindings. Break one and the magic begins to fail. But dismantle them all and the country returns to the surface."

Loulie's gaze flickered to the black sky. Right now, all *she* could see was the failing magic. Her eyes landed on a gold streak suspended ominously above her that had not been there before. It looked like splintered glass. She thought back to the tremor in Dhahab she had caused. How was she to know the ifrit was telling the truth?

"And what if the magic fails faster than the land rises?" she asked.

Nabila gave her a hard look. "There is no *if.* I will be faster."

Loulie swallowed. Even if Nabila *was* telling the truth and they managed to make it back to the surface this way...what would Nabila do when she returned? Loulie could still remember the visions she had seen while she was possessed. Nabila's memories of the war, and her rage as Qadir turned away from her. She remembered what the shadow attendant had said about the ifrit's mission to wreak havoc on the surface.

Nabila frowned when Loulie asked the question. "What happens afterward is none of your concern. There is only one choice for you to make. But I will give you time to consider. Four days, until we reach al-Malath."

Loulie remembered the vanishing hideout on the Wanderer's map. "Al-Malath?"

"Home," Nabila said. She offered no further explanation, simply handed the knife back to Loulie and turned on her heel, vanishing in much the same way she had appeared, her body breaking into currents of wind that re-formed at the ship's wheel.

With the rest of the sailors studiously ignoring her, Loulie was left alone with her thoughts. Mazen's horror-stricken face returned to her then. She hoped that he and Rijah had escaped the queen's wrath. That they would be safe until she found her way back.

When she was no longer able to bear the sight of the city shrinking into the distance, Loulie fled below deck. No one followed her, and Loulie was grateful for it. She did not know where she was going. Her only thought was to get as far away as possible from the ifrit.

Eventually, she came to what appeared to be the ship's hold, packed full of supply crates and barrels. Loulie wedged herself between two barrels and, with nothing but her scarves to shield her from the cold, buried her face in her hands. She did not know how long she sat there heaving in gulps of air as her mind spun helplessly in circles, only that eventually, the moan of the wind died into a murmur that sounded a bit like a familiar lullaby.

Loulie nodded off to that serenade, humming as a restless sleep took hold of her.

—⁂—

The dhow was so stark a change from her usual surroundings that, for the first time since she'd started journeying with Qadir, Layla forgot her grief. The feeling was eclipsed by a greater emotion: wonder. For though she had heard many stories about what it was like to sail, she had never had the chance to board a ship herself. At first, she was convinced she would fall off, unsteady as the deck was beneath her feet. But then the seafarers unfurled the sails, the ship began to crest the waves, and Layla's fear slid through the boards like sand through a sieve.

Standing on board the dhow with the wind gently tugging at her clothes, Layla could almost believe she was another person, untouched by the tragedy that had destroyed her life. She could believe she was a journeyer on her way to find fortune in Madinne.

She was in so good a mood she did not notice, at first, that Qadir had disappeared. The jinn usually stood behind her, a loyal shadow, but now he had vanished. Layla searched the dhow until she found him sitting with his back against the cabin door. His eyes were closed, and there was a concerningly deep furrow between his brows.

She shuffled toward him on unsteady feet. "Qadir?"

He lifted an eyelid to peer at her. "Mm?"

"Why are you sitting here? Don't you want to look at the ocean?"

"No." The eyelid dropped closed once more. "We will be at sea for many days yet. There is no rush to gape at the water."

"I wasn't gaping—"

"Go. Enjoy the sights. You do not need my permission."

Qadir was nothing if not calm, but now Layla perceived an unusual tension in his shoulders. Something occurred to her then, something that made her gasp. "You're not afraid of the water, are you?"

"There is a difference between fear and aversion."

Layla recognized a deflection when she saw one. Glee bubbled in her at the realization, and she laughed before she could help it. Qadir opened his eyes at the sound, expression softening slightly. "You would not laugh if you knew how deep the ocean is."

"No one knows how deep the ocean is. That's what makes it such a marvel."

Qadir lowered his head with a sigh. If Layla hadn't known better, she might have thought he was trying to hide a smile. "I am well past the age of being wonderstruck by such things."

"It's because you're an old man," she said.

Qadir simply shrugged, but Layla could read his amusement in the upturned corner of his lips. The sight instilled a surprising peace within her. For the first time in a long time, she dared to hope she would not be left behind.

—⁂—

Loulie woke to a horrible moaning sound. The first thing she remembered was where she was and why. The second realization was that the moaning was not a person, but the ship, which creaked beneath her. And then, the last thing she noticed: she was not alone.

The marid sailor, Duha, sat cross-legged in front of her, absently drumming her hands on the floor. Even in the dimness of the hold, Loulie could make out the slashes of scales on her face. This close, she saw those scales glimmering beneath her clothes as well, traveling up her arms and stretching between her fingers as a soft gold webbing.

Duha paused her drumming when she saw Loulie had woken. "You looked like you were having a pleasant dream."

"How long have you been watching me?"

"I came down the moment curfew fell to make sure you had not been flattened by a barrel." She laughed at Loulie's glare. "Some of those barrels weigh more than you do, you know. If they fell on you, they would crush your bones."

Loulie scowled. "You seem very invested in making me aware of my mortality."

"That is not my intention. You are just so—"

"Small, yes, I know." Loulie rose to her feet with a grumble, setting a hand on a barrel to balance herself. She noticed Duha had risen in the same moment. Standing so close to her, Loulie realized the marid was tall. Not as tall as Nabila, but big enough to dwarf Loulie.

She grumbled as she turned her attention to the door. "What's happening outside?"

"Curfew," the sailor explained with the same nonchalance one would use to describe the weather. "Everyone is inside when the darkness falls, no exceptions. Nokhitha's orders."

Loulie glanced around the swaying ship. "Then who's steering the ship?"

Duha blinked at her. "Nabila, of course."

"She can *see* in this?"

"Nabila has her own ways of seeing."

Loulie processed this. She was no sailor, so she knew nothing about navigating the waters, but perhaps the jinn understood the Sandsea in a different way than the ocean. Still, the thought of their ship pushing through the thick darkness made her uneasy. She glanced at her hand, searching for Firas's eye tattoo, but it had vanished when they left Dhahab.

The capital had been filled with ashfire—what kind of protection did they have on the ship? When she asked Duha, the marid gestured toward the ceiling. "We use ashfire too."

Loulie squinted into the darkness until she found the faint light Duha was pointing to. She pinpointed four sources—slivers of glass built into the ceiling that glowed with cool blue light. At Loulie's look of bewilderment, Duha explained, "The glass is a prism that reflects the ashfire we have on deck. It is a scarcer resource outside of Dhahab, so we use it carefully."

Loulie eyed the fragile glimmer of light on the ceiling. Seeing how weak that light was, she understood why jinn would flock to the city.

Duha was frowning at the light as well. "Ziyad has already sent ships after us; I hope Nabila will be able to lose them in her storm."

Loulie blinked. Her mind caught on two things. First, the casual use of Ziyad's name. Second, the casual mention of the storm. She remembered the unnatural cyclone tearing through Dhahab and shuddered. She was beginning to understand why no one had ever captured the ifrit.

Duha must have misread Loulie's unease as awe. She grinned with clear pride. "Nabila lets no one stand in her way."

"No," Loulie said bitterly. "She just kidnaps them."

Just as Duha's smile faltered, the ship lurched beneath them. It was a sudden motion that sent Loulie skidding across the floor. Duha caught her and held her steady as, above deck, there came an ominous booming sound.

Duha chuckled, but it was a humorless sound. "My brother's ships are tenacious as always, it seems."

"Brother—wait, are you talking about Ziyad?"

"In a way. We are kin born in the same waters. Is that not what family is?"

Family. The word was a string of faded memories in Loulie's heart. Her tribe, Qadir...they had all been stolen from her by Omar. Always by Omar. The thought made her heart burn with rage.

Duha seated herself on a barrel, her gaze contemplative as she tugged on a loose end of her turban. "Before the war took our home, Ziyad and I acted as advisors to the same ruler."

Loulie thought back to the map of the realm she had seen in the archive. She remembered the Eastern Marid City, abandoned but not lost.

Duha's gaze softened when Loulie brought it up. "Yes. The city was our home, but it was different back then. There was no east or west; it was one city." She cupped her palms in front of her. "But then the ifrit sunk the realm, and our city was split in two. Half stayed above the sands; half fell beneath it." She lowered one palm, offering the impression of a severely tilted scale.

Loulie pondered this, trying to place the Eastern Marid City on a human map. If it had been split in half . . . then the part of the city still on the surface must have been Ghiban, the city of waterfalls, which had been conquered and remade by humans.

She frowned. "You said you once served the same ruler. And now?"

"After the city fell, the marid scattered. Our queen vanished, and with her, all allegiances. For reasons unbeknownst to me, Ziyad bent his knee to the Usurper of Dhahab. I chose to follow Nabila—I have believed in her cause for a long time. So you see, even when we marid avoided participating in the war, we still became a part of it. Just as you have."

Loulie shook her head. "I want nothing to do with your politics."

Duha only gave her a pitying look. "Even the mightiest of us are moved by greater powers." She set a cold hand on Loulie's shoulder. "But I assure you that Nabila is not the nefarious power that has caused this world's demise. These lands were sinking long before her interference and have been ever since they fell beneath the Sandsea."

If what Duha said was true, then Qadir had not just sunk this realm; he had made it so no one could save it in his absence without the dagger. But—no, how could that possibly be the truth? The Qadir *she* knew would never have been so heartless.

And yet—

The words he had spoken to her on a rooftop in Dhyme returned to her: *I am not accustomed to facing my mistakes. Always, I have run from them.*

Loulie trembled as Duha headed for the door. The marid paused on the stairwell and threw a glance over her shoulder. "It is best you remain here until the curfew passes." She smiled—a soft, sympathetic look. "Return to your dreams, al-Nazari, and take solace in the knowledge that they do not have to be dreams for long."

She opened the door and walked out, leaving Loulie to weather the tempest in her heart.

21

MAZEN

Though the storm in Dhahab had cleared, the one in Mazen's mind had yet to pass.

All he could see was Loulie al-Nazari, stepping off a roof. Loulie al-Nazari, bleeding through her fingers as she was whisked away by a mad ifrit. He had feared their plan would go awry, but not like this. Never like this.

My fault, said a voice in his mind. *My fault, my fault.*

If Rijah were here, they would have chided him for the thought and told him to *do* something. And so he had. Shortly after Loulie had been kidnapped, Mazen had chased the queen and her leaders out into the city and to the docks. Their purpose here was twofold: while Ziyad had been communicating with the ships he had sent after Nabila, the queen had come to search the jinn leaders' ships for any evidence of correspondence with her.

Mazen angled his head past the crate he was hiding behind to peer out at the docks. From here, he could make out the leaders lined up by the gates. Though none of them were shackled, it was clear they were at the mercy of the soldiers overseeing the search, Hayat among them.

Of all the zuama'a, the zaeem of Kharjem was the most angered by the turn the night had taken. "Your Majesty, I beg you to cease this folly. The wazir already discovered the humans' involvement in Nabila's scheme. You have an *ifrit* locked up! Your suspicion is wasted on us."

Mazen flinched. He thought of the flaming bird that had appeared during the disaster—the creature *he* had somehow summoned. What would have happened had the bird not appeared? Would the jinn have still turned on him and Rijah? Would he have been able to work together with the queen to rescue Loulie?

As it was, he was relieved to have escaped capture. While fleeing the palace, he had realized his shadow cloak did not just hide him from pursuing soldiers—it also concealed him from Firas's surveillance magic. If not for the shadow, he would have already been caught. It was the reason he had elected to wear it even now, in hiding. He would take no chances.

"Your Majesty!"

Mazen looked up at the sound of Ziyad's voice. The marid had just returned from one of the ships. In one hand he held a cage. And in the cage was a bird.

The zaeem of Kharjem grew pale. "That bird does not belong to me."

"No," the queen mused as she took the cage from Ziyad. "But you must know its owner."

Mazen remembered what the queen had told them about Nabila's birds. *Messengers and spies*, she had called them. And if one of them had been found on the zaeem's ship, then...

The queen's face was terrible in its blankness. "I had wondered how Nabila passed the barrier. But with an accomplice, she could easily enter the city through the gate."

The earlier bravado had vanished from the zaeem's eyes. "No," he said as the other jinn peeled away from him. And then again when the soldiers grabbed him: "No!" He struggled and was strong enough to throw the soldiers off. But he was severely outnumbered, and it was not long before they regained their footing and handcuffed him.

Still the zaeem of Kharjem yelled, his body engulfed in a fire that made his eyes burn red. Even with the iron shackles suffocating his power, he put up a fight, but it was a short-lived struggle, cut short when one soldier coated his feet in rock, holding him in place.

The queen approached, wraithlike in her quiet. The zaeem was still screaming, insisting he had nothing to do with the ifrit and that it was the *godsdamned humans* who had let Nabila into the city. The queen did not react to these claims. She stopped before him and said, "Will you tell me the truth?" When he glared at her, she said, "Do you not feel the ground trembling beneath your feet? Your secrets will sink us all."

"I have told you nothing but the truth," the jinn insisted. "Nothing—"

With a flick of her wrist, the queen slashed a knife through his throat, cutting off his words. Blood splashed the boards, silver and bright. Mazen flinched back at the sight of it, his gasp held between chattering teeth as the jinn fell to his knees. But the queen was not done.

She stabbed the zaeem of Kharjem—again and again—until his silver blood stained her skin up to her elbows. It was only then, standing in the splashes of gore, that she stopped.

The port had gone eerily silent during the butchery. It was Hayat who tentatively broke the silence. "Shall I sit him up, Your Majesty?"

When the queen nodded, Hayat and another soldier leaned the corpse up against a wall. Mazen watched with horrified fascination as the queen stepped back. She closed her eyes, took a deep breath, and then when she opened her eyes again, her irises were black and shiny, like river stones. She curled her fingers, beckoning. "Rise."

Mazen nearly choked on his gasp when the corpse sat up, its eyes lifeless and milky. There was no recognition on its face as it looked at the queen.

"Tell me Nabila's plan," she commanded.

The corpse did not respond. It stared at her with glazed eyes.

"*Speak*," the queen hissed through clenched teeth.

Again, the corpse simply gazed at her. It did not blink as silver blood oozed from its lips onto its neck. Where it dripped onto the floor, weeds peeked through the blood-drenched wood.

The queen tried a different approach. "We found one of her birds on your ship. Tell us what message it delivered."

The corpse met her hateful gaze with hollow eyes. And then, in an awful, shredded voice, it said, "She offered me a deal. The same deal she offered all of us."

"What deal?"

"My assistance for hers. If I helped her into the city, she would rescue my citizens."

"Your citizens..." The queen frowned at him. "They are in danger, are they not?"

"My lands are sinking," the corpse said without emotion. "They will sink with it."

The queen was right, it seemed. The zaeem of Kharjem *had* betrayed her. But if he had done so for his citizens, what would happen to them now that he was dead? Would an ifrit that had heartlessly stolen Loulie away make good on such a promise?

"Such a shame." The queen eyed the corpse, deadpan. "You may have convinced yourself that you betrayed me for the good of your citizens, but in the end, it is your betrayal that doomed them. They will die because of it."

With a flick of her fingers, she severed the connection. Without any magic to animate it, the body promptly slumped over. In the ensuing silence, the queen crouched beside it. She untangled a chain from the zaeem's belt—one glittering with a bright red ruby—and handed it to Ziyad. "His relic," she explained. "You may find some use for it."

She rose to face the rest of the zuama'a, who had watched the exchange in muted terror. "Well? Will the rest of you tell me about this 'deal,' or will I have to interrogate your corpses?"

They all spoke at once, yelling over each other to be heard. The queen held up her hand. "I will hear your explanations in the throne room. But for now..." Her gaze flitted to Ziyad, who looked like he was holding back a yawn. "All preparations have been made to pursue Nabila?"

He tipped his head in acknowledgment. "The soldiers are boarded, Your Majesty."

The queen nodded, dismissing him as she turned back to the cowering leaders. Mazen hesitated as he watched Ziyad walk away. If he followed the marid onto his ship, then he could go after Loulie. But if he left, he did not know when he would be back for Rijah.

He wavered, uncertain. What would Rijah say if they were here? Most likely, they would take offense that Mazen was concerned for them at all. They would tell him that they were the mightiest of jinn and could handle themself.

And yet...

No. Mazen steeled himself. He would come back for Rijah, but he could not—*would not*—turn his back on Loulie.

I'm sorry, Rijah. I'll be back.

Making sure his shadow was secure, Mazen drew himself to his feet and chased after Ziyad.

—∞—

As a child, Mazen had often wondered what it would be like to stow away on a ship. In his mother's stories, it had seemed a romantic notion. The stowaways were usually heroes fleeing some terrible fate, and when they were discovered aboard the ship, their existence was a pleasant surprise, celebrated in earnest by the sailors they had tricked.

Mazen's own experience was not nearly as pleasant. After all, *he* was a criminal. It was a sobering thought, that he had been painted a villain not just on the surface, but in this country as well. His father had been right—what had his bleeding heart ever given him but trouble?

Loulie's face came to mind then. He remembered the glimmer of hope in her eyes when he had insisted their survival was a miracle. Mazen had to believe that was true—not just for his sake, but for hers. He had to believe he would find her.

He clung to that hope as the ship set sail. Though the vessel was the same one he and Loulie had boarded when they came to this realm, it felt foreign to Mazen. With the boum swarmed with soldiers, his safest hideaway was the hold, where his only company was the caged bulbul Ziyad had found on the zaeem's ship. The bird, thankfully, did not alert anyone to his presence, though Mazen often felt it staring at him through the crates.

The hours bled together as they traveled. Mazen spent most of that time caught in a nightmare-ridden sleep. Every time he closed his eyes, he was assaulted by visions: His city, burning. The sultan, dying beneath his hands. And now he saw Loulie's face in his dreams too. Sometimes she died in his arms, the life fading from her eyes as her blood ran through his fingers. Other times, he reached out to grab her as she fell through the sky, only to miss her.

He had no idea how much time he passed trapped in his own mind, only that at one point there was an obvious turn in the weather—a storm he felt shudder through the boards of the ship. Mazen looked up at the ceiling as something heavy slid across the deck. Hope kindled in his chest when he heard the sailors yelling.

A storm had stolen Loulie away. If they'd sailed into one, then maybe they had found her.

Mazen moved toward the door, his shadow thrown over his body for cover. He was navigating himself out of the labyrinth of boxes when the ship banked, throwing him across the room. Out of the corner of his eye, he saw the birdcage begin to topple. Unthinkingly, he grabbed it before it could fall, but the bulbul inside still released a terrified squawk.

Mazen was trying to steady them both when the door opened.

A familiar figure stood in the entryway. Ziyad, who was staring right at him. Mazen realized his shadow had fallen from his shoulders when he'd reached for the cage.

"Mm." Ziyad tapped his chin. "I had wondered when you would reappear, Yousef."

Mazen staggered back. The cage door jostled, having come loose during the fall. It occurred to him, suddenly, that the bird might return to Nabila if he freed it. Which meant...

It will find Loulie. It will tell them what happened.

The moment Mazen pried the door open, the bird fled, shooting past the marid and out the open door. It vanished into the sky before any of the startled soldiers could capture it.

Mazen knew better than to struggle when the jinn came to restrain him. There would be no fleeing in the middle of the Sandsea.

Ziyad regarded him with an exasperated smile as they bound his wrists with enchanted rope. "Is this a pastime of yours? Sneaking on and off ships?"

"This is all a misunderstanding."

"You stowing away on my ship is a misunderstanding?"

"No, my—our crimes. Layla and I are not working with Nabila. She was *kidnapped* by her." His gaze swept hopefully past Ziyad to the door. "Have . . . have you found her yet?"

Ziyad's smile vanished. "We spotted Nabila's ship, but her storm stopped us from getting close." He regarded Mazen coolly. "Do you know you're a wanted criminal now, Yousef?"

"Please, if you would just listen to what I have to say—"

"You lie as a profession. What reason do I have to believe you when you have been telling untruths this whole time?" Ziyad threw a glance over his shoulder at the soldiers behind him. "Take him away. We shall see if he gains us anything as a hostage."

Mazen's faith dimmed as the soldiers guided him away. With the storm gone and Nabila escaped, he harbored one last hope: that the bird he had freed would return to its master.

22

AISHA

Aisha bint Louas was accustomed to the weight of grief. Years ago, when her village had been slaughtered by jinn, the creatures had carved the deaths of each of her family members onto her arms as a reminder. Rather than cave beneath that pain, Aisha had learned to sharpen her resentment into a blade. For years, she had fought bitterly against heartache and prevailed.

How strange, then, that the loss of Umm Jaber lay so heavy on her. *Have I truly grown so soft?*

The thought prickled at her sleep-addled mind, worsening her headache as she and Hakim neared their first detour after five days of travel. The town, called Bhurj, was humbly sized, minuscule in comparison to the grand cities of Dhyme and Ghiban. Devoid of any awe-inspiring architecture and greenery, it was hardly a place people wove poetry about. In fact, while it existed on most maps, Aisha knew many travelers avoided the place. As a stopover well off the beaten path, it did not offer much in the way of comfort or convenience.

If there were any stories told of Bhurj, they were of the lone sidra tree planted in the settlement. Though the tree itself was reported to be impressive in size, it was its nature the stories warned of, for they claimed the tree was not just dead but haunted. Any who passed beneath the sidra's sagging boughs were doomed to hear the whispers of malevolent jinn, and the few travelers who had braved the walk claimed they had barely survived possession.

Hakim confessed to being intrigued by the stories. Aisha thought they were drivel.

At first, she was disgruntled the mapmaker was taking them there. But he insisted it was the safer path, leading them past Dhyme and making it easier to avoid both Omar's thieves and the rumors that had likely spread of Aisha's betrayal.

Eventually, she and Hakim came to the fence bordering the small town. There, they were met by a young scout with shifty eyes. At first, Aisha feared he might recognize her from some wanted poster. But there was no scrutiny on his face when he asked them their business.

"We are just passing through," Aisha said. "And will be gone come morning."

The scout eyed the sinking sun, then glanced between the two of them. His gaze lingered on Aisha's face. Her returning scowl was one-eyed—she had opted to part her hair to the side so that it curtained her darker eye.

The scout conceded, leading them through the ramshackle town to an inn with a lopsided sign. When Aisha handed over the requested coin to the innkeeper, he waved a hand toward the corridor and said, "Only one room."

Aisha grabbed the key and started down the hallway with Hakim. When she saw the cramped room they were to share for the night, she wondered if sleeping in the open desert might have been the better choice after all. They had come here for comfort, but there was only a single cot in the room. Other furniture included a chest with a broken lock, a cupboard with a slightly unhinged door, and a threadbare carpet that looked as if it had been burned in a fire.

Aisha threw their supplies on the ground with a sigh. "You take the bed."

"No. You are the one who is injured."

Aisha glanced sharply over her shoulder, but the mapmaker had one of those hard, unyielding looks on his face. "You think I don't notice the way you lean in your saddle? You almost fell off your horse four times."

She frowned, annoyed that he had perceived she was still recovering from the injuries the Resurrectionist had sealed. "Speak for yourself. You've been favoring a leg this whole time."

Hakim ignored her, brushing the dirt off his tunic as he settled himself on the edge of the bed. He spoke without meeting her eye. "This exhaustion—it came over you before, when you defeated those raiders in the desert with your magic. Jaber said that you fainted." When she did not answer, the thoughtless fool probed further. "The power takes a toll on you, doesn't it?"

Aisha pressed her lips together and said nothing. The only other person who had paid so much attention to her was Mazen bin Malik, and dealing with him had been exhausting. *This* prince was tiring in a different way.

In the end, Aisha forced Hakim to take the bed. The man was stubborn, but even he saw the foolishness in objecting once she started spreading her blankets on the floor. Not long after he had settled, Aisha heard the telltale susurrus of his breathing as he drifted off to sleep. Soon after, she collapsed beneath the weight of her own exhaustion.

In her dreams, Aisha was transported back to the Asfour campsite. She was in the shed, standing in front of Umm Jaber's corpse and staring at the sickle-shaped gash around her neck. Jaber's desperate words echoed in her mind: *You can bring her back. Please, bint Louas.*

Aisha could feel the Resurrectionist's magic humming in her bones, her ears. It was not just a feeling this time, but a song. A melody, from somewhere deep in her memories.

The stars, they burn the night
And guide the sheikh's way . . .

Aisha did not realize she had put voice to the lyrics until the corpse craned its neck to look at her. It smiled—an awful, bloody smile—and said, "You sing beautifully, murderer."

When Aisha startled awake, it was still dark outside. She sat up and dragged her hands across her face with a silent groan. The last time she'd been assaulted by such nightmares, it had been after her family died. Those dreams had plagued her for years, filling her mind with corpses and blood and burning fields. And now a near *stranger* was haunting them?

She forcefully pushed the memory of Umm Jaber away as she glanced toward the bed, which she noted was empty. That Hakim had left the room without her hearing was disconcerting. She decided to wait up for his return.

Running from your dreams, hunter? There was amusement in the Resurrectionist's voice.

Aisha glowered at the ceiling. "Are you so bored you would haunt them now too?"

They are our *dreams now.*

Empty words. Their union was not coexistence; it was a war constantly being waged.

Still, in the silence of the quiet room, Aisha found herself suddenly wondering, If the Resurrectionist could pry open the doors to *her* memories so easily, could Aisha do the same? The thought repulsed her the moment it crossed her mind. The ifrit, ever observant, just laughed.

Your mind is a fortress, thief. You limit yourself by keeping the gates closed.

Aisha would not be fooled. If the ifrit was so eager to tear down the walls between them, then she would continue to reinforce them. She was still frowning up at the ceiling when she spoke again. "If you are so eager to talk, tell me about that gods-awful song you always sing."

I told you before that is an old song from Dhahab. But if you are so curious about its origin . . . why ask when you can simply take?

The taunt was crystal clear. Aisha could feel the ifrit's memories lying dormant in her mind like a pool of still water, but to dive in would mean surrender. Aisha was not that desperate. She would not be like Prince Mazen, whose curiosity had nearly gotten him killed.

The thought of the prince made her remember Hakim, who had still not returned.

Aisha stood with a sigh, grateful for an excuse to end the inquisition. She strapped on her knives, fastened her cloak, and set out. The inn was eerily quiet as she exited, the innkeeper nowhere to be seen. Remember-ing the mapmaker's curiosity for the sidra, Aisha decided to search for the tree. Finding it was surprisingly easy. The settlement was small and cramped, and it was not difficult to spot the single tree in the center of the town. It was as enormous as purported, its gnarled branches stretch-ing so wide they cast long, limb-like shadows on the sand.

Aisha found Hakim staring up at the branches. He did not look up when she called his name. "Any reason you've decided to go sightseeing in the dead of night?"

"I prefer the stars to a ceiling," he said.

She supposed he would after all those years he'd spent trapped inside. But still, the tree was a peculiar place to visit. Aisha did not believe the stories, but even she had to admit it was an ominous sight…and the wind *did* make a strange sound passing through the branches. She was reminded of the undead muttering she often heard in the desert, the sound that she tried valiantly to block out with the rest of her magic.

"You'd have a better view of the sky beyond these branches," Aisha said.

At that, Hakim finally turned. "I was just thinking Mazen would be fascinated by this tree."

"He is fascinated by *most* things." Even now, she could imagine him standing beneath the sidra, excitedly pointing at the branches as he shared its story with all the useless details. The thought sent a bewildering pang of concern through her.

Hakim smiled. On his face, it was a distinctly somber look. "I wish, sometimes, that I could still see wonder in the world the way Mazen does."

"Some would call that naivete."

"Others would call it faith. Mazen has always believed in the good in people. That belief is a rare thing, and all the more precious for it."

"And what about you?" Aisha crossed her arms. "What do you believe in?"

"I believe in that which I can see with my own two eyes." Hakim paused, breathed out softly. "Before I was brought to Madinne as a child, I had a mentor who taught me to read those truths, both in people and in my surroundings."

"You had a teacher?"

Hakim nodded. "He was a cartographer, and I was his apprentice while he still lived." It was the most he had ever divulged to her, and he seemed to realize it the same moment she did. He paused, perhaps debating whether to share more, before adding, "The knowledge he left behind is invaluable. Without his guidance, I would not possess half the skills I have."

It was uncharacteristically high praise coming from Hakim, and Aisha was curious despite herself. But before she could probe further, a sudden crack startled her from her thoughts. She whirled in place, searching for the disturbance.

She spotted the dead branch on the ground first, and then the intruder who had snapped it underfoot. It was the scout who had welcomed them. But he was no longer alone. A whole band of people, including the innkeeper, stood behind him. Aisha did not miss the glint of their weapons.

Her hand hovered at her belt. "Masa'a al-khair," she said in a clipped voice.

The scout ventured forward slowly. "Masa'a al-noor." He paused beneath the swaying branches. "I realized earlier I may have come off as a brute, not introducing myself. I think it would be the hospitable thing to do—trading names."

Aisha scoffed. "Is hiding a blade behind your back your idea of hospitality as well?"

The mapmaker shifted uneasily behind her. Perhaps he had just now noticed the weapons himself. Aisha inched toward him protectively as the vagabonds formed a circle around them.

One of them, a woman with a gaunt, hateful face, pulled a knife from her pocket. "A lone woman armed to the teeth and a man with striking hazel eyes... Your appearances match the wanted posters perfectly."

Aisha cursed under her breath. So there *were* wanted posters. She had been a fool to think this place was safe.

"Perhaps we can strike a deal," the scout said. There was hunger in his eyes. "If you are a jinn hunter, then you must have relics on you. Give them to us, and we'll spare you."

Hakim made a soft sound of protest. His distress must have been answer enough, because the vagabonds gave them no time to consider their deal. The scout moved first, rushing toward Aisha with a yell. Another came right after, charging from a different direction.

Aisha withdrew one of her weapons. When the scout came at her with a staff, she met the impact with the flat of her sword, then shoved him backward. She rammed an elbow into his face before he could recover, knocking him to the ground before facing the next attacker. Though she missed the edge of their blade, the hilt caught her in the hip. She stumbled back, and the mapmaker called her name in concern.

Too late, he realized he'd drawn attention to himself. Aisha muttered a curse as two of the vagabonds moved to capture him. She turned to see two more crowding her.

The tree, bint Louas, the Resurrectionist snapped. *Focus on the tree.*

Aisha balked at the command. It was nonsense.

One of the assailants grabbed Hakim, holding a knife to his chest in warning. Aisha glanced past them to the sidra. She was close enough to hear the whisper of the wind through the branches. Through her darker eye, she became aware of faint gold threads stretching across them like a spiderweb. She could do more than feel the links; she could *grasp* them.

It took her a moment to realize why. It was not that she could feel the tree. It was that she could reach the souls of the dead jinn whose blood had been used to *make* that tree. These souls, unbound to relics, had instead burrowed into the land itself. Aisha forced herself to concentrate on them as the Resurrectionist's magic hummed beneath her skin.

"*Move*," she commanded.

Her mind stretched with the instruction, pulling her toward the tree and its sprawling branches. She could feel them like phantom limbs, and all she had to do to grasp them was tug...

The tree gave an unearthly screech. The vagabonds froze as the dead branches shook themselves out of their stupor. Aisha aimed at Hakim's captor. The branch snapped him across the face, knocking him to the ground.

Aisha grabbed for Hakim, her attention split between pulling him away and commanding the branches. She flexed her fingers, curling them into a tight fist that the branches mimicked as they gripped another of the assailants.

With every command, Aisha's mind sank deeper into the dead tree. When she swallowed, she felt dirt in her throat. When she moved, she felt the dead tree's roots in her legs, her arms.

At some point, she must have stopped moving, because she felt Hakim grab her hand and guide her away from the revolting tree. Her mind was still nestled within the rotting trunk as he led her back to the inn, throwing nervous glances over his shoulder all the while. But the way was clear; Aisha had struck the fear of a living curse into these people.

Only when Hakim set a hand on her shoulder did Aisha remember herself. Her limbs felt stiff, and her fingers were locked into trembling fists. The mapmaker made no comment, just left her to gather herself as he went to grab their horses. By the time he had returned, Aisha's exhausted body was her own. Her mind, however, was a different story.

Long after they had escaped Bhurj, part of her remained connected to the possessed tree. When they were a safe distance away, Hakim insisted she sever the connection. He turned to face her in his saddle, worry plain in the furrow of his brow. "Bint Louas—"

"Keep riding," she said. "We are not safe until that cursed place is behind us."

They continued traveling in silence, and Aisha was glad for it. It took all her concentration to untangle her mind from the tree, and afterward the effort left her feeling frighteningly empty. Had the mapmaker pressed her, he would have seen through her bravado.

Aisha was not trying to outrun the vagabonds. She was trying to outrun her magic.

23

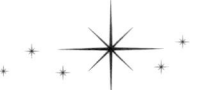

LOULIE

Loulie spent the next few days on Nabila's ship learning the ropes of the vessel.

Nabila let her stew in her misery for all of one night before shoving a crate at her and saying, "Make yourself useful. Every body counts."

When Loulie retorted that she was not a *willing* body, the ifrit's responding glare had been icy enough to chill the air. Still, Loulie had resisted her demands until Duha called on her to assist with the nets. She was the only one on the ship Loulie did not have the heart to deny.

Perhaps it was because, unlike the others, Nabila's first mate weathered Loulie's questions with patience. When Loulie asked her about the sinking land, Duha explained that the continent had been fractured for hundreds of years and that it was only recently the Sandsea had swallowed so much of it. She said Nabila speculated the turmoil had something to do with the well-being of her fellow ifrit—that their bindings had broken with their deaths. It would explain why there had been only four bindings on the map.

Loulie would have liked to hear the story from Nabila herself, but the ifrit was rarely on deck. At first, Loulie thought she was ignoring her. But then on her second night, she glanced up at the crow's nest and saw the phantom outline of Nabila in the breeze. As she watched, the ifrit's form dissipated into a gale that swept through the sails.

Later, when she asked Duha about this, the marid explained that Nabila preferred to drift on the wind when she was not needed. "Even leaders need to relax," she said. "*This* is how Nabila rests. She is incapable of staying still, even for a moment."

This became more evident to Loulie as the days went on. Even when Nabila lacked a physical form, she was ever present on the ship. Like a nahhām on a human ship, she sang for the sailors, leading them in song while they worked. She was the magic breathing beneath the planks and the gust tugging at the sailors' clothing, nudging them toward one task or another. Whenever Loulie did something Nabila found impermissible, the wind hissed a warning in her ear.

By the time the sun had risen on the third day, Loulie had grown distrustful of the breeze. She was eager to reach al-Malath. The sooner she unsealed this binding, the sooner she could be free of Nabila and return to Mazen, Rijah... and Qadir, whose fate was still a mystery to her.

Had he been captured by Omar or fallen victim to some other unexpected misfortune? Loulie had no way of knowing, not when Qadir refused to speak to her outside of the bindings.

She swallowed her unease as she circled the deck, surveying the Sandsea from the rails. She walked until she reached the ship's rukh figurehead, pausing only when she noticed Duha seated between the bird's wings. Loulie grimaced at the steep drop beneath her feet.

Duha, for her part, looked thrilled to see her. "Al-Nazari! Come to join me on lookout?"

Loulie raised a brow, thinking of the ship's perfectly usable crow's nest. When she brought it up to Duha, the marid only laughed and said, "Yes, but *this* is the best view on the ship. You should see it for yourself."

"I'll pass. I would rather not make it easier for Nabila to push me overboard." She sighed as she turned her attention to the Sandsea.

The godsforsaken stretch of sand was as empty today as it had been yesterday; there was still no sign of al-Malath on the horizon.

The anxiety must have been plain on her face, because the marid tried to console her. "Do not look so glum, human! You are out of Dhahab, the golden prison. Surely that is cause for celebration..." The words faded as her eyes caught on something in the sky.

Loulie glanced to the horizon and saw...a bird? A bulbul, flying rapidly toward them.

A sliver of unease sickled through her at the sight of it. "One of Nabila's spies?"

Duha nodded as she slid from the figurehead. "A messenger sent to the zaeem of Kharjem."

The whole crew had paused to watch the bird alight on the crow's nest, where Nabila had already materialized. The ifrit held out a calming hand to the bird, which flitted to her wrist. She said something to it—something that the wind did not carry to Loulie's ears. She heard only the bird's response: a high-pitched and frantic squawking.

The sound made her shudder. "What's it saying?"

Duha shook her head. "I do not know. Only Nabila speaks to the birds."

It looked less like a conversation than a shrieking monologue, but the sailors were just as invested as Loulie was. They all stood watching, waiting, until the ifrit turned to look at them. Loulie's blood ran cold when Nabila called her name. Time seemed to slow as she climbed up to the crow's nest to meet her.

Both the ifrit and the bird frowned at her. "This little one told me he was on a ship chasing after us," Nabila said. "He told me he was freed by a human."

The human could only be one person. Loulie wanted to kick herself. If the ship was pursuing them, it had to be one of the queen's vessels. While she had been bemoaning her inability to return for Mazen, he had come after *her*. If he had freed the bird, did that mean he was in danger? In hiding? She could not turn her back on him.

"That human is my companion," Loulie said. "He must have escaped the city. We need to go back for him." She forced herself to speak calmly, even as panic squeezed her heart.

"You speak of the man who was calling your name," Nabila said. She said nothing when Loulie nodded, just quietly stroked the feathers of the bulbul to calm it. When the bird finally quieted, she shook her head and said, "I am not turning back."

The refusal hit like a punch to the stomach. Again, the terrible memory of the storyteller's scream cut through Loulie's mind. They had survived sandstorms and ghouls together, had escaped sinking ruins and terrible odds. She would not leave him behind. She would *not*.

"Then let *me* go." She stepped forward, and she was close enough now that she had to crane her neck to meet Nabila's stormy eyes. "Let me save him."

The ifrit did not yield. Somehow, her gaze had grown frostier. "Do you have sand in your ears? I am not turning my ship around. Not for you, not for anyone."

Loulie's patience broke. "You have to—"

"You *dare* command me? I am the nokhitha of this ship." The ifrit's voice was a roar in her ears. Loulie fell back, startled. "I will not repeat myself. The ship stays its course."

Nabila vanished with the dismissal, abruptly ending their conversation. Loulie's eyes swept the deck, seeking a sympathetic ear, but the sailors had all gone pointedly back to their work. Even Duha had left to chase after the bird, which had flown off with Nabila's disappearance.

Loulie resisted the urge to scream. Instead, she took a deep breath and focused on the horizon as she considered her options. The choice was simple: obey or disobey.

In the end, it was an easy decision to make. Loulie did not balk at low odds, and she did not surrender to authority. She was the Midnight Merchant, Loulie Najima al-Nazari, and she was the master of her own damned fate. She did not need Nabila's permission to save a prince.

She would save him herself.

—₥—

The sky had lightened to a rotting purple by the time Loulie gathered her supplies and snuck toward the ship's pinnace. The small boat did not inspire confidence. Though she had witnessed a couple of sailors floating across the Sandsea in it over the last few days, she could not help but harbor doubts that the magic would hold for her, a human.

Loulie had just begun to lower the boat when a soft cough sounded behind her. She whirled, Qadir's knife in hand, and froze when she came face-to-face with Duha.

The marid was untroubled by the dagger. "Masa'a al-khair, al-Nazari."

Loulie froze. If she tried to escape now, the marid would certainly overpower her. Would she tell Nabila of her deceit? Or was there a deal she could cut to keep her quiet?

Duha slunk against the mast. With her ankles crossed and head gently inclined, she appeared the portrait of nonchalance. "What are you thinking, ya sayyida?" There was no reprimand in her voice. Just curiosity, as if she were genuinely interested in Loulie's escape plan.

Loulie lowered the knife. "You heard me before. I'm going to save my companion."

"Why? Is he that important?" A sudden spark came into her eyes. "Is he your husband?"

"What? *No.* We are only friends." The word had an unexpected weight to it. She realized she had rarely used it. Other than Qadir, she'd always had associates, acquaintances, connections—but *friend* contained a different warmth, one that felt almost like an embrace.

The marid drummed her sharp nails against her arm. "And after you rescue him, what is to stop you from vanishing on us before you break the bindings?"

Loulie did not answer. She imagined Duha could read her reticence from the quiet. This could end one of two ways: either she tried to escape and Duha chased her, or she failed to make it off the ship and the marid dragged her kicking and screaming back to her captain.

But much to Loulie's surprise, Duha defied expectation and chose a third option. Instead of turning on her heel and calling for Nabila, she reached past Loulie for the rope and, with a hard tug, dropped the pinnace closer to the Sandsea.

Loulie blinked at her, baffled. "Why are you helping me?"

Duha's expression was serene as she lowered the pinnace to the Sandsea. "Because without me, you *will* perish, and your death would be both a tragedy and an inconvenience." She flashed a bright smile as she reached for the rope ladder. "And make no mistake, al-Nazari—even if you managed to evade capture, Nabila would find you again. She is just less likely to smite you with lightning if I am there to plead for clemency."

Loulie's thoughts whirred as she followed Duha down the ladder into the boat. No sooner had she seated herself than the marid reached into the sinking sand and made the vessel *move*.

When Loulie scrambled to hold on to the edges, Duha only laughed. "You realize that there is water in the Sandsea, sah? I may not be able to swim in it, but I can shift it with effort."

Loulie gaped. The sand didn't *look* wet. "There's water in the Sandsea?"

"Why do you think it is called the Sand*sea*?"

With the enchantment and Duha's mysterious magic at work, the ship cut across the sand. Loulie had no idea where the marid was drawing this water from, but evidently, the sea of sand was more like an ocean than she had imagined. That being said, it was a less smooth trip than it would have been with Nabila's magic. Many times, Loulie feared the boat would tip into the sinking sand for how erratically it moved.

Duha seemed unconcerned. She was looking past Loulie to the long stretch of Sandsea, a wistful look on her face. "You should have seen me and Nabila on the ocean. When we were together, we were a perfect storm. No one could survive our magic. No one could survive *us*."

"You clearly would do anything for Nabila. So why are you dis-obeying her?"

The marid looked at her, amused. "Because you would have left regardless. You are like Nabila that way, too prideful to back down once you have made a decision. Besides..." She winked. "Unlike my nokhitha, I can never resist a gamble. The more perilous, the better."

Bizarre reasons aside, Loulie was grateful for her assistance. "Shukran," she muttered.

Duha laughed. "Do not thank me yet, al-Nazari. We still need to make it back alive."

24

LOULIE

The moment Loulie saw Ziyad's ship on the horizon, she recognized it.

The last time she had boarded the boum, it had been when she and Mazen first came to the jinn realm. It had seemed their only means of rescue then. Now it was a trap. The closer they came to it, the more it loomed, blotting out the night sky above them.

Loulie was a bundle of nerves. Duha, on the other hand, appeared to be not only calm but in good spirits. "This is Ziyad's ship?" She smiled in appreciation as she gazed upon it.

Loulie nodded. "At least, I think so. Most ships look the same to me."

"The same! Have you never stopped to appreciate the craftsmanship of each vessel? Every builder pours his soul into his work; each ship has her own heart."

When Loulie raised a brow in response, Duha dropped the subject with a sigh, then reached for something around her neck. "Here. This will help you sneak on board."

Loulie blinked in surprise as the marid held out a necklace that had been hidden beneath her scarf: a single unblemished pearl hanging from a string. She eyed the accessory with suspicion. "What is this? Magic?"

"A gift from Nabila. If you do not return it, I will hunt you to the ends of the world to reclaim it." Though the proclamation had the levity of a joke, Duha's smile was vicious.

Loulie accepted the pearl. The moment she cupped it in her palms, a strange lightness overcame her, and she swayed in place, suddenly unsteady on her feet. "What manner of enchantment is this?"

"Hold the pearl in front of you, like this." Duha demonstrated by curling her fingers into a fist and extending it inches before her.

The moment Loulie mimicked the motion, she felt an abrupt push at her back and stumbled forward, running right into the marid in the process. Duha laughed as she steadied her. "Do you understand now?"

"All I understand is that I suddenly can't walk in a straight line." She grimaced as she righted herself, but even when she braced her feet, she felt unbalanced. The feeling was familiar in an odd way. It reminded Loulie of the looseness that came into her limbs when she'd had too much to drink. But her mind was still clear; it was just her limbs that had become unwieldy.

Duha's eyes shone with amusement. "Nabila does not create wind; she redirects it. The enchantment on the pearl grants you the same magic. With it, you can shape the breeze around your body as she does." The marid grinned at her befuddlement. "When we get close to the ship, use the wind to propel yourself on deck. All you must do is imagine the pearl as a target. Where it moves, the wind follows. Do you understand?"

Loulie did not comprehend anything beyond the basic theory of the magic, but Duha gave her no time to ask questions. The moment Loulie offered an uncertain nod, Duha leaned back toward the Sandsea and began speeding the pinnace forward again. "You remember the plan? I will create a distraction. You sneak on board. We save your lover."

"Friend," Loulie snapped. And then: "I *can* trust you . . . sah?"

"I suppose you have no choice," the marid said cheerfully.

The wind was whipping so fiercely at their boat that Loulie did not even have the breath to sigh. She forced herself to focus on Ziyad's ship as they cruised into its shadow. Duha's smile faded as she glanced at Loulie. "Are you ready?"

Loulie was not, but she knew they were running out of time. Soon, the sailors would notice the pinnace. She had to make sure she was off it before they did. With a deep breath, she faced Ziyad's ship. The pearl felt terribly small in her palm, and as a last-minute safety measure, she clasped it around her neck and twisted the string around her fingers.

"Al-Nazari," Duha whispered urgently.

Loulie curled her fingers over the pearl and raised her hand. The effect of the magic was immediate. Moments ago, she had felt unmoored. Now she was *weightless* as the wind that had moments ago tugged at her clothes suddenly pushed her up.

There was a terrifying, breathless moment when Loulie felt as if she were pinwheeling through the air. But then the gusts steadied into a solid current, pushing her up toward the deck on a gentle draft. Loulie barely had time to process the experience before the deck rose up to meet her and she remembered to lower her palm.

But the motion was too quick, and the wind did not lighten so much as vanish. It was all she could do to grab the rails before she plunged into the Sandsea. Loulie hung over the hull, breathless and shaking, as footsteps sounded on deck. Sailors, no doubt coming to investigate.

Her mind whirred with panic. If she let go, she would fall into the Sandsea. If she climbed up, she would be spotted.

Shit. What could she do? What could she—

The ship tilted, hard enough to flatten Loulie to the hull and make the sailors on board stagger. Loulie heard them curse loudly as the boum swayed, the Sandsea suddenly tumultuous.

Duha's work, Loulie assumed. Sure enough, not moments later, Loulie heard her voice above the crashing waves. *"Akhi!"* she was yelling. "Will you not come greet your sister?"

The footsteps on board receded as the sailors rushed off to deal with the intruder. Loulie waited until she was certain they had left, and then, with a wheezing gasp, she pulled herself over the rails. The minute her feet touched solid ground, she slumped into a crouch.

As she'd hoped, Duha had drawn the attention of the sailors, but Loulie was still vulnerable. Her eyes darted to the nearest crate, which she gracelessly threw herself behind as another sailor rushed on deck. Though she missed his face, Loulie recognized his pristine coat. Thankfully, Ziyad's gaze never strayed as he strode toward the prow.

"Ukhti!" he yelled back. "I thought I recognized your magic. Have you finally decided to leave your terrible nokhitha?"

His voice faded as he walked away. Cautiously, Loulie ducked her head out to observe the chaos on deck. While a few of the sailors had gone to join their captain, the others were working to secure nearby objects. Loulie glanced toward the cabin door, still hanging ajar.

It was now or never. She sprinted across the deck, hand outstretched toward the door—

Only to collide headfirst with something very, very solid.

Loulie stumbled backward as the obstruction—the *sailor*—who had just stepped through the entryway stared at her in shock. The moment Loulie saw his mouth open, she did not think. She placed her palms on his chest and shoved him back the way he had come. The sailor flailed on the staircase, then toppled.

Loulie flinched at the loud thud his body made. She could already hear the telltale shuffle of investigating footsteps. If the crew had not known there was an intruder on the ship, they would certainly know now.

With a curse, she rushed down the steps, Qadir's dagger clutched in one hand and the pearl in the other. She and the investigating jinn spotted each other at the same moment. Soldiers, she realized when she saw their uniforms. One pulled a blade on her. The other did not need a weapon; with a flick of his wrist, his nails lengthened into wicked-looking claws.

Loulie gripped the pearl with a grimace. *Time to see what you can do.*

The soldiers came at her at the same time, but Loulie was ready for them. Concentrating on the wind at her back, she swerved, yanking the pearl right with the motion. With the magic, she meant to send the jinn careening into the wall.

But the moment she moved, she knew she had miscalculated. The wind roared with purpose—and threw *her* across the room. A sword passed inches above her head as she crashed into the wall, where she crumpled to the ground with a wheeze.

The jinn stood frozen at the foot of the staircase, watching her with confusion.

Loulie's head throbbed as she staggered to her feet. *Damn magic.*

The soldier with the claws recovered faster. He came at her, slashing a vicious arc through the air that would have torn her face had she not rolled to avoid it. On the ground, she aimed for his legs. He retaliated by aiming a kick at her gut.

Loulie gasped in pain as Qadir's dagger slipped through her fingers. Alarm shot through her as the soldier lunged for it. The first thing she thought to do was use the pearl. This time, when she thrust it forward, the radius of wind caught the weapon, sending it skittering across the floor.

The force pushed one jinn to his knees and swept the other across the room. Loulie saw her opening and pressed it. She pushed forward with the magic, letting herself be propelled by its momentum. Neither sailor was ready for the sudden gale, but Loulie was.

She braced herself against the staircase as she directed the wind into a tempest, gritting her teeth against the magic as it threw one soldier over the fallen body of his comrade and the other against the wall, hard enough to knock him out. Though the remaining jinn struggled valiantly, the gale was relentless, pressing until it had stolen the air from his lungs. It was only when he collapsed that Loulie released the magic.

For a few moments, she stood trembling in the aftermath of the tempest, stunned by its ferocity. Then she turned away, swapping the pearl for her compass as she plucked the dagger off the floor and rushed down the corridor. She whispered to the instrument, "Show me where Mazen is."

The relic led her down a swaying corridor to a weathered door. Loulie paused just long enough to press her ear to it. When she heard nothing, she tucked the compass back in her pocket, wrapped the necklace around her fingers, and entered with the knife raised.

The first thing she saw was Mazen, tied to a beam in the center of the room. His face was bloodied and bruised, his fine clothing torn—and there was terror in his eyes when he saw her.

"Behind you!"

She spun just in time to see a hidden soldier lunge at her from behind the door.

Loulie just barely evaded the slithering rope in his hands. The movement sent her back against one of the walls, where she knocked into a floor mirror. She briefly faltered when she saw the glass *waver* but had no time to process the sight before the soldier rushed her.

With a sidestep, she avoided his blade as it crashed into the glass. It ought to have cracked the mirror. Instead, it made the surface ripple like disturbed water. The sight was evidently more shocking to Loulie than to the soldier, because he whirled on her without pause.

This time, Loulie reached for the pearl around her neck. The wind was not as powerful as it had been outside, but still, the soldier had not been expecting it. With the magic, Loulie blew him away and out of the room, giving her enough time to secure the bolt behind her.

She turned to see Mazen staring at her, slack-jawed. "You're... unharmed?" he said.

Loulie's heart constricted at the worry in his eyes. "I'm fine." She cast a wary look at the mirror, which was still rippling oddly. "What is that thing?"

"I think it is Ziyad's magic. He uses the water to communicate with the queen."

Had she the time, Loulie might have investigated the water-mirror to see how it worked. But time was the one thing they did not have. She knelt beside Mazen and began to carefully cut at the ropes on his wrist. "I didn't mean to leave you behind."

"I know. The ifrit—she kidnapped you."

"She is apparently incapable of asking people for favors *without* kidnapping them."

"A favor?"

The door shook violently on its hinges. Loulie forced her shaking hands to unravel the ropes. She worked on them until, with one final slash, they gave beneath her knife. Mazen had just stumbled to his feet when the door burst open and the soldier rushed inside.

Loulie pressed a palm to Mazen's back. "There's a boat on the sea. Go!" She pushed him away as the jinn charged forward with a blade.

She was relieved when Mazen ducked out of the room. Before the soldier could give chase, Loulie rushed him with the dagger, aiming a strike at his shoulder that he deflected. The ringing impact sent her stumbling back, and she tripped on the writhing rope and fell.

Something crashed to the ground and rolled away from her. Loulie caught a flash of white.

The pearl.

She scrambled toward it, realizing too late when her fingers closed over it that she had put herself directly in harm's way. She tensed as the jinn raised the weapon above his head.

But the strike never came. Suddenly, the soldier keeled over with a gasp, hands reaching for his stomach. Loulie stared, uncomprehending. He looked as if he was being pulled...back?

Mazen.

The realization snapped into place when she heard the storyteller's harried breathing. She'd forgotten he had his shadow. His disembodied voice came out a rasp: "Use the rope."

Loulie reached for the rope-snake squirming on the ground and faced the jinn. Though he struggled against Mazen's grip, Loulie was able to tie both his arms and legs. Her fingers worked from memory, securing knots in the careful way Duha had taught her.

It was a shoddy solution, but it would buy them time. After shoving the jinn into the room, the two of them ran. The corridor slanted precariously beneath their feet as they exited, the ship swerving so violently Loulie crashed into a wall. She heard the wind howling outside, along with the ominous hiss of the sand. Was this Duha's doing?

No.

Loulie recognized the shriek of a storm. This was not Duha's magic; it was Nabila's. Loulie could feel it through the floor—could feel the whole ship shuddering, *capsizing.*

The sailors must have realized their ship was sinking. In their panic, she and Mazen were forgotten. Loulie used the chaos to her advantage, darting past the panicking masses toward the staircase. It was disorienting not to see Mazen running beside her, but she could hear his breathing, a pained, labored wheeze.

They made it to the staircase before a figure stepped in front of them. Ziyad, standing in the entryway with his arms crossed. "Layla." He said her name with enough venom to make her flinch. "I knew you would return for Yousef. Where is he?"

Invisible, she thought with some relief. To his eye and hers. This time, she did not have to worry about him being in danger.

She held up her knife. "Get out of my way."

Loulie charged him before he could react. If they could just push past him, then—

She did not see the strange, sparkling knife hidden up his sleeve until it was too late. Loulie was dimly aware of its sharp blue edge as it flashed through the air toward her neck.

But the blow never came.

She heard the tear of flesh. A gasp of pain. But it was not her reaction.

At first, neither she nor Ziyad understood what had happened. His eerie blade seemed to be suspended in midair. Then, inexplicably, its tip turned a dark crimson.

Loulie heard heavy footfalls. A terrible, wet cough as something fell into her, knocking her to the ground. She felt the warm press of a body. A heartbeat that was not her own. And then: red. *Blood*, dripping through her fingers. But she was not bleeding.

No.

Loulie drew shakily to her knees. The invisible weight shifted with the movement, and the shadow that had been coating Mazen's body fell away, revealing a weeping gash of red across his chest. Loulie saw the torn clothing, the shredded skin, and the *knife* in his chest.

The present faded as she clambered forward. Now that his shadow had fallen, she saw how much blood was coming from his body. Saw it pooling on the ground beneath him.

No.

The ship tilted, hard enough for her and Mazen to go sliding. This time, the sound was accompanied by an angry howl. It was a familiar sound—one Loulie had heard on the rooftop of an ancient archive. Ziyad seemed to recognize it too. He spun toward the door, but too late. Before he could flee, Nabila's wind had blown the wood off its hinges. The force of her storm threw him across the corridor, where he crashed into a wall and went still.

The ifrit stood before them, eyes flashing with rage. The moment she spotted Loulie, her lips curled into a sneer.

"Please," Loulie whispered. Her bloodstained hands were shaking. "He's injured."

Nabila lifted him up and off the ground as if he were light as air. "Move," she commanded, and when her wind pulled Loulie toward the door, she did not fight it.

While Loulie had been below deck, the rest of the ship had been torn apart. The soldiers who remained on deck lay scattered and unconscious beneath the debris. Nabila walked amidst the bodies like some vengeful god, tracking bloodied prints across the wood— blood that was spilling from *Mazen's* injury. Loulie slowed at the realization, terror spiking through her.

"Did you not hear me?" Nabila threw a stormy glare over her shoulder. "This blade is poisoned. The longer you delay, the longer the venom runs its course. His life is in your hands."

Loulie obeyed.

Stupid, stupid man. She blinked and felt tears on her lashes. *What kind of person throws himself in front of a fatal strike?*

But she already knew the answer to that question.

Mazen bin Malik. Prince. Storyteller. Fool. She would never forgive him if he died.

And if he did, she would never forgive herself.

25

AISHA

The entrance to Madinne's underground tunnels was located on a small plateau just outside of the city, in a nondescript place surrounded by cacti and scraggly bushes of arfaj that thrived in the sun. The location of the trapdoor was not immediately apparent; Aisha and Hakim had to dig in a specific spot for nigh on a half hour before it finally revealed itself.

Despite being thoroughly weathered by the elements, the door did not yield beneath their touch. Hakim was prepared. Without explanation, he pulled a small key loose from a stitch in his robe and used it to open the door. They both stared at the blackness on the other side.

"You first," Aisha said.

She grimaced as she watched Hakim descend a thin rope ladder. The darkness unsettled her less than the murmurs emanating from it. Unlike the voices of the lost souls in the desert, these memories pulsed beneath Aisha's eyelids like a headache.

The Resurrectionist hummed in her mind. *All this time, and still you are not accustomed to the sounds of the damned and the dying?*

Aisha ignored the ifrit as she followed Hakim down into the depths. The mapmaker had already lit one of the lanterns hanging on the wall and was exploring the tunnel. He ventured at a careful pace, sometimes sweeping his feet or hands across the rocky surface to check for traps. If there *were* traps, Aisha could not see them in the dark.

Though she would never admit it aloud, she realized it would have been impossible for her to navigate the tunnels alone. It was not just the darkness that thwarted her sense of direction but the pathways themselves. The longer she and Hakim wandered, the more difficult the trails became to follow. The pathways twisted and turned, cutting through rocky walls and over abysses and splitting in various directions.

That Hakim could traverse the paths without putting himself in peril was a miracle.

"How long did you wander this place before you made it out the first time?" she asked.

"I am not certain. A full day, perhaps."

Aisha considered the crude shape of the branching pathways. It was nothing short of incredible that a labyrinth this massive existed under Madinne. Even more impressive was that it had, from her understanding, been crafted by humans rather than jinn.

Hakim turned a bend and paused. In the light of his lantern, Aisha could make out the nexus they had stopped at. A network of branching roads stretched before them, some built into the outcrop of a second landing. Aisha glanced between the landscape and the map Hakim was holding. The twisted lines were blurred in the darkness, smudging into a winding circle.

Aisha shook her head. "How in nine hells can you read that thing?"

He offered an infuriatingly dispassionate shrug. "Practice."

Aisha trailed him down the westernmost path, keeping pace with him as they journeyed deeper. Whenever they came to a steep landing, she would climb ahead and hold out a hand to help him over. If a crossing was precarious, she would tread it first to ensure its stability.

"The sultan tried to discern the layout of this place for years," Hakim told her later. "You would not believe the number of men he sent here to die, all so he could attempt to map it."

Aisha thought of the people the man had forced into his quest for magic. She thought of Loulie al-Nazari, sent on an impossible mission to find an impossible relic.

"I can believe it." She peered at the mapmaker's back, noting his stooped posture and lowered head. "You never call him 'Father.' Is it because he treated you like dirt?"

Hakim's smile looked particularly grim in the dark. "Before Mazen's mother, Shafia, died, he *did* treat me like a son, at least publicly. But that was a long time ago. I have referred to him as the sultan for many years."

Aisha considered this. Where family was concerned, Hakim's mother had been hanged soon after her son's birth, leaving him with just his mother's tribe and . . .

Her eyes flitted to the rings on his fingers. "What about your mentor?"

Hakim brightened at the mention of him. "He was more like a grandfather to me, wise and long suffering. He was a good teacher who taught me to study the landscape by making me search for him in it. If I was able to locate him, he would educate me on the geography."

"It sounds like a frustrating education."

"Do you think so?" Hakim glanced at her over his shoulder. As far as Aisha could tell, the curiosity in his eyes was genuine. "To me, he seemed to value passion. An eager student who pursues what they love is more likely to learn than a reluctant one made to practice daily."

He had a point. Never mind that Aisha herself had never had such a mentor. When she'd been a child, she'd learned everything by doing—by helping her brother work the fields, her mother cook, and her sisters weave. Her one and only "teacher" had been Omar, and he had always been more of her commander than a mentor.

Still, he had seen the potential in her and helped her foster it. It was because of him she knew how to wield a sword with efficiency. Because of him that she had any life at all.

It is because of him that you are filled with hatred, the Resurrectionist said.

"No," Aisha muttered. *That* rage was directed at the jinn who had destroyed her life.

The ifrit sighed. *So you say. But are you not now bent on revenge against your king?*

A retort sat on the tip of Aisha's tongue, but she swallowed it when she noticed Hakim watching her. Too late, she realized she had spoken aloud. But there was no alarm on his face, just mild curiosity. She was not sure whether to be mortified or relieved when, instead of probing about the ifrit, he inquired about Omar instead, asking her how long they had known each other.

"Nine years," she said. The words felt like a confession. Nine years the two of them had worked together, and now she was trying to kill him.

She searched the mapmaker's face for pity and was relieved to see none. There was just the usual thoughtfulness as he said, "Then you understand what I mean about resolve. You would not have tolerated Omar for so long if it had not served your ambitions."

Aisha's immediate impulse was to object. She had done more than tolerate Omar; she had respected him. But she stopped when she realized she was defending him. Hakim was correct. She *had* respected Omar—she would never have worked for him otherwise—but the two of them had often been at odds. Different tactics, different goals.

And in the end, he *had* used her. He'd seen her determination and used it to his advantage. The thought made her chest burn, and she cut the conversation short with a decisive, silent nod. Thankfully, Hakim dropped the subject.

Aisha was grateful for the silence as they continued traveling, and even more relieved when, not an hour later, Hakim told her they were nearing their destination. "I recognize this area," he said. "We are close to the entrance I came through."

Aisha's stomach twisted with anticipation. Hakim had not given her his contact's name; she knew only that they were someone from the black market and someone Ahmed himself had trusted. It was little information to go on, but it was too late to turn back now.

Hakim had begun to press forward with more certainty, moving so quickly Aisha had to rush to keep up.

They had just made it to an upward slope in the tunnel when, abruptly, the ground rumbled and Aisha tripped. She braced her feet before she fell, but the tunnel remained unsteady.

Her heart dropped. "Shit."

Hakim froze, glancing around with wide eyes. When the tunnel began to quiver more visibly, Aisha shoved him forward and launched after him in a run. She gritted her teeth as the shaking intensified, forcing herself to focus on the end of the tunnel as the walls creaked and dust coated the air. The mapmaker wasn't moving *fast* enough.

She put on another burst of speed, aiming to push past him and drag him behind her, but the landslide was already coming, the rock cascading down the walls and into their pathway like a wave. Aisha reached out a hand, yelling at Hakim to retreat—

And then she noticed the falling debris *parting* before them.

At first, Aisha did not understand what she was seeing. One moment the mapmaker was rushing into a blocked path. The next, it was as if the sediment had been pushed away by some invisible hand, the avalanche of rock curving *away* from Hakim like water parting around a boulder.

The mapmaker was evidently just as shocked as she was. When he realized what was happening, he froze, face blanched. Only when Aisha grabbed his hand and yanked him forward did he stumble after her. His palm was clammy in her hand, his fingers so warm they were nearly burning. She glanced down, perturbed, and witnessed something even stranger than the landslide.

One of Hakim's rings, previously silver, had changed to a dull emerald. Something flashed across the surface. Aisha tugged his hand up to read a strand of words: *Everything I have seen once, I know in perpetuity.*

Bint Louas. The Resurrectionist's voice trembled with shock. *That is* ifrit *magic.*

Aisha could believe it. The proof was in the magic; it had become an invisible force field around them, strong enough to shatter debris on impact. She was filled with equal parts wonder and terror at the sight. What kind of magic was this, that it could shape the land so?

The magic remained until the earthquake subsided. By that point the two of them had reached the trapdoor Hakim had been leading them to. Neither of them spoke. The only sound was Hakim's muttered prayer as he took out his key and reached for the lock on the ceiling.

Aisha stared at his hands. At his ring, which was once again silver. "What was *that*?"

"I don't—" He nearly dropped the key in his trembling hand. "I don't know what just happened."

Looking at his ashen face, she believed him. Hakim was imperturbable; that he was so visibly distressed was a testament to his shock.

How? she asked the ifrit. *How does a sheltered mapmaker have* ifrit *magic? And why did I not sense it earlier?*

This whole time, while Omar had been searching for ifrit relics, Hakim had been using one right beneath his nose. Had he or the sultan known? Did *Hakim* know?

She could feel the Resurrectionist's own astonishment clouding her mind. *I suspect the magic was concealed from us. It seems the sultan's family is filled with secrets.*

Hakim slid the latch open before Aisha could interrogate him. Somewhere above ground, Aisha heard the soft chime of a bell as a ladder dropped down. The mapmaker was up and gone before she could ask about the bell, and Aisha had no choice but to follow him into what appeared to be a storage room filled with casks of wine. A sharp cough drew their attention to the doorway, where a middle-aged woman with amber eyes and long black hair tied into a knot stood. Her face was a stern, assessing mask.

Hakim's contact, Aisha assumed.

"Mapmaker," the stranger said coolly. "I didn't expect you back here so soon. Good to see the quake didn't bury you." Her eyes pinned Aisha next. "And who are you?"

"Hakim's traveling companion," Aisha responded tartly.

The stranger studied her cautiously. "I've seen your face before. On the wanted posters. You're one of bin Malik's thieves."

"A thief no more," Hakim said. "Otherwise, she would have killed me." He still looked unsettled, his fingers curled over his ring, gaze cast away from Aisha as if to avoid her eyes.

Aisha peered at the woman suspiciously. "And who are *you*?"

The stranger crossed her bulky arms. "Dahlia bint Adnan. Tavernkeeper and overseer of the Night Market." Her eyes sparkled with a dare. "If you are with Hakim, I trust you enough to let you stay. For a price, that is." She held out an expectant hand.

With a groan, Aisha dug into her satchel and slapped a coin onto the tavernkeeper's palm. Dahlia tucked it away with a smirk. "Welcome back to Madinne, Aisha bint Louas."

26

LOULIE

For the three remaining days of their journey, Mazen did not wake. At least, not fully. There had been one time, when Loulie visited him in the ship's cabin, when his eyes had been open but unseeing. He had been muttering under his breath in that half-lucid state, whispering a string of words Loulie interpreted as a prayer. Shaking him had done nothing; the storyteller had been wholly trapped in his sleeping mind. Even when his eyes had fluttered close, fear etched permanent lines into his face.

Though Nabila had begrudgingly sealed the wound he'd sustained with her own blood—Loulie had been shocked to see she *could* bleed, incorporeal as she often was—the poison in Ziyad's dagger still coursed through his veins. Duha tried to reassure her, insisting he would be fine until they arrived at al-Malath, where she could find the resources to help him.

Loulie wondered if the captain and her first mate might argue about this. On the night Loulie had returned from Ziyad's sinking ship, Nabila had been furious. When she had seen the pearl around Loulie's neck—the magic she had gifted Duha—she had snapped it off with such vehemence it had made Loulie cower. Thinking back on it, none of Nabila's wrath had been directed at her first mate. Whatever the relationship between the ifrit and the marid, it seemed

Duha had not been lying when she told Loulie she could soften the edge of Nabila's anger.

The marid, for her part, seemed unbothered by the sinking of her brother's ship. When Loulie had tentatively asked about Ziyad, Duha had just smiled and said, "It takes more than that to kill a marid. Ziyad will be back; you will see."

She offered no further explanation, which did little to settle Loulie's already frayed nerves. It was impossible to erase the memory of Mazen throwing himself in front of her. If he died because of her... it would be like Ahmed all over again, and she would never forgive herself.

The guilt sat heavy and dark in her chest when al-Malath finally appeared on the horizon their fourth day at sea. Nabila materialized at the helm of the ship as they approached.

The vanishing isle was a marvel of architecture, a valley stretched between two identical cliffs. Trees and bushes dusted the golden crags, which cast gentle shadows against the beaches. The land itself floated idly upon a patch of water carved incongruously within the sinking sands.

Nabila glanced at Loulie over her shoulder and said, "Welcome to al-Malath."

"Why is it called that?" Loulie shaded her eyes as she squinted into the distance.

"Because while many isles have been lost to the Sandsea, this place remains. I have made it into a haven for those escaping the sinking lands," Nabila said.

"And how can you be sure it will not sink as well? Are you holding it up with magic?"

"Not my magic. The island has its own zaeem. It is by his generosity we can take refuge here."

On Nabila's command, they prepared the dhow for docking. Swaying on the deck with a rope clutched in her hands, Loulie could have been on a ship in the human world arriving at some remarkable new city. But then, if this had been a voyage on the surface, she would not have been alone. Qadir would have been there with her, never mind his aversion to water.

Duha came to stand beside her as they moored at a pier with shoddy pillars and pilings. "It is beautiful, no?"

Loulie looked past the docks to the towering cliffs and sparkling beaches. It *was* beautiful, but it was difficult to appreciate the view under the circumstances. Duha must have noticed the heaviness of her nod. She set a reassuring hand on Loulie's shoulder. "Leave your companion to me. Ziyad's knives are made from marid scale; I know how to dilute that venom."

There was little Loulie could do but trust her. When they docked, Duha called on a volunteer to help her deliver Mazen to Nabila's abode. Loulie followed them off the ship, down a rickety gangplank, and onto the beach.

It was not long before the terrain changed beneath their feet, sand giving way to rich soil as they came into a village dotted with ashfire-lit torches. Loulie let her gaze wander as Duha led them down a path that cut between weather-beaten homes crafted from straw and reed. The single-story buildings were small, squat, and packed past capacity.

Perhaps that was why most of the jinn they passed were lounging outside, conversing on decks or beneath the shade of palm trees. When they saw Duha walk past, they greeted her with waves and smiles, seemingly unperturbed by the unconscious human she was carrying.

Loulie, they regarded with curiosity. "The human with the borrowed magic," they whispered behind her back. "The Ashfire King's human ward."

In Dhahab, those claims would have been uttered with disdain. Here, Loulie was surprised to see wonder in the islanders' eyes. Wonder and—

Hope.

Her stomach twisted. She was no king's ward. There was no mantle for her to don, no debts she owed to these jinn. Nabila may have dragged her here for some maniacal plan, but the ifrit could not *make* her break the bindings, not when the dagger's magic worked only for Loulie.

Her only goal was to return to the surface. To *her* life, and to her realm. After Mazen was safe, she would find a way to get them off this cursed island.

Still, the guilt festered. Loulie averted her eyes as Duha greeted the jinn on her behalf.

The next time the landscape transformed, it was littered with trees rather than houses. Loulie might have thought the forest beautiful—serene, even—if not for the uncomfortable number of *birds* alighted on the branches like sentinels. Some of the birds Loulie recognized—the little zarzours perched on stone walls, the pigeons cooing at one another across branches, the cranes flocked at the edge of a pond. She recognized the bulbuls chirping playfully at each other across the lip of a birdbath and saw a red knot soaring above her head.

But there were other birds too—creatures Loulie had never seen before, with shimmering wings and strange beaks. She saw birds with eyes that shone like gemstones, birds so well camouflaged they blended into trees and nests, and birds that sang in foreign languages.

She was so taken aback by the sight that she nearly missed Duha grinning over her shoulder. "I recognize the wonder in your eyes. The splendor of Nabila's Garden often has that effect on visitors."

Threatening atmosphere seemed a more appropriate explanation, but Loulie kept the thought to herself. "If this place belongs to Nabila, does that mean all these birds are spies?"

Duha laughed. "Of course not. Some of them are residents. Nabila has always kept birds as companions. They are easier to talk to, she says."

Loulie shuddered. This affinity was, she decided, yet another reason to distrust Nabila.

Eventually, they arrived at their destination: a large, walled-in compound at the crest of the hill. Beyond the gateway was a hawsh, a simple courtyard connecting two buildings. *The fortress*, Duha called it, a long-abandoned watch post that had been used during the war. The marid led Loulie to the much smaller second building: an austere single-story abode with only three rooms that had once belonged to the guards stationed at the fortress. It was here she deposited Mazen on a threadbare divan in what appeared to be the diwan.

While Duha went searching in the other room for supplies for her antidote, Loulie restlessly paced the diwan. Every time Mazen so much as stirred, her gaze snapped hopefully to his face, but he never opened his eyes. It was discomfiting to see his normally expressive face so slack.

She leaned forward to touch his forehead and grimaced when she felt the heat radiating off his skin. When she gently brushed a strand of hair off his brow, he shuddered, a motion so violent it shook his entire body. Even then, he did not wake.

Loulie swallowed. "Wake up. You can't just..."

Leave me behind. Like Ahmed had. Like Qadir had. How many times had she kept herself separate from others so that she could avoid this? This terror? This guilt?

The storyteller did not respond. Loulie had never felt more helpless than she did now, watching him struggle against himself. But none of the magics she had on hand would help him. Not Qadir's dagger, which remained ever silent, and not the compass. Even so, she found herself reaching for the relic out of habit, her hand dipping into her pocket to find—

Nothing.

Loulie froze, confusion muddying her mind as she searched her other pockets. But though the dagger was accounted for, she could not find the compass.

"Looking for something, human?"

Nabila stood in the doorway, her arms crossed. Loulie sprang to her feet. "Have you seen my compass?" Her voice cracked with her fear, but she did not care. If Nabila had managed to filch it from her, she would grovel to see it returned.

But the ifrit just shook her head. "Nothing is ever lost on my ship."

The claim, uttered so flippantly, only sharpened Loulie's desperation. She fell to her knees and threw off her robe to tear through the pockets again. But they were empty. All empty.

She refused to accept it. "You can't know that for certain. One of your sailors may have stolen it at sea, or they—"

"Nothing is ever lost on *my* ship." There was a cold certainty to the ifrit's words. It was only then, hearing her repeat them, that Loulie understood what she was saying.

Dread sank its claws into her heart. "You think I lost it on Ziyad's ship."

Nabila's expression remained dispassionate. "This is your own fault. I told you not to go back for the human."

"I went back because *you* wouldn't take me!" She stood, adrenaline scorching through her veins like fire. "You stole me from Dhahab in the first place. All of this is your fault."

Nabila glared at her. In the dimness of the diwan, she was little more than a phantom with glowing eyes. "Careful, al-Nazari. You do not want to pick this fight with me."

But Loulie *did*. Devoid of her magics, anger was all she had, and the emotion was rising inside her like an unruly tide, sweeping away reason. "Maybe if I had lost your pearl in the Sandsea, you would know what it meant to have something precious stolen from *you*." She knew the words were petty and petulant, but they burst from her lips before she could stop them.

Irritation slashed through Nabila's eyes. The building creaked as she stepped forward. The walls, the floor, even the air itself seemed to shudder as the ifrit paused before her. "You cannot begin to comprehend the depths of my loss." She took another step forward, driving Loulie back into a wall. "Before you humans came along, my tribe lived here peacefully. But because of your ancestors, they are *dead*, my home in ruins. You cannot fathom—"

"Nokhitha?"

Duha stood behind them, a glass in hand. When she saw Loulie crushed against a wall and Nabila looming over her, she sighed. "You are both far too alike for your own good."

Unbothered by the stormy atmosphere, Duha strode past them to kneel beside Mazen. Loulie was still shaking as Duha eased a tonic down his throat. The moment he shifted, Loulie was on her knees beside him, hand pressed again to his forehead. His skin was warm beneath her touch, but she could finally feel his breathing begin to settle.

"We will have to wait for the antidote to take full effect," Duha said. "But you may rest easy; his condition is stable."

All the adrenaline rushed from Loulie's body in one breath. Mind fuzzy with exhaustion, she turned to face Nabila, but the ifrit had vanished. "Where did she go?"

"To calm herself, most likely." Duha frowned. "It is unwise to antagonize your host."

Loulie laughed. It was a choked, bitter sound. It made her realize, much to her horror, that she had begun to cry. "You are not hosts. You are abductors. Criminals." She stood, vaguely aware of the tears collecting on her lashes. Even through her blurring sight, she could perceive Duha's expression. She expected anger or hurt, but the disappointment on her face was worse.

Loulie needed to get away. She needed to be alone.

Bereft of both her compass and any sense of direction, Loulie fled the fortress.

27

LOULIE

It did not take Loulie long to realize she was being followed.

Though no one stood in her way as she charged across the island, she did not miss the movement in the trees. Whoever—*whatever*—was chasing her did not seem to care for stealth. At the cusp of the forest, she turned to apprehend her tail, but nothing emerged.

And then she noticed the bird watching her from one of the branches.

In a forest filled with the creatures, it would have been easy to dismiss the myna, but she had spotted the menace enough times in Dhahab to recognize it. How foolish, to think she would be free of Nabila's spies when she arrived at her hideaway.

The minute she laid eyes on the bird, it snapped its beak and made an agitated squawking sound. Loulie's frustration was a burning match; it surged dangerously bright as she turned away. But the bird would not let her leave in peace. When it shrieked at her again, the sound was the final strike of flint against her anger.

She whirled, jutting a finger at it. "I am *not* going back to your despicable master. Now leave me be!"

The myna stood its ground, beady black eyes boring into her. It made a low, threatening sound in its throat that was unlike anything she had ever heard from a bird before.

"If you touch even a single hair on my head, I will roast you on a skewer," she spat.

The bird shot into the air, where it circled mockingly. Loulie stomped away with a growl. What did it matter if she was being followed? There had been eyes on her since she came to this realm. And now the compass, the one magic *she* had looked to for guidance, was gone.

The revelation slammed into her again, unbalancing her. There was no escaping the reality: she had lost her—and Qadir's—most precious heirloom because of her own carelessness. It had slipped from her pocket like a misplaced *trinket*.

Frustration warred with grief as she retraced her steps past the village to the shoreline. Loulie's feet automatically took her to the water, a comforting familiarity in this bizarre world. She focused on the rise and fall of the waves, timing her breaths with the water to steady the harried beating of her heart. It worked; the tide was gentler than the wave of emotion roaring through her and helped calm her as she walked the shoreline.

This late at night, the beaches were mostly deserted. The few jinn Loulie passed were fishermen checking traps in the water, and though they looked puzzled by her presence, they thankfully did not engage her in conversation, choosing instead to observe her from afar.

On a whim, she kicked off her shoes so that she could wade directly into the surf. She welcomed the shock of the waves against her ankles, the crunch of the wet sand beneath her feet. For a moment, walking through the water, she could believe she was back on the surface. But she could dam the flood of loss inside of her for only so long.

The compass is gone. The realization pounded through her mind. *Gone. Gone.*

She remembered when her father had first given her the relic. Remembered sitting knee-to-knee with him by a campfire and gasping in delight as he handed her a flat disc made of wood and glass. *It does not work for me*, he had said. *But perhaps it will guide your way.*

She remembered Qadir, crouching before her in the ashes of the burned Najima campsite. He had gestured at the compass—at the red arrow pointing at her—and said, *Layla Najima al-Nazari, it seems saving your life was my destiny.*

The compass had guided her to safety and fortune. To magic and coin. It was not just some magical trinket, but a *relic* containing the soul of one of Qadir's most precious friends. And she had lost it in the damned Sandsea.

Gone. Gone. Gone.

In that moment, Loulie was grateful for the roar of the ocean against the shore. No one—not even she—had to suffer the sounds of her heartbreak as she began to cry.

—⁓—

"You are certain about this?" Qadir stood between her and the ravine, disapproval clear in the downturn of his lips.

Layla grinned at him. "I've never been more certain of anything in my life."

At present, "this" was walking on a thin, rocky pathway across an abyss to get to the relic on the other side. When Qadir didn't budge, Layla showed him the compass. She pointed at the arrow directing them across the ravine and said, "You told me it was never wrong."

"You know that is not what I am asking." He looked pointedly at the perilous path.

Layla shook her head. Dahlia bint Adnan had given her thirty days to prove she could be more than a messenger by finding a magic she could sell. It had taken her and Qadir ten days to piece together rumors of the nearest magic. Seven to find it. And now that she was here, she would prove to Dahlia that she could claim that magic herself.

"Where's your sense of adventure?" Layla handed him the compass for safekeeping.

The jinn frowned at her. "My job is to keep you safe. I can easily cross the ravine path myself." When she shot him a skeptical look, he added, "In my lizard shape."

Layla was insulted. "I have two perfectly good legs."

"And you have one *life."*

Layla waved him away. What would she prove to anyone if all she had done on this journey was follow a compass? There was no point if she didn't collect the magic herself.

Thankfully, Qadir did not question her again. Instead, he shifted into his lizard shape and scrambled up her arm to settle mulishly by her ear. "Fine. Then we will do this together."

Layla hid a smirk beneath her scarves. And he called her *stubborn.*

Together, the two of them crossed over the ravine. The path was, much to Qadir's dismay, just as perilous as anticipated. And yet the fear that burned through Layla's veins was exhilarating. For the first time since her tribe's passing, she felt capable. She felt alive.

She was laughing when she arrived at the other side, where their target—an unremarkably plain and dusty vase—stood on a rocky platform. The vase was filled with water. Layla quickly discovered its magic when, after she tipped a small amount onto the ground, the jar immediately refilled. A replenishing magic such as this would be priceless in the desert.

She was grinning as she pulled the compass from her pocket. Qadir was right—this small, seemingly unspectacular tool could lead someone to their destiny.

"People will pay a fortune for this magic," she said. "They will pay me *a fortune."*

"I told you the compass was useful."

Layla cupped the relic protectively in her hands. "More than useful. Priceless."

When her father had first given it to her in the desert, he had said he hoped it would guide her way. She wished she could tell him that it had led her to fortune. That it would.

"Qadir." She smiled. "I have an idea."

—◊—

Loulie did not know how long she wandered the beach with only her memories for company, just that it was long enough for her mind to grow fuzzy with exhaustion. Some part of her knew she ought to return to the fortress, but the more stubborn part would have rather collapsed here in the sand than face Nabila again.

Loulie let her eyelids drift closed. The cadence of the waves was hypnotic; she considered how nice it would be to lie there on the beach and fall asleep. It seemed to her that it was not just the water that encouraged it, but the wind and the sand as well. The breeze was gentle and caressing. And the sand was warm and ... breathing?

She blinked her eyes open to stare at the ground. It was the slightest of sensations, one she had at first mistaken as the ebb and flow of the waves, but the ground beneath her *was* shifting. She was pondering the phenomenon when she noticed a figure in the surf. She turned, expecting Nabila, but was met with the sight of the marid instead.

"Al-Nazari." Duha wore her usual smile as she approached Loulie in the water, wading deep enough for the surface to ripple around her thighs.

Loulie backed away to the shoreline. "Did Nabila order you to bring me back?"

"No, she has gone to gather intel from her birds. But I must report to the zaeem even in her absence." She tilted her head. "Since you were so eager to leave the fortress, I thought you might like to accompany me."

Loulie hesitated. She still felt the remnants of anger and despair coiled deep in her chest, but grief had smoothed the edges into a dull resignation. Besides that, Duha had acted as her accomplice on the ship—it was not *her* fault the compass was lost.

The marid looked pleased when Loulie nodded, and purposefully slowed her steps so that Loulie could keep pace with her on the shoreline. Loulie was grateful Duha did not attempt to lift her spirits; perhaps she realized it would be a fruitless endeavor.

She turned the conversation to the zaeem Duha had mentioned. "You said before that his magic keeps the island afloat. Is that the shifting I'm feeling beneath my feet?" She eyed the sand again. Now that she had noticed it, she could not stop feeling the sensation.

"Indeed. This land breathes with his will."

"I have no idea what that means."

The marid just winked at her. "You will after you meet him."

As they walked, the beach changed. The seashells vanished, replaced with jagged rocks that curved up like jaws beneath the water. The obstacles would have slowed a human, but Duha traveled as easily in water as Loulie did on land. When Loulie darted a glance at her, she could not help but notice the patchwork of scales on Duha's legs. The scales themselves were not noteworthy; the strange, murky glow they had taken on beneath the waves was.

Duha noticed her looking and smiled. "Ask your question, al-Nazari."

"Your scales—they're different?"

"Under water, everything is different." Her grin widened, revealing the long, curved fangs at the bottom of her mouth.

"How so? What do you look like beneath the water?"

The way Duha's eyes sparkled, she looked almost pleased by the question. And then she cheerfully said, "I am what you humans would call a monster. You remember on the ship when I said I could crush your bones if I wrapped my arms around you?"

Loulie bristled at the reminder. "You will not let me forget it."

"In my true form, I *would* crush your bones. All I would need to do is get you between my teeth, and I could tear your body limb from limb." She clenched her jaw as if to demonstrate, her teeth clicking together to form a perfect grimace.

The nonchalant discussion of violence made Loulie queasy. She was glad when they arrived at their destination and Duha dropped the conversation. They had stopped at a low, rocky outcrop that stretched into the ocean. At Duha's insistence, Loulie climbed the rock. When Loulie finally made it to the marid's side at the top, Duha pointed back at the island. As far as Loulie could tell, she was gesturing to a shoreline farther out, one that stretched back into a cove.

Loulie frowned. "What are we looking at? Is your master some cave-dwelling hermit?"

Duha looked like she was trying not to laugh. "*Cave* is not quite right. Look closer."

Loulie squinted past the greenery into the slim darkness, narrowing her eyes until she could make out…*something*. She did not know how to describe it other than that it looked like holes floating incongruously in the darkness. Black, shiny, blinking—

"Are those *eyes*?" Loulie's voice cracked on the word. She could not grasp how enormous a creature would need to be to possess such large eyes.

Duha grinned. "You still don't see it?" She pointed again, this time at the rocky overhang fringing the cove. Loulie's gaze swept over the curve of it. She had not noticed it when she was walking, but now she saw the island did have a strange curve to it. Almost like…

A shell.

She became only more certain when she marked the rest of the island's geography. The strangely identical cliffs on either side, the cave with the eyes, the *breathing* beneath her feet…

"This is the zaeem of the island," Duha said matter-of-factly.

Loulie whirled on her. "The master of al-Malath is a giant *crab*?"

It did not matter that the evidence was right before her eyes; Loulie could not believe it. Still, now that she had seen the island in its entirety, there was no mistaking its unusual shape. And those eyes in the darkness—those were the eyes not of some hidden creature, but of the island itself. The crab—the *zaeem*—was the very foundation of al-Malath.

"The reason people can't find you is because your island is on the back of a massive *crab* that can travel through the Sandsea?"

Duha clicked her tongue. "It is respectful to call him the zaeem of al-Malath."

Loulie took in the island with renewed awe. It was no wonder the queen had been unable to capture Nabila. Who would have ever thought she was riding on the back of a gigantic crustacean? Loulie was literally looking the creature in its eyes and could not comprehend it.

"How is this possible?" Her voice was faint.

Duha shrugged. "The zaeem and I made a deal. When Nabila's home was sinking, I begged him to carry it upon his back so that it would stay afloat in the Sandsea."

"What kind of deal could you make with a..." She gestured emphatically at the island.

"I offered to be his eyes and ears. The zaeem may be mighty, but we marid have always had a knack for gathering intel across the waters. In exchange for safety, I give him reports."

Loulie hesitated. "And he doesn't care that he's sheltering two humans right now?"

Some part of her hoped that the crab would have reason to reject their presence. If Nabila was here by his mercy, then perhaps it would be his mercy that set her and Mazen free.

But Duha just shrugged. "Why would he? What kind of sanctuary would this place be if he turned away humans?"

Loulie thought of all the jinn packed into the homes on the beach. There had been no wariness when they regarded her, only curiosity. Perhaps they had thought her a refugee as well.

She swallowed. "You call this place a sanctuary, but *I* didn't come here of my own will."

"You think any of the refugees here left their homes because they wanted to? The queen claims she does not have space to shelter them in Dhahab, so Nabila brings them here."

Loulie opened her mouth to object. Their situations were not the same. These jinn had been saved when their islands were sinking. She had been *kidnapped*. But the words stuck in her throat as she glanced back at the cluttered shadows of the houses.

Collateral damage, she thought, and was reminded of her own tribe. Her family, who had died simply because they were in the wrong place at the wrong time. They had not deserved that fate, and neither did these jinn.

The weight of that realization pressed the air from her lungs. She knew she was being manipulated. Even so, she could not bring herself to argue. How selfish would she be, to compare her grievances to a refugee's plight?

She wished she could ask Qadir, *Did you know this would hap-pen? Is this the mistake you ran from?* And then she would ask him, *Are you running from* me *too?*

The marid clapped her hands, pulling Loulie from her thoughts and proclaiming that she had delivered her report to the zaeem. When she saw Loulie's confusion, she tapped her temple and explained that the crab spoke mind-to-mind rather than in words.

Duha turned back to the island. "If you have cleared your head, I suggest we return. We do not want to leave your companion for long. Where strangers are concerned, the birds are sometimes too curious for their own good."

The myna circling above their heads gave an affirmative chirp. Loulie did not have the energy to be angry. Not at the bird or at Nabila. Though the walk had cleared her mind, it had done little to dissipate the storm clouds in her heart.

Her fingers tightened on the dagger. *What do I do, Qadir? What would* you *do?*

But Qadir, as always, was silent.

28

MAZEN

Mazen was drowning.

It was a terrifying thing, to drown in your own mind. Normally, dreams were like mirages; once you had determined their nature, you could see past them. And yet Mazen could not escape his nightmares. He *knew* they were figments of his sleeping mind, but try as he did to wake, slumber held him prisoner.

In one of his dreams, Omar locked him in the Bowels. In another, Mazen searched futilely for Hakim and Aisha in a fire. But the worst dream was the one that put him back on Ziyad's ship. In that vision, he was too slow to save Loulie. He witnessed the moment the marid's knife cut into her throat and the life left her eyes. That nightmare, more than the others, seemed a plausible reality.

Please, he said to no one. *Please let me wake.*

He whispered those words as his world burned and blurred and shattered until finally—

Mazen resurfaced from his visions with a pained gasp. His senses returned to him in fragments: the sound of a crackling fire, the scent of salt and brine, the stifling warmth of blankets thrown over him. His vision was the last thing to settle, and when it did, the world that appeared before his eyes was completely foreign to him.

Not Ziyad's ship. His body relaxed by degrees, his breaths evening out when he realized the floor beneath him was not that of a moving boat. *It was a nightmare. Just a nightmare.*

The room he had woken in was sparsely furnished, and the only light came from ashfire burning in a small hearth. When he strained his ears, he thought he could hear... the ocean? Where *was* he, and where had Loulie gone? The last time they had spoken, she'd told him Nabila had kidnapped her for a "favor." Did that mean they were at her hideaway, the vanishing isle?

Though he was alone in the room, surely there had to be someone in the building he could ask. He was just about to investigate when he paused, his attention caught by a flicker of motion in the hearth. At first, he dismissed it as the erratic movement of the ashfire.

But then he realized the fire was staring at him.

Mazen drew back with a gasp. As he watched, it shifted into a defined shape with a beak, a tail, talons, and wings made of burning feathers. By the time the flame had settled into its new contours, Mazen recognized it as the firebird that had appeared in the queen's diwan.

He tensed, searching the room for a weapon, but there was nothing here that would protect him. It was just him and the bird, staring at one another.

In Dhahab, the bird's appearance had been a herald of doom. The wazir had claimed it was one of Nabila's spies and that Mazen must be working with her. He had not known what to make of it then and was at a loss now. Bizarrely, the creature seemed smaller than it had in the diwan, its size more reminiscent of a canary than a bird of prey.

Mazen eyed it nervously. "What are you?"

The bird cocked its head at him, a curious but otherwise unthreatening motion. Mazen watched it, uncertain. It seemed harmless enough, perched quietly on the hearth. And if the bird *was* Nabila's spy... then it had no reason to harm him, right?

When he crawled closer to it, the bird fluffed its fiery wings but did not flee. "I don't suppose you can speak?" he asked it.

The creature looked at him, deadpan.

He held back a sigh. "I thought not."

Convinced his life was not in immediate danger, Mazen turned his attention to his injuries. Whoever had taken care of him had dressed him in a new tunic, but he could feel bandages underneath, obscuring the wound. A wound that, when he gently prodded at it, was still tender. But the injury was undoubtedly scabbed over. Had he been healed with jinn blood?

He glanced at a pile of clothing folded nearby. Mazen recognized the vest he had been wearing in Dhahab. With bated breath, he reached into the pocket where he had hidden the crescent earring. His heart stuttered with relief when his fingers closed over the relic. The magic was as unresponsive as always, but the important thing was that it was still in their hands.

Was it Aliyah's plan to hide herself away in the hope that Omar would eventually steal her relic back? Mazen supposed it didn't matter so long as the magic remained inert.

The bird made a soft trilling sound as he tucked the earring away, drawing him from his thoughts. It had hopped closer, its head tilted in silent question. Mazen smiled despite himself. "You must have an owner. Is it Nabila?"

When the bird merely clicked its beak in response, Mazen hesitantly reached toward it. This time, it did not move. Mazen's heart beat in his throat. If the ashfire had been created by Qadir, then perhaps the magic would not harm him? Perhaps—

"*Mazen?*"

Mazen turned so quickly he pulled at his wound. He flinched, blinking through the sudden pain until he could make out the familiar figure in the doorway. Relief surged through him at the sight of Loulie al-Nazari. The moment she saw him, her eyes widened, her lips parted, and Mazen experienced the rare phenomenon of seeing unguarded shock on her face.

"You're okay," he said hoarsely.

"You're *alive*."

He was taken aback by the emotion in her voice. And then she was rushing toward him, her gaze sweeping over him in search of injuries. Before Mazen could think of how best to reassure her, she had crouched down beside him and pressed her palm to his cheek. The warm touch of her fingers sent a jolt of shock through him.

If Loulie noticed, she said nothing, just turned his head to examine the other side of his face. "The bruising is gone," she muttered. She was close enough he could count the lashes ringing her eyes. Close enough he could feel her breath on his cheeks.

Mazen's own breath was suddenly trapped in his lungs. Loulie always kept herself carefully apart, separate. That she had breached the space between them herself was a surprise.

In the end, it was a stranger who interrupted them. "Ah, the storyteller wakes at last!"

Loulie drew away so quickly it was as if she'd been burned. Even her cheeks were flushed with heat as she glared at the newcomer. "How long have you been there?"

The smile on the stranger's face was sharp as a sickle. "The whole time."

Mazen got a better look at her as she stepped inside. She had the look of a sailor, her skin sun bronzed, her sheared scalp half-hidden beneath a tattered scarf. He focused until he could make out her face—the shining black eyes devoid of any whites, the faint brown brows, the sharp cheekbones. He realized there were patches of glittering scales on her body.

A marid?

"Masa'a al-khair," the stranger said, and the warmth of her voice was so unexpected it made Mazen gape. She laughed at his shock. "Sit any closer to that fire and it will burn you."

It was only then Mazen remembered the firebird. But when he threw a glance over his shoulder, the bird had vanished. The ashfire burned steadily in the hearth, seemingly unperturbed. Based on Loulie's own nonreaction, it must have disappeared before she entered.

The stranger addressed him: "Yousef, was it?"

He nodded, hesitant. "And who are you?"

She gasped. "He speaks!" The sound of her laughter was genuine enough to relax his nerves. "My name is Duha. I am Nabila's first mate."

Mazen processed this information slowly. He had expected to wake to shackles and interrogations. But the first mate, Duha, made no move to restrain him. She remained leaning against the entryway, one ankle crossed over the other. It was a relaxed pose.

Mazen tried another question. "Where am I?"

It was Loulie who responded resignedly: "On the back of a gigantic crab."

She delivered this information unflinchingly, with the jaded exasperation of someone who was accustomed to dealing with magical surprises. Of all the revelations Mazen had confronted since waking, this was the only one that stunned him into complete silence.

Duha looked amused by his reaction. "I will allow your companion to enlighten you," she said with a grin. "Nabila is sending a message; I will let her know you have woken."

After flashing one last mischievous smile, she left them alone. Or, well, nearly alone. Mazen had just now noticed the myna bird watching them from the windowsill. He wondered if it was the same bird from Dhahab and if it had been following Loulie.

The moment the door closed, Loulie faced him. "We won't have full privacy with that damned bird watching us, but I can give you the facts."

And so, perfunctorily, she did just that over the next half hour, filling him in on what had transpired since the kidnapping. She told him about Nabila's goal, about the rescue on the ship, and about coming to al-Malath—a shelter for refugees she claimed was floating on the back of a massive crab. Mind-bending as that truth was, Mazen did not doubt it for a second.

Afterward, when Loulie asked him what had happened in her absence, he told her about the queen's diwan, the firebird, and the docks. Loulie listened quietly, her expression growing stormy when he recalled the zaeem of Kharjem's murder, as well as the "deal" that had sealed it.

"So in the end, even *his* blood is on Nabila's hands," Loulie muttered. "I don't trust her. She may act a hero, but she's full of hatred. Toward humans, and..." She swallowed. "And Qadir. She didn't bat an eyelash when I told her his compass was lost."

She seemed to sink into herself with the confession, her fingers curling into fists on her lap. Instinctively, Mazen set his hands atop them. "I'm sorry about the compass. Truly."

Foggy-minded as he was, it occurred to him only belatedly that he had touched her without thinking. He expected her to withdraw. Instead, he was surprised to feel her hands loosen. Some of the tension eased from her shoulders as she whispered, "I am too."

For a few moments, the two of them sat in amiable silence, processing the information they had exchanged. It was Loulie who broke the quiet first. Loulie who caught his eye and said, "You shouldn't have thrown yourself in front of a blade for me."

He met her gaze unflinchingly. "You were in danger."

"You were passed out for *days*. When you didn't wake, I feared..." She trailed off, then shook her head, decisive. "It doesn't matter. Don't ever do that again."

When he opened his mouth to argue, she gripped his hands tightly, fingers laced around his palms in a vise. "Promise me," she said. "We both need to make it out of here alive."

Mazen's thoughts scattered at the warm press of her fingers, at the quiet intensity of her gaze. She did not relent until he nodded, and then she pulled her hands away and rose, suddenly looking restless. "You must be hungry. I'll bring you back some food."

She had nearly made it to the door when Mazen called out to her. "Wait." With an effort, he managed to stumble to his feet. "I'll come with you."

He straightened at her wary look, trying to channel some of Rijah's cockiness into his slouch in the hope that it looked casual rather than exhausted.

Loulie looked unimpressed. "Your legs are shaking."

He steadied himself against the nearest wall. "I just haven't used them in a while." When she frowned at him, clearly unconvinced, he was insistent. "I want to see the island with my own eyes. And..." He managed a faint smile. "You know how restless I get behind locked doors."

Her expression softened somewhat at that, the last of her resistance crumbling with her sigh. "Fine." She pulled open the door, pausing only to glower at the myna as it shot out ahead of them. "Try to keep up, Mazen."

—⟶—

Mazen's first impression of al-Malath was that it was filled with more birds than jinn. Yet for as impressed as he was, he could not stop himself from searching for one particular bird.

It must have been obvious to Loulie which he was looking for. "You should ask Nabila about the firebird," she said. "I haven't seen it myself, but it has to be on the island somewhere."

Mazen tucked the resolution away as they came into the village. The moment he beheld the cluster of huts, he reflected that the settlement was crowded in a different way from Dhahab, the buildings pinched into rows rather than stacked high in tiers.

Most of the inhabitants were outside, lounging beneath trees and reclining on cushions in shaded pavilions. Mazen was struck by the serenity of the scene. He'd expected a heated reception after Dhahab, but the islanders only watched him inquisitively.

They walked until they arrived at a large pavilion where food was being distributed. After a brief exchange with the jinn passing out the portions, Loulie secured two bowls of a fish soup for them. At Mazen's insistence, they ate their meal in the pavilion.

Mazen was curious about the islanders, but even more than that, he was curious about Loulie's relationship with them. Over the course of the hour, she was approached by many jinn. The food distributor, a fisherman's son by the name of Hatem, came to tease Loulie for her lack of fish-related knowledge. A child named Yazid shoved a shoddily made oud into her hands and laughed when her playing elicited a string of painful twangs. A tired mother with seven children deposited her youngest with them, apologizing as she explained that he refused to return home until he saw the fabled humans for himself.

Loulie was gulping down the last of her soup when she finally noticed Mazen smiling at her. "What? Do I have something on my face?"

"You look like you're enjoying yourself."

Her cheeks flushed. "The soup is surprisingly edible today."

"You were enjoying the *company*."

Loulie set her bowl down with a sigh. "Yes, well, if I'm forced to be on this godsforsaken island, then the least I can do is gather intel about its inhabitants while I look for a way off."

Mazen would have continued teasing her if they had not been interrupted by another visitor. The jinn introduced herself as Zabiba. She wore rings of leaves around her wrists and neck, and atop her head like a crown. She regarded Mazen with the unabashed wonder of a child.

"Do you possess ifrit magic like Loula?" she asked.

The merchant's eye twitched. "*Loulie*," she corrected. "And Yousef is a storyteller. He does not need magic when he can hold an audience captive with his words."

Mazen blinked in surprise. Though Duha had called him by his alias, he had wondered if Loulie meant to stop using them when he'd heard the jinn call her by her name. But perhaps she had realized "Yousef" was more than just a disguise to him; it was an escape. A refuge.

He flashed a grateful smile at her before obliging Zabiba's request for a performance. He was in a good mood, after all, and the tale of the firebird was already on his mind. This time, when he told the story, his mind lingered on the details of the bird as he had witnessed them. He described in detail its majestic shape, its magnificent feathers . . .

He was so invested in the telling that he did not at first notice the fire in the center of the pavilion wavering—not until Loulie grabbed his arm, yanking him away just in time to avoid the ashfire as it surged into a shape that was at once fearsome and familiar.

Mazen blinked, stunned, at the firebird.

Now, as in Nabila's abode, the bird manifested in a smaller, canary-like shape. But it was no less magnificent, its fiery form blazing the brilliant white blue of ashfire.

Panic unfurled in the pavilion at the bird's appearance. Zabiba, who had been seated in front of Mazen, crawled away with a whimper. Many of the jinn fled the pavilion, while others warily circled from the outskirts. Loulie had already leapt to her feet, dagger in hand.

Mazen reached out in panic. "Wait, Loulie, I think it's safe—"

A powerful gust swept through the area, strong enough to make the firebird flicker. Mazen turned to see a woman standing at the pavilion entrance. Or at least, she looked like a woman, if a woman could be crafted from wind. Mazen was immediately struck by the brightness of her eyes, which flashed like mirrors as she stepped forward.

Nabila? The ifrit matched Loulie's nebulous description.

The pirate ignored them both, her eyes trained on the bird. "Come down from there, little one." Her voice was gentle, coaxing. "This is a safe place. I promise."

She began to hum as she approached. It was a strangely familiar song; Mazen remembered Loulie singing it on the balcony in Dhahab. He could tell from her expression that she recognized it too. Her suspicious gaze remained pinned on Nabila as the firebird slowly drifted toward them—toward *him*.

Mazen yelped as the bird swooped down to nestle in his hair. He swatted frantically at the creature, but it refused to budge, squawking with agitation every time he tried to knock it off.

It occurred to him only belatedly that its fire did not burn him.

Nabila's song died on her lips as she scowled at him. "How did *you* summon that bird, human?" Her words were clipped—with jealousy?

Mazen shook his head. Though the fire did not burn him, it still warmed his skin, and he felt sweat rolling down his neck and into the collar of his shirt as he mumbled, "I don't know."

Two times he had told this story, and two times the bird had appeared. Was it possible the story was a means of summoning it? He did not know enough about the magic to speculate.

Now that the immediate danger had passed, the islanders had begun to drift warily back into the pavilion. Still, they kept their distance, watching him and the bird from afar.

But then: applause.

Mazen looked up in surprise as Duha entered. The marid was clapping, a bright smile on her face. "Aywa! This must be what they call a storyteller's grand introduction!"

Her enthusiasm was contagious, and it was not long before the bystanders joined in on the ovation. Mazen stood frozen, uncertain of whether it was appropriate to bow. He glanced helplessly at Loulie, but she looked just as flustered, her attention flitting uncertainly between the bird and the ifrit approaching them.

Nabila paused before them as the crowd dispersed. "When Duha told me you had just woken, the last thing I expected was to see you putting on a show."

"I—I assure you it was entirely unplanned, sayyidati." Mazen tried futilely to peer at the bird, but it was impossible with the creature on his head. "I still am not sure how this happened."

"Is it not obvious, storyteller?" Duha still wore her mischievous smile as she came to stand beside her captain. With her fingers laced behind her head, she looked completely at ease. "You shaped the ashfire with your words. Your will. It is drawn to you."

Nabila bristled at the suggestion. "With what magic? The ashfire is not his to command."

"Ya nokhitha, you know just as well as I that magic can take many shapes. Al-Nazari commands the fire in her blade; is it so strange Yousef can shape it with his words?"

The idea seemed absurd to Mazen. Certainly, stories could move hearts and influence minds, but how could they possibly craft a bird out of *fire*? Hesitantly, he reached a hand toward the creature.

This time, when it pecked at his fingers, it was more of a probing, quizzical motion. Mazen managed a wavering smile. Though it was difficult for him to wrap his mind around Duha's explanation, he supposed he was flattered the fire had reacted to him at all.

"I have a question for you," Loulie said. She was frowning suspiciously at Nabila. "Just now, you tried to captivate the bird with a song. I recognize that melody because Qadir always sings it, but how do *you* know it?"

"I know it because it is my song."

Whatever answer Loulie had been expecting, it was clearly not the one Nabila offered. Her eyes widened. "What do you mean *your* song?"

When Nabila merely raised an unimpressed brow, Duha seated herself by the still-crackling fire with a sigh. She glanced at her captain and reached for a discarded food bowl. "You have yet to eat, nokhitha. Why not take the time to reminisce before you share the news from the Sandsea? Perhaps you can win the bird over with your own story."

It was difficult to read the ifrit's transparent expression, but Mazen thought he saw her features soften at Duha's suggestion. She relented, seating herself beside Duha with a glower. "Fine. I will share with you the inspiration behind the song."

"She will share it as a *story*," Duha said. "Nabila used to be the most renowned performer in this country. She could enchant whole crowds with naught but a song. She could hypnotize them with a single dance. And her stories, they were—"

"Duha," Nabila warned, but Mazen did not miss the faint quirk of her lips.

Slowly, so as not to disturb the bird on his head, Mazen settled himself on the ground beside Loulie. The merchant shot the creature a quizzical glance but said nothing. She had been uncharacteristically quiet since Duha brought up the idea of the story.

Nabila turned her attention to the brazier. With an easy wave of her hand, she sculpted the flame into a shape with her wind—a single two-legged figure. "Listen well, humans, for this story, unlike your human fictions, is truth. It is the tale of a king who traveled the desert in search of his destiny, and who found his beloved on that path.

"This"—her voice rose with the wind—"is the tale of his never-ending journey."

The Tale of the Never-Ending Journey

Neither here nor there, but long ago...

There lived a jinn wanderer who traveled alone, with nothing but his magic and a simple knife to aid him. Unlike other jinn, who journeyed in search of lands to conquer, this nameless nomad wandered the desert without purpose. Such was the nature of his travels until, one day, he chanced upon a message written in the sand beneath a talha tree.

The message said, *You who wander the desert without succor, find me and know your destiny.*

Beneath the words was an arrow, pointing him toward the cliffs. The traveler was mystified by this turn of events. He muttered aloud to himself, "Who is this stranger that would claim to know my ambitions? Is their message a sign or a trap?"

Knowing there were no answers to be found in the desert, the traveler decided to heed the mysterious directions. He followed the arrow north to a palisade of cliffs, where he began to climb, searching all the while for the mysterious messenger.

But though he passed all manner of creatures during his ascent, none showed any interest in him.

Day shifted to night as the traveler climbed, and by the time he had reached the top of the cliff, the sky was scattered with stars. Before him lay a gigantic nest and inside it were three eggs, each five times the size of his body. The traveler immediately recognized their unique color.

"This is a rukh's nest!" he proclaimed. "What destiny could possibly await me here?"

No sooner had he spoken the question aloud than the traveler saw a pattern of cracks in the eggs. He was shocked to see the fissures formed a set of instructions: *You who wander the desert in search of your destiny, you may find me by way of starlight.*

The traveler was puzzling out this clue when he heard a loud screech in the distance and turned to see a rukh approaching. He quickly dove into the nest, lying so still in the bramble the rukh did not notice him when she burrowed amongst her eggs.

There the traveler remained for the night, barely breathing for fear the massive bird would sense him. Because he could not sleep, he pondered the stranger's clue, turning the directions over in his mind until an answer came to him. Had he been able to gaze upon the night sky, he would have seen a cluster of stars: Qalb al-Asad, a constellation he used often to guide himself through the desert. He decided he would follow those stars and see where they led.

And so on the morrow, when the rukh took flight, the traveler departed. He kept his eyes trained on the sky as he descended the cliffs, and when the stars once more glimmered above his head, he followed the constellation to a nearby oasis. But like the cliffs, the oasis was empty.

Exhausted and travel weary, the jinn collapsed at the water's edge. He addressed his reflection: "What twisted game is this! Do these trials serve some greater purpose, or is it my destiny to chase a phantom through the desert?"

His reflection, of course, had no answer for him. The traveler sighed at the silence, and then he knelt by the water and studied the constellation on its surface. After scrutinizing the reflection for a long time, he realized one of the stars did not belong. The glow he had mistaken for a star at the center of the lion's chest was no star at all, but a glowing clam.

Carefully, he plucked the clam from the water and pried it open with his knife. Much to his amazement, another clue had been inscribed upon the inside of the shell: *You who wander the desert in pursuit of your fate, you shall find me in the shade.*

Seeing this third instruction, the traveler was filled with despair. But for as much as he feared that he would never reach the end of his journey, he knew he had come too far to turn back now. And so the next day, his search continued.

Every time the traveler arrived at a new destination, he unearthed another clue. This went on for many years, and the clues the stranger left became more and more difficult to decipher. Soon, it was not just puzzles in the terrain the traveler was tasked to solve, but riddles of the mind and heart. The clues led him through battlefields and ancient ruins, encouraging him to end conflicts, protect the weak, and outwit conniving beasts.

When the traveler realized his journey had transformed him from a nameless wanderer into a hero, he was aggrieved. "How cruel are the fates to put this responsibility on me!" he cried. "Is it my destiny to serve some faceless master for the rest of time?"

As it was, the traveler did not have to ponder this long. Days after this outburst, the stranger stopped leaving their clues. The traveler recognized the silence for what it was: an ending. It was a devastating realization. For decades, he had found his purpose chasing the promise of his destiny, but now that his guide had vanished, he had nothing and no one.

Or so it would have been had he not met so many others on his travels. The jinn, whose life had once been lonely and aimless, now found himself at the center of a web of favors. Unexpectedly, the desert dwellers he had saved soon began to seek him out for advice, and he decided he would settle in a humble abode to advise them.

As news of his wisdom spread, the single visitations transformed into dense crowds. With so little space to accommodate his guests, the traveler called upon acquaintances he had met during his journeys to help him construct a shelter.

It is said that all great things have humble beginnings, and so it is with the city of Dhahab, which began as a sanctuary for the travel weary and transformed over the years into a prosperous city fashioned from gold and magic. Every year a new wall was built, a new building erected, a new courtyard plotted, until the settlement became a sprawling city.

The glittering city was the most remarkable metropolis ever constructed. And yet as the walls grew higher and the streets more crowded, the traveler recognized the place for what it had become: a prison. For while he had built the city to shelter those aimless wanderers like himself, he knew now that they looked to him for guidance.

Knowing he had just one last chance to escape this destiny, the traveler decided to steal away in the night, taking nothing with him but his knife. He made it as far as the city gate before a figure strode into his path. Small and fine-boned, the stranger at first appeared meek and unassuming with her doleful brown eyes. But then the traveler saw the sad smile on her face and knew that she had been expecting him.

"Salaam," she said. And then: "Finally, I have found you."

The traveler was overcome with great emotion then, for he realized the jinn standing before him could be none other than the stranger who had eluded him for decades. Who else could so well predict his actions?

"I have been looking for you a long time," he told her. "Please tell me: Why have you evaded me for so long?"

The stranger's smile vanished with her sigh. "Because I am a coward. I am an erafa, you see, able to foretell destinies ordained by the gods. For years, I knew our futures would align, and so I became determined to delay our meeting for as long as possible."

The traveler was dismayed. "Do you hate me so much you would run from me?"

And the erafa responded, her voice heavy with misery, "It is not the future that terrifies me, but the inevitability of its ending. But then I saw you leaving the city and knew I could turn away no longer. You have met your destiny time and again. Now I must meet mine."

She stepped forward and bowed, and the gesture was filled with such deference it made the traveler flinch back. The stranger said, "In the future, you will know me as Khalilah. Now I offer myself to you as your most humble advisor. When others look to you for counsel, I will stand beside you and provide aid. We will weather the burden of your crown together."

The traveler recoiled. "You are mistaken. I am a wanderer, not a king."

Khalilah lifted her head and smiled. It was an expression of such pity it made the air catch in his lungs. Khalilah, who had known this would happen, took his hands in hers. "You see? Few who know their destiny would willingly face it. But in this, we are together. You need no longer chase your fate. Now I will guide you to it."

And so Khalilah led him back to the city. She remained at his side when he was crowned, and she was there when he was given a name that would cement his destiny.

The Ashfire King, he was called, named for his fire, which never burned out.

The stories say that by accepting his crown, the king accepted his responsibility. But even after centuries passed, he still resented the shackles of his governance. Every day, he stepped onto his palace balcony and let his gaze fall on the distant horizon, where he yearned to escape.

Many would have said it was inevitable that when war eventually came to his city, the king grew tired of living for others. That instead of using his magic to save the city, he decided to bury it beneath the sand and escape to the surface, where he could once again wander.

But remember: a crime forgotten is not a crime forgiven.

29

MAZEN

Mazen's first thought when the story ended was that too much of it was missing. Though Nabila was an engaging storyteller, her contempt for the Ashfire King bled into her performance, sharpening each of her words to a brittle, venomous point.

As for the history itself, Mazen could not reconcile the legendary king in the story with the bodyguard who had saved them on the surface. But then, all Mazen knew of Qadir was his relationship with Loulie, and if his experiences had taught him anything, it was that it was foolish to assume things about people based on the stories told about them.

It was as his mother had once said: there was no such thing as a single truth.

At the story's end, he glanced at Loulie. The merchant sat with her hands clasped tightly in her lap, watching Nabila with an inscrutable expression. But Mazen had become good enough at reading her tells to notice the stiffness in her posture.

"Did Qadir tell you that story?" she asked.

Nabila shook her head. "Khalilah did. She did not believe in secrets as he did."

She went on to explain how the king's history had inspired her story and her melody, and how, the first time she had traveled to

Dhahab with her father, she had performed the song in the king's throne room. But Qadir had not approved of the lyrics.

"He said they were false," Nabila said bitterly. "He told me that Khalilah was not his lover. She was—"

"His dearest friend," Loulie muttered. Her expression had softened with the explanation, and now she was looking at Nabila with something akin to pity. "But Qadir remembers your song. He hums it all the time, saying it reminds him of home."

Nabila's gaze snapped toward her. "If he truly cared about his *home*, he would not have left it to decay beneath the Sandsea. He had the opportunity to make things right when Khalilah freed him. To return these lands to the surface. Instead, he stole her away and disappeared."

She spoke the accusation with enough venom to make Mazen and Loulie flinch. Even the firebird, which had been idly nesting in Mazen's hair, released an affronted squawk. It darted toward the brazier, where it began to restlessly peck at crumbs on the ground.

Duha said nothing, merely brushed her hand across Nabila's in comfort. It was a subtle touch, there and gone, but it seemed to relax the ifrit.

Loulie was the first to speak into the quiet. "What happened after? When Qadir left?"

Again, the ifrit turned to the fire. Using her wind, she shaped it into seven distinguishable figures. The bird gave another indignant squawk at the manipulation. This time, it fled the pavilion entirely, swooping out to watch them from a rooftop nearby.

Nabila spared the bird a brief, vaguely offended glance before turning back to her display. "When he left, so did the others. My old *companions*." Another sharp wave, and all but one figure disappeared. Mazen recognized Nabila by her undulating coat and hair.

"I alone was left to bear the burden of our crimes," Nabila continued. "At first, I fought to seize the throne the king had promised us. But though I struggled for years, the queen was more tenacious still. She survived—battle after vicious battle—and emerged victorious with her twisted magic.

"After that, I had no choice but to retreat. Until..." Threads of fire unspooled beneath Nabila's fingertips as she brushed a hand through the air. The flaming pattern stretched above the figure like a barrier. And then it cracked. A broken binding, Mazen realized.

Nabila inclined her head. "One day, I saw a break in the sky. I thought it was a tear in my king's magic and that I could bring the tribes back to the surface if I shattered it completely." With another gesture, she split the single figure into a crowd. Jinn, rushing up through the crack to the surface.

Loulie reached out a hand as if to touch the fire, then seemed to remember herself. Her face was ashen in the light of the flame. "And then what happened?"

"And then...I failed." Nabila closed her hand into a fist, and the figures collapsed back into formless fire. "The crack was but a temporary breach, and only some of the jinn escaped." She scoffed. "The devious queen assumed that *I* had broken the magic and that I was gathering an army against her. She sent soldiers to chase the innocents even as they fled to the surface."

Mazen's heart plunged to his feet. Even Loulie sat frozen, staring in horror. When she spoke, her voice was faint. "I heard rumors that your goal was to invade the surface."

"My only *goal* is to bring us back home."

Home. Mazen thought of the jinn who called the desert their home—the same jinn who were ruthlessly murdered for their blood and magic. What would Nabila say if she knew that such a fate had befallen those survivors? He suspected that conversation would end badly.

"Now do you understand?" The ifrit's silver eyes had frosted over to an icy white. "The queen would blame me for this country's collapse, but the bindings have always been anchored to us ifrit. That they are breaking now means that my companions are dying."

Mazen remembered the bindings on the Wanderer's map. Now he understood why there had been only four of them.

"Only three bindings remain," Nabila said. "The binding on this isle, which contains my magic. The binding in the Eastern Marid

City, which contains the Tide Bringer's. And then there is the Ashfire King's magic, which takes a unique form and is contained within his ashfire." Her expression dampened. "The news from around the Sandsea is grim; we are running out of time."

It was at that point she reviewed the intelligence her spies had delivered that morning. The creatures had witnessed the zaeem of Kharjem's death, and they had watched the queen interrogate the other island leaders. And during those questionings, the birds had spotted—

"Rijah?" Mazen blinked, stupefied. The last he'd heard, Rijah had been imprisoned. If they had been seen at the queen's side, did that mean they had regained her trust?

"The Shapeshifter is speaking poison into their ears." Nabila seethed. "*I* am the one who promised the zuama'a safety and retribution, and yet Rijah's words have confused them."

As concerned as Mazen was about Rijah's sudden involvement in this scheme, his attention caught on something else Nabila had said: What did she mean about *retribution*? Against whom? What if the rumors were true and Nabila *was* bent on ravaging the human cities?

"Well, al-Nazari?" The ifrit turned to Loulie. "Will you look away from the truth of your bodyguard, even now? Or will you finally agree to assist me? My plan benefits us both; if you help me break this magic, we will all return to the surface together."

Loulie did not answer. Her gaze was carefully vacant as she rose to her feet. "I would like some time to think," she said quietly.

She left before Nabila could object, the myna trailing her obediently from the sky. There was no sign of the firebird; Mazen assumed it must have flown off during their conversation.

Nabila scowled at Loulie's vanishing back. "What is there to think on? Is the Ashfire King's influence over her so great that she would refuse to see what is right in front of her?"

Mazen did not know what to make of this talk of influence. To him, the king in Nabila's story had not seemed craven or cruel. He had seemed desperate. Mazen knew what it was to spend your whole life being ushered toward an unwanted destiny. He had, after all, constructed an entire persona to avoid his responsibilities as Prince Mazen bin Malik.

Perhaps Qadir had done what he had not because it was a good choice, but because it was his only choice. Mazen's father had often told him that when it came to ruling, there was no such thing as appeasing everyone.

Mazen drew slowly to his feet. "I'm going to go check on her."

He turned his back on the frowning ifrit to go searching for Loulie.

—⁂—

Mazen found the merchant sitting on the shoreline among a group of children, gathering sand into her palms. He understood what she was doing only when he saw the mound in front of her. He paused, so taken aback by the palace she was building that he momentarily forgot why he had come looking for her.

At first, the palace was just a hill with a leaf on top that Loulie had placed there as a flag. But then the children—there were three of them—began to assist her. One of them flattened the mound with his magic, shaping the sand into elaborate turrets and domes. The second built a deep trench around it. The third carved elaborate symbols into the walls, declaring it a binding that would protect the structure from evildoers. After some consideration, Loulie moved her barely visible leaf to the entrance of the palace and proclaimed it was a tree.

The laugh that had been building in Mazen's chest finally escaped him. He grinned when Loulie turned, cheeks flushed. "The tree-leaf is a nice detail," he said.

Loulie grumbled something under her breath as he approached. The children watched, bright-eyed and triumphant, as he gasped at the details of their work. "This is the most remarkable palace I have ever seen," he said. "And I have seen many of them."

"Of course it is," the child who had built the moat said. "It has *water* around it."

"Not sinking sand," the symbol carver piped in. "Because this palace is on the surface."

The childish claim, spoken so matter-of-factly, sent a pang through Mazen's chest. Even Loulie looked morose as the children squabbled over the technicalities of this.

Mazen remained after the children left. He watched Loulie mindlessly trail her fingers across the sandy turrets. "Can I ask you a question?" The softness of her voice betrayed her nerves. "What would *you* do in this situation? The jinn are in danger here, but if we return them to the surface..." She shook her head. "I worry about Nabila starting another war."

Mazen knew what his father would have said. He would have told Loulie that war was unavoidable, that if the jinn infiltrated the surface, he would have no choice but to respond with violence. But that was the thing about his father—when he'd surveyed Madinne from his balcony, he had not had the luxury of seeing people as people. To a sultan, his subjects were a faceless mass. It was easier to label jinn *enemy* when you could not see their faces.

"I think..." Mazen faltered, but Loulie only waited patiently. She trusted him, he realized, and that emboldened him to speak his mind. "I think the war between humans and jinn never ended. Humans blame the jinn for the barrenness of the land, and the jinn blame humans for their sunken cities. I think *both* of our worlds are dying, in different ways, because they are divided.

"In the absence of the truth, people make up their own stories. That is why there is so much hatred. That is why, even now, jinn blood paints the human desert and ifrit like Nabila pray for war. You know as well as I that there are people who do not believe in those stories—people who are caught in the middle that only wish for peace. But when we think about war, we forget about those people. We forget that there might be an alternative to violence."

Loulie was quiet for a long moment, the words hovering between them. Finally, she said, "That wasn't an answer, you know." She held up a hand before Mazen could speak, her lips twitching into a wry smile. "It's all right; I know you prefer allegories to straightforward answers."

The soft look faded as she glanced back toward the village. "You're saying these refugees are the ones caught in the middle and that it would be unfair to turn our backs on them. And..." Her eyes drifted back to him. "You think a war is avoidable?"

"I don't know. But I don't think avoiding one should come at the cost of innocents who are suffering right in front of our eyes."

He knew it wasn't an answer his father would have appreciated, but Mazen did not want to be like the sultan, who had let rage eclipse his compassion. Perhaps it was foolish to want to keep his heart. But once, his mother had told him such a thing was valuable in their desert.

He expected Loulie to scold him for his lofty ideals. But the smile had returned to her face when she said, "It's good to have you back, Mazen bin Malik." She stood, brushing the sand off her robes. "We'll break these bindings, then. I'll ask for Qadir's forgiveness later if I must."

Something twinged in Mazen's chest. "We're going to help them?"

"I'm going to help the *islanders*. I refuse to let anyone be collateral damage."

Seeing the resolve in her eyes, Mazen wondered if she was thinking of her tribe. Her family, whom Omar had once called collateral damage because they were in the wrong place at the wrong time.

"Come on." Loulie started walking. "We're getting off this island one way or another."

30

AISHA

Her first night back in Madinne, Aisha slept like the dead.

It was a testament to her exhaustion that she slept through even the riotous singing in the tavern that went on past midnight. She was alarmed when she woke with sleep-crusted eyes and a foggy mind, her nightmares from the evening before a blur. She ran a hand through her hair as she rose, narrowing her focus to her surroundings.

The room Dahlia bint Adnan had given her was a simple space, empty of everything but the bare necessities. This suited Aisha just fine, as the bed was the only luxury she'd missed.

She dressed and headed downstairs. The creaking steps announced her arrival long before she made it to the bottom floor, where she was unsurprised to see both Hakim and Dahlia at the bar, waiting for her.

The mapmaker inclined his head at her approach. "Sabah al-khair, bint Louas."

Dahlia looked up from polishing a glass but said nothing, only eyed her warily.

Aisha slid onto the stool beside Hakim's and addressed the tavernkeeper. "Tell me what's happened in my absence. What has Omar done to the city?"

The tavernkeeper scowled. "I shelter you under my roof, and the first thing you do is demand information from me? You're a terrible guest."

The comment shouldn't have bothered Aisha. *Wouldn't* have bothered her if it hadn't reminded her of Umm Jaber.

The tavernkeeper sighed at Aisha's muttered apology. "Your goal is to best the sultan, isn't it? I'm afraid you won't find information about him in a run-down tavern."

"No, but I'd hoped the owner of the notorious *Night Market* might have information."

When Dahlia only gave her a flat stare in response, Hakim cleared his throat and cut in, "Ya sayyida, I told her—"

Dahlia set her bottle down on the counter with a sharp thud. "I told you, mapmaker, that I would provide you with sanctuary if you returned to the city. Nothing more, nothing less. If your disgraced thief wants information on the sultan, she can pay me to gather it for her."

The woman was insufferable; Aisha could not help but feel a grudging respect for her.

"Fine." She tilted her gaze to meet Dahlia's defiant frown. "Do you have clothing I can borrow, or will you take coin for that too?"

"I would pay *you* to leave me in peace and not loiter when the guests arrive," Dahlia said. It wasn't an answer, but when the tavernkeeper turned and headed upstairs, Aisha was hopeful.

In Dahlia's absence, she turned to Hakim, who was staring intently at one of the liquor bottles. It was clear from the intensity of his gaze that he was trying to ignore her, but Aisha would not allow him to avoid the subject of their escape.

"Are you going to tell me about your magic, or will I need to steal your ring?"

Hakim shot her a sharp look. "Your threats are unamusing."

"As are *your* secrets."

The two of them frowned at each other. The mapmaker did not cave. She had learned very quickly that if Omar was temperamental as quicksand, Hakim was obstinate as stone.

The Resurrectionist's voice filled her mind like smoke. *Why bother with these mind games when there is a simpler way to steal your answers?*

Aisha could feel that "way" humming beneath her skin, a current of electricity pulsing behind her right eye and through her ears. How simple it would be to tap into that magic and reach out to the relic in Hakim's possession. With it, she would be able to hear it.

It was painful to shove the magic down, away. Her voice was hoarse when she said, "How many secrets have I shared with *you* to prove my reliability?"

It was a low blow, but Aisha much preferred the twinge of guilt to the flood of poisonous magic in her veins. Thankfully, the comment had the intended effect on Hakim. He regarded her thoughtfully for a moment before raising his hand. "I told you before about my mentor, yes? His name was Jubayr. The relic was a gift from him before he passed."

Aisha considered. Most would have assumed the relic had been a keepsake of his teacher. But Hakim spoke about the magic as if it were an heirloom, not a thing stolen. Which could mean only one thing. She stared at him, baffled. "Your teacher was a *jinn*?"

An ifrit, if the Resurrectionist was correct.

A slim smile touched his lips. "Do you see why I was not eager to tell you, a hunter?"

Aisha withheld a retort about Hakim's teacher already being *dead*. After all, Omar's forty thieves had been in the business not just of hunting jinn but also of stealing their relics. She forced her guilt away and asked another question, this time about how the magic functioned.

Hakim confirmed what she had suspected: that the ring could help him "see" the lands his teacher had once passed through, albeit in their present form. It was, in essence, a relic that contained a mapmaker's memories. Of course, that meant that only a mapmaker could understand them, and that this particular ring had been given to Hakim to guide him.

Hmm, so Jubayr gifted his magic to a human, the Resurrectionist mused. *Interesting.*

To Aisha, it was unfathomable. "Did your tribe know?" she asked. "That he was jinn?"

Another nod. "I am too young to remember the day myself, but I was told he found us during a vicious sandstorm. In exchange for shelter, he led my tribe through the storm."

"And then he stayed," Aisha muttered. She thought of the jinn her tribe had entertained. The same jinn who had then murdered them and painted the sand with their blood. The same jinn who had carved the proof of her family's deaths into her arms.

"And then he stayed, and we were all glad for it." The mapmaker held up his hand once more, brow furrowed. "I have used the ring to help me map the landscape for years. But what happened in the tunnels . . . I did not know the relic could *change* the landscape."

His voice cracked at the confession, and Aisha knew he was telling the truth. Curiosity swept through her. Deep in her mind, she could sense the Resurrectionist's memories of Jubayr lying dormant. If she wanted to find out more about him, all she had to do was let those memories sink in and . . .

She came back to herself with a shudder. *Foul creature, stop trying to fill my mind with your demented visions!*

The Resurrectionist's annoyance snapped through her, sudden and cold. *Those* demented *visions would give you the answers you seek, yet even now you turn away. This is idiocy.*

I do not want your knowledge, Aisha shot back.

She noticed that Hakim was staring at her, perhaps confused that she was scowling at nothing. He looked like he might say something, but the sound of footsteps made them both pause. It was Dahlia bint Adnan, returning with a bundle of clothing.

"We'll finish this conversation later," Aisha muttered as the tavernkeeper unceremoniously dumped the attire in front of her. From what she could tell, the robe would be a bit short at the ankles, but it would suffice. She rose from the table. "I'll be back."

She departed to make herself ready in her room, easing out of her travel clothes and into the heavy robe. Despite its weight, the attire was loose and would be easy to move in if she needed to act quickly.

Thankfully, Dahlia had also provided a shawl that would hide her features.

When Aisha returned downstairs, Dahlia and Hakim were deep in conversation. The tavernkeeper looked up as Aisha walked past her to the door. "Hakim has told me of your intention to break into the Bowels. I have a contact who can give you information about the prison. You can expect to see him when you return."

Aisha turned, brow raised. "You'll help us break into an unbreakable prison, but you refuse to track down information on the sultan?"

Dahlia scoffed. "I owe *Hakim*, not you. You really are an ungrateful guest, aren't you?"

Aisha turned away with a sigh. Based on what little she had gleaned of Dahlia's personality, she assumed there must be something in this rescue for her as well. The woman did not seem the type to hand out favors without demanding something in return.

She stepped outside and began to make her way to the central souk, where she would be able to eavesdrop on recent developments within Madinne. It did not take her long to realize the city had changed. She saw veins of greenery running through residential spaces that had once been barren, and trellises of flowers growing down walls and winding through streets.

Lush was the first word that came to mind as she beheld the large trees shading the stalls in the main square and the flowers hanging over balconies. The nature was not the only abnormality. As she wandered deeper, she saw a fountain filled with odd silver water that reminded her of the surface of a mirror. When curiosity bade her to look inside, she saw not her own reflection, but that of a stranger. A child, who let out a silent, gleeful cry as Aisha retreated.

Her heart beat in her throat as she drew away. Her blood had begun to hum in that telltale way that let her know a relic was nearby. Sure enough, her suspicion was confirmed when she saw a green gemstone sparkling on the centerpiece of a fountain.

Please, the voice in the relic said. *Please have mercy. Please, please, please...*

Aisha turned away before anyone noticed her staring. Now that she had opened her mind to the voices of the dead, she could hear others screaming beneath the din of the crowds.

It seems your sultan likes to flaunt his wealth. The Resurrectionist's words were bitter.

"Flaunt" was an understatement. Every whisper led Aisha to another relic. She saw a performer cut glowing shapes into the air with an enchanted rod, a wooden bird flit above the crowds' heads echoing news from a crier, and an enchanted tapestry hanging from the meeting hall, showcasing different decrees from the council at every angle. It was magic, out in the open.

To any normal citizen, such magics would have seemed remarkable. But to Aisha, the relics were more than just objects—they were *souls* with histories, and the memory of the agony they had endured when slain by hunters was all the more unbearable because she was the only one who could hear it.

She was so overwhelmed by the cacophony that she did not at first realize her feet had taken her down a familiar path through the noble quarter toward the palace. She might have followed that road to its end had she not become distracted by a picture on the wall.

Aisha turned to see her own face staring back at her on a wanted poster.

Despite the unnatural sharpness with which her features had been rendered, it was a frustratingly accurate depiction. Aisha tugged her shawl up to better hide her face as she regarded Hakim's poster beside hers. His likeness too was striking.

Though her features were covered, Aisha felt suddenly exposed on the empty street. Cursing herself for her foggy mind, she began to retrace her steps. She had not made it far when she felt eyes on her back. But when she darted a look over her shoulder, no one was behind her.

She might have convinced herself that her nerves were playing tricks on her, but she had always trusted her instincts. Eventually, her suspicion was rewarded when she saw a flutter of motion above her. Aisha continued walking as she lifted her gaze to the roof behind her.

A large man garbed entirely in black stood watching her. Though his face was covered, his broad-shouldered figure and relaxed posture were familiar to her.

Samar?

The last time she had seen the easygoing thief, it had been before she set off on the quest for the lamp. She had noted the injury on his arm, healed unnaturally fast. It was only later she'd found out he was a jinn.

Aisha knew she ought to turn away. That she was as good as giving herself away by acknowledging him. But in the end, it was Samar who turned away first, leaving her to stand alone in the alleyway. Had he recognized her beneath her shawl? It was impossible to tell.

Dread weighed Aisha's footsteps as she made her way back to the tavern.

31

AISHA

True to her word, Dahlia's black-market connection was waiting in a room upstairs when Aisha returned. The merchant was a vaguely familiar man by the name of Rasul al-Jasheen. She assumed their previous encounter must have been brief, however, for she would never have forgotten this egoist of a man otherwise. He was either oblivious or ignored her annoyance; her glares slid off him like water, and he took no offense at her brusque commentary.

Such was the nature of their interaction as they leaned over Hakim's in-progress map of the Bowels, the terrible underground prison where Qadir was being kept. Though Aisha herself had never visited the prison—her targets' bodies had always been used as fertilizer, after all—she had not worked with Omar for nine years without hearing anything of their structure.

The Bowels were not just a labyrinth; they were a death trap.

Those unlucky enough to land themselves inside were thrown into dark, claustrophobic shafts nailed shut with grates. Aisha had heard horror stories of the corpses the guards hauled up from the depths. As for the prison itself, all she knew was that its halls were notoriously serpentine. She did not like their odds of breaking in with only an estimation of the layout.

That was where Rasul al-Jasheen came in.

Though the man himself had never been in the Bowels, he knew a friend of a cousin of a customer who had bought information about the prisons from a palace soldier for some outrageous sum. Naturally, the soldier who had overshared had been locked in the Bowels for his loose lips. Not long after, the friend who had purchased the information had been thrown in with him. But not even the threat of death could halt the spread of gossip, and so the information had been passed down to merchants who could pay the right coin for it.

Rasul al-Jasheen was, apparently, a merchant of very good means.

He was enjoying flaunting those means now as he described in detail the layout of the prison. "The Bowels run deep," he was saying. "There is only one entrance: a single narrow staircase accessible through the surface building. It is open during patrol shifts, but the jailor does thorough checks of his men, so there is no chance of entering in disguise."

Having delivered that unfortunate news with great certainty, he moved on to describing the floors. "There are seven levels in total, each accessible through a single door..."

As the merchant spoke, Hakim sketched details into his rudimentary map. "These chambers here"—he tapped a series of squares—"are the prison cells in the Bowels?"

Rasul nodded. "Each chamber is sealed shut with an iron door. I have heard there is a special locking mechanism for each one, specially designed by the sultan. Your friend is likely *here*"—he indicated a chamber at the end—"the cell with his most recently commissioned lock."

Hakim's fingers stilled on the map. "Do you know anything about these locks?" When Rasul shook his head, Hakim frowned, then turned questioningly to Aisha.

Aisha offered a noncommittal shrug. She certainly had experience with Omar's special locks but knew he would not be foolish enough to reuse the same mechanisms.

Rasul gave her an appraising look. "I admit I thought it a fool's errand when Dahlia told me you were considering breaking into the prisons. But I suppose if anyone can outmaneuver the sultan, it would be one of his thieves."

He flinched when Aisha stabbed her dagger into the table. "*Former* thief."

Dahlia swatted the back of her head. "You ruin my furniture, you pay for it."

Aisha resisted the urge to slap the smile off Rasul's face as she wrenched out her dagger. The merchant turned to Dahlia. "This man you're trying to save must be important."

"He is more important than you can imagine," the tavernkeeper said.

"Oh? Why are *you* interested in him, bint Adnan?"

Dahlia's responding smile was pressed thin in warning. "Ya Rasul, you know better than to interrogate me. After a betrayal like yours, my trust is not so easily regained."

Rasul recoiled at the words. It was then, seeing his guilty expression, that Aisha knew why he was familiar. He was the merchant who had given away the location of the underground market so Omar's father could find Loulie. While it seemed Omar was turning a blind eye to the market's existence, Dahlia had evidently not forgiven Rasul's duplicity.

The merchant told them what he knew of the patrol shifts, the corridors, and where the guards kept their key rings, which would include a single iron key used to open the Bowels. He explained that the most dangerous prisoners—usually the jinn—were kept in the bottommost cells, where they were shackled and placed in iron-coated rooms.

Aisha's mood darkened as the explanation went on. Though she was a thief, stealth had never been her preference, and the thought of sneaking through such a maze exhausted her.

An hour later, the map was complete. Hakim had drawn a sprawling network of lines and circled the approximate area they anticipated Qadir would be. As far as Aisha could tell, they would need to tunnel through several layers of security, pass through an unreasonable number of locked doors, *and* unlock a grated shaft to get to him.

The impossibility of their mission dawned on them as they scrutinized the map. It was Dahlia who spoke first. "If this plan succeeds, it will be more than just a prison break."

"Yes," Rasul agreed. "It will be a miracle."

The dour mood lingered after the merchant departed. After muttering something about needing space to think, Hakim vanished to his room. Dahlia excused herself shortly after. Alone once more, Aisha decided she would return to the city to gather information. Though she was unsettled by the run-in with Samar, she refused to let the encounter scare her.

But no sooner did she exit her room than she paused, noticing one of the doors at the far end of the hallway, always closed, had been left ajar. Curious, Aisha peered inside. She was immediately taken aback by how lived-in the space looked, stuffed full as it was with furniture and accoutrements. Upon closer inspection, she realized she was standing in a sitting room that connected to a bedroom. It seemed more an apartment than a guest room.

Dahlia sat on a divan by the window, frowning at her. "Intrusive as always, I see."

Aisha shrugged. "Open door, open invitation. Is this your room?"

The tavernkeeper shook her head. "It belongs to a long-term tenant." Her lips curled into a wry smile as she glanced around the room. "The same man you're breaking out of the Bowels, actually, though he shares the space with someone else."

The realization dawned on Aisha as she took in the room. The maps, the wall tapestries of the desert, the shelves cluttered with sundries and tomes—she saw now whose room this must be. Last night, Dahlia had introduced herself as the owner of the Night Market. Loulie al-Nazari was a *merchant* of the market. Aisha should have drawn the connection between them sooner.

"I remember seeing you riding beside Loulie and the prince at the farewell procession," Dahlia said. "At the time, I thought he was *your* prince, the King of the Forty Thieves. It was not until later, when Ahmed bin Walid arrived, that I realized he was a different man."

Aisha remembered what Hakim had said about Ahmed's efforts

to unravel Omar's plot. If Dahlia knew of Omar's deceit, then she must have been working with Ahmed—and with Hakim.

She leaned against the doorway. "You were plotting with Ahmed and Hakim, then?"

The tavernkeeper nodded. "The wali was a perceptive man. Not long after he arrived in the city, he discovered my connection with Loulie al-Nazari. That is why he started coming to me when he began unraveling Omar's plot, and why he brought Hakim here when he realized the prince was keeping his brother's secret."

It *would* have taken a perceptive man to draw all those connections. It was a shame Ahmed's astuteness had not been enough to save him in the end. But that was the way things were with Omar. No matter the opponent, he always had the superior strategy.

Not this time, Aisha thought. *This time, I will best him.*

She crossed her arms. "And the tunnels—you showed them to Hakim?"

"I showed him the entrance and told him I would shelter him if he returned to the city."

"Why?"

Dahlia gave her a pointed look. "Because our interests align. One thing you should know about us merchants: we will do anything to protect our investments."

Aisha raised a brow. *Investment* seemed a peculiar term of endearment, but Aisha thought she understood. Umm Jaber had shown her affection in a similarly jaded way. And Aisha—

You are too proud to call anyone your friend. There was a smirk in the ifrit's words.

Aisha ignored her as she cast her gaze over the room. It was hard to believe one of the ifrit Omar had been searching for all those years had been living right under his nose.

Of course, even he had fallen prey to Omar in the end.

Aisha might have lingered to converse with the tavernkeeper had Hakim not called her from his room across the corridor. Dahlia excused Aisha before she could excuse herself, waving her away with a muttered "You have better things to do than listen to me reminisce."

Aisha's chest tightened at the remark. It sounded like something Umm Jaber would have said—and she hated that even now, the comparison made her heart ache. What would the matriarch have said, she wondered, if she'd known she was leading Hakim into such danger?

With one last glance at the abandoned space, Aisha crossed the corridor to Hakim's apartment. The mapmaker sat cross-legged on the floor, two maps stretched in front of him. The first, Aisha recognized as the diagram Hakim had just produced of the prisons. The second, more complicated map was the one he had used to lead them through the underground tunnels.

She came to stand beside him. "What's this?"

"The beginning of an idea." He glanced at her, a sparkle in his eye. "You know what they say about the tunnels here, bint Louas? That they stretch beneath the entirety of the city?" He slid the map of the prison over the map of the tunnels, overlying them at the edges.

Aisha searched the intersections of the lines. Though the maps were mostly unreadable to her, she could discern repeating patterns between them. Lines bleeding into one another. Understanding dawned as she glanced between the two pieces of parchment. "They overlap?"

Hakim nodded. Now she understood the gleam in his eyes, the frenzied energy. "It is not a direct path, but so long as I know the lay of the land..." He fingered the ring on his hand. "I should be able to carve a path into the prison from underground."

It was the most brazen plan Aisha had ever heard. And yet it was no secret the Bowels were well guarded on the surface. No one would expect intruders from *under*ground.

Aisha smiled. A grim smile. "Who needs miracles when you have magic?"

32

LOULIE

The day she and Mazen set out to unseal the second binding, they met Duha, who was to be their guide, at the base of one of the cliffs. Loulie was unsurprised. Given the small size of the island, she had expected the magic to be hidden in some high location. Still, she groaned as she beheld the towering rock face. *Are* all *these bindings in such inconvenient locations?*

Duha grinned at her frustration. "I promise the view is worth the perilous climb."

The journey up the cliffside was every bit as exhausting as anticipated. The three of them climbed a long time—long enough for the sky to darken from a gentle azure to a crimson red. Though they had made certain to embark after the curfew darkness lifted, Duha still carried an ashfire-lit torch to illuminate their path.

As they walked, Loulie watched Mazen. She'd said she could handle the binding on her own, but he had insisted on accompanying her. Try as he did to hide the discomfort from his injuries, his fatigue was plain. By the time they reached the plateau, he was trembling like a leaf.

Stubborn fool, she thought fondly.

Knowing he would not ask for a respite himself, Loulie settled herself on the ledge to "catch her breath." He flashed her a grateful smile as he slumped down beside her. At first, neither of them could spot the "view" Duha had promised. But then she pointed farther up, and they saw an entire *city* built into the cliffside.

Loulie gaped when she caught sight of the ruins. "What is this place?"

"This," Duha said with a grand wave of her hand, "is Nabila's old home."

Loulie was awestruck. Her eyes swept over elaborate columns and slanted roofs, across patterned walls and staircases built directly into the cliffside. Rock balconies punctuated the spaces between the edifices, trellised in vibrant greenery.

The marid smiled at their wonder. "It is nothing but ruins now, but before the war, it was a bustling city. Nabila's father was so renowned an entertainer it was said travelers came from across the ocean to see the performances he put on. Now this place is . . ." She paused, considering. "Have you ever held a shell to your ear and thought you could hear the ocean in it?"

Loulie nodded, thinking of the seashells she had collected off Madinne's beaches. The first time she had pressed a conch shell to her ear and heard the echo of the waves inside, she had thought it an enchanted object. Never mind that the shells were merely amplifiers for surrounding noises; she had always thought the sound was something akin to magic.

"The ruins are like those shells," Duha said. "Nabila has preserved the memory of her tribe in the echoes of the wind; you will understand when we enter."

The mood dampened with her warning, and by the time they reached the staircase leading into the ruins, Loulie was on high alert. They had just started making their way up when Duha abruptly paused, head tilted as if she were listening for some sound on the wind.

A few moments passed before she said, "The zaeem is calling for me. I must heed his summons." Though her expression was calm, Loulie noted a twinge of unease in her voice.

"What, right now? I thought the bindings were our priority."

"And they still are. You will go on ahead of me to meet with Nabila." Duha handed the torch to Loulie and pointed straight above her, to a plateau so high up they had to crane their necks to spot it. "Do you see that balcony? Nabila will meet you there."

Mazen cast a nervous look at Loulie as the marid ran off. She responded with what she hoped was a nonchalant shrug. At this point, what choice did they have but to continue?

The wind changed as the two of them climbed, pitching from a low murmur to a more disconcerting howl. The sound made Loulie's skin prickle. Was this what Duha had meant by memories trapped in the wind? She forced herself to focus past the sound as she ventured into the nearest building. In the torchlight, she made out twisting corridors.

The loss of the compass hit her again then. While Loulie had navigated ruins like this many times before, she'd always used the relic to guide her way. Without it, she felt unprepared.

But there was no use mourning now. She told herself, *If the wind is the only foe I have to face here, then I don't* need *the compass.*

But her conviction faltered when, as she and Mazen wandered deeper into the ruins, the haunting breeze pitched into a bloodcurdling *scream*. The sound was so unexpected it made her jump. Beside her, Mazen froze, staring around the building with wide eyes. They both waited with bated breath, but the sound did not come again.

"What in nine hells was *that*?" Her voice cracked.

Mazen glanced nervously behind them. "One of the memories Duha mentioned?"

As the terrible sound reverberated through the halls, Loulie thought of her own tribe. Though she kept the memory of them close, she would have given anything to forget the moment of their deaths. If Nabila was holding on to memories like this, it was no wonder she was so filled with hatred.

"It sounds awfully loud for a memory," she finally managed.

Mazen nodded quietly. She could tell by the way his head was tilted that he was watching her, brow furrowed with clear concern. Was her grief that obvious?

She did her best to suffocate the feeling as she led them up a crumbling stairwell to the second floor. From there, they came out onto another plateau. Loulie saw lifeless gardens filled with weeds and insects, and buildings filled with ash and dust. Much to her horror, the screaming grew louder as they ascended to the higher levels. Through the wind, Loulie experienced an entire battle. She heard the harsh clang of metal and the smell of burning flesh, the heartbreaking sobs of children and the whispered pleas of the dying.

The sounds were familiar to Loulie. Her own mother had begged like this before she was run through with a blade. In her mind's eye, Loulie could still see her bloodied corpse on the ground. Could feel the smoke stinging her eyes as the thieves' fire engulfed the camp—

She startled when Mazen reached out to steady her hand. She had not realized she was trembling. One second later and the torch would have slipped through her fingers.

"Allow me to take the torch for a bit?" he offered.

Wordlessly, she handed it to him. For a long moment, Mazen stared at it, his eyes narrowed with concentration. Loulie blinked in surprise when the ashfire atop snapped into the familiar shape of the firebird. The tiny bird fluffed its wings and chirped at them.

A bright smile broke out on Mazen's face. "It's you." He glanced up at Loulie, golden eyes glimmering with wonder. "I was thinking about what Duha said about summoning the bird with words; I wondered if it might appear if I simply thought of the story."

Loulie recalled what Hayat had told her in Dhahab: that this realm was so touched by magic the jinn did not give its existence thought. Perhaps that was why the fire had responded to Mazen's story; it was alive in a way no other flame could be.

Loulie glanced between the storyteller and his bird. Seeing the smile on Mazen's face, she felt... at ease. If he had meant to distract her, then he was doing a good job of it.

"You should give it a name," she said as they continued walking. "Maybe then you can call it directly."

Mazen warmed immediately to the idea. He pondered as they

traveled, mumbling names under his breath until a sudden spark came into his eyes. "What about Azhar?"

Shining. Bright. It was such an obvious choice for a name it made Loulie groan. But the creature seemed to enjoy it. It tweeted—a sweet chirrup that made Mazen laugh. The trill even made her smile.

"Azhar, then." He grinned at the bird. "Can you light the way?"

With a tweet, it obeyed, sweeping ahead of them into the dark. Not wanting to lose its light, Loulie hurried after it. Mazen easily matched her footsteps with his longer strides.

"Shukran," Loulie mumbled. She hoped he knew what she was thanking him for.

Mazen just nodded, his eyes crinkled in a silent smile as they followed Azhar.

—⁂—

The moment they reached their destination, it became apparent the balcony was more than just a plateau overlooking the cliffs. Stairs sloped down from the entryway, curving toward a crescent-shaped stage. Behind the stage, a crumbled balustrade ringed the edge of the platform.

Mazen breathed out in awe. "An amphitheater?"

Loulie could see it too. As they stepped outside, she could also make out Nabila seated in one of the lower rows.

The ifrit stood at their approach. "Where is Duha?" When they relayed what the marid had told them, she looked unsatisfied but did not question them further. Instead, she turned to the stage behind them. "The binding is here." She pointed to the faint streaks on the ground.

Carefully, Loulie approached the markings. They glowed as she drew nearer, reacting to Qadir's dagger. "What is this place?" she asked.

There was silence at first. When Nabila finally did speak, her voice was soft with remorse. "It was where I performed, in my youth. My father would entertain dignitaries here."

Loulie cast a glance back at the ifrit. Though Nabila's body was as ethereal as always, there was a heaviness to the wind that formed her limbs. "When first I bowed my head to the Ashfire King, it was as a performer," she said. "My father offered me as tribute."

Loulie stared at her. "Tribute?"

"What better way to secure favor with a king than to offer him your own daughter as a personal entertainer?" She shrugged—or at least, that was how Loulie interpreted the snap of the wind around her shoulders. "Such is the way of politics. I never judged my father."

Loulie caught Mazen's gaze. The storyteller looked just as flummoxed as she did. Perhaps the ifrit read their pity from the silence. With a curt wave of her hand, she dismissed the subject and ordered Loulie into the binding.

Mazen walked with Loulie to the outskirts, holding up the torch where Azhar now roosted. He glanced over his shoulder at Nabila. "Why carve a binding all the way up here?"

"Because this is where the wind is strongest." Nabila regarded the fiery threads with a cold blankness. "When I helped the Ashfire King craft the magic here, he told me it would keep the island safe. But when I returned from the war, the last memory the wind had trapped was my family's murder. Can you imagine what it is like to return to such a reality?"

Loulie swallowed. She could imagine because it was the last memory she had of *her* tribe. Loulie understood Nabila's wrath—it was one of the reasons it terrified her.

But she had agreed to do this.

She returned her attention to the binding. Though the fire was familiar, she noted the nature of the markings was different. These threads spiraled inward, pulling at her clothing.

As she moved to step inside, Mazen reached for her hand. "Loulie." His bright eyes had clouded over with worry. "Be careful."

Loulie squeezed his palm—whether to reassure herself or him she was not sure—and entered the binding. The moment her feet passed over the fire, the wind around her grew turbulent, ripping at her hair and clothing with a startling tenacity. It was not just the flames that rose around her, but a storm of smoke and cinders.

Loulie wrapped her scarf more tightly around her mouth to keep out the smoke. She narrowed her burning eyes as she waded through the whorls of magic.

It was only at the center that things calmed. *The eye of the storm,* Loulie thought.

Despite the roar of the fire, she could hear Nabila's voice. Even now, it seemed, the ifrit had the ability to speak on the wind. *"Look down, human."*

Loulie lowered her gaze to the ground. The center of the binding was a simple circle, a barrier holding the rest of the wind at bay. If this binding worked like the one on the archive roof, then the magic would shatter if Loulie broke the middle.

Her fingers tightened on the dagger. Even now, the weapon was quiet. When she tried reaching for Qadir, she felt only the memory of his pain. Knowing him, he had severed their connection to protect her against it.

The thought made tears gather in her eyes. *Infuriating creature. Why must you hide things from me? Why can you not trust me as I trust you?* Was it so wrong to confide in her like she had always confided in him?

Loulie shoved the thought aside. If he would not talk to her, then she had no choice but to press on. Qadir had entrusted her with his dagger; *she* had to decide how best to use it.

She crouched in the center of the binding, one hand on the ground and the other wrapped around the knife. She could feel a thrum beneath the storm, a heartbeat.

Before she could lose her nerve, Loulie broke the circle.

As she had expected, it was like unleashing a storm. The amphitheater grew suddenly unstable, shaking so hard Loulie was thrown to her knees. When she tried to crawl away, the pressure of the wind beat against her body, blowing her backward.

And then she saw fire—ashfire—burning on Mazen's torch as he stepped into the now-broken binding. He had one hand on the balustrade, another outstretched toward her. Though Loulie could not hear him over the storm, she read the shape of her name on his lips.

With a grunt, Loulie threw herself at him, holding tight as the wind tore through the amphitheater, screaming in their ears and lashing at their bodies.

And then, abruptly as it had started, the tempest stopped.

Loulie could make out the sound of her breathing mingled with Mazen's. She could not tell if it was her heartbeat or his beating in her ears. Slowly, she peeled herself away from him. She spared a glance at Mazen's torch, but it appeared Azhar had vanished during the storm, for the ashfire was still. It was stiller, in any case, than the trembling ground beneath them.

Another quake, Loulie realized. Her stomach knotted with dread.

It was not just the ground that had become unstable, but the sky as well. When Loulie glanced up, she saw the illusion flickering, the crimson red already beginning to bleed into the ominous black of curfew.

A shudder ran through her as the darkness encroached. What did it mean that the magic was falling again so soon? Would they be able to make it off the cliffs before it engulfed the sky completely?

Loulie returned her attention to the broken binding. Where the center had minutes ago been, Nabila now stood.

Stood. For the first time since Loulie had ever seen her, Nabila was stationary. Details she had never spotted in the wind revealed themselves to her. Loulie saw brown skin, cloudy-gray eyes, and waves of hair that hung *down* Nabila's back rather than snapping in the air.

Perhaps because she was so visible, Loulie noticed something else on Nabila's face that she had never seen before: fear. The ifrit shivered, and the motion traveled from her shoulders down to the soles of her feet. "My magic..."

It was Mazen who said, "What's happened to the wind?"

The wind had not just grown weak; it had *died* completely.

Nabila said nothing. She slowly lifted her hand to flex a perplexingly tangible wrist. When she called the wind, only a weak gust responded, barely fluttering their clothing.

But even on that faint wind, Loulie heard something. Duha's voice, little more than a panicked whisper. And then the breeze was gone, Duha's words with it. Nabila stood frozen in what had once been the center of the storm, her hands clenched into fists.

"What?" Loulie's voice came out soft, trembling. "What's happened?"

The ifrit's eyes were dark as storm clouds when she looked up. "We have been found."

33

MAZEN

We have been found.

The meaning of those words became apparent when they arrived at the beach and saw the ships looming on the horizon. The armada was an encroaching storm; it had already pushed past the barrier of wind Nabila had erected around the island, and was bobbing onto the water.

Duha was waiting for them on the shoreline. The moment she saw Nabila—saw her *tangibility*—her eyes widened with alarm. "Your body—"

"I am fine." The ifrit spoke through gritted teeth as she walked to the shoreline. Mazen could not help noticing how heavy her footsteps were without her magic. Normally, Nabila seemed to glide across surfaces. Now she left unmistakable prints in the sand.

When Duha shot them a baffled look, Mazen said, "After Loulie broke the binding, the wind started to fade." He could feel it in the air—the strange absence of the breeze.

"Never mind the wind," Nabila said sharply. "Explain the situation."

Duha turned to the water with a grimace. "I do not know how, but Ziyad has found us. Some of the sailors have gone ahead to slow the soldiers' progress on the water."

Mazen followed her gaze past the line of ships to the turbulent waves on the horizon. Ziyad's magic, he assumed. He glanced at Nabila. "Was it one of your birds?"

There was fire in Nabila's eyes when she glared at him. "No. They would never betray me." She said the words with enough certainty to close the door on the possibility entirely.

For a few moments, they all stood staring despondently out at the water, taking in the overwhelming sight of the ships pushing toward the island. Mazen could tell from the thick weight of that silence that even Nabila was at a loss.

It was Loulie who spoke first. Her voice came out soft, almost tremulous, but she said, very clearly, "The compass led them here."

Nabila's gaze snapped up to meet hers. A dozen emotions seemed to war across her expression, but the one that settled was rage. When she took a threatening step toward Loulie, the merchant stood her ground, meeting her wrath head-on.

"This isn't my fault," Loulie said. "You told me the compass was gone."

Mazen quickly interceded, stepping in front of Loulie with his hands raised in a gesture of supplication. "I swear we are not working with Ziyad. On the ship, he nearly killed me. He... made it clear what happens to traitors." He set a hand to his chest, over his sealed wound.

The ifrit looked like she might argue before Duha said, softly but firmly, "Nokhitha." They turned to see her standing ankle-deep in the surf. "This is not the first time Ziyad has found us, and it will not be the first time we escape him."

"They have never been this close," Nabila said. "Close enough to sail on the water."

"Then we will have to hold them back. We are more than capable."

Some of the spark faded from Nabila's eyes as she glanced out at the village. "And what of the island? If the soldiers make it past us to the shore, there will be no defending it."

"Can we not move it?" The suggestion was out of Mazen's lips before he had even thought it, but if the zaeem was al-Malath itself, the vanishing isle, could they not make it move on their own terms?

Nabila frowned. "Only Duha can speak with him. She and the zaeem have a deal."

He considered. Did that mean the crab would be amenable to another deal? Was there something they could offer him? Perhaps they could give him a relic? A story? Or...

"I'll go."

They all turned to look at Loulie. She was staring out at the ships, her lips pressed into a thin line. "I know how to bargain. Let me cut the deal."

Even Nabila seemed surprised by the offer. Surprised and then suspicious. "Your compass is on one of those ships—you would leave it in Ziyad's hands?"

For a few moments, Loulie looked uncertain. Her eyes flitted between the village behind them and the ships before them. She wavered, took a deep breath. And then she said, almost too softly for Mazen to hear, "A stolen object can be recovered. A stolen life cannot."

Mazen could tell how much it pained her to say those words. And yet she stood tall, resolute. When Mazen saw her determination, an idea began to form in his mind as Nabila and Duha discussed their plan. Duha declared that she would go after Ziyad while Nabila attacked the ships. They would not be able to defeat such a massive force, but they would be able to buy Loulie enough time to speak with the zaeem. As for Mazen...

Nabila pointed to the ashfire-lit torch in his hand. "You can serve as a guide. The villagers will already be heading to the fortress, but they will need all the help they can get."

Mazen recognized a dismissal when he heard one. It was not that he doubted he could be of assistance, but the villagers knew al-Malath better than he did, *and* they already had the ashfire-lit torches to guide them. They did not need him, not for this.

In a way, it was a relief to know Nabila was trying to sideline him. It made it easier to lie, to nod along when she gave the command.

When Loulie ordered him to stay out of danger, he repeated the sentiment back at her. Thankfully, she did not notice how distracted he was before she rushed off, heading back in the direction of the zaeem's cave. Mazen watched her go until he heard the unmistakable sound of a storm behind him.

He turned and was surprised to see wind pulling at Nabila's clothing. But it was clear the magic was weaker. Nabila's body remained corporeal, which meant he could see the strain on her face as she used her magic.

"Duha," the ifrit called. "I am going ahead to slow the ships."

With one last nod to the marid, she charged across the waves, no longer the wind itself but its conductor. In her hands, the gale became a blade, cutting through the water and parting the waves. Mazen watched the gust travel to the nearest ship, where it slammed into the hull so forcefully the whole vessel listed.

Duha had just started to give chase when Mazen grabbed her by the arm. She turned, startled, and Mazen spoke before he lost his nerve. "Take me with you. Please."

Her brow furrowed with confusion. "You intend to disobey Nabila's orders?"

"I will not get in the way, I promise. I just want to take back Loulie's compass." When her expression only grew more incredulous, he pressed: "You see now how dangerous it is for the magic to be in Ziyad's possession. Let me steal it back."

The marid looked at him, thoughtful. "You say that, but you are not doing this for us. You are doing it for Loulie."

Mazen flinched. He supposed there was little point denying it when she had seen through him so easily. He nodded.

He feared she would refuse him outright, but the marid surprised him by *laughing*. "I knew it! Nabila did not think you had a spine, but I knew you would put up a fight for Loulie." She gently peeled his hand off her arm. "Fine. It would be in everyone's best interest to take it back. I can get you to Ziyad's ship, but you must find your way back. Can you do that?"

Mazen did not have a plan. But did that matter when so many of their plans had gone awry anyway? He didn't have the time to falter now. He nodded. "I'll find a way."

Duha seemed pleased by his moxie. With a smile, she gestured him toward one of the boats docked at the pier. Mazen followed after setting the torch aside, stepping into the skiff as Duha ducked beneath the water. He had just leaned over to search for her when the boat lurched forward, nearly sending him overboard.

His heart beat in his throat as he held tightly to the edges of the skiff. By all appearances, the boat was moving by itself. Only—

The surface of the water bubbled with Duha's laughter. When she spoke, her voice echoed in Mazen's head. *Hold on, storyteller.*

Mazen could do little else as the boat sped across the churning waters.

34

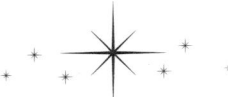

MAZEN

The waves had grown even more unruly by the time he and Duha approached the queen's fleet, the water's surface made choppy by Nabila's magic. It was not a true storm, not like the one Mazen had witnessed in Dhahab, but Nabila was still a force to be reckoned with, using the wind to keep her afloat as she tore through the ships with her magic.

All the while, the armada pressed forward.

Rather than navigating through the chaos, Duha circled the battle from the outskirts. In the growing darkness, their boat was little more than a smudge, difficult to spot. Mazen was comforted until he remembered it was not just the ships he had to worry about, but the water.

At first, he thought it was Nabila's wind making the waves turbulent. But then, from a distance, he saw the water rise—and rise and rise—stretching into a long, twisting shape that loomed above the ships. Mazen did not understand what he was seeing until the thing turned and he perceived liquid scales, a muzzle, and *eyes*.

With a roar, the water serpent crashed back into the water, shaking the ships in the vicinity. Mazen held tight to the skiff as it jumped on the waves. His whole body trembled as he glanced behind him. "What was *that*?"

Duha's response was a sigh in his mind. *That is my brother.*

It took a moment for Mazen to recall what Loulie had said about Duha's family. "That..." He shot a nervous look across the water. "*That* is Ziyad's magic?"

Ziyad had told him that he could communicate and travel through the water, but he had said nothing about shaping it into such monstrous forms.

My brother favors trickery over brute strength, Duha said. *We have always been different that way. He fights with intellect rather than instinct; it is why he avoids his true form.*

Had Mazen the time, he would have asked Duha what she meant by *true form,* but they were fast approaching Ziyad's ship. They had nearly reached the vessel when the water beneath them shuddered. Feet away, the serpent had emerged from the depths, disturbing the surface.

Before Mazen could react, the skiff was in the air. His scream caught in his throat as he crashed through the waves.

By the time he had managed to kick back to the surface, the skiff lay in pieces around him. Thankfully, he was close enough to Ziyad's ship to latch on to the nets thrown over the hull, but when he frantically searched the water for Duha, she was gone.

Where she had been, a gigantic shadow was beginning to spread beneath the waves. Mazen stared in terror at the layers of scales emerging beneath his feet. It was all he could do to cling to the nets as the shadow shot away, rocking the ship.

Mazen stared after it. *Duha?*

Was this the other form the marid had spoken of? Mazen could only imagine how massive her body must be beneath the water. He shuddered as he turned his attention to climbing. The nets were rough, chafing his fingers, and his feet were slippery against the wood. By the time he had made it onto the deck, the ropes had torn lacerations into his palms.

Mazen ignored the cuts as he grabbed for his shadow. The few sailors who might have noticed him were on the other side of the deck, pointing in alarm at Duha's fleeing shadow. Mazen searched

the ship for a familiar coat but saw nothing. If the serpent was far-
ther out, then perhaps Ziyad was controlling it from another ship.
That meant now was Mazen's best chance to recover the compass.
He only hoped Ziyad had not taken it with him.

Muttering a prayer under his breath, Mazen inched his way
across the deck and into the belly of the ship. At first, he was greeted
by an empty corridor. But his relief was short lived, vanishing when
he reached the end of the hall and heard approaching footsteps.

Mazen pressed himself into a wall just as a soldier rounded the
corridor. Even beneath his shadow, he felt exposed as the jinn passed
him with an ashfire-lit lantern.

There is nothing to see here, Mazen thought desperately. *Keep moving. Keep moving.*

But it seemed his luck had finally run out. The soldier had
stopped in front of him and was turning in a slow circle. It took
Mazen a moment to piece together what he was looking at: Footprints. *Wet* footprints.

Mazen wanted to kick himself. The shadow may have hidden
him from view, but he had not accounted for his wet clothing and
shoes, which even now were dripping onto the wood.

He held his breath as the jinn glanced at the shadows on the
walls. Mazen's own attention snagged on the fire casting those
shadows—the ashfire in the jinn's lantern.

"Azhar." The firebird's name was nothing but a faint whisper on
his lips.

And yet the creature still came. One moment the ashfire in
the lantern flickered weakly. The next, it had shaped itself into the
firebird, which announced its presence with a shriek. The soldier
whirled, holding up the lantern as he tried to locate the disturbance.

When he saw the firebird staring at him from inside the glass, he
panicked and threw the lantern to the ground. Mazen lingered just
long enough to be certain Azhar had already disappeared before he
edged away. He kept his back pressed to the wall until he felt a door
behind him. A few turns of the knob, and he was inside the room.

Mazen closed the door softly behind him. He glanced around

the room, taking in the maps and the mirrors on the walls—the many, *many* mirrors—all missing his invisible reflection. When he reached forward to touch one of them, his fingers came away wet.

Not a normal mirror, he thought. *This is Ziyad's magic.*

Which meant this had to be the captain's cabin. But what was the marid using all these mirrors for? Was he communicating with the other ships? With his queen?

Mazen glanced at the single ashfire-lit lantern on the desk. "Azhar?" he whispered.

The firebird popped into existence with a soft chirrup. When it peered quizzically around the room, Mazen realized it could not see him beneath his shadow. The moment he threw the magic off his shoulders, it hopped excitedly on its perch.

He leaned forward to unlatch the lantern door. "Help me look for the compass?"

The firebird flitted to his shoulder, where it could better illuminate his surroundings.

Mazen managed a weak smile. "Shukran."

Azhar chirped its pleasure.

With the magic bird on his shoulder, it was easier for Mazen to examine his surroundings. He checked the desk and then the shelves, rifling through an assortment of sailing tools. His attention paused on an object that glittered in the light. Not the compass, but a rubied chain. With a start, he remembered the relic the queen had stolen off the zaeem of Kharjem's corpse. This was definitely his magic. After some consideration, he decided to take it with him.

The bird shuffled restlessly on Mazen's shoulder as he browsed until...

There.

Loulie's compass was on the bottommost shelf. Cracked and plain though it was, Mazen would never mistake it. Relief surged through him as he tucked it away. But the respite was brief, lasting only as long as it took for him to hear the footsteps in the corridor. Panicked, Mazen reached for his shadow, but it was too late. The door burst open before he could don the magic.

Mazen blinked, dazed, at the figure in the doorway. *"Rijah?"*

Rijah was just as shocked to see him as he was to see them. "Human?" They quickly shut the door behind them. "What are you doing here? I was told you were on Nabila's island!"

"I . . ." Mazen paused to take in their sudden appearance. From a distance, he might have mistaken Rijah for one of the queen's soldiers in their crimson uniform. Up close, he could never have missed their eyes. Much to his relief, the ifrit appeared unscathed.

When Rijah hissed impatiently, Mazen gestured helplessly at the shelves. "I was looking for Loulie's compass. What are *you* doing here?"

"I am here to rescue you."

Mazen stared at them. Al-Malath was about to be invaded, he was in *danger* on an enemy ship, and the ifrit was spontaneously here, claiming to save him? He stepped back, overwhelmed. "I don't understand. The last time I saw you, the wazir used your lamp to . . ."

To hurt you.

Rijah's expression soured. "After you left, the queen discovered one of the zuama'a was involved in Nabila's scheme. She questioned me afterward, and the two of us reached an agreement. Neither of us wants to see the cities sink; I told her I would bring you both back to help keep them safe. That I would rescue you from Nabila."

So in the end, even Rijah had struck a deal. What would Loulie say if she were here? Would she want to go back to Dhahab now, when she had already agreed to help Nabila?

Rijah's eyes narrowed at his hesitation. "What has Nabila said to you? You felt the earthquake in Dhahab, and now the wind is weakened! I would have thought you *wanted* to be rescued from this."

"What if Nabila is right and breaking the bindings is the only way to save this place?"

Rijah's eyes flashed with alarm. "Do you remember what I said in the archive? Nabila has always been selfish—she is playing mind games with you."

Mazen did not know what to believe when it seemed *everyone* was playing that game with them. But the situation was different now. Loulie was here; Mazen would not leave her.

"Rijah." He swallowed. "Please, trust me?"

The ifrit seemed taken aback by his pleading. Their eyes wandered, for the first time, to Azhar. "I had wondered what that soldier was blathering about. But that bird—is it the same one you summoned in the diwan? Is it Nabila's bird?"

"I too am most curious."

Mazen jumped at the sound of a new voice behind him. He turned, heart in his throat, and was shocked to see Ziyad.

At first, he did not understand how the marid had snuck up on him. But then he realized Ziyad was watching him from *inside* one of the mirrors, his smiling visage so tangible it looked as if he were in the room with them.

In his hands, he held Rijah's lamp.

"Yousef." Ziyad looked amused to see him there. "I had heard a bird made of fire was running amok on my ship. It sounded familiar." His eyes landed on Azhar. "Is this creature tied to the ashfire? A binding? Her Majesty is most curious..." He reached out a hand.

Mazen stared in horror as Ziyad's scaled fingers emerged from the mirror's surface.

Azhar shot off his shoulder with a cry. Mazen yanked the cabin door open, but Ziyad's cold hand came down on his shoulder before he could escape after the bird.

The marid stepped out of the mirror and into the room. "I admit I am surprised to see you alive. Did my sister heal you?"

Mazen struggled against Ziyad's grip. "How are you here? I saw your serpent—"

"And now I am here, dealing with *your* disturbance. Duha can wait." Ziyad glanced at Rijah, who stood frozen in the doorway. "Well? Do you plan on capturing the human, or..." He held up the lamp. "Will I have to punish you for your disobedience?"

Rijah's eyes darted uncertainly between Mazen and the lamp. In that beat of hesitation, Mazen acted, shoving himself into Ziyad with enough force to make the marid stumble. Mazen slid out of his grip, peeled his shadow off the wall, and threw it over his head.

Ziyad's eyes went wide as he vanished. "What kind of magic—"

This time, Ziyad did not see the assault coming. When Mazen pushed him again, the marid lost his grip on the lamp. The moment it clattered to the floor, Mazen swept it into his hands and rushed past a still-stunned Rijah into the corridor. Smoke coated the air, but Azhar was nowhere to be seen.

When the bird didn't respond to its name, Mazen rushed outside. On deck, he was greeted by the terrible sight of the firebird clutched in one of the soldiers' hands. The fire was burning the jinn, but he held tight even as it scorched his skin. Mazen did not understand why Azhar had not disappeared. Was the bird incapable of evanescing when it was trapped?

His mind reeled. What could he do? If he could not call the firebird back, then . . .

His eyes fell on the lamp.

A prison, his father had always called it. A prison containing the mightiest of jinn.

But the lamp was more than that. In the story of Amir and the lamp, it had been not just a trap, but a vessel. Amir had confined fire, wind, and even stars in it.

Perhaps in the wrong hands the lamp was a prison. But Mazen could be better than his father. Better than his brother. Remembering the words Amir had spoken in the tale—words echoed by his own brother—Mazen held up the lamp.

"Azhar!" His voice carried across the deck. Both bird and jinn froze when they saw him. Mazen could have sworn the bird's hollow-eyed gaze snapped up to meet his as he said, "You are bound to me, and you will serve me."

He felt the lamp burn beneath his fingers, reacting to the blood on his hands. Felt the soft hum of a heartbeat that may have been Rijah's. One moment the firebird was trapped in the jinn's hands. The next, it had vanished.

Two things happened then.

The first: the binding on the lamp flashed a vivid blue as the vessel warmed in his hands.

The second: the ashfire the bird had streaked across the ship suddenly went out. And it was not just the fire on the ship. When Mazen glanced out across the water, he could see *all* the distant specks of ashfire vanishing. The fire on the boats, the island—gone.

Mazen had not just trapped the firebird. He had trapped the *ashfire* it was made of.

The world went pitch black.

35

LOULIE

Loulie was almost out of the forest when the sky went black.

The curfew darkness fell abruptly, taking her senses with it. Suddenly, she could no longer feel the ground beneath her feet. She could not tell whether she was breathing and if her body had stopped moving. The darkness pressed down on her, crushing—

And then her dagger flared with ashfire. Loulie's vision swam as she surveyed the forest in its meager light. It took her a moment to realize that though the blade was aflame, the ashfire around the island was gone, leaving it at the mercy of the sudden darkness.

A sudden chill descended on her. The unnatural darkness wavered and rippled like water, smudging her surroundings into twisting shades of muted gray. It was not just Loulie's sight that felt subdued, but her hearing. Even the usual birdsong was absent, the trees eerily silent.

Loulie turned in place, staring around her in horror. *Is this... my fault?*

The last time she had broken a binding, she had caused an earthquake. This time, she assumed the binding had taken the wind with it. Had it extinguished the ashfire too?

Loulie steeled herself as she continued through the forest. As she navigated the shifting pathways, she reflected that she had never missed her compass so much. The relic would have guided her in this unnatural dark. Her eyes flicked to the flaming dagger, but though it had ignited with fire, she could not sense Qadir's presence. Had he lit the weapon himself, or had the enchantment reacted automatically to the darkness?

Focus, she chided herself. She could figure out what to do about the vanished ashfire once they had moved the island. Right now, she had to make sure they escaped the armada.

Still, even with the goal in mind, it was difficult to concentrate. Unable to hear both the sounds of the forest and her own footsteps, Loulie suddenly felt unmoored. She did not know how long she had been walking when a sound broke the darkness. The sharp crack of a branch.

Loulie spun, dagger raised. She saw a figure emerging from the trees. In the darkness, his body was distorted, his face oddly blurry and shadowed. But still, there was no mistaking his crimson uniform. He was one of the queen's soldiers.

If he was already here on the island, then . . .

Loulie's grip tightened on the dagger. *I was too slow.*

There was a moment when she and the jinn stood blinking at each other with shock. And then his expression cleared.

Panic muddied Loulie's mind as he came at her with his blade. She dodged. It was a sluggish motion, but thankfully, the soldier's movements were just as confused as hers under the influence of the magic. When his blade whistled past her shoulder, Loulie aimed a strike at his head. Her slash went high, arcing into the tree branch above him instead.

The impact loosened a flurry of leaves, and Loulie backed away as the jinn swatted ineffectually at the air. She was planning her next move when another figure crashed through the trees behind her. And then there came a fourth, a fifth.

She froze, horrified, at the sight of the villagers.

When Loulie saw the soldiers they were fleeing from, she quickly shifted targets, lunging at the nearest pursuer. The movement was panicked, unfocused, and she was surprised when the jinn crumpled so easily beneath the weight of her blade.

Loulie was still recovering from the attack when a scream cut through the forest. The sound made her blood run cold. Why did it sound *familiar*?

She looked up just in time to see another shadow dart into the clearing. Loulie recognized his golden eyes, round with fear.

Mazen?

When a soldier came crashing through the trees after him, Loulie threw herself at the jinn unthinkingly. The two of them tumbled to the ground in a heap. The jinn was dazed but had managed to keep his grip on his blade. With a strangled scream, he drove the silver edge through Loulie's arm, tearing her skin above the elbow.

Pain shot through her body in an agonizing current. Loulie was vaguely aware of her own scream as she rammed an elbow into the jinn's face. This time, he went down, and Loulie had enough time to pin him beneath her and brace the knife above his heart. Blood seeped down her arm as she struggled to steady her trembling hands.

But just as she was about to plunge the knife into his chest, she paused. The soldier was . . . crying? She blinked, startled. The jinn's shadowy visage wavered, difficult to focus on, but Loulie did not miss the tear tracks on his cheeks. And his voice—

It was a child's voice.

She lowered the dagger to his face, throwing off the shadows that had masked his features. She stared, aghast, at the fisherman's son, Hatem.

This was no soldier. It was one of the villagers wrapped in illusion, and she had nearly killed him.

Loulie rolled off him with a gasp. Now she understood why the soldiers' movements had been so slow. They were not warriors at all, but villagers pitted against each other. The darkness had twisted their minds just as it had twisted Loulie's, making them see each other as enemies.

Loulie pressed a hand to her wound as she searched for Mazen. Had he ever been here, or had his appearance also been a mirage?

She turned back to Hatem, who was still staring at her with fear.

It was only when Loulie waved the dagger in his face that his gaze cleared. Once she was certain he was lucid, she moved on to the next jinn. With her dagger, she cut through their shared nightmare, illuminating the fogginess in the villagers' eyes until they could all see clearly.

It was not lost on her that without the ashfire, the darkness might have killed her. Hayat had told her jinn lost their senses in it—now Loulie understood what she meant.

Cursed magic.

She let her anger surge through her, let it burn away the clouds in her head as she gathered the villagers around her. Some of them, she could see, bore injuries. But no one had been fatally wounded, and the jinn at least had the magic to heal their injuries.

Short of any jinn magic herself, Loulie tore off a piece of her scarf and used it to stanch her wound. She tried not to flinch as blood seeped through the fabric. At least the pain from the injury kept her clearheaded.

She glanced back at the huddled crowd. It was a small group, no more than a dozen jinn. Loulie searched but did not see Mazen among them. Still, she could not stop herself from asking, "Have any of you seen Yousef?"

The villagers exchanged baffled looks. The youngest of them, Zabiba, stepped forward and shook her head. "We have not seen him in the forest, ya sayyida."

Loulie was disquieted. If Mazen was not here, then where *was* he? There was no time to search, not when there was still the very real possibility Ziyad's force would make it onto the island. Mazen was remarkably tenacious; Loulie had to trust that he had kept himself safe.

Moving as quickly as she could under the influence of the twisting darkness, Loulie guided the jinn toward the fortress. By the time they arrived at the gate, she felt fatigued. The cloth around her arm was drenched with gore, and the pain had built into a sharp agony in her veins. Even the adrenaline that had kept her going had been replaced with a numbing exhaustion.

In the end, only Hatem lingered outside the gate. He eyed her injury guiltily. "You are hurt because of me. Let me help you?"

Loulie was shocked by the offer. Shocked and . . . grateful. Carefully, she unwrapped the cloth around her elbow, revealing the vicious gash on her skin. When Hatem set his bloodied hands atop the injury, she hissed in pain. The surge of magic prickled like a needle beneath her skin, but the blood did its work. When Hatem pulled his hands away, her injury was sealed.

The jinn hurriedly shoved his torn hands in his pockets, looking abashed. "Do not tell my father? He would chide me for the blood loss."

Loulie nodded. She still felt weak, but at least now she could focus beyond her pain. "It will be our secret." She paused, then added, "Shukran."

The jinn tilted his head with a smile. "May the gods guide your path, ya sayyida."

It was the last thing he said before he entered the fortress and pulled the gate shut behind him. Alone in the dark, Loulie glanced at her sealed injury. Other than Qadir, no jinn had ever willingly healed her. She pressed a palm to the wound in wonderment.

A stolen object can be recovered. A stolen life cannot.

With one last glance at the enshrouded building, Loulie darted back into the dark.

36

MAZEN

Darkness swept across Mazen's vision. It was total, obliterating. In that absence of light, he lost not just his surroundings, but himself. He walked, or at least he tried to, but he could not perceive the weight of his own footfalls. There was no sky, no deck. Even Mazen's thoughts had abruptly faded, leaving no space in his mind for anything but terror.

But then: light.

He blinked, vision hazy, until he was able to make out a shape in the darkness. A figure, limned impossibly in ashfire. Rijah had ascended to the deck of the ship, their body outlined in glowing blue light. A startled sound left their lips as they gazed down at their burning hands. Mazen stared, uncomprehending. How was it possible for Rijah to use a magic that harmed other jinn? Unless—

The lamp.

He had trapped the ashfire in a vessel that was bound to Rijah, which must have meant it was now tied to the ifrit too. But Mazen's wonder was quickly eclipsed by horror when he remembered it was *his* fault the world had gone dark.

The realization seemed to dawn on Rijah in the same moment. Their eyes—glowing now as they never had before—darted anxiously across the water, but the curfew had swallowed the battlefield entirely, reducing the ships to gray streaks. The sounds of combat were gone too. It was as if the whole world had frozen.

The soldiers on board gazed at the ifrit with a mixture of fear and confusion. Mazen could not blame them. Rijah was, after all, the only source of light on the ship.

And then the screaming began.

The unnatural darkness shuddered with the sound. Mazen's gaze snapped toward the water. He could faintly make out the sounds of ringing metal and the boom of magic. Had the battle resumed?

He stiffened when Rijah whirled on him, burning eyes narrowed. Remembering their endeavor to capture him, Mazen backed away. "Please, Rijah. I can't leave Loulie behind again."

The soldiers pressed closer. Mazen considered his options. He could throw himself into the water, but what good would it do him if he could not see? Besides that, Ziyad was still somewhere on the ship, which meant the water was just as unsafe.

Rijah approached slowly, as if Mazen were a spooked animal. As they moved, the ashfire hazed around their body, creating a double mirage in the air. "You are the same as always, foolish human. You would follow Loulie al-Nazari anywhere, regardless of the danger."

The soldiers had formed a circle around the two of them, their attention torn between the standoff on deck and the sounds on the water. A nervous silence hung in the air as the ifrit paused before him. Mazen saw a glimmer in their eyes. Not determination, he realized, but *mischief*. In one swift motion, they threw out their hand, coating the area in ashfire.

The soldiers scattered with the magic, quickly turning their weapons on Rijah. The ifrit smirked. "Fine," they said. "For the gift of the ashfire, I choose to trust you."

I choose to trust you.

The declaration stunned Mazen. He gaped as the ifrit shifted to offense, transforming into a broad-shouldered jinn who could easily crack a skull with their hands. Wisely, many of the soldiers fled their assault. Unfortunately for Mazen, that meant *he* was the easiest target.

A soldier lunged at him with a blade. The edge just barely missed Mazen's neck as he staggered back—into another body. The second jinn shoved him, hard enough to send him toppling to the ground. The lamp fell from his hands, along with the zaeem of Kharjem's ruby.

Mazen scrambled toward the magics, managing to snatch them off the deck as another soldier approached. But before he could regain his footing, the jinn kicked him hard in the stomach, knocking the breath from his lungs and making him collapse.

Mazen rolled onto his back just in time to see the soldier raise his blade. One moment Mazen's attacker was about to run him through. The next, the soldier was . . . frozen, expression suddenly gone slack.

Terror held Mazen in place as he waited for the strike to come, but the jinn did not move. He had the look of a sleepwalker, swaying unsteadily on his feet as he stared at Mazen with vacant eyes. Cautiously, Mazen rose to his feet. The jinn's eyes followed him as he moved.

No, Mazen thought with a start. *He's not looking at* me.

He was staring at the ruby in Mazen's hands. At some point, the gemstone had begun to glow. When Mazen lifted the chain, the soldier's blank gaze followed it as if it were a target. Mazen backed away before the spell broke. As he fled, he glanced at the ruby. He'd stolen it from Ziyad's cabin knowing nothing of its magic, but now he could not help but wonder . . .

When another soldier came at him, Mazen raised the glimmering ruby in front of him as if it were a shield. Again, the jinn froze, captivated by the sight. When Mazen swung the ruby left and right, the soldier's eyes tracked its motion through the air like a pendulum.

A hypnotizing relic?

It was, he soon found out, a very temporary magic, more a distracting flash of light than a full compulsion. But a distraction was all Mazen needed. While the soldier blinked in confusion, Mazen stole his shadow off the ground and used it to conceal himself. It was none too soon, for Ziyad had finally made it onto the deck. The moment the marid saw the fiery destruction Rijah had wrought, he stopped, dazedly taking in the sight of his burning ship.

He snarled when he spotted the ifrit in the chaos. "I told my queen you were not to be trusted. Hope has made a fool of her one too many times."

The marid cut a hand through the air. The ship shuddered with the motion, and Mazen had to steady himself against the rails to keep from losing his balance. His gaze caught on the water, which had begun to rise in front of him in the form of a serpent.

Ziyad gestured across the darkened waters. "You said you were going to save this realm, but do you think any of the jinn will *thank you* for extinguishing the ashfire?"

Rijah said nothing. Their glowering attention was fixed on the watery creature looming above them. The serpent was massive; it could have easily wrapped itself around the boum if Ziyad commanded.

The soldiers had already scattered, but Rijah did not cower. Their eyes flashed with challenge as they said, "You think you can defeat *me*?"

Abruptly, the ifrit pivoted away from the serpent to rush the marid. Midmotion, their body blurred into the shape of a large black panther. But they were too slow.

With a flick of his wrist, Ziyad sent the serpent crashing down onto the deck. The creature's head hit the surface like an anvil, shattering the wood beneath Mazen's feet. He quickly staggered away.

At first, it appeared the ifrit had vanished—and then Mazen saw the shadow struggling in the confines of the serpent's body and realized the serpent had swallowed Rijah whole.

Ziyad approached with a grimace. In his hands he held one of his glimmering knives. "You interrupted a good fight, you know. I was moments away from finally besting my sister."

Rijah did not respond. Could not respond. They were struggling in the serpent's body. *Drowning* in it.

Mazen reached for the lamp. He had told Loulie he would not throw himself in front of a blade again—but perhaps he did not need to. He set a hand on the lamp and whispered, "Azhar!"

The lamp glowed beneath his touch. This time, when the firebird surged forth from the ashfire burning on deck, it was as big as it had been in the queen's diwan. Big enough to cut a fiery scythe through the serpent's neck, severing it from its body.

Ziyad fell back with a curse as Rijah staggered out of the water. Mazen rushed toward them, heedless of the fire. He was halfway across the ship when an ominous boom rattled the vessel, sending him headfirst into the mast.

The force of the impact made stars dance across his vision. He weakly grabbed for the mast as the ship slanted.

The tremor came again. It could not be the water serpent, which had melted on deck, and Mazen could tell from the confusion on Ziyad's face that it was not being caused by *his* magic.

"Sayyidi!" One of the sailors was pointing at the water. "It is Nabila's first mate—"

This time, there was a terrible creak as the thing in the water crashed headfirst into the ship's hull. Mazen held tight to the mast as boxes and containers went sliding across the wood.

When the fourth blow came, Duha punched a *hole* through the ship. Murky scales flashed across Mazen's vision as the marid sprang from the water in the form of a massive fish, tearing into the deck. Mazen saw fathomless black eyes, a rictus of teeth—and then he was free-falling, the floor slanted so drastically it had become a wall behind him.

Ziyad's ship was capsizing.

Mazen did not have enough air in his lungs to scream. He scrambled for something to hold on to—anything—but the deck was slippery beneath his palms. He felt himself sliding, slipping, until his hands once again found the mast. He clung to the beam for dear life.

"Duha!" Ziyad had climbed over the rails and was balancing on the upturned prow of the ship. His black eyes shone with malice. "What kind of depraved victory is *this*?"

Mazen's arms trembled as he glanced beneath him.

He immediately regretted it.

There was no water under him. Instead, Mazen saw a ring of sharp teeth. An open mouth, soundlessly swallowing the sailors that fell overboard. Mazen's mind clouded with terror. He was vaguely aware that he was hyperventilating, that his vision was dimming with his panic.

If this was what Duha meant by fighting with instinct, then he doubted she recognized him in that form. To her, everyone on the ship was prey.

Which meant if Mazen fell, he would die.

Mazen's arms were beginning to weaken. His palms slid on the beam, chafed and bloody. Somewhere above him, the firebird restlessly circled, but there was nothing it could do to save him.

"HUMAN!" A large shadow streaked through the air beneath Mazen's feet, shooting above the marid's open mouth. He recognized Rijah's voice. *"WHAT ARE YOU WAITING FOR? JUMP!"*

Mazen did not jump so much as faint, falling through the air with a soundless scream. He landed, hard, on Rijah's feathered back. The ifrit gave him no time to recover. With a sweep of their wing, they shot away from the sinking ship, leaving Mazen scrambling to hold on.

Azhar shot after them. In the firelight cast by the bird, Mazen saw the two marid. One a gigantic monster in the water, the other standing poised atop the bow with an uncanny grace. Mazen spotted a gleam of silver in Ziyad's hands. He had acquired a spear and was now aiming it at one of Duha's eyes.

Mazen grasped Rijah's feathers. "Rijah, take us back."

"HAVE YOU LOST YOUR MIND? LET THE MARID DESTROY EACH OTHER."

"One of those marid is a friend." Mazen patted frantically at his pockets until he found what he was looking for. His fingers closed around the chain. "Please. I have an idea."

With an agitated click of their beak, the ifrit obeyed, swerving back toward the capsizing boum. Mazen cupped his hands around his mouth and yelled Ziyad's name. The captain paused, gaze darting past the sinking wreckage to land on him. Mazen pulled the zaeem of Kharjem's relic from his pocket and held it up in the air.

The moment Ziyad spotted the swaying ruby, he froze.

That split second was all Duha needed. With a decisive snap of her jaws, she tore the ship in half. Mazen spotted Ziyad falling amidst the shattered wood, but he did not linger to witness his fate. He had done what he could for Duha. Now they just had to make it back to the island before it disappeared.

As the three of them cut across the dark sky, Mazen reached into his pocket to check for Loulie's compass. His fingers curled protectively over the relic as they flew.

I'm coming, Loulie.

37

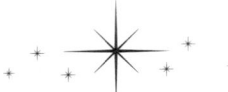

LOULIE

In the curfew darkness, it took Loulie longer than anticipated to find the cove where the zaeem resided. Wandering through the soundless dark, she had no way of knowing how much time had passed and what was happening out on the water. But she could not think about the armada now; it had taken all her concentration to simply focus past the hallucinations.

Now she followed the thin, sandy pathway around the water to the cove Duha had shown her. She walked until she came to the cave where she had seen the crab's eyes. As she stepped inside, a strange weight fell on her shoulders. Her neck prickled at the feeling of being watched. That sensation, more than anything else, was how she knew she had found the right place.

The dark shifted as she entered, peeling away to a sudden brightness. Loulie squinted as she tried to comprehend what she was seeing. It was only when she raised Qadir's dagger that she realized there was sea glass on the cavern walls reflecting the ashfire at her from various angles. The sight was as eerie as it was enchanting, the ashfire so vivid it nearly burned her eyes.

Loulie brushed off her apprehension as she wandered into the cave. The deeper she went, the more overbearing the zaeem's presence became. Soon, she could feel his breathing beneath her feet, that same steady rumble she had felt on the beach before, only magnified.

She spoke quietly into the darkness: "Can you hear me, sayyidi?"

A soft buzz was the only response. Loulie felt it pushing against...her mind? It was less a physical breeze than a feeling. She had the strange impression the crab was sighing at her.

When he said nothing else, she tried speaking her request aloud. "Mighty zaeem, I need you to move the island." Her voice echoed hollowly in the empty cave. Loulie waited, but if the giant crab heard her, he gave no indication.

She recalled what Duha had said about speaking to the creature with her mind and closed her eyes, concentrating until she could call forth an image of the island. She showed the giant crab a vision of Nabila shooting across the waves toward the armada. Showed him the curfew darkness pitting the island's inhabitants against one another. And then she showed him her request: the island, moving away from Ziyad's force.

The zaeem's response bled slowly into Loulie's mind. Though the vision possessed a faded quality, the details were sharp enough that she could tell she was watching a memory. She was still in the cave, but the light was different, and the ground was stained with what looked like silver blood. Duha leaned heavily against one of the walls. From the way she was standing, Loulie suspected she was supporting an injury.

"Please." The memory of Duha slumped against the wall with a shudder. "I beg of you, sayyidi: sanctuary for protection. She has lost her entire tribe—I am all that remains." Her eyes grew foggy. She must have been "seeing" the crab's reply the same way Loulie was now.

Duha laughed. It was a weak, humorless sound. "If it is a bargain you want, then it is a bargain you shall have. Carry Nabila's life for me, and I will carry yours."

The memory was so tangible, so *real*, that Loulie could not help but reach out to the marid. She had never witnessed an expression of such raw anguish on her face. But the memory was just that: a memory. When Loulie tried to touch Duha, the image wavered like smoke, and Loulie's hand passed right through her.

The next time she blinked, she was alone. But now she understood what the creature wanted. It was asking her for a bargain. Well, Loulie was experienced with such deals. The trick was to oversell your offer, to make it not just appealing, but a necessity.

She closed her eyes and recalled one of her own memories. In it, she was standing on the edge of Rasul al-Jasheen's ship, arms stretched to catch a breeze in her sleeves. She remembered the gentle sway of the ship beneath her feet and the dark, unfathomable depths of the ocean—the *real* ocean. What lay in those depths, no one knew.

A creature like the zaeem would fit right in.

Loulie conveyed that—or she hoped she did—in that vision.

This time, the zaeem's response was immediate. Loulie stumbled as the ground rumbled beneath her. The motion seemed to shake the darkness itself. Within it, the zaeem's attention pressed on her, waiting, *wanting*. So Loulie put a voice to her resolve.

"Zaeem of al-Malath," she said. "Move this island and I will give you the ocean."

Loulie felt a strange hitch in her chest when she uttered that promise. A hook, yanking her heart up into her throat. She'd had just enough time to marvel that she had spoken to a *giant crab* when the walls shuddered. The sea glass flashed around her, blue with the firelight.

Before Loulie could piece together what was happening, the chamber was *falling*. She screamed—or tried to—but when she crashed to her knees, she was in . . . water?

A cold murkiness enveloped her sight as she struggled, reaching desperately toward the surface of the water as it closed over her head. But there was nowhere for her to go.

The island of al-Malath sank, and Loulie sank with it.

38

AISHA

Aisha was beginning to resent that the underground was the solution to all her problems. After the last quake, she was not keen on venturing back into Madinne's subterranean tunnels. But given the Bowels' notorious security, this was her best choice. It would not get her to the prison where Qadir was being kept, but it *would* see her past the unbreachable entrance patrols.

She turned her plan over in her mind as she followed Hakim through the tunnels. He strode ahead of her, with nothing but a dim lamp to light the way. She called to his back, "How much longer, mapmaker?"

He was focused on his map and did not so much as glance at her. "Not long."

Aisha had no choice but to abide the ensuing silence. She had noticed the weight of it was different here, the hollowness of the walls making her voice echo eerily. Even the mutterings of the dead reverberated strangely in this place.

The dead do not speak, she'd once reassured herself. It had been easier to kill a man when she knew his corpse could not hold a grudge. But the Resurrectionist's power had made that impossible. Now death was an ever-encroaching presence—a literal, immortal ifrit who was even now rifling through her thoughts as easily as if they were tomes on a shelf.

Death is *inescapable*, the Resurrectionist chided. *Better to command it than fall prey to it.*

As frustrating as it was to admit it, the ifrit was right. Aisha would not have made it this far without her magic—would not be *alive* without it. The thought sent a wave of disgust through her. She had become an abomination, a human reliant on twisted, godsforsaken magic. If she had known before she set off on this quest that this was what she would become, then . . .

"Bint Louas?"

Hakim had stopped at a wall. "This is our best entry point into the Bowels. It will not take you into the cells themselves, but it should get you close."

Aisha regarded the rock with skepticism. As far as she could tell, nothing differentiated this wall from the rest. But then, *she* could see nothing beyond the surface.

"What happens now?" she asked.

Silence. At first, she thought Hakim was ignoring her, but then she noticed the furrow between his brows and the sweat beading his forehead. "The magic is normally passive." His voice was thin, pinched like his expression. "I do not know how to shape it to my command."

Aisha's already frayed patience thinned. "I did not come all this way for you to fail."

The mapmaker had no retort. A muscle feathered in his cheek as he stared at the wall, but he was otherwise motionless. Still, the ring did not glow. The longer Aisha watched him, the more frustrated she became. Standing here doing nothing would drive her mad.

Then why not help him? the Resurrectionist said. *You wield magic as well as swords.*

Aisha's knee-jerk reaction was to object; she did not manipulate the ifrit's cursed magic so much as succumb to it. But then she thought of the tethers that connected her to the dead, the ones she herself could control.

She turned to Hakim and tried a question. "What shape does your magic normally take?"

"It is a map, unfurling behind my eyes."

Aisha remembered the phrase inscribed on his ring: *Everything I have seen once, I know in perpetuity.* The words made something click in her mind. "You see what exists then," she said. "But what if instead of drawing what you see in your mind, you alter the course of the lines?" She pointed at the rock wall. "Imagine that as an outline to be erased."

Hakim frowned at her. "That...is not how cartography works, bint Louas."

She said nothing, only glared at him until he returned his steely gaze to the wall. Aisha watched in silence as he touched his fingers to his ring. Long minutes passed before the relic began to glow and the phrase inscribed upon its surface became visible. It was the only warning the magic gave before the wall crumbled *inward.*

Aisha startled. It was like watching an explosion in reverse, the sediment falling into itself rather than out. It happened so fast she did not even have time to step away from the radius of the blast until it had already happened.

Afterward, Hakim stared wide-eyed at the chasm in the wall. "*I* did that?"

"The magic did that." Aisha stepped forward to pat at the walls of the newly formed tunnel, testing its stability.

She could feel Hakim watching her back. "You would make an awful teacher," he said, but she knew him well enough now to read the mirth in his voice.

"Experience is the best teacher. I have no interest in teaching anyone anything." It was a waste of her time to hold others' hands when she needed both of hers to swing a blade. But...

She cast a glance at him over her shoulder. "I would have loved to see the look on Rasul al-Jasheen's face when you performed your so-called *miracle.*"

Though Hakim's lips did not so much as twitch, his eyes betrayed his smile. "It would have been gratifying, I'm sure." The softness on his face faded when he noticed Aisha peering through the hole. "Are you certain you want me to wait here for you? I can help."

With his magic, perhaps he could, but there would be no time for staring at walls once they breached the prison. It would be stealth, not magic, that saw Aisha through this endeavor. The last thing she needed was to free one man and doom the other.

She shook her head. "Stay here. And if you hear someone, close the hole."

Aisha did not want to imagine what would happen to her if her only escape route was blocked, but she had lived her whole life with the certainty that she could survive any situation, no matter how dire. If she had survived death, then she could survive this.

Hakim consented with a reluctant nod. "May the gods guide you, bint Louas."

Aisha smiled wryly to herself. Gods, ifrit, they were all the same to her.

The Resurrectionist smiled in her mind. *Together, then.*

They began their climb.

—⚏—

Aisha's first impression of the Bowels was its smell. It was a rank scent, a mingling of excrement and blood and rot that immediately clogged her throat. But she had smelled death before and could handle the onslaught. The second thing she noticed was the cold. The air was *freezing*, the concrete so frigid beneath her hands she half expected her fingers to come away with frost. But it was the third revelation that alarmed her most.

At first, she could not place the sensation. It was like an itch in the back of her mind, but the feeling grew more tenacious as she moved through the tunnels. It pressed on her limbs until it was no longer an itch but a physical *weight*. It was only when she tried to reach for the ifrit's magic that she understood what was happening. The impressions that defined her magic—the tethers, the voices—had all faded to a disturbingly dull throb in the back of her mind.

Ifrit? She reached for the Resurrectionist. *What's happening?*

The ifrit's response was alarmingly weak. *The iron, bint Louas.*

Aisha recalled Rasul's warnings about the prisons being coated in iron that suppressed magic. She had expected that iron to be contained to the cells, but now that the Resurrectionist had mentioned it, Aisha could not stop feeling the metal in the walls around her.

She forced herself to focus as she peered beyond the bend into a stairwell. She had studied Hakim's map long enough that she was immediately able to place her location within the prison. The Bowels were made up of various "blocks," each divided into stairwells and rooms. She was currently in the easternmost block, the one closest to the cells. Since Hakim had brought her in from a lower floor, she was close to the guards' room, where they kept the cell keys.

Aisha squinted into the darkness. There would be no way to anticipate where the guards were—she would simply have to dispose of any that came her way and hide the bodies.

No sooner had she thought this than she heard footsteps on the stairs. The sound was oddly muted to her ears. It took her a moment to realize it was her own hearing that was the problem; even her breathing sounded as if it were coming through ears stuffed with cotton.

What kind of iron is this that it can suffocate even my human senses?

Aisha eased herself up the staircase, pausing only when she spotted the guard. She pressed herself against the wall and waited with bated breath for him to descend. When he had drawn close enough to capture her in the halo of light cast by his lantern, she slashed his throat.

It was only afterward, looking at his body, that she realized hiding the corpses would not be so simple. She could only hope it would be a while before anyone noted the man's absence.

After moving the corpse, she continued up the stairs. The weight of the iron pressed on her body as she walked. By now, it had compounded into an unbearable heaviness in her limbs.

Ifrit? When she felt only a feeble stirring, she tried her name. *Amina? Are you there?*

This time, when the ifrit responded, her voice was barely a murmur. *Your mind is distant, thief. Because my magic is not meant for your blood, your body bears the weight of the iron here more heavily.* She paused and then added softly, *Be wary. Our connection grows tenuous.*

Aisha had no time to linger on the warning before she passed from one floor to the next. She heard the two guards talking before she saw them in front of an open door. The fools did not hear her approach, not beneath the sound of their own laughter.

The first guard she ambushed from behind, stabbing a knife through his neck. She shoved the dying body at the second man before he could react, then used the moment of surprise to carve a fatal blow through his heart. Afterward, Aisha dragged the bodies to a more discreet corner of the dim hall. But it was impossible to miss the trails of blood on the floor.

Don't stop. Keep moving.

Aisha ducked into the guards' room and scanned the walls. She found one of their key rings on the far back wall, half hidden behind a tower of crates, then backtracked the way she had come. She made it down two floors before she heard the ring of an alarm.

Shit.

She tore through the tunnels. If the guards had already found the bodies, then it was just a matter of time before they cornered her. She had to free Qadir before that happened.

By the time she had reached the iron doors leading into the cells, the alarm had dulled to a muffled wail in her mind. Her limbs, she noted dully, were trembling with fatigue. Her hands shook as she fumbled through the keys on the ring, searching until she found the one that burned her fingers—the single iron key—and stabbed it into the lock.

Inside, Aisha slammed the doors shut behind her with a grunt. The force of the iron was staggering here, an acute *pain* shooting through her body. Aisha had to balance herself against one of the walls until the ache passed.

Per Rasul's instructions, she found the door with the newly commissioned lock at the end of the hall. Like every other cell door, the surface was large and imposing, and cold beneath her touch. But then Aisha saw the lock. Surprise flared through her at the sight of the familiar mechanism. It was a variation of the lock on the thieves' tower.

Seeing that lock, Aisha had no doubt that this was a trap. Omar had expected her to come here. Had made it *possible* for her to come here. He was playing with her, but Aisha did not know his game. At this point, however, she had no choice but to press forward.

With shaking hands, she worked at the complicated device until it clicked and opened. On the other side of the door was a small room with dirt walls. Most of the floor was taken up by a large hole. Iron bars stretched across it, thick enough it would be impossible for any human—or jinn—to slide through them.

Aisha crouched beside the hole. When she focused beyond the bars, she saw thick iron needles jutting from the walls like crooked teeth—a jinn trap. A wave of nausea rolled through her as she leaned forward to peer at the figure slumped at the bottom. Encased in iron and coated in blood, the man looked like a corpse. But then, when Aisha squinted, she saw that his face was tilted toward her. And she saw that his eyes were *glowing*.

Aisha stared. "Qadir?"

He blinked at her blearily, as if coming out of a trance.

Aisha set her hands on the bars experimentally. She pulled away with a hiss when she felt the burn against her skin. Even had the iron not been an issue, she would not have been strong enough to break these bars. Not even with a blade.

She addressed Qadir again. "Is that you, ifrit? I'm here to save you."

Aisha was certain his eyes widened then, but he did not move. One wrong shift and he would be impaled. She glanced past the needles to his body. She saw shackles around his wrists, his ankles, even his neck. How could she possibly hope to free him?

A memory came to her as she was thinking. She remembered Mazen telling her about a black lizard who had sat on his shoulder in Ghiban, making the fire dance in a lantern.

Suddenly, she had an idea.

"If I throw you these keys, could you climb up yourself?"

With all the iron here it would be a miracle if he could shapeshift, but he was an ifrit, wasn't he? Aisha's magic was a borrowed thing, not meant for her body, but if the ifrit's eyes could still glow, he might have enough magic to free himself so long as he had the keys.

It was difficult to say if the ifrit was nodding at her when he tilted his head. Aisha held the keys above the bars. If this plan failed and Qadir was too weak to climb up the walls in his lizard shape, then . . .

Well, she would be right back where she'd started, wouldn't she?

Still, her stomach dropped when she released the keys. When they landed on a needle above Qadir's head, she cursed but then was shocked into silence when he reached up with his shackled hands to grab them. The iron tore gashes through his arms, but he never made a sound.

Aisha watched as he slowly unlocked his shackles. As time passed, she wondered, Was it luck that the guards had not found her yet, or was this also a part of Omar's trap?

There was no sound more relieving than the final click of Qadir's shackles. But when Aisha peered into the hole, she saw . . . nothing. Where Qadir had been, there was only blood.

At first, she feared the ifrit had somehow spirited himself out of the prison without her. But then she saw movement on the needles—a small black lizard, scrambling up the walls. She offered a palm, but the jinn instead climbed all the way up her arm to her shoulder, where he curled up against her neck with a shudder.

Well, at least I didn't have to lug a corpse out of the cell.

With an effort, Aisha stumbled to her feet. Her exhaustion had worsened while she had been in the cell, the pain building into a pressure that left her feeling feverish. A pang of real terror ran through her as she shakily brushed beads of sweat off her forehead.

This was more than just exhaustion; it felt like her whole body was revolting against her. In a moment of clarity, she remembered something the Resurrectionist had said to her in the desert: *Our deal did not bring you back from the dead; it saved you from it.*

When Aisha had put on the collar, she had been on the verge of dying. She'd assumed the Resurrectionist's magic had healed her, but had the Resurrectionist not also said Aisha's life was no longer just her own? Aisha had not been saved by the relic; her life was *bound* to its magic.

The ground slanted beneath her feet with the realization. Aisha was suddenly extremely aware of every stuttered heartbeat and pained breath. How long did she have until the iron drained the magic keeping her alive? How long did she have until it *killed her*?

Her dread was a physical weight as she exited the cell. Beyond her panic, she became aware of the thick silence that had overtaken the cellblock. It was the quiet before a storm, a breath held before a kill. Aisha knew immediately that danger was coming for them.

But no hidden figures surged from the shadows. The corridor was empty.

Until it wasn't.

The roar was distant at first. Nothing but a faint rumble. But as it drew nearer, Aisha's heart clenched with fear. She knew that sound. It was the sound of rushing water.

Qadir, quiet up until that moment, whispered on her shoulder, *"Run."*

39

AISHA

The torrent surged after Aisha, swallowing everything in its path.

Not a force of nature, she thought, but man-made. Tired as she'd been, she had not noticed the grates on the ceiling, the shutters of which were now open to release a cascade of water.

This was the trap. Omar had found her.

She shoved her trepidation aside. If Omar had sent his thieves, then they would know better than to underestimate her. If they were smart, they would use the water to draw her out of the cells and ambush her. The only question was how many lay in wait.

But there was no time to think, no time to plan. Adrenaline was the only thing pushing Aisha forward and toward the doors. On the other side, she had just enough time to bolt the lock as the flood of water crashed against it.

Aisha braced herself as she turned to face the opponents who had been waiting for her.

She had been right. Thieves, three of them, stood in a line, poised to attack her. These were faces she recognized, though she had rarely worked with them herself.

Aisha raised her blade. "Are you so incompetent Omar had to send *three* of you?"

One of the thieves stepped forward with a snarl. "He is the sultan now."

"Sultan, thief, king..." She scoffed. "He is just a man."

The thieves rushed her. Unexpectedly, the first came at her with a blade. Aisha took his strike head-on. The fool laughed when she fell back, only to balk when he realized it was a feint. Aisha aimed for his legs, knocking him to the ground. But the moment she lunged, the second thief grabbed her from behind.

Aisha threw an elbow back into his face, stumbling out of the way with a curse when his blade drew blood on her arm. She barely had time to react as the third thief charged toward her.

It was not lost on Aisha that none of the jinn were using magic. Perhaps they too felt the effects of the iron. But right now, they did not need magic to best her. As the battle wore on, Aisha realized she was at a disadvantage. It was not just the odds that were stacked against her, but the prison itself. She could barely see past the dark spots blooming across her vision.

"What are you doing?" Qadir hissed in her ear.

"What are *you* doing?" she snapped as she fell away from another strike. "Are you not a legendary king? Where is your magic?"

The lizard dug his nails into her shoulder as she rolled to dodge another blow. His voice was sharp with frustration when he responded, "The iron has diminished my power."

Aisha could imagine the way the Resurrectionist would have laughed had she been here. Her voice was so clear in Aisha's mind she nearly mistook it for the truth.

"You cannot win this fight," Qadir warned. "You must flee."

The realization had already dawned on Aisha. In a normal fight, she might have been able to hold her ground. But she could not endure this for much longer, not when the prison was actively thwarting her. So the next time she saw an opening in the battle, she fled.

But escape was no simple thing. Now that she'd been noticed, the prisons had transformed from a labyrinth into a death trap. Around every corner lay a group of soldiers waiting to ambush her, and Aisha could not afford to fight them all.

Moment by moment, the iron chipped away at her senses, blur-ring her sight and weakening her body. Aisha knew this feeling. She had experienced it before, when a banished thief cut her throat and left her to bleed out in the desert. Magic had saved her life then. But now, as that magic seeped away, her body was beginning to expire.

This prison was killing her.

It was desperation that fueled her as she lashed out with her blade. Desperation that coursed through her veins in the absence of magic, forcing her body to act beyond its limitations. Her swordplay, normally as defined and tactical as her brushstrokes, descended into mindless thrashing. She had to get out of here. She had to *escape*.

At the next nexus, four men blocked her exit. When Aisha tried to lift her blade, her hand quivered, her fingers so numb on the hilt she could barely keep her grip on it.

The guards approached, a menacing blockade.

"*Thief.*" Qadir's voice was a hiss in her ear. "You must move. Now."

Aisha knew it, but her body would not obey her. When her blade fell, she could do nothing but stare in horror as the thieves pressed forward—

The ground rumbled, hard enough to rock her assailants off their feet. Aisha, unable to hold her balance, crumpled to her knees as the quake rolled through the passage. When she saw the looks of confusion on the men's faces, she knew it could not be their doing.

They were all still searching for the source of the disturbance when the ground beneath them began to *melt*, the dirt opening into a sinkhole underneath their feet.

Aisha scrambled away from the hole as it swallowed the scream-ing men. Her heart was in her throat as she reached for her blade and ran. It was only when she had escaped from the tunnel that she realized what had happened.

"That magic...," Qadir muttered. "I recognize it."

"Jubayr's," she said, remembering the name of Hakim's mentor. And if the ifrit's magic had shaken these halls, then...

Aisha turned at the sound of footsteps. Just as she had antici-pated, Hakim stood behind her. He looked harried, his shoulders rising and falling with his thin breaths. Beads of sweat trickled down his flushed face, and he was frantically twisting at the ring on his finger. Aisha could make out the strands of words shining around his finger.

"You came," she muttered. It was both an accusation and an expression of gratitude.

"I heard the chaos and suspected you would need assistance." Hakim glanced down at the ring, his brow faintly furrowed. "The relic's magic barely works here. It took a great deal of concentration to shift the ground." He looked up. "Where is Qadir?"

In response, Aisha tilted her head toward the lizard on her shoulder. Hakim's eyes widened at the sight of him. "Is that...?"

"A legendary jinn king, yes."

Hakim's surprise was fleeting. He turned, squinting down the corridor. When Aisha strained her ears, she could hear the faint echo of footsteps. "We are being pursued," Hakim noted. And then: "They are blocking off my exit."

He sounded disturbingly calm for a man in peril. Aisha found herself oddly grateful for it. It was easier to pretend she still had the upper hand when her companion believed in her. But then she moved—staggered—forward, and Hakim finally noticed her fatigue.

When she tripped, he rushed forward to steady her. Alarm flickered across his expression as his gaze swept over her, searching for an injury that did not exist. "Are you well?"

"I'll be fine when we make it out of this hellhole." With a groan, she peeled herself away from Hakim to stand upright. "We need to go, now. Can you make us another exit?"

For a few moments, the mapmaker looked uncertain as he fiddled with the relic. But then he nodded, guiding her in the opposite direction of the footsteps and into another corridor. At this point, Aisha barely had enough energy to follow.

Two floors down, they came to another obstacle. A wall of black. Thieves.

Aisha's whole body shuddered at the sight of them. She could not raise her blade. The thieves must have known this too—she could see their smirks beneath their scarves.

"Bint Louas." One of them stepped forward.

Aisha startled at the sight of Samar. The last time she had seen him, he had been watching her from a rooftop. Samar, the thief who had often visited her in her tower room. Samar, a man who was in actuality a jinn.

"Samar." She greeted him stiffly.

A sad smile cracked his miserable expression. "Long time no see, Princess."

She bristled at the familiar nickname. "Where is Omar?" she demanded.

"The *sultan* is busy with other, more important matters," another thief said. "We have been charged with your capture."

Aisha frowned. If she *was* captured, then they would drag her out of this awful place to Omar's feet. Her once king would not kill her—not immediately—but she would be free of the iron. Free from a more immediate death, at least.

But she could not let them have Qadir.

She caught Hakim's gaze. From his calm, it appeared that he had come to the same conclusion as her. He nodded in compliance.

Aisha tilted her head toward Qadir, obscuring him from sight behind her hair. "Ifrit," she whispered. "You must leave. We saved you from this place—I expect you to return the favor."

Qadir did not respond. At least, not in words. One moment he was on her shoulder. The next, he had disappeared, climbing down her arm and scuttling away. In his lizard shape, he was invisible. In his lizard shape, he could make a quiet escape.

Still, Aisha would have to make sure he had enough time.

With a bravado she did not feel, she faced the thieves. Her lips pulled into a smirk as she said, "You want to capture me?" She held up her blade in challenge. "I dare you to try."

40

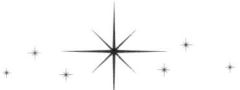

LOULIE

Loulie woke with salt on her tongue. Her memories returned in fragments. She recalled the sensation of drowning as the world turned upside down, of dropping into an ocean that should not have existed.

Her body trembled as she sat up. She swallowed, expecting liquid in her throat, but though the air was saturated with brine and sulfur, the cave bore no signs of having been submerged. When she ran her fingers through her curls, she found, oddly, that they were caked with sand rather than water. The realization perplexed her.

"Salaam, al-Nazari."

Loulie was still blinking sand from her lashes when she looked up to see Nabila sitting cross-legged before her. At first, she could not discern why the sight of the ifrit alarmed her. But then she noticed her body—her still very *solid* body—and the labored rise and fall of her chest. Rivulets of ash ran from Nabila's temple down her neck, streaking soot across her brown skin.

She held up a hand before Loulie could say anything. "I am tired, not dead."

Loulie swallowed again, mouth dry. She was grateful when Nabila handed her a waterskin. "What happened?" she asked. "When I spoke to the zaeem, I thought we'd sunk in water." She glanced past Nabila to the beach. She was relieved to see the curfew darkness had lifted. The ocean too was empty of ships. "My companion, Yousef—is he okay?"

"Your storyteller is fine. He and Rijah"—her lips twisted into a grimace when she said their name—"are waiting for you on the beach."

It took Loulie a few moments to process what she had said. "Did you just say—"

"Yes, Yousef found the Shapeshifter on one of the ships. Ask him for the story." If Nabila's cold tone was any indication, then she was not pleased to see Rijah on the island.

She deftly redirected the topic as she took back the waterskin. "As for your question about the zaeem's magic—memory is just as strong as magic. The zaeem roamed the ocean long before he traveled the Sandsea. Undoubtedly, it was his memory of the water that influenced your perception when he sank beneath the sand."

Loulie stared at her. "*Sank?*"

"How else do you think our island is able to vanish?"

It was an incredible magic. One that, if Loulie was being honest, she could not fully comprehend. But then, she had begun to accept such magics were not made for her mind.

Loulie glanced toward the empty shoreline. "So the queen's soldiers are gone?" She remembered the dread she had felt when she saw the illusions on the island.

"We lost them during the plunge. Duha and I kept the battle on the water to avoid losses, but we could not entirely avoid injuries." Nabila paused, silver eyes boring into Loulie with a strange intensity. "Hatem told me you guided his evacuation group to the fortress when the curfew fell. They are all grateful."

She did not, Loulie noticed, express her own gratitude, but what did it matter? Loulie was not doing any of this for Nabila. Still, she had to ignore a sting in her chest when she asked after Duha. She was relieved when Nabila confirmed she was resting and would make a full recovery.

"And you?" Nabila probed. "You are not harmed?" Her frown eased at Loulie's nod. "Duha tells me the zaeem does nothing for free. What deal did you make with him?"

Loulie shrugged. "I promised him the ocean."

The ifrit looked momentarily stunned. And then, amazingly, she laughed. It was the first honest laugh Loulie had ever heard from her. "Smart human, offering him what you already promised me." She rose to her feet and held out a hand.

Loulie was briefly surprised by the coldness of her skin. It occurred to her only when Nabila scowled down at her palm that she was just as unnerved by her tangible state. She thought back to the disappearance of the wind after the binding had broken. "The reason your body is still solid...Is it because I broke the binding here?"

"The wind has grown weaker, making it difficult for me to manipulate." Nabila sighed as she turned away. "It is yet another consequence of these dying lands."

Loulie remembered the cracks of gold she had seen in the sky. She thought of the curfew, a magic that obliterated all other magics. Then, with a start, she remembered the ashfire guttering out during the attack. When she asked Nabila what had happened, the ifrit's eyes darkened.

"Come. You should see it for yourself."

Loulie paused briefly at the entrance to glance behind her. A single pearlescent orb stared back at her, shining like a jewel. One of the master's eyes. She dipped her head in silent gratitude. Perhaps it was just her imagination, but she thought the earth rumbled beneath her feet in acknowledgment as she exited.

Outside, Nabila stood on the shoreline, frowning at the horizon. The scenery was different than it had been before, the distant isles replaced with a wall of sand. Loulie stared for a long time before she realized what she was seeing: the edge of the realm.

And then she saw the markings *above* the sand.

She stared, shocked, at the web of fractures across the sky. She had spotted them before, but never stretched so wide. And never so *many* of them.

"The cracks appeared after your friends put out the ashfire," Nabila said. At Loulie's blank stare, she sighed. "During the battle, your companion trapped the firebird away in a vessel, which trapped *all* the ashfire in the realm. Do you remember what I said about the Ashfire King's binding? That it was tied to his ashfire?" She pointed to the cracks in the sky. "I believe this damage is evidence enough that his binding has been broken."

Loulie suddenly felt faint. Given that none of them had understood the nature of Qadir's binding, she had not anticipated breaking it so soon. And she had never thought *Mazen* would be the one to shatter it. What in the world had happened during that battle?

Her fingers curled around Qadir's dagger, but there was, as always, no responding warmth. She hoped whatever Mazen had done to the ashfire had not hurt him.

"Why the long face?" Nabila cocked a brow. "This is good news. Only one binding remains."

With a shudder, Loulie recalled the darkness that had swallowed her senses. Had she not had Qadir's dagger, she would have been killed by an illusion. "The ashfire kept everyone safe. Without it, things are going to become very bad, very fast."

"Did I not tell you from the beginning that our undertaking is an urgent one?" Nabila crossed her arms. "One more binding, human. And then this will all be over."

—⁂—

Just as Nabila had promised, Mazen was waiting on the beach. It was impossible to miss him; the storyteller stood in the shade of a thatch-roofed pavilion, gesticulating dramatically as he recalled what had happened during the attack. What little Loulie heard did not make sense. He spoke as if he had been out on the water, not on the island—but how had he gotten there?

It was then she saw Rijah. Though the ifrit was in an unfamiliar shape, a body with broad shoulders and a square face, Loulie recognized their smile, sharp and mischievous. And she could never miss the telltale color of their eyes—especially not when those eyes were *glowing*.

When Rijah held up their hand and summoned ashfire to their palm, Loulie's mouth fell open in shock. She was torn between wonder and disquiet as the villagers applauded.

Nabila's eyes narrowed at the sight. "*Shapeshifter.*" The title was brittle on her tongue. "You can summon that cursed fire now too?"

Rijah, who had been in the middle of preening, paused to look at her. They met her frown with a smirk. "Why are you so surprised? I *am* the mightiest of jinn." They clenched their fingers into a fist, extinguishing the fire. "How many centuries has it been, Nabila?"

"Not nearly enough." The stale wind picked up around Nabila as she moved, throwing a sharp chill across the area and kicking up sand with her every footstep.

Rijah sighed. "I see you have not outgrown your tantrums."

"Do not condescend to *me*, whelp." The wind snapped at that last word, throwing sand in Rijah's face. They stepped back with a growl, rubbing at their eyes.

Nabila parted the crowds as easily as if they were water. When Mazen moved to stand in front of Rijah, she shoved him away without even looking at him, her gaze trained on Rijah.

Loulie rushed to Mazen's side. "You were on one of the *ships*? Why? How?"

His expression softened with relief at the sight of her. "Loulie! I was—"

"You are not welcome on my island, traitor."

They both looked up at the sound of Nabila's voice. The pirate stood feet away from Rijah, close enough to glare into their face. Rijah met her wrath head-on, their bright eyes narrowed to slits. "How am I the traitor when *you* are the one destroying our king's magic?"

"You abandoned this realm!"

"I followed my king to the surface. Because I was loyal."

Nabila laughed. It was a sharp, jagged sound, one that swirled the sand beneath her feet. "What honor is there in remaining loyal to a king who *ran* from a war he could have won? You all vanished and left me to bear the burden of his deceit!"

There was a flicker of shame on Rijah's face, but it was quick to vanish. Loulie expected whatever came out of their mouth to be a defense of their king. She was surprised when they instead said, "I know. And I am sorry."

Nabila, who had clearly been expecting a fight, seemed to deflate at the apology. The wind died around her, leaving her standing, vulnerable and shaking, in the clearing. "You knew," she echoed softly. "You knew, and still you hid on the surface for all these years."

"If by 'hid' you mean I was trapped, then yes."

She eyed them warily. "What do you mean *trapped*?"

Rijah held out an object. The lamp, which Loulie was shocked to see cradled in their hands. "I was afraid of death, so I bound myself to the first object that came into my possession. A human used it against me and made me his prisoner. Now, because of my own foolishness, I am bound to his bloodline. This lamp is both my relic and my prison."

A stunned quiet followed this confession. The islanders glanced between each other, murmuring in shock. Mazen stood frozen, expression blanched. Never mind that he'd had no hand in Rijah's imprisonment; he was the only one in his family who felt any guilt about it.

Even Nabila briefly seemed at a loss for words. When next she spoke, her voice had softened with confusion. "Even when you were trapped, our king did not return for you. He left you behind—and still you trust him?"

Rijah nodded without hesitation. "Is that not what loyalty is? To believe in someone even when they have made a grave mistake? Our king trusted us the same way we trusted him."

Nabila shook her head. It was a wild, desperate motion, as if she were trying to clear Rijah's words from her mind. "No," she said. And then, louder: "*No*. You may be foolish enough to trust a liar, but I never will. And I have no reason to trust you either."

Rijah did not so much as flinch as they set the lamp down and stepped forward to meet Nabila on the sands. Their body rippled, wavered—and then Rijah was wearing a new shape.

Loulie had the impression she was gazing upon a foggy reflection. The face Rijah had taken was Nabila's, but it was different. *This* face had a gentle smile and soft eyes. She wore her hair in beautiful waves and draped her curvaceous figure, unhidden by a coat, in jewels and gold. Coins tinkled at her hips and ankles as she walked.

The real Nabila reeled back as if she'd been slapped. "You... How *dare* you."

Rijah grinned at her. It was disconcerting to see their roguish grin on Nabila's face. "This is the Nabila I know," they said. "You were a performer. Exuberant, confident, and cunning."

"That is not who I am anymore." The words were barely more than a whisper. When Nabila looked up, Loulie saw something she had never seen in her expression before: hurt.

Rijah's smile slipped. But Nabila held up a hand before they could apologize. "I do not want your pity. I want answers. Tell me: What do you want, Shapeshifter?"

It was only then Rijah seemed to remember Loulie and Mazen. Their gaze fell on them as they said, "My king tasked me with protecting the humans. Where they go, I go."

"And if I do not allow it?"

The ifrit met her cold gaze in challenge. "Then I will take them with me."

Nabila tensed. For a moment, Loulie feared she might fight Rijah. But as she gazed upon her old comrade—at the faded memory Rijah had wrapped themself in—her anger seemed to dissipate. "Fine. You may stay, but know that if you get in my way, you will regret it."

She turned away before Rijah could prepare a retort, leaving them on the beach with the stunned crowd. Quiet blossomed in her absence, the islanders obviously unsettled by the altercation. But then Rijah shifted back into their previous shape with a flourish, and the jinn once more became distracted.

As Rijah began an impromptu performance for the crowd, Loulie turned to Mazen. "I missed your story," she said. "What happened?"

He smiled at her. It was a strangely subdued look, almost

embarrassed, and Loulie did not understand why he was making such a face until he reached into his pocket and withdrew—

She gasped at the sight of the compass in his hands.

Her compass.

Loulie stifled a cry as she grabbed it from him. The moment she felt its magic humming beneath her fingers, she grinned. Even had she wanted to, she could not have smothered that smile. "You went back for the compass?"

"You came back for me. It was the least I could do."

Joy surged through her, so bright it cut through the gloom cast by Nabila's warning. Loulie was swept away by the feeling. "Shukran," she said, but the word was too small to express her gratitude. Before she realized what she was doing, she had leapt forward to embrace him, wrapping her arms tightly around his waist.

Mazen froze against her. She heard his heart stutter. Felt the surprised intake of his breath as his chest rose against her cheek.

When Loulie's mind caught up to what she had done, she froze, her body flooding with heat, but she resisted the urge to step away. She was glad for it when, in the next moment, Mazen's arms came to rest around her.

"I would do it again in a heartbeat," he said.

His dedication flummoxed her. But then she realized she felt the same way. She did not know when it was she had come to rely on Mazen bin Malik, but at some point, the thought of losing him had become unbearable.

But he was safe. *They* were safe.

For a moment, Loulie let herself believe it. She leaned her cheek into Mazen's chest and thought, *I refuse to lose anyone again.*

Somehow, she would make certain of it.

41

MAZEN

Following Rijah's arrival on al-Malath, an uneasy atmosphere came over the island. Nabila was as moody as a storm, her temper short and easy to summon. And, though the islanders were charmed by the Shapeshifter, they were also unsettled by the circumstances of their arrival. It was hard not to be when the world had begun to visibly decay around them.

It was not just the air that had gone stale in the days following the attack. The change was in the water, which had grown murky and dark, and in the trees, whose leaves had begun to wither. With every passing hour, the fractures in the sky stretched larger and longer, and the fall of the curfew became more erratic, the illusion-festered darkness lingering more frequently.

Looking at the cracks in the sky, Mazen had the odd impression of being trapped in a glass prism. He was reminded of the bottles of colorful sand he sometimes saw in the Madinne souk. In those vessels, artists meticulously crafted entire landscapes made from colored sands. The jinn realm, Mazen thought, was like one of those bottles. But now the glass was breaking, and the sand inside was slipping through the cracks. And when it broke...

He did not want to think about what would happen, but they could not avoid the future forever. On the second day of Rijah's stay, Nabila's spies delivered alarming news: the islands, which had already been falling into the Sandsea, were now sinking faster. Kharjem in particular was in dire straits, but when Mazen asked Nabila if she would help the inhabitants as she had promised, she waved the question away with agitation. They could not afford the detour, she said, especially not when that evacuation was likely to take longer with the erratic curfew magic.

The situation had grown disastrous enough to impact Dhahab. According to the birds, the queen had her hands full dealing with riots that had broken out after a particularly worrisome earthquake.

"We are running out of time," Nabila said. "We must depart at once for the next binding."

The night before their planned departure, Loulie called a secret meeting. At first, there was the question of where their rendezvous would happen. The island, filled with Nabila's spies, was hardly a place any of them could talk discreetly.

Rijah waved away their concerns. "We will not have to worry about her spies. Trust me."

The meaning of those words became apparent when Rijah showed up at the fortress, their meeting place, in Nabila's form. Even more shocking was that they were using her voice—her *singing* voice—to placate the birds.

Rijah looked amused by Loulie and Mazen's shock. They winked as they shut the door behind them, locking out the creatures. "The birds will not bother their master."

Mazen gaped as the ifrit seated themself. "You've even mastered her singing voice?"

Rijah shrugged as if that was a given. The more Mazen saw of their abilities, the more he understood why they had been given the title of Shapeshifter.

Loulie sighed. "Can we focus? I want to talk about what happens at the final binding."

Rijah's brows shot up. "You think this is the last? Have you forgotten about my king's?"

"*You* were the ones to put out his ashfire!"

The ifrit looked exasperated by her. "Is your memory truly so short? It is as I said before: it may be possible to chip away at a binding's magic, but to unseal it—"

"You have to break the center," Mazen finished. Nabila had assumed Qadir's binding was gone because Mazen had locked his ashfire away, but it seemed the fire was just an extension of his magic. Which meant that somewhere, there was another binding to unseal.

When Mazen asked about its location, Rijah told them they had felt a pull from Dhahab ever since gaining command over the ashfire. Though they would not be able to pinpoint the source of Qadir's binding themself, Loulie might be able to track it with her compass.

Loulie had a thoughtful gleam in her eyes. "This is good, I think. It gives us some leverage over Nabila. Let's keep Qadir's binding a secret from her."

Mazen's skin prickled with unease. "Why?"

"I want to see what she'll do after I unseal this next binding. I've been trying to interrogate her before we return to the surface, but I don't think she'll be honest with me while I still have some use to her."

Rijah regarded her curiously. "You don't trust Nabila."

"No. Nabila has only ever treated me as a means to an end. I think..." She swallowed. "I think she resents me for the relationship I have with Qadir."

Mazen could not blame Loulie for her distrust. Not after what the ifrit had said about retribution. Not after what she had done— or not done—for the zaeem of Kharjem. Even after his death, the ifrit's promise to him remained unfulfilled.

His hand went absently to the ruby relic around his neck. Reluctant to relinquish the relic to Nabila, he had decided to tuck it away beneath his collar. It was tragic to think the relic would never make it back to Kharjem. Even worse to know the zaeem's sacrifice had meant nothing.

Nabila may have promised them all a return to the surface, but who knew how many oaths she had broken to get what she wanted?

Loulie must have noticed his silence. When she saw his hand

wrapped around the chain, a glimmer came into her eyes. "You asked Nabila about Kharjem, didn't you?"

The last time Loulie had looked at him so intently, she had been concocting a plan to break into the archive. Uncertain of what she was getting at, Mazen nodded.

He was alarmed when she started *smiling*. He recognized the look. It was her merchant's smirk, the one she wore when she had closed a particularly lucrative deal. "I think the two of you should offer to go. If the curfew is a hindrance, you can use the ashfire to help evacuate the islanders. Nabila will not see it as a detour if *you* travel to Kharjem while I deal with the binding. And she has no reason to deny the request if it earns her favor with one of the zuama'a."

Rijah's confounded expression mirrored Mazen's own. They eyed Loulie warily. On Nabila's severe face, the look was especially cutting. "What are you scheming, human?"

"I have a plan. But I'll need your help with it."

Mazen shook his head. "If what you were saying is true, then you could be in danger after you unseal this next binding. We should all go to the marid city together and—"

"If I go alone, then I am the *only* person in danger. And..." Her lips curled. "It means you two will be unaccounted for, which will make staging a rescue easier."

Mazen hesitated. The last time he and Loulie had tried to plan for contingencies, their scheme had fallen apart. But Mazen had trusted Loulie then, just as she'd trusted him. Just as she trusted him *now*. They had depended on each other this whole time; he would not disappoint her.

"What do you have in mind?"

Loulie grinned at him. "When you're on Kharjem, I want you to tell a story."

42

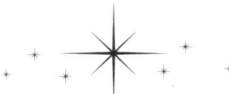

AISHA

The palace courtyard was more garish than Aisha remembered. The sparkling rose beds she had thoughtlessly strode through so many times before suddenly seemed unnaturally bright, glowing an eerie silver beneath the sinking sun as she was marched to the throne room. Even the topiaries shaped like fantastical creatures resembled hollow monsters, their concave eyes glaring down at her as Samar led her through the courtyard.

A grim nostalgia swept through her as she treaded paths she had once traveled side by side with Omar. Months ago, the two of them had shared an apple in the orchard here as comrades. Or something like it. But now all Aisha could think about was how much she wanted to see the sultan bleed.

She swallowed a knot in her throat as they approached the throne room. She felt bereft without her weapons. Even her hidden blades had been stolen from her; Omar's thieves knew her well enough to find them. It was maddening, to be matched in skill.

And it was not just the loss of her blades that unnerved her, but the absence of Amina's magic. Though she could feel it humming beneath her skin again now that she was out of the prison, the iron shackles the thieves had set on her wrists had silenced her voice.

Had Aisha's mind always felt so empty without the ifrit?

She shoved the thought away as she glanced between the thieves barring her escape. Perhaps she could take them, even with the shackles on her wrists. Omar, however, was a different story. Aisha was certain if she fought him in her current state, she would die.

But she knew Omar. He never killed his targets outright; he'd always preferred to play with them first. It was that knowledge, more than anything, that Aisha counted on to save her. She only wished she could determine the mapmaker's fate with the same sureness.

No sooner had concern for his safety crossed her mind than she chided herself for losing focus. She forced her gaze up as the throne room doors opened.

It had been a long time since she'd entered this place. The first time she had been admitted was when she'd been officially recognized as one of Omar's thieves. She remembered thinking the gargantuan chamber had felt more like a showroom than a seat of power, but now the room was completely changed.

The gifts from the nobles had been retired, the beautiful tapestries pulled from the walls. Where there had once been furniture, there was now an abundance of foliage: vines entwined with razor-sharp flowers and bloodred roots growing through the tile. Aisha had no doubt the greenery stemmed from spilled jinn blood. She glanced to the back of the room, where a throne sat between two vine-coated columns. And on that throne...

Aisha was unable to put a name to the emotion that seized her when she beheld the sight of Omar bin Malik. He was both familiar and not, his practical attire replaced with expensive finery. The cotton had been exchanged for silk, the silver rings on his fingers were studded with gemstones, and his belt of daggers was now a strand of leather glittering with gold. He had wrapped a star-embroidered scarf around his head and set a silver circlet atop it.

In that moment, he looked every bit the Stardust Thief.

But he was no longer just a king of thieves. Now he was the sultan, and his smug smile and relaxed posture made it apparent that he had already sunk into the role. Gods knew he'd been preparing himself for it long enough.

And yet Aisha was surprised by how small she felt in his presence.

Omar's smile remained fixed on his face, a perfect mask, as Aisha was brought before him. His grin only widened as they forced her to kneel. Aisha kept her scowl affixed. She refused to let him see how much his presence rattled her.

She and her once king stared at each other for a long time. Aisha found herself at a loss for words. What did one say to a man who had given them the means to enact revenge, only to become the target of it? The last time they'd spoken, she had promised to kill him.

In the end, it was Omar who broke the silence first.

"What's wrong, Aisha? Am I not your sultan? You ought to bow." The words dripped with mockery; Aisha recognized the question from their last conversation.

One of the thieves—not Samar—forced her head down. The other rammed a boot into her back. Aisha snapped at these indignities, throwing both men off with a hiss. When they moved toward her again with drawn blades, Omar raised a hand to halt them.

He smirked. "Do not waste your time. Aisha would sooner suffer torture than bow."

Aisha leveled her glare on him. It was easier to feel in control when she let her rage burn away all the tangled and confused emotions inside of her. "I would sooner stab out *your throat.*"

The thieves tensed behind her, but Omar just laughed. "How I have missed your honesty. This court is not the same without it."

Aisha surveyed the greenery that had sprung up in her absence. "You are right. It isn't the same. Because you have changed it."

"For the better." Omar rose from his throne. Aisha stilled as he sauntered toward her, twirling one of his black knives. "That is the thing about you, Aisha. You have always been narrow sighted. Samar tells me you toured Madinne before your infiltration. You *saw* what I accomplished. I have not changed Madinne: I have improved it."

As much as Aisha wanted to object, she could not. Making jinn magic a public amenity had clearly worked in Omar's favor. He had given the populace yet another reason to see him as a hero. The sultan had never been a good man; it was easy for Omar to be better.

But Aisha didn't care what a bunch of starry-eyed fools thought of him. They didn't know Omar the way she did. He may have been full of dazzling smiles and soft laughter, but it was the poisonous hatred concealed beneath his charm that made him dangerous.

Aisha scoffed. "You think I care? I have never been interested in your antics."

"How sad, to lack a cause."

"Better to be untethered than a puppet."

The smile slid from Omar's face. "It is unlike you to be so self-pitying."

"Don't insult me by pretending you care about me, bin Malik. I know the truth of you. Your words are gilded but your tongue is barbed. You may be able to convince this city, but you could never fool me into thinking you care about anyone but yourself."

The bastard laughed at her. "That might be the most eloquent thing you've ever said, Aisha. I see how my brother may have rubbed off on you."

The beginnings of a retort formed on Aisha's lips, but the words caught in her throat as Omar touched his blade to her chin. With frightening nonchalance, he tilted her face up.

Their gazes locked.

"You say you know the truth of me? Then you know what comes next. You have seen what I do to traitors, and you know the punishment I inflict upon thieves who have stolen from me is especially severe." His eyes wandered to the collar, exposed at her throat.

Too late, Aisha realized what Omar was about to do. His fingers were around her neck before she could retaliate, his grip unyielding. Aisha tried to shove him off, tried to knee him in the stomach and get him *away* from her, but Omar was unmovable. Aisha's blood sang with panic.

Desperate, she threw her weight into him, suddenly enough he did not anticipate it. The motion unbalanced him, but before Aisha could attack him, arms encircled her from behind, holding her frozen. Samar. The thief's grip tightened as Aisha writhed uselessly in his grasp.

The grin snapped back onto Omar's face, an alarmingly automatic motion. "You seem frazzled, Aisha. Tell me—what happens if I steal that relic from you?"

I would die. Some small, traitorous part of her wondered if Omar would be less likely to take it from her if he knew it was keeping her alive.

Omar read her answer from the silence. "Ah, your fraternization with the jinn suddenly makes more sense. I wondered why you would work with one after betraying us."

"You betrayed me first," Aisha said coldly. "You lied to me."

Omar raised a brow. "You learned you were working with jinn— so you conspired with *another* jinn to obtain your revenge?"

Aisha hated how easily he made her feel like a fool. He was right to be puzzled. Had she not been forced to make a deal with the Resurrectionist to save her own life, she would have gone on killing jinn and refusing to use their magic for the rest of her life.

She glared at him. "What do you want from me, bin Malik?"

"*There* is the thief I know. The one who refuses to suffer idle chatter." He stepped back, considered her thoughtfully. "I would like to recruit you."

The air caught in Aisha's lungs. Samar had let her go, but the room spun around her so wildly she nearly stumbled back into him. She remembered the last time Omar had recruited her. The disbelief, followed by the flare of pride. But now there was only dread. This clearly was not an offer; it was a threat.

"I *stole* from you," she snapped. "I freed your prisoner!"

Omar shrugged. "What is stolen can be returned, and you are much more valuable than any prisoner." The intensity in his eyes, so at odds with his casual posture, threw her off guard. It was a trick, a lie. And yet there was a despicable part of her that softened at his words. It would be so much easier to return to the way things had been. To obey rather than question.

There was a faint hum from the collar, a flicker of warmth against her throat. A reassurance that she was not alone. Omar must have seen the defiance rekindle in her. He stepped away with a sigh. "If *I* cannot convince you, then perhaps someone else can."

With a gesture, he bade the guards at the entrance to open the doors. Aisha braced herself as Omar's pawns dragged another prisoner into the throne room. Her conviction faltered when she saw who it was.

Hakim looked as if he'd been dragged from a battle. His face was bloodied and bruised, his clothing torn. He was in such a bad state that the soldiers restraining him were also holding him up. The mapmaker's face filled with hatred at the sight of Omar. Her once king simply smiled at the look, as if it brought him personal vindication.

The guards held Hakim by the door. He was close enough for Aisha to see, but far enough away that she could not have spoken to him unless she pitched her voice into a yell. She whirled on Omar with a glower. "What have you done to him?"

"We had...a conversation." Omar played with one of the rings on his fingers. A *familiar* ring. "Like you, he was unwilling to part with his relic. I admit I was less patient with him."

Aisha's stomach twisted as she beheld the ifrit relic on Omar's finger. Did he know how to use it? What was he going to use it *for*?

"I would encourage you to reconsider my offer," Omar said. "You may choose to fight me, but know your defiance will result in casualties." He brushed his fingers against the collar. "We both know how easy it would be for me to end your lives right now."

Aisha gritted her teeth against the shudder that racked her body. If she refused, he would steal both the relic and their lives. If she accepted, she would be only as important as the magic around her neck. She would be a tool once more.

She suddenly felt boneless, exhausted. Her heart deadened to a dull thud as she said, "If I agree, you spare the mapmaker."

Omar dipped his head in a nod. "Swear your fealty, bint Louas."

The last time he had spoken that command, she had eagerly knelt. It had been an easy choice when anger was all she had. Omar had taught her how to sharpen her rage into intent, into power. But now Aisha's anger was a dying flame.

To bow was to succumb. But Aisha had no choice.

The fire inside of her died as she lowered her head and said, "I will do as you command, my king."

43

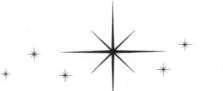

LOULIE

The absence of the wind on the day of their departure felt like an omen.

Loulie could not shake the feeling as she glanced back at al-Malath from the docks. The decaying land did not so much as shift; there was no breeze to move the ocean, no gale to flutter the dead leaves. Even the birds seemed unnaturally stationary, their movements lethargic.

Not an omen, she thought with dread. *This is what a dying world looks like.*

She certainly felt like she was marching to her doom as she trailed Nabila down the pier toward her ship. The crowd that had gathered to see them off did not inspire confidence. There was a stoniness to their eyes, less resilience than resignation. Loulie understood that distrust; it was hard to hope for a better future when the present was so dismal. And yet...

Her attention wandered to Mazen. The storyteller walked beside her, matching her hurried footsteps at a more leisurely stride. He carried with him two birds: the firebird, housed in the lantern he held in his hand, and Rijah, who sat atop his shoulder in their hawk form.

Loulie raised a brow at the ifrit. "You could have chosen *any* other form."

"Yes." Rijah clicked their beak, a motion Loulie interpreted as a beleaguered huff. "But this shape annoys Nabila the most."

Mazen coughed to clear a laugh from his throat. Seeing the suppressed smile on his face, Loulie grinned despite herself. It was easier to pretend the situation she was heading into was not so perilous when easy banter preceded it. But then she saw Nabila's ship looming ahead. She saw the sailors already on board, readying the vessel, and her nervousness returned.

Everything that happened next, she would have to do on her own. Before, she might have fooled herself into thinking she preferred the solitude. But she was not so stubborn anymore.

It is not weakness to rely on others for help, Qadir had once told her. How unexpected that it had been Mazen, of all people, to remind her of the truth of those words.

Too soon, they arrived at the gangplank. This was where they would part ways, Mazen to Kharjem and her to the Eastern Marid City. Loulie knew their plan, but she could not bring herself to move.

This is not farewell, she reminded herself. *And he's not alone this time. He has Rijah.*

But even so, she stalled. She had led Mazen astray in Dhahab; what if something went amiss when he came after her this time as well?

But when she caught Mazen's gaze, he looked unconcerned. "Trust me," he said.

Had he asked that of her when they left Madinne months ago, she would have hesitated. Now his resolve sent a shock of warmth through her. She nodded, an automatic motion, and when he beamed at her, she mirrored the smile back at him, exasperated.

How far they had come since they'd set out on their journey, she and this lying prince.

Rijah, not to be forgotten, said, "Trust *us*. And stay alert." They shot a pointed look above them at Nabila, who was barking commands at her sailors.

Before Loulie could respond, Duha called her name from the rails. Loulie's chest tightened at the sound. She was seized by a sudden resolve. At this point, she was no stranger to leaving others behind, but she was tired of walking away with words left unsaid. She jutted a finger at Mazen's chest. "If you put yourself in danger again, I'll murder you myself." She frowned at him until he nodded, and then, in a softer voice, she added, "You promised me that we would survive together. So stay safe. If not for yourself, then for me."

When he just stared at her in surprise, she turned away before she could make a fool of herself, stomping up the gangplank and onto the ship. It was only when she had put some distance between them that she looked back. Unsurprisingly, Mazen was smiling, and when he cupped his hand to his mouth and called a farewell, the calm in his voice made her feel that he had taken her seriously after all.

Slowly, the sails began to unfurl themselves, Nabila's stilted magic breathing life into them. The sailors greeted her with a surprising warmth, breaking out into a jaunty song that brightened the mood as they set out on the Sandsea. Even Loulie could not help but smile when she heard Nabila's voice beneath the din of the tune, a deep and steadying undercurrent.

Loulie was still watching al-Malath fade into the distance when a hand came down on her shoulder. Duha stood behind her, wearing her usual smile. This close, Loulie saw that the wounds she had sustained during the battle had healed over to scabs. She wondered vaguely if marid could heal in a similar way to jinn, or if Nabila had taken care of her.

Duha grinned, revealing all her sharpened teeth. "How do you feel about a celebration?"

Loulie blinked at her. "What could we possibly be celebrating?" She gestured at the ominous sky, the decaying land.

"Not what. *Who*." She thumped Loulie on the back.

Loulie staggered with the force, flushed. "What have I done?" She had not been on the front lines of the battle. Besides that, *she* had been the one to draw the armada to the island.

"Do not ask ridiculous questions, binding breaker. Besides, we need an excuse to bring out the alcohol." When Loulie stared at her, appalled, she sighed. "It is *because* the situation is so dire that we need this. Think of it as a distraction. We have time yet before we reach the city."

She went to spread the news after that, leaving Loulie to pass the time doing chores while the sailors began their preparations for their so-called celebratory meal.

That night, when they brought out the food, it was apparent they had been anticipating this "celebration." Platters of fresh zubaidi and rice were served, along with an assortment of sauces. Someone had even prepared some kind of date-and-flour dessert.

The mood was festive as they ate, the air filled with laughter. At Duha's insistence, Loulie seated herself at the head of the gathering and recounted how she had broken the binding. She told the sailors about the firebird, the ruins, and the ferocious gales. When she got to the bargain she had struck with the giant crab, the sailors' delight fueled her own good mood.

Their cheer persisted when Nabila finally appeared, looking morose as a storm cloud when she saw what they were celebrating.

"Are we commending the *human*?" Nabila's skeptical gaze cut toward her.

In response, Duha held up a liquor bottle and flashed one of her brightest smiles. "We are celebrating victory." She laughed at Nabila's wary look. "Come now, nokhitha; your body may not bear physical injuries the same way ours do, but you are clearly heartsick after the battle. Treat yourself to a drink."

Nabila did not take the bottle immediately. It was only when the rest of the sailors loudly voiced their encouragement that she caved, swiping the draft with a grumble. "Fine. *One* drink." She raised the jug to uproarious cheering and proceeded to down it all in one go.

Loulie was impressed despite herself. Did Nabila not feel the effects of the alcohol, or was the drink lighter than she expected? She watched in surprise as the ifrit sank gracefully onto the deck beside Duha and gestured for another bottle.

Nabila must have noticed her staring; her eyes narrowed as she glanced at Loulie. "Where is *your* drink, human? Or are you too weak to handle it?"

Loulie bristled at what was clearly a taunt, but shook her head. She could not afford to let her guard down.

Nabila merely shrugged as she accepted a second drink from one of her crewmates.

As the night wore on, the ifrit's taciturn disposition softened. The storm in her eyes cleared to a gentle azure, and by the time they had started on dessert, Nabila was *laughing* at her crew's stories. At some point between her third and fourth drinks, she had shucked her coat and let her hair down, which lent her a more brash, youthful appearance.

When Duha caught Loulie staring, she winked. "I told you we all needed a break."

Loulie was disconcerted. "She smiled at me just now. She's *never* smiled at me."

"Nabila has little reason to smile these days. But..." Her gaze wandered back to her captain, who had just broken into song. It was a melancholy melody, filled with longing, and Loulie saw that same yearning reflected in Duha's eyes. "Sometimes, I can make her remember. What she—what we—were like before."

Before. Loulie did not have to ask what the marid meant. Instead, she said, "The first time you met her—was it when she was performing in Dhahab?"

Duha shook her head, a twinkle in her eye. "I met Nabila long before she performed for the Ashfire King. Back when she still lived with her family, she used to sing when she was out on the ocean, and the wind would carry her voice to me beneath the waves."

It sounded like the beginning of a romance tale to Loulie. She could imagine the questions Mazen would ask if he were here; he seemed the type to appreciate such stories.

Loulie did not want to pry, but seated before Duha, it occurred to her that the marid had once lived in this city they were sailing to. Perhaps she would be able to tell Loulie about the binding there. She gently probed: "By 'beneath the waves,' you mean the marid city? You said before that you and Ziyad lived there and advised the same queen. Does that mean you knew about the binding there? Do you know anything of the ifrit who crafted it?"

"You speak of Ramiz, the Tide Bringer."

Much to her surprise, it was Nabila who responded. Loulie had not expected the ifrit to overhear her from the other side of the circle; she should not have underestimated her hearing.

She faced the captain. "His name was Ramiz?"

"It was what he called himself when he came to Dhahab." Nabila had a faraway look in her eyes as she swirled the liquor in her bottle. "He was the most tolerable of the ifrit, I think."

Duha grinned. "You only say that because you saw him the least."

A faint smile touched Nabila's lips as she shrugged. Not a denial, then. If she knew Ramiz—if he had been one of her comrades—then perhaps she could give Loulie information.

Loulie asked another question. "Why did you see so little of him if he served Qadir?"

"Because he lived with *us*," Duha said. "In the marid city."

Nabila looked amused by the puzzlement on Loulie's face. "His is a strange story. One I have not told in a long time." She glanced at Duha, as if asking for her permission to share it.

But the marid was already ushering for her to continue. She grinned at Loulie. "You are in for a treat, al-Nazari. Not many know Ramiz's story, and Nabila tells it best."

The other sailors chimed in, raising their glasses and egging her on. Even though Nabila rolled her eyes, Loulie could sense she was pleased by the attention. The ifrit set her bottle down on the deck with a hard thump and quieted the sailors with a wave of her hands.

"Fine. If it is a story you want, then it is a story you shall have. Listen well..."

The Tale of Ramiz and the Wish

Neither here nor there, but long ago . . .

There existed three kingdoms. The Court of Jinn was over-seen by the Ashfire King. The Court of Man met beneath the shrewd gaze of a human sultan. And lastly, there was the Court of Marid, ruled over by a queen in the ocean depths.

Our tale begins in Dhahab, with a most unusual criminal.

One day, a jinn citizen strode into the Ashfire King's court to discuss a matter of great urgency. When the king bade him to speak, the stranger bowed his head and said, "I beg your forgiveness, Your Majesty, for my business is a sordid one." He held out his hand, and upon his palm lay a single scale, glittering with blood. "I have come to confess to murder."

The court erupted with cries and gasps then, for it was no simple scale in the stranger's palm but a marid scale, proven as such by its venomous edge and unique, ever-shifting color.

The king saw the scale and shook his head. "I am afraid your confession is not for my ears. Your victim is one of the marid, so you must beg for mercy from their queen."

A stunned hush fell over the crowd, for none in attendance had never seen the Marid Queen. But they had all heard the stories that said she was as large as the jinn palace and ten times more ferocious than their king. The criminal knew these stories as well, but he did not balk when the king ordered him onto a ship to the queen's underwater kingdom. For seven days and nights, they traveled across the ocean, and the criminal uttered not a word of his confession.

On the seventh night, the king finally broke the silence. "At least tell me your name," he insisted. "So that I might announce you to the queen."

The stranger bowed his head in deference. "They call me Ramiz, Your Majesty."

The king committed the name to memory, and when at last they arrived at the whirlpool that was the gateway to the marid kingdom, he walked to the bow of the ship and called out, "Mighty queen, I bring before you a jinn criminal named Ramiz! His offense was inflicted upon your kin, which means his crime is yours to judge."

Ramiz was ushered onto a small sambuk and, on the king's command, released into the whirlpool. Even when the boat began to spiral into the depths, Ramiz remained calm. He neither wept nor screamed, but instead accepted his fate with the resignation of the guilty.

The boat sank deeper and deeper into the waves until it drifted into an enchanted room filled with air. At the back of the chamber was a massive throne made from sea glass, and stretched atop it was a gigantic scaled creature who was as beautiful as she was fearsome. Ramiz knew immediately this must be the Marid Queen and that the shadowed, black-eyed creatures on either side of her must be her advisors. He lowered his forehead to the ground in respect.

"You may rise." The queen's voice boomed through both the throne room and his mind. Aloud, it was a strange cacophony of echoes and shrieks. Yet in his mind, her voice was smooth and melodic. She asked him, "Your name is Ramiz?"

When he nodded, her mouth pulled into a grimace wide enough to reveal all seven rows of her sharp teeth. "It is brave of you to stand before us. Now tell us: What is your crime?"

And so Ramiz began his story.

"My tale begins on the ocean, Your Majesty. One day, as I was delivering my wares across the waters, the ship I was traveling on was hit by a terrible storm. By chance alone, I drifted to a nearby human settlement on a piece of driftwood.

"There, I was mistaken for a sickly sailor and offered a place to recover. For three days the villagers watched over me, and in return, I performed errands for them. On the third day, a fisherman put me to work. I trailed him to the beach, and while I prepared the nets, I caught him rubbing a strange, cracked jar and muttering to it as if it was some charm.

"I confess my curiosity got the better of me, and when the fisherman left to collect his haul, I decided to open the jar. But no sooner had I uncorked it than I witnessed a strange sight: two pitch-black eyes, staring at me from the depths!

"The moment the jar was opened, the creature inside materialized before me. On the beach, he took the shape of a two-legged being with sleek gray skin and sharp teeth. The moment I saw the scales and barnacles upon his body, I knew him to be a marid.

"I immediately prostrated myself on the ground, but the marid was understandably angry. He jutted a finger at me and cried, 'Three hundred years I have been trapped in that jar, fulfilling the wish of any human who possessed it. And now *you* sit before me, sniveling jinn, with that same jar in front of you. Give me one reason I should not smite you!'

"I begged the marid for mercy. 'Please, mighty marid! If you spare me, I will take your jar when I leave and throw it upon the ocean. There, away from the fisherman, you will be free.'

"To this, the marid reluctantly agreed. After promising me one wish in exchange, he vanished into his prison. When the fisherman returned, I said nothing to him. The next morning, as I had promised, I stole the jar and escaped on a boat, eager to set the marid free. But the fisherman must have suspected me, because when I looked back at the island, I saw him approaching on a ship. Human archers stood at the rails, ready to shoot me with iron arrows.

"Desperate, I threw the jar onto the water, where it shattered into a thousand pieces. 'Oh, mighty marid!' I cried. 'I have freed you and ask for but one wish in return: I want to survive!'

"The marid surged out from his prison in the form of a fearsome fish, charging through the water to sink the ship. But though he succeeded in ravaging the vessel, he was too slow to dodge the archers' arrows, which plunged through his eye. The creature let out a terrible roar, and when he sunk beneath the waves, I knew my wish had killed him.

"Desperate to save him, I dove into the water, but my magic was naught but a guttered flame in the depths. It was all I could do to pry a scale from his body before it was lost. Now I stand before you with the proof of his life and await your judgment."

The whole time Ramiz had spoken, the queen had listened with rapt attention. At the end of his story, she glanced to her two advisors and asked their opinions.

The first advisor flashed a menacing smile from the darkness and said, "He ought to suffer, Your Majesty. I suggest you stab him with iron and send his corpse to the bottom of the ocean. There, his soul cannot be bound into one of the jinn's precious relics."

The second advisor flashed a twin smile, though hers was filled with more mischief than cruelty. "I think it would be more interesting to test him, Your Majesty. Have him participate in one of our games, and if he wins, he shall be released with his life."

The queen considered both their suggestions. In the end, she said, "I offer you this deal, Ramiz: for seven hours, you will be shackled in iron chains and sunk beneath the waves. If you, a being of fire, can survive for that long in the depths, then I will return you to the surface. But if you perish in the water, then that shall be your punishment."

Ramiz, who had already accepted his death, agreed to the queen's challenge without complaint. He allowed himself to be locked in iron and did not struggle when the queen's advisors bound him to the seafloor. There, he waited seven hours to die.

After the first hour, the fire in his blood began to freeze.

After the second, his heartbeat slowed to a faint and fluttering hum.

After the third, his skin began to gray and wither.

After the fourth, there was hardly any air left in his lungs.

After the fifth, he felt himself slipping into what he knew would be an endless slumber.

After the sixth, he began to choke on the water.

The seventh hour had not yet passed when Ramiz began to die. He gazed at the marid scale clutched between his fingers one last time and thought, *A wish for a wish and a life for a life. This is a just punishment for my heinous crime.*

He had just made peace with his death when he noticed the marid scale, moments ago cold, had begun to burn in his palm.

When Ramiz looked down, he saw that it had dug itself into his palm. Then, before his eyes, the single scale began to unfold across his arms and neck like a living moss, coating his body in thick armor.

At the end of the seventh hour, Ramiz began to breathe, but now it was not air that filled his lungs, but water. Where there had once been fire in his blood, there was now a different, more ancient magic. He realized then that the marid's magic had saved him from beyond the grave: Ramiz had wished to survive, and the marid's scale had protected him.

When Ramiz returned from the depths, the queen's advisors were shocked to see him alive. The queen merely smiled when she saw the scales that had grown over his body. "I see he chose to fulfill your wish in the end. Had he believed you were stealing, his scale would have poisoned you. Instead, it kept you alive. As promised, you are free to go."

But the honorable Ramiz was reluctant to depart. "Your Majesty, my life was saved at the expense of one of your kin's. Please, allow me to serve you in his place."

Again, the queen asked her advisors their opinion. With a vicious snarl, the first proclaimed, "Your Majesty, he is a *jinn*! He does not deserve a place at your side."

But the second advisor laughed. "He may be a jinn, but he is the only one who has ever survived our waters. Surely he would be useful to you, Your Majesty."

Again, the queen pondered. After some consideration, she cracked off a piece of her throne, shaped the sea glass into a spear, and offered it to Ramiz. "I will make you another deal, ya Ramiz. You may serve at my side, but because you are not marid, you will only ever act as my envoy. You will be allowed to travel our paths and use our magics, but you may only do so to deliver messages to the jinn king. Do you understand?"

Ramiz bowed low as he accepted the queen's spear. "I understand, Your Majesty."

And so the deal was struck. With the marid magic the queen had gifted him, Ramiz traveled back to Dhahab. At first, there was an outcry when the court saw his scaled flesh, but the king recognized Ramiz's fiery eyes, undampened by the marid magic. "You have returned!" he proclaimed in wonder. "And with a marid's magic, no less. How did this come to be?"

No longer bound by silence, Ramiz told him his story. The Ashfire King was pleased that the queen had chosen him as an envoy. "The marid have always avoided communicating with us," he said. "You will be a welcome messenger between us."

With his blessing, Ramiz performed his duties in the centuries to follow. For his abilities, he was given the name Tide Bringer, for with a sweep of the queen's enchanted spear, he could command tides and travel between any bodies of water. There are some who say he was cursed, as he was a servant to the marid. Others say he was blessed, for he had been gifted great power.

But as it is with most stories, no one knows Ramiz's true loyalties. He, like the other ifrit, vanished during the war. Did he mourn the destruction of his city? Or was he the one to sow it?

To this day, no one knows the answers.

44

LOULIE

The tale of the Tide Bringer was nothing like Loulie expected.

Of all the ifrit—or *jinn kings*, as the stories called them on the surface—he had been the most enigmatic, a shadowed monster wreathed in scales. Now, listening to his story, Loulie could not help but feel a pang of remorse for him. In a way, the ifrit reminded her of Mazen, internalizing guilt for crimes he had not committed.

"What happened to him?" Loulie asked when the story was over.

Duha fell back on her palms with a shrug. "No one knows for certain. He has not been seen since the war. Some believe it is because he remained on the surface."

Loulie frowned. If that was true, then it meant Ramiz had been in the human realm when Ghiban was seized by humans. Had he fought to protect the marid? That his binding was still intact meant he had survived, but Loulie had heard no stories of him from human storytellers.

Nabila's sigh cut through Loulie's pondering. "Does it matter? In the end, he left just like the others. Though I barely knew him, messenger that he was."

Loulie thought of Ziyad, who had become the envoy to a jinn queen. Was it a coincidence she had chosen a marid the same way Duha's queen had chosen a jinn? When she asked Duha, she looked thoughtful. "Ziyad never told me why he chose to serve the usurper. It was always baffling to me, given how he despised the jinn."

Nabila scoffed. "I would not be surprised if the jinn queen has some blackmail over him."

Given the queen's threats, Loulie would not have doubted it either. Still, she was curious. Based on what Duha had shared of her and Ziyad's history, the advisors Nabila had described in the story must be...

"You and Ziyad are the advisors in the tale," Loulie said with some awe. She had thought their dispositions were familiar.

Duha winked. "Who do you think shared the story with Nabila?"

The ifrit nudged her, but there was a fondness in her eyes. "You spoke with Ramiz more often than I did. Perhaps I did not mind him so much because of your stories."

Glancing between the smiling marid and the ifrit, Loulie was struck by a sudden uncanniness. She forgot, sometimes, that the creatures she had met in this realm were ancient, that they had lived centuries before she even existed.

She cleared her throat to recapture their attention. "What happened to the Tide Bringer's spear? The one that contained the queen's power?"

"It disappeared, of course," Duha said. "Vanishing ifrit, vanishing spear."

Nabila scowled. "Perhaps the usurper queen has it on her wall of stolen weapons."

Loulie had nearly forgotten about the throne room filled with blades. Now she tried to recall the sight. Had she seen the spear there? Or was she misremembering?

Duha shoved a cup at her, startling her from her reverie. "Why the gloomy look, al-Nazari? You ought to drink!"

Loulie pushed her hand away with a grumble. "I was asking about the story—"

"The time for stories is over," Nabila said. "You will see the marid kingdom soon enough. We can search for the binding when we arrive." She pointed insistently to the glass. "It is an insult to reject the food offered to you by your host."

"Alcohol is *not* food."

Loulie's protests fell on deaf ears. When the sailors continued harassing her, she knew there would be little point in denying them. With a sigh, she snatched the cup from Duha. At first, she cringed at the taste of the alcohol, sour and far more potent than any of the liquor she'd had at Dahlia's tavern or Ahmed's estate. But the longer she drank, the more soothing the liquid became. By the time she had finished the drink, her mind was fuzzy in a pleasant way.

She slammed the cup down on the deck and said, "Another."

And the sailors, gods bless them, obliged her.

Had Qadir been here, he would have snatched the second cup away from her. But he was not, so Loulie drank to her heart's content. The more she indulged, the brighter the present became. The crude banter between the sailors was suddenly the funniest thing she'd ever heard. Every slurred joke drew a laugh from her, and she felt no shame joining in on the merrymaking.

She was downing her third cup when the conversation turned to song. Though her mind was too foggy to make out the lyrics of whatever Nabila was singing, Loulie nonetheless found herself clapping along with the sailors.

Instruments were retrieved. One sailor played a nay, another a tambourine, and even Duha took up a mirwas drum. The energy on the ship grew to a fever pitch that brought the sailors to their feet. The liquor was forgotten as the jinn shuffled and spun across the deck.

Eventually, it was Loulie's turn.

She sprang up with a grin, laughing as the world tilted beneath her feet. Letting the music buoy her steps, she twirled and tossed her head, beating her heels against the deck with the music. And when the jinn applauded, she timed the beat of her feet with their clapping.

The present blurred. One moment Loulie found herself performing the debka routine with Ahmed bin Walid. The next, she was trading steps with Mazen, grinning as she avoided his feet.

And then, suddenly, she was dancing not with a man, but with the wind itself. She did not realize Nabila had risen to join her until she saw the flash of her teeth. She was grinning—such a bright, dazzling smile it made Loulie startle even in her haze—and then she twirled away, matching Loulie's steps with exceptionally more confidence and grace.

Faced with the sight of the dancing ifrit, Loulie suddenly lost her concentration. She stopped and stared as the ifrit twined her hands through the air in delicate, hypnotic motions. The ship swayed with her movements—everything from the ashfire in the lanterns to the sails and the sand they crossed.

Loulie was enchanted. Even more so when Duha rose to join Nabila, spinning into her sphere and matching her motions with an enthusiasm that was unrefined but no less contagious. The two converged and parted like waves, moving around each other with such a frenetic energy it had all the sailors whooping and cheering.

Watching them, it occurred to Loulie that the two of them moved not like dancers performing a routine, but like two halves of a whole that had fallen back into synchroneity. Loulie had never seen anything like it before. A new emotion flared beneath the wonder. It was sharp and bitter and reminded her of the gaping absence she felt between her memories.

The feeling was loneliness, and it prickled against her skin. It was a phantom hand brush against her arm, a tickle of warm breath in her ear. All the kinds of touches she had once shied away from in Ahmed's diwan because the promise of his proximity had scared her.

But now, looking at the captain and her right hand, she wondered, Was it possible to find someone who would not tie down her heart but would instead set it free? Someone who would welcome her into their life without forcing her to give up her own?

Inexplicably, her mind wandered again to Mazen bin Malik. Their lives had not been entwined long, and yet she felt as if she knew him in a way she had rarely known anyone else. She had the creeping suspicion that he had come to know her just as well. It was a startling realization, one that left Loulie feeling uncomfortably vulnerable.

Thankfully, the musing evaporated with the music, leaving Loulie exhausted. Someone grabbed her arm before she could slump onto the deck. Much to her surprise, it was not Duha.

Loulie blinked bleary eyes at Nabila. "Your dancing was beautiful," she blurted. "Is that why they refer to you as the Dancer in the stories?"

Nabila sighed as she guided Loulie toward the cabin. "I did more than dance. I was a spymaster, a warrior. But the stories always paint me in simple shades."

The world grew fuzzy around the edges. Loulie was vaguely aware that she had been lowered onto a bed. "Maybe it's because you look happiest when you dance. You wear an honest smile, unlike when you're…" *Fighting. Destroying.* The words slipped from her tired mind.

Nabila sighed again, but it was not the beleaguered sound that had earlier escaped her lips. This was a sad, wistful noise, and it lingered in the air as Loulie settled against the pillows.

"Happiness is a hard-earned battle," the ifrit said. "But someday in the future, perhaps, I will lose myself in dance again." She paused, long enough for Loulie to assume she had drifted from the room. She was surprised when the ifrit leaned forward to tuck a strand of hair behind Loulie's ear. "What about you, human? Who were you thinking of when you danced tonight?"

In the haze of her fatigue, Loulie struggled to remember. She recalled dancing on a ship in Ghiban. A smile so bright it was contagious. She draped an arm over her eyes. "A man," she said.

The ifrit hummed. "The storyteller?"

Loulie nodded. She could still see the determination in Mazen's golden eyes. Could still feel the weight of his words—*Trust me*—as they sank into some small crevice of her heart. It had been a long time since she trusted anyone besides Qadir. It had been easier to assume everyone would leave her behind, that their lives would slip through her fingers like her family's had.

But this whole time, she had been lying to herself. Perhaps she and Qadir had that in common—they were both so scared of reliving the past that they had done everything to avoid repeating it.

Trust me, Mazen had said.

This time, she would.

At some point, Loulie heard the light patter of Nabila's retreating footsteps. "Rest well, al-Nazari." The door creaked open. "You will need it before we arrive at the city."

45

MAZEN

On the crab's back, it took them mere days to reach the island of Kharjem. Or at least, that was Mazen's estimation. Ever since the ashfire had been extinguished, a nearly perpetual darkness had engulfed the sky, stretching the nighttime hours into an infinite blur.

Mazen remembered when Loulie had told him being in this realm made her miss the stars. But Mazen's greatest yearning was not for the constellations but for the sun. He missed the natural warmth of the light on his skin, missed the way it soaked into the landscape, crystallizing the desert into a delicate collage of sands and cliffs and foliage. It was hard to believe *these* lands had once existed on the same plane and under the same sun.

If we make it out of here alive, it will be just like that again—one country.

The uncanny musing lingered as Mazen caught sight of Kharjem on the horizon. His first perception of the land was that it looked... flat. There were no cliffs, no dunes, no hills. What scant vegetation coated the island was yellow and withered, which contributed to its appearance as a hollowed-out husk. This was not a place decaying, but an island already starved.

Rijah came to stand beside him on the prow of the boat, their body limned in the unmistakable haze of ashfire. "We came just in time," they said. "This place does not have long."

Mazen cut a glance at the darkening sky, at the cracks running like splinters across the invisible barrier. "I worry that's true of the entire realm."

Every time he looked at those cracks, it seemed they had grown wider. What would happen when Loulie broke the next binding? What if they did not have time to unseal the last?

"No," Rijah said fiercely. "It will not sink. Not while I still draw breath."

Despite the arrogance of that claim, Mazen believed it—believed them. But the haywire magic was not his only concern. His mind drifted to Loulie. It always did, in these moments of quiet. He remembered her parting words to him: *Stay safe. If not for yourself, then for me.*

Mazen wished he could parse the depth of those words. Was she concerned for him because they were comrades? Friends? He had thought he'd read something else in her expression before she stormed away, but it was difficult to tell with Loulie.

"I can tell by your forlorn expression that you are thinking of the merchant." Rijah raised a sharp brow. "You ought to focus."

With a sigh, Mazen returned his attention to the task at hand as they docked. It was immediately clear they were expected. A group of soldiers—at least, Mazen assumed they were soldiers based on their uniforms—awaited them on the shoreline. At the head of the procession stood a tall, elegant jinn draped in glittering yellow shawls that, by all appearances, looked like liquid gold. Mazen took one look at her fine attire and the soldiers' deference and assumed this must be the new zaeema of Kharjem.

He bowed low. "Sayyidati. It is an honor to be in your presence. Nabila sent us to—"

She held up a hand. "Let us not waste time on formalities. I know why you are here and am grateful." She glanced between them, noting first the flaming bird on Mazen's shoulder, then the halo of ashfire around Rijah. Her lips pulled into a wry smile. "A human and an ifrit...I had heard rumors the ashfire found a new master, but what strange masters it has chosen."

Chosen was an odd way of paraphrasing the events that had led them to this moment, but Mazen knew the power of a good story.

He reached a hand toward the bird, smiling as it nuzzled its head against his palm. "I have met many incredible magics on my journeys, but none so brilliant as the firebird. I am humbled it trusts me." His eyes flitted to Rijah over his shoulder. "Even more impressive is Rijah's ability to *use* the magic."

The ifrit did not miss their cue. With nothing but a flick of their fingers, they summoned the ashfire to their palm. The soldiers tensed, glancing warily at their leader, but she remained poised at the sight of the fire. "Impressive" was all she said.

It was difficult to tell if she meant it. Mazen awkwardly cleared his throat. "Since Rijah has mastery over the fire, they can guide everyone onto the ships and to al-Malath."

"And you?" She arched a brow. "Why are you here?"

"I am here to help oversee the evacuation." He paused, then added, "There is a matter I would discuss in private, sayyidati. It is about what transpired during the queen's summit."

The soldiers immediately objected, but the zaeema silenced them with a decisive wave of her hand. "Leave us. Show the Shapeshifter to the boats."

Rijah eyed Mazen quietly, a clear question in their eyes: *Will you be okay?*

Mazen dipped his head with a forced smile. Rijah didn't look convinced, but they did not argue as the soldiers led them toward the shoreline. After lighting a torch for Mazen, Azhar followed from the sky to brighten their way. After, only one jinn remained, a burly soldier with a face hard and rigid as stone. Mazen assumed he was the zaeema's personal guard.

The zaeema of Kharjem looked at him expectantly. "Yousef, was it?"

Mazen had grown so accustomed to the name he did not even

have to think before he nodded. "And you? Is there a name by which I should refer to you?"

The tired smile returned. "Before my husband died, I had a name. But now that I have taken his place, you may call me what you called him: the zaeema of Kharjem."

A soft pang ran through Mazen's chest. "I'm sorry about your husband."

She inclined her head in acknowledgment. "My husband is the matter you wanted to discuss in private, sah? Speak."

At the crack in her voice, Mazen's story, so clearly laid out in his mind, suddenly fell to pieces. His hand hovered uncertainly at his satchel. He *knew* she was grieving. What kind of monster would he be if he used that grief to his advantage?

If Loulie were here, she would have laid out the terms of the deal persuasively and decisively. But as Mazen wrapped his fingers around the necklace—around the relic that contained the soul of the zaeema's husband—he realized he would be asking for a favor in exchange for a life. He could not bring himself to do it.

"I was there at the queen's summit," he started. "I was there when the binding was broken, and I was there when your husband . . . passed."

"When he was killed," she corrected.

Mazen flinched at the coldness in her voice. Of course that news had already reached her. Knowing there was little point in trying to comfort her, Mazen withdrew the chain he had recovered from Ziyad's ship and held it out to her.

Her expression slackened with shock. "Where did you get that?"

"As I said, I was there when the queen attacked your husband. I stole his relic off Ziyad's ship before I escaped. I thought you might want it."

A favor for his relic. That was the bargain he was meant to strike. And yet, even knowing their plan hinged on this deal, Mazen could not bring himself to put a price on such a precious item. When the zaeema reached for the relic, he relinquished it without a word.

In the long, silent moments that passed, Mazen wrestled with his decision. Even when the stakes were this high, even when Loulie was in danger, his bleeding heart had failed him. What kind of noble was he, that he could not manipulate others?

"Look at me, Yousef."

His eyes flitted nervously to the jinn. He saw that she had already clasped the ruby around her neck. The gemstone now rested between her collarbones.

"I owe you a debt," the zaeema of Kharjem said. "Name it."

Mazen was startled by the offer. He must have worn his shock openly; she looked annoyed with him. "Do you think us such duplicitous creatures that we would never offer our own bargains?" She shook her head. "I saw the look in your eyes—you want something from me, and I would not have you still your tongue because of pity."

"That was not my intention—"

"Then speak."

Mazen drew in a deep breath, steeling himself. "Do you still possess the marid water that allows you to speak to Ziyad?"

She raised a sharp brow. "Why do you want to speak with the queen's envoy?"

Mazen could have made up some elaborate lie. But honesty had served him well thus far, so he simply said, "Because I want to save someone important to me."

"And what does your companion have to do with Ziyad?"

"I want to make a bargain with him," Mazen said carefully. "I promise it will not interfere with your evacuation. I need only to speak to Ziyad, and afterward, I plan to meet up with my companion. If it would ease your suspicion, you can listen to our conversation."

The zaeema shot a look at her guard, whose rigid expression echoed her caution. She glanced back at Mazen. "This has the sound of deceit to it."

"No deceit, sayyidati. Just desperation." He held her gaze, hoping she would see his sincerity.

The zaeema's fingers twitched as she touched the ruby resting above her heart. For a few moments, she considered him quietly, eyes narrowed. Mazen was relieved when she relented. "Fine. But I will oversee your discussion."

With her bodyguard trailing behind them, she began to guide him through the forest toward her manor. In the dim torchlight, Mazen witnessed the decay of the island up close. The trees were long dead, the palm fronds drooping low and ashen to the ground. Dead leaves crunched beneath Mazen's feet, and shadows writhed across the forest floor, twisting away from the glow of the ashfire as they traveled.

The few jinn who remained inland passed Mazen with vacant expressions on their faces. Many of them bore visible injuries, which was strange given how easily jinn could seal their wounds. When the zaeema saw his unease, she said, "This darkness weakens not only our minds, but our magics." She idly tapped the jewel around her throat. "The fall of the curfew is the fall of anarchy; there is little we can do to protect ourselves against such illusions."

Mazen remembered what Loulie had told him about curfew fall on al-Malath. Those illusions had twisted her mind and painted the islanders as soldiers. It had made them into enemies. He wondered if that darkness had devastated the other islands in a similar way.

By the time they arrived at the manor, Mazen's blood was humming with anticipation. Unlike the rest of the forest, this place still buzzed with activity, the servants rushing through the corridors to clean out rooms. They stuffed bags with an impossible number of items and then loaded those deceptively small sacks onto wagons outside the manor.

The zaeema passed all this without comment. Her bodyguard remained outside as she led Mazen into one of the barren rooms. Based on its spacious size, he guessed it had once been a bedroom, but it was hard to tell with the furniture cleared. There was only a brazier and a table left, both pushed to opposite corners of the chamber. Incongruously, there was a platter of steaming cups on the table.

Chai for the servants, the zaeema explained when she saw Mazen staring. She gestured in invitation. He plucked one of the cups off the tray to be polite but could not stop himself from staring uncertainly at the drink.

A flicker of amusement crossed her face. "It is not poisoned."

"Sorry, I did not mean to insult your hospitality. I just have, ah, terrible luck."

Mazen saw the briefest flash of teeth—*A smile?*—on the jinn's face before it vanished. "Unlike my late husband, I do not much see the appeal of subterfuge."

Regret washed over Mazen. He drank to avoid responding. When he lowered the cup, he was surprised to see the zaeema still watching him. "I admit you are not what I was expecting. The queen said you were a conniving criminal, but I see no malevolence in you."

Mazen's fingers curled tighter around the cup. "I never meant any of you ill will."

"I believe you." The zaeema gestured him over to the brazier on the other side of the room. Like the containers in the queen's throne room, it was filled with water rather than fire. "The water is enchanted by the queen's envoy. His magic is still active, which is why I plan on leaving it here. To call on Ziyad, all you must do is tap the surface."

Her gaze bore into Mazen as he leaned over the brazier. "You will not tell him the location of al-Malath?"

"I swear I will not say a word."

Her shoulders loosened. "Then I will hold you to your promise." She turned, heading for the doorway, but then paused to glance back at him. "I assume Nabila knows nothing of this correspondence?"

Mazen had not been expecting the direct question. He faltered, but the zaeema just shook her head. "It is just as well. I am grateful to Nabila for her assistance, but I do not care for the deal she struck with my husband."

Deal. The word gave Mazen pause. Back in Dhahab, the zaeem of Kharjem had confessed that Nabila had offered a bargain to all the zuama'a: safety for their cooperation. Now he tentatively said, "He mentioned that she would offer sanctuary for his assistance?"

The sardonic smile was back on the zaeema's lips. "If only such debts were so easily paid. Nabila saved our lives; she will be expecting us to use them in service of her ambitions."

The zaeema did not clarify what she meant, but Mazen had his suspicions. After all, Nabila had promised the zuama'a not just a return to the surface, but justice. If she had been recruiting them for that cause, then perhaps the queen was right to fear her.

If so, Mazen would *not* let Loulie be another of Nabila's discarded tools.

As the zaeema moved to watch him from the entryway, Mazen turned back to the still water in the brazier. It did not look enchanted, but he knew Ziyad's magic was unassuming.

I'm doing this for Loulie.

With a deep breath, Mazen leaned over the brazier and tapped the water.

46

AISHA

Aisha's room was exactly as she'd left it.

There was her bed, the sheets still made, with all the bare necessities surrounding it—the cupboard, the chest, the simple rug. Even the sheets of henna remained on her walls. Only her blades, which had once hung from hooks around the chamber, were gone.

Looking at the room, Aisha was struck by the absurd thought that whatever space she'd carved for herself in Omar's force had yet to be filled. But that was impossible. She *knew* how easily replaceable she was. Omar had made that clear to her in the throne room.

At Samar's gesture, she trudged into the room with bound wrists and seated herself at the edge of the bed. She looked at the thief, who regarded her wearily. "What, here to reminisce?"

The faintest of smiles touched his lips. "It truly has not been the same around here since you left, Princess."

There was that feeling again—that sensation of sliding back into an old, comfortable routine. She turned away, angry at herself for the sentimentality.

She could feel Samar still watching her. "Why did you betray us, bint Louas?"

Because you betrayed me first.

She didn't bother lifting her gaze, just glared at him beneath her lashes. "Omar lied to me. I refused to be a tool for him any longer." For as heated as the words were, they lacked potency. They were, after all, now an empty claim.

Aisha recalled her encounter with Samar in the Bowels. Remembered the sad smile on his face when he had greeted her, and the way he had apologized when he bound her hands. If she didn't know better, she would have suspected he cared what happened to her.

She raised her chin to look at him. "What about you? Why would *you* kill other jinn?"

Samar's expression was torn between frustration and grief. "Because the jinn we kill are criminals. Anyone who makes it to the surface is deemed as such."

"And what is their crime?"

"Escaping."

Aisha stared. It was a surprisingly cold response coming from Samar. But then, he *had* always carried out his hunts without complaint. Despite the blood on his hands, he had always returned with a jovial smile. Now, however, he was guilty enough to avert his gaze. "Those jinn who make it to the surface are not just deserters, but traitors."

She arched a brow. "And who are they betraying?"

For a few moments, the thief looked like he might answer her. But in the end, he settled on a deflection. "I'm afraid I am not permitted to share that information with you."

With those remorseful words, he turned back to the door. "Ma'a salaama, bint Louas." He shut the door behind him.

In his absence, Aisha slumped against the bedframe. She had known for years that Omar was seeking ifrit relics and had his eyes set on the throne. She also knew that he was a tenacious bastard. That, like her, he would chase his goals to the end of the world if need be, and willingly sacrifice others to obtain his heart's desire.

But now she realized she had only ever known half of the story. After all, Omar had never told her about his alliance with the jinn.

Had never told her that many of the thieves she was working with were jinn themselves. What had he said in the ruins beneath the Sandsea when she had first discovered his betrayal?

The jinn who flee into the human lands are criminals in their world. Is it so strange I would work with jinn who want to exterminate them?

But who were those jinn exterminators? What deal had Omar struck with them?

Aisha rolled the possibilities over in her mind as she worked at the manacles on her wrists, but there was little information to go on. She fared no better puzzling out the shackles. They were iron, clearly made for jinn, and they burned against her wrists and made it impossible for her to reach the Resurrectionist.

She turned her attention to her surroundings. She soon found out the door would not budge; whatever lock had been put on it was too complicated. The window was also not an option. She was too high up, and the nearby wall had no scaffolding to hold on to.

Aisha paced her cage until evening fell. She realized how much time had passed only when she noticed the darkness suffusing the room. A pang ran through her chest when she glimpsed the moonlit sky outside. Back when she had *willingly* been a thief, she would have used this time to sharpen her swords in her window alcove. But that time had long passed.

Aisha turned away with a huff, only to freeze at the sight of the open door.

Omar bin Malik leaned quietly against the doorframe, arms crossed. Aisha had not heard his footfalls. She had not even heard the door open.

Alone in the chamber, Omar looked more himself, dressed in a black bisht and stripped of all his jewelry but for Hakim's ring on his right hand. But he was more than just a hunter now. He was the godsdamned *sultan*, and she'd been a fool for thinking he would not use her as a tool to gain power in this twisted court.

Omar's lips curled in an infuriating smile. "How rare to see you at a loss for words. And after I came all this way to see you."

Aisha reflexively stepped back. Her first instinct was to reach for her swords, but the only weapon she had at her disposal was the collar, and the iron dulled the magic to a useless thud.

It was as if Omar could read her mind. His smile slanted into a smirk as he inclined his head toward the doorway. "Follow me."

Though she bristled at the command, she had little choice but to obey. Thankfully, it was a quiet, uneventful walk. Aisha used the time to take in the palace. It was unsettling, how deceptively serene the place was. If, as Hakim had claimed, this courtyard had been the scene of Omar's coup, there was little physical evidence to suggest it. The architecture seemed whole, the courtyard vibrant beneath the lanternlight—perhaps even more so than it had been before.

And yet despite that tranquility, it still had the feeling of a battlefield. The wandering servants were jumpy as soldiers awaiting a skirmish, and the landscape felt strangely hostile. Trees loomed, once-straight pathways suddenly seemed winding and treacherous, and the sound of the wind through the trees was a dreary, forlorn sigh.

It occurred to her that this courtyard had been a graveyard for a long time, and that Omar's coup was only the most recent massacre to have taken place upon its grounds. Before that, dozens of jinn had been bled out on this soil to create the beautiful greenery they were roaming through. And before that, the sultan had murdered his many wives here in cold blood.

Though Aisha's magic was muted, she could spot the golden glimmer of lost souls in the ground. It seemed not all the jinn who had been killed here had been bound to relics.

"Amazing, isn't it?" Omar was watching her out of the corner of his eye. "This soil is saturated with blood, but not a single corpse has left its mark here."

"A single *human* corpse," Aisha muttered.

Omar only looked at her, amused. "Did you rediscover your conscience while you were away, Aisha? How unfortunate."

Anger mingled with shame as Aisha turned away, putting an end to the conversation.

Thankfully, it was not long before they reached their destination:

the royal quarters where the sultan's family was housed. Of course, only one member of the family lived here now, and so the corridors were eerily empty. Aisha remembered how, not long ago, she had met Prince Mazen in this courtyard. How little he had known then. How little they had *both* known.

She shoved the thought away as Omar led her into the building that housed the sultan's apartments. Inside, he guided her through sparkling corridors to a pair of magnificent silver doors. Two soldiers stood guard outside but stepped aside at a gesture from Omar.

Omar bade her to enter first. Inside, Aisha took in the rich furniture and the large, canopied bed. She imagined the previous sultan lying limp on the sheets, bleeding out through a tear in his throat.

The doors thudded closed as Omar stepped into the chamber. He smiled. "It was a quick death," he said, reading her mind. "I was uninterested in conversation, so I slit his throat."

"What did he look like?" The question came from her lips, unbidden.

His lips curled into a faint smile that did not reach his eyes. "He looked anguished. Confused. I was wearing a different face, after all."

Mazen's face. Aisha could not stop seeing the prince in her mind, bright-eyed and smiling. She had wondered before how he had remained soft in this place filled with vultures. Was he still the same way, even now? To survive loss was one thing. To survive betrayal was another.

"Why did you not declare victory over him with *your* face? Your voice?"

Omar laughed. It was a humorless sound, stark and cold. "Come, Aisha. You know me better than that. With the sultan, it was never about victory. I wanted him to suffer."

There was a bitter vitriol laced beneath his words. Aisha had never asked Omar for his reasons, but they were not difficult to infer. The sultan had killed Omar's mother. The sultan had known Omar possessed jinn blood and used him for it, the same way Omar had used Aisha.

They were the same. All of them, monsters. Only Mazen had been innocent, and now he would be haunted by imaginary blood on his hands for the rest of his life.

Omar gestured her through the room into a branching chamber. Aisha had expected a diwan, but this seemed more a storage room filled with shelves of musty objects and scrolls. Her attention went to the long camel-hair rug that was the room's centerpiece. The embroidery so reminded Aisha of the henna Umm Jaber had painted on her arms that she had to turn away.

Much to her surprise, she saw the room was not empty. A man sat on a rickety old chair, thumbing through a tome. Recognition shuddered through Aisha at the sight of him. She would never forget this man—this *jinn's*—corpse-like face with its sunken features. The last time she had encountered him, it had been in Dhyme, when he'd scolded her for losing the Resurrectionist's collar.

Junaid's lips slanted into a gruesome smile at the sight of her. "Long time no see, traitor."

"It has not been long enough, *jinn*," Aisha responded coolly.

Omar chuckled. "How nostalgic." He shut and locked the door behind him. Aisha tensed as he slid the key into an inner pocket. "As much as I enjoy your barbed tongue, I did not bring you here to throw insults at fellow thieves, Aisha."

She eyed Junaid as he rose from his chair and silently stalked through the room, watching her with that awful smile. Standing between the two thieves, Aisha felt cornered. She forced her gaze back to Omar. "Why *did* you bring me here, then? What is this place?"

"The sultan kept his own special collection outside of the treasury. As for the why . . ." He tapped his neck. "I require your assistance."

There was no mistaking what the gesture meant. For as cold as the collar had grown around Aisha's neck, she thought she felt an urgent vibration from it in response.

When she said nothing, Omar continued, "You should be grateful. I have been looking for these relics a long time. That I would let you keep one is the highest honor."

Not an honor. A leash.

So long as she wore the relic around her neck, he could threaten her, control her with iron. Which was why what he said next shocked her. "I can release you from your shackles," he said. "But only if you give me your word you will not try to escape." He gestured toward Junaid, who had taken up a sentinel position at the door. "If you do, I will have Junaid steal it from you."

Aisha was insulted. "You think *Junaid* can match my speed?"

The thief's dreadful grin widened. "Try me, bint Louas."

Aisha glared at him, perplexed. Junaid was nimble—this she knew. Long ago, he had been proclaimed the fastest rider in their band of thieves and deemed Omar's most reliable messenger. But that was on horseback. He did not look so spry now with his gangly, creaking limbs.

Still, she was curious. Curious enough to assent. She stood statue still as Omar withdrew another key, this one specifically for her shackles, and began to unlock them. Aisha drew in a deep breath as the iron fell away from her wrists and the magic—magic she had so long denied—flooded through her body once more.

She reached hesitantly for Amina. *Ifrit?*

Thief. The Resurrectionist's presence rekindled in her mind like a flame. *I am here.*

And then Aisha felt a different source of heat: Omar's fingers, encircling her wrist. He was standing close enough she could see the hunger in his eyes. "What is it like, bint Louas, to share a body with an ifrit?"

His touch was like ants crawling up her skin. Aisha could feel the ifrit's own displeasure radiating through her blood as she breathed with Aisha's lungs. *We should kill him*, she said.

But Omar's grip was like a vise, and he, unlike her, had many weapons at his disposal. His wit, his knives, and Hakim's ring, all at his fingertips.

Without flinching, Aisha answered, "Annoying."

The answer seemed to take him by surprise. He withdrew with a laugh. "Perhaps you have changed less than I thought." He gave her a measuring look. "You can speak with the ifrit?"

"I can speak for her," she returned cautiously. "What do you want from us?"

She braced herself as Omar strode across the room toward the shelves. The objects on the shelves were relics, she realized. She had not heard them before beneath the roar of the iron, but now she could discern their final pleas and screams, and the sound filled her with revulsion. She expected Omar to grab something from the shelf and ask her to read its memories. Instead, he knelt by the rug. With a hard tug, he pulled the fabric from the tiles, revealing...

A terrible buzzing filled Aisha's mind at the sight of the intricate etchings on the ground. Though she did not know why, her body had begun to quiver with dread. She did not know what those markings were, and yet—another part of her *did* know.

Thief. The Resurrectionist's voice was strained. *You must listen.*

And for the first time, Aisha let down her mental walls and listened. The ifrit's memories overtook her with the violence of a tempest. In them, Aisha saw those same etchings carved on different soil with magic. *Bindings,* Amina told her. And then Aisha looked down and saw those markings on her—*no,* on the Resurrectionist's skin.

This was a memory, the markings having been lost when Amina "died," but the magic on Aisha's skin felt real. She had carved them into herself, a connection between her and the bindings her king had drawn across the realm.

A magic to trap magics, she thought. *And a magic to connect them.*

As quickly as it had crashed down upon her, the flood of memories stopped. Through it all, Aisha had been staring blankly at the binding on the ground. "How?" Her voice was faint, cracked through with the Resurrectionist's horror.

Omar gave her a smug look. "Are you surprised, mighty ifrit? Surprised a lowly *human* could craft such magic? Your fallen king was too. Like a fool, he ridiculed me.

"When I told him I would claim your relics, your power, for myself, he told me I would never find them all." His fingers went absently to the ring on his finger. "And when I discovered the glowing markings etched into his skin reacting to some distant magic, he told me I did not have the power to replicate it. But my mother was no simple jinn."

Aliyah, Aisha remembered. Aliyah, the sultan's forgotten wife. Aliyah, the Mystic. Omar's mother was not just a jinn, but an ifrit. And though Aisha had never seen him use magic beyond the crescent earring he no longer possessed, what did *she* know of his abilities?

With a wry smile, Omar yanked up one of the sleeves of his bisht. Aisha jerked back at the scars on his skin. Most of them were short and jagged, and shaped like bursts of fire. She thought of her own scars, which had been carved into her by jinn. But these marks were self-inflicted, the desperate attempt of a man reaching for a power that was not his own.

"Why?" she demanded. "Why would you do this to yourself?"

Omar shrugged as he let the sleeve fall. "Because it is my magic by right."

She glanced again at the binding, trying to reconcile what she had learned with the ifrit's knowledge. The markings were familiar. She had seen them before—but where?

Remember, the ifrit said urgently. *Remember when Qadir used his magic.*

The first time she had seen the bodyguard use his power, it had been as they were trying to escape a horde of ghouls. She remembered the magic burning on his arms. These etchings—they were the same ones on his skin. Which meant...

"You carved my king's magic into your body," the Resurrectionist said through her.

Omar smiled. "An astute observation."

He tapped the markings on his arm, thoughtful. "The first time the ifrit's markings glowed, I did not understand. Locked in iron, the bodyguard should not have been able to use his magic. But then I realized the markings were reacting to something else. His magic, in a different world. That was when I understood the nature of the magic. It does not just connect magics—it can trap them as well. Trap them in an object, a body...an entire world."

Aisha had already gathered from the Resurrectionist's memories that it was the bindings that kept the jinn realm alive. That they were the only reason it still *existed*.

You couldn't have spoken to me about this magic before? Aisha hissed in her mind.

Your ignorance is your own fault, the ifrit snapped. *How many times have I told you that there is no divide between us, that we are one and the same? But you refused that invitation.*

Aisha felt a twinge of regret. She had always kept the walls around her mind up because she had assumed the ifrit would destroy her autonomy. But now she realized Amina had never done more than toe that divide as she waited for her to accept her presence.

Omar was still talking. He had always liked to hear himself talk, Aisha thought. Now he gestured toward the binding on the ground. "This magic will allow me to enter that realm and regain what has been taken from me," he said.

Aisha thought of the earring the merchant had stolen from him. "Aliyah's magic?"

He inclined his head in acknowledgment. "The relic. And the cities."

Aisha stared at him. "You already have a throne."

"My father's throne," Omar said. "But that is not my only birthright."

Sudden grief surged through Aisha. It was not her own, but the Resurrectionist's. While she had no recollection of Omar's mother, Amina had known her as the Mystic. And she knew, from her memories, that Aliyah *had* expected a throne. Qadir had promised them all one.

"The human and jinn realms are two sides of the same coin," Omar continued. "But I will do more than lead them both. I will unite them."

Had it been Mazen proclaiming such a thing, it might have sounded like a declaration of peace. From Omar's mouth, it could be nothing but a threat. Over the years, he had done nothing but steal jinn magic. For himself and now for this city. Any union he promised would be won with fear, not peace.

"You would start a war?" Aisha's voice was faint.

"Are we not already at war? All I am doing is eliminating players from the board." He toed the binding. "At least, that is my intention. But I am missing something."

Ah, so the binding did not work for him. Not yet.

He needs magic, the ifrit whispered in Aisha's mind. *He believes that he has trapped Qadir's magic in his body, but that is wrong. In his blood, there is only poison. He needs a source. A relic or... a jinn he can draw magic from.*

"Well?" Omar arched a brow. "Will you tell me how to finish this, Aisha?"

What would he do if he knew the truth? Would he bleed one of his thieves dry for their magic? Would he steal the relic from her neck and siphon magic from it the same way she was now borrowing the queen's magic?

Omar seemed unbothered by her silence. "I will give you some time to think." With a gesture of his hand, he ushered Junaid forward. The thief moved so fast, Aisha barely had time to blink before he clasped the shackles back on her wrists. The iron immediately burned through the ifrit's voice, her magic.

Aisha's mind went quiet once more.

"Remember, Aisha: my patience is finite." Omar tapped the circlet around her neck. "And if you do not take my threat seriously, *your* time will be finite too."

The terrible smile remained etched on his face as Junaid led her from the chamber.

47

LOULIE

In the days leading up to their arrival at the Eastern Marid City, Loulie sought out whatever information she could find about the sunken metropolis. The sailors, who clearly enjoyed spinning gossip in their free time, regaled her with tall tales.

The city was built in the skeleton of a gigantic dendan, they said. The water it had sunk beneath was dark—so dark you would not be able to spot the deadly jellyfish in the waves until the swarm surrounded you. Dive deep enough, they claimed, and you would find yourself amongst the bloated corpses of marid that had perished during the war.

Loulie was bemused by the dramatizations. When Duha surreptitiously started listening from a distance, Loulie smiled at her mock fascination.

"A gigantic dendan!" she exclaimed. "You think our city was so *small?*"

After the sailors had rushed off with muttered apologies, she turned to Loulie and said, "Well? Do *you* have any stories of the mythical marid city?"

Had Mazen been here, Loulie had no doubt he would have some story to share. As it was, the only ones she knew were of Ghiban. And those stories—the tales of marid being massacred and then bled out to make the waterfalls surrounding the city—were clearly not worth sharing.

Perhaps Duha knew this. When Loulie muttered that all she knew were falsehoods, she sighed. "You would be surprised by how many lies I have been told about my own kind. Jinn are like humans that way, so steeped in their own biases they believe the lies they speak."

When at last Nabila called them to the prow and pointed west toward the city, Loulie was confused. She could see no city, just an archipelago of mountains dotted across the Sandsea. It was only when Nabila called on Duha to guide them that Loulie realized the location they were looking for was *between* the mountains. As far as Loulie could tell, she was guiding them by memory, easily pointing Nabila through the winding straits until they came to the island that appeared to be their destination.

The majority of the rocky terrain was taken up by a large saltwater lake, which they entered through a lock in the waterway. A single building constructed from multicolored glass sat upon the surface, illuminated as if by some unnatural glow. But the most remarkable thing about the construction was not the material from which it had been created, but the way it rose directly from the lake. The building lay at the heart of a network of glass bridges that, as far as Loulie could tell, floated on the water without foundation or support.

She stared at the massive tower. It was magnificent, to be sure, but it was hardly a city. Based on Duha's and Nabila's accounts, she had expected the city to be underwater; she could not make sense of this ruin.

Once they had reached the clearing, Nabila stilled the wind in the sails and said, "We shall have to continue on foot to the Audience Hall." She looked at Duha. "Watch the ship?"

The usual smile was absent from Duha's face as she gave her assent. She remained on the ship with the sailors while Nabila led Loulie down one of the bridges to the hall. Loulie glanced up at the building as they walked. "If this is the Audience Hall, where is the rest of the palace?"

"Underwater. The Audience Hall is the only building the marid built on the surface."

Loulie had been tiptoeing carefully across the glass. Now she stopped, taken aback. "Why?"

"Why not try to puzzle this mystery out yourself for a change?" The ifrit sighed as she continued ahead, her normally soft steps ringing sharply against the fragile glass.

By comparison, each of Loulie's strides was a slow, heavy plod. Was it just her imagination, or was the glass shuddering beneath her? Seeking a distraction, she turned her mind to Nabila's explanation. If the Audience Hall was up here... then it was likely because it needed to be. Perhaps this was the only place the marid entertained land-dwelling guests.

And yet...

Her eyes wandered to the water. At first, it was impossible to make out what she was looking at. Not because the water was dark and foggy, but because her mind refused to piece together what lay in the depths. Then, fragment by fragment, she discerned the gleaming constructions. The glittering roofs, the silt hills, the forest of coral growing between stone walls...

This was the fabled marid city.

As beautiful as the cityscape was, it was pervaded by an eerie stillness. The place had the look of a locale that had been left to decay. Now all that remained of it was a pretty, lifeless shell. A memory of grandeur. It certainly *looked* like a cursed place.

"Al-Nazari." Nabila had reached the front doors of the tower and was looking back at her. "You have the compass? I will let you lead the way."

With a breath, Loulie pushed open the doors, revealing a massive chamber. She was immediately taken aback by the interior—by the stained-glass windows splintered with more fractures than colors, by the seashell-lined alcoves eroded by water and time, and by the chipped coral traveling up the walls toward a ceiling looming above reef balconies.

At the far end of the chamber sat what she thought must be a throne, though it looked less like a chair than a large pedestal over-grown with algae. Naturally, it was where the compass led her. As she walked, a familiar glow began to fill the room. A familiar *magic*.

The ifrit lingered at the edge of the chamber as Loulie ventured forward. As the fire from the binding rose around her, she noted that this light was different than the others. It was dimmer, almost smokelike, and Loulie had the strange impression it was rippling around her like water.

No, not ripples. A vortex.

If the binding in Dhahab had been a labyrinth and Nabila's binding had been the eye of a storm, then this magic was a whirlpool. Loulie could feel its push and pull as she moved. Walking through it was like wading through the ocean, each step heavy and slow.

At the center of the binding, she pulled out Qadir's dagger. As it had before, the fire flickered to life at her proximity to the center. But something was different. She knew it the moment she pulled the blade from its sheath and it began to hum. She watched in aston-ishment as the darkness on the blade peeled away to reveal glowing dots on the surface.

Eyes.

Loulie's breath caught in her throat when those eyes found hers. "Qadir?" she whispered.

And for the first time in weeks, the jinn responded in her mind, *"Loulie, where are you?"*

The shock of his presence crashed down on her like a wave. "I'm . . ." She faltered, mind scrambled with shock.

"Loulie." His voice was gentle but urgent. *"Tell me."*

She blinked back sudden tears on her lashes. Her heart was pounding so loud and hard in her ears she could barely hear herself say, "The Eastern Marid City. Where are *you*?"

But he did not answer. Instead, he said, *"Wait for me."*

Then his eyes were gone, the fire once more eating up the surface of the blade. Loulie stared at the edge in shock. After all this time, he had spoken to her. What if it had been a dream? Her desperate mind playing tricks on her?

Dimly aware of Nabila calling her name on the outskirts of the binding, Loulie forced herself to concentrate on the magic. She discerned that the walls of fire had grown higher as she made her way to the center, almost as if she was descending into the binding as she walked.

It was then she realized the vortex she was in went deeper than this floor. The true center of the binding lay at the center of a whirlpool *beneath* the building.

When Loulie exited the binding and told Nabila this, her focus was scattered. She could not stop thinking about Qadir. Qadir, who had finally spoken to her.

Qadir, who was *coming* for her.

Or was he?

How far away was he? Would he be able to reach her before she unsealed the binding?

Loulie's mind was still reeling when Nabila spoke. "It seems we will need to dive into the city, then," she said. "I have an idea."

—◊—

Nabila's "idea" was to tie Duha to the anchor of the ship.

Much to Loulie's bafflement, neither the ifrit nor the marid thought this a problem. Because Duha's scales were venomous to the touch, this was apparently the best solution. The plan was a simple one: Nabila would drop the anchor, and somehow, Duha would sink the ship down into the depths with her magic. The enchantments Nabila had placed on her ship would keep the air in their lungs while they dove, and then they would search for the binding together.

"Only the marid can navigate their cities," Nabila said. She spoke defensively, as if she was trying to convince herself as much as Loulie that drowning Duha was a good idea.

Duha, for her part, seemed perfectly amenable to the plan, even when it involved Nabila wrapping her body in thick ropes. Or perhaps, Loulie thought, she was only acquiescent because it was her captain who had made the request of her.

As far as Loulie could tell, Nabila handled Duha's entrapment with all the gentleness one could manage while securing someone's body in rope. More than once, Loulie caught her brushing her fingers gently against the marid's shoulder or cheek, a light caress most would have mistaken for an accidental touch.

Watching her, Loulie was struck by a sudden idea. When Nabila reached for the last of the ropes, Loulie slid her dagger carefully up her sleeve and grabbed the rope first. "Allow me. Duha taught me how to tie knots."

The ifrit looked incensed by the suggestion, but she could not complain when Duha offered her assent. "Let her do it, nokhitha." She grinned. "I am eager to see her progress."

At Duha's insistence, the ifrit begrudgingly helped Loulie onto the anchor, where she balanced herself on one of the prongs. The sight of the imprisoned marid unsettled her. Duha cut an imposing figure when she wanted to, but suffocated in ropes, she looked unbearably small.

When Loulie told her this, Duha actually laughed. "Small," she mused. "If your concern is that I will be too small to pull on these ropes, then cease your worrying."

Loulie's heart beat in her throat as she leaned over to secure the knot around the anchor. Thankfully, Duha mistook her nerves for concern. "Do not worry, al-Nazari! The ropes may be thick, but they are looser than you think. You shall see."

Loulie steadied her quivering hands as she looped the knot between Duha's collarbones. "I don't know if I'll be able to see much of anything beneath the water."

"Oh, you will. The city has its own source of light."

Loulie slid Qadir's knife from her sleeve. "Is it magic?"

"Of a sort. I would rather it be a surprise."

"Even at a time like this you would think of surprises?" She raised her hand—raised the knife—as her fingers found the clasp of Duha's pearl necklace. Sweat beaded her forehead.

"*Especially* at a time like this. You are unlikely to witness such a sight again."

With a breath, Loulie flicked the knife, severing the cord. Carefully, she slid the pearl into her sleeve. When the marid tensed, Loulie feared she would accuse her of theft. But Duha just released a hoarse laugh. "All right, I admit it. The ropes are a bit tighter than I would like."

As soon as Loulie had tied the final knot, the ifrit reappeared beside them, one of her corporeal hands gripping the shank. She leaned close—close enough to press her forehead to Duha's. "Had-han muwaffaq," she said softly. "I will see you when it is over."

"And beyond, nokhitha," Duha responded immediately. "I will follow where you lead."

With those parting words, the ifrit returned herself and Loulie to the deck and ordered the anchor lowered. Loulie tucked her hands into her sleeves, fingers gripping the pearl, and watched Duha. If the marid noticed Loulie had taken her necklace, she said nothing, her gaze focused on the water. Even when she vanished into the depths, Loulie forced herself to watch.

Behind her, the sailors muttered into the quiet, whispering about marid magic and doomed depths and their beloved first mate, swimming with corpses.

But then: a hard tug on the anchor.

The deck shuddered with the motion, unbalancing her. Loulie stumbled into the rails, then searched the water for any signs of Duha or magic. But the lake was still dark and calm.

Loulie was on the verge of voicing her concern when the ropes gave another tremendous yank and the ship *lurched*. They were capsizing, she realized with horror, the whole starboard side poised to hit the water. Nabila's voice was a roar above the rising tides. "*HOLD ON*," she said.

And Loulie did. She scrambled to grasp the rails as the anchor—and whatever Duha had become—pulled the dhow into the water.

Loulie managed one last breath before the haunted waters swallowed the ship whole.

48

AISHA

Over the next few days, Omar summoned Aisha back to his chamber multiple times. Though he clearly called on her with the purpose of soliciting answers, he never began with an interrogation. Instead, he did one of the things she despised most: he made idle conversation.

The first time she was brought before him, he told her at length about what had happened when he took over Madinne. He told her about the wali of Dhyme, who had died for being foolish enough to stand against him, and about the bloodshed in the courtyard. Afterward, when he asked her if she had anything to say and she remained silent, he sent her away.

The second time he called for her, he reminisced. "Do you remember the first time we met on the streets?" He smirked. "You had the same nerve as you do now, trying to steal coin from my pocket. You haven't changed, have you? You are *still* stealing from me, after all."

Again, she offered no response. Again, he sent her away.

It continued this way for three days, and every time Aisha came and went, the thieves seemed more and more agitated by Omar's patience with her. Aisha paid them little mind; if they had no information to offer her, then she had nothing to offer them.

Only Samar ever visited her, though his conversations were brisker than his sultan's. Always, he brought with him an air of mourning. Aisha did not care to ask why. She felt no sympathy for secret keepers, most of all when they were keeping secrets from *her*.

But then, on the third day, something between them shifted. Ever since her arrival, Aisha had been searching for an opportunity to escape. But there were no cracks in Omar's guard. It was no wonder, then, that on that day, something finally snapped in her.

This time, when Samar came into the room, she greeted him: "If you will not tell me why you are here, then I have no interest in talking to you."

He paused in the doorway, considering her with doleful eyes. "Would you believe that I am here for the pleasure of your company?"

She scoffed. "You ought to hate my guts. You know I hate yours."

Samar seated himself on a stool beside her bed. The last few times he had visited, Aisha had considered tackling him and searching his pockets for keys. But it was a foolish impulse. The jinn was a rock wall; Aisha had no doubt he would overpower her.

The two of them sat staring at each other—her with her glower and him with that damned pitying smile. "I do not think I have ever seen you so indecisive," he said.

Aisha bristled. "What do you know of my situation?"

"I know you have magic in your veins that the sultan wants." He lifted his shoulders in a shrug. "And I know you have yet to surrender it to him. If it were any of the rest of us holding out on him, he would have killed us already."

Aisha turned away. "You know that is not Omar's way. He never kills anything outright, not when he can maim it first."

She had no doubt that was what he was doing. It was not tolerance that stayed Omar's hand but some sick, twisted game. He would not have spared her otherwise. Would not have put on such a show when she had defied him in the throne room.

But Samar shook his head. "You are special to him, bint Louas."

Special. The word sent a visceral loathing through her. Omar bin

Malik did not care for anyone, least of all her. He judged people for their worth. She had only ever been a tool to him.

Samar leaned forward. "Do you know why are you special to him? It is because you were one of the few thieves chosen by him."

Omar had told her that before, but she had always thought it empty flattery, a ploy to win her loyalty. Now she wondered. Omar had said more than half of the thieves were jinn. If *he* had not chosen them, who had?

She glanced at Samar out of the corner of her eye. "Why serve him, then?"

At first, Samar said nothing. Aisha was not surprised; she had posed the question to him many times and received no answer. But now the thief *did* respond to her. "Because the queen *I* serve has seen fit to work with him," he said. "But..."

"But?"

"But we have not heard from her in a long time. Not since Omar lost communication with her messenger." He looked suddenly skittish, his eyes darting to the door as if he worried someone might overhear them.

Aisha frowned. Who were this queen and this messenger Samar spoke of? He would not offer names when she asked, so she tried another question: "What does your queen want? Why is she working with Omar?"

A muscle feathered in Samar's jaw. "She wants to cull the traitors who have made it to the surface. And she wants magic. Ifrit magic to protect..." He broke off at a knock on the door.

A servant—the only one who had interacted with Aisha since her arrival—entered the room, interrupting their conversation. The woman was stockily built and had an air of no nonsense to her. Despite the warm color of her eyes, her expression was always cold, her hair pulled back into a bun that rendered her frown more severe.

Samar rose, once more composed. "I shall return when Omar summons you." He paused, then added, "If I were you, I would tell him what he wants to know today."

He left the room as the servant set down the usual spread of food. She caught Aisha's eye as she straightened. "Sayyidati, if you continue to ignore the food, you *will* starve."

Aisha frowned at her, then the food. "Your sultan is not above poison."

Where Omar was concerned, it was a relatively mundane form of torture, but Aisha would take no chances. She was surprised, then, when the servant unflinchingly helped herself to a serving of all the food on the platter. The rice, the chicken, the marag sauce—all this she tasted for Aisha's benefit. Afterward, she raised her brows and said, "You ought to eat."

Her insistence was perplexing. Aisha eyed the food suspiciously after she had left.

She had just begun to scoop up the rice with her hands when she felt something cold between her fingers—an object with metal teeth. A thrill of shock ran through her as she pulled a *key* from the clump of rice. Upon closer inspection, she saw it fit perfectly into her shackles.

Aisha glanced at the doorway, but the servant had already departed, taking any answers with her. Aisha considered using the key to unlock her shackles but, after some consideration, slid it into the seam of her cloak instead. It was better, she thought, to wait for the right moment.

For the next hour, she pondered whom the servant might be working for. She was still thinking when the door opened again and Samar entered.

"The sultan will see you now."

As she had every day, Aisha followed Samar through the silent courtyard to the sultan's chamber. But this time when she entered, Omar was not alone. Her once king was seated at the table, a bored expression on his face as he twirled one of his black daggers in his fingers.

And sitting in front of him, blood running down a fresh cut on his cheek, was Hakim.

"Salaam, Aisha." Omar was smiling when he looked at her, but it was a flat smile. "I thought you might appreciate company today."

The mapmaker turned his head to look at her. He looked more than disheveled. While Aisha had been blatantly ignoring Omar with little consequence, Hakim looked as if he had been tortured for his silence. Bruises bloomed across his neck and face, and blood dripped from a split lip. His sleeves were rolled up, revealing injuries on his arms.

Her blood boiled at the sight. "Why is he here?"

In answer, Omar raised a hand. A single ring gleamed dully on his left hand. "I thought the mapmaker might be more willing to speak to me about his magic today."

Hakim lifted his head and said, "I have nothing to say to you."

Omar made a humming sound as he tapped his dagger against the table. "Stubborn as always. You only ever did speak up for Mazen, didn't you?"

He spoke Mazen's name with such vehemence it made them both cringe. Hakim's expression shuttered further at the mention of his brother. "I only ever spoke to *you* because of Mazen. Now I have no reason to."

"Oh?" Omar flipped the dagger in his hand. "How do you suppose he would respond if I dragged your corpse in front of him? He was so impacted by our father's death; I would be curious to see how much *your* death would break him."

Aisha stepped forward. "Enough with the dramatics."

Both men stared at her, Omar with mild annoyance and Hakim with surprise.

Aisha straightened. "Ask me your question, sayyidi."

She did not know what had come over her. With Samar at the door and Omar in front of her, there was no chance of her escaping the room. Perhaps if she could pull the key out from her clothing and unlock the shackles before Omar came for her, or if she could attack him first . . .

Omar stood from his chair. "Fine. Then I will ask again." He closed the space between them, moving close enough he could have sliced her throat in a single stroke. "Tell me what I am missing from the binding, Aisha."

Magic, she needed only to say. *You are missing magic.*

On its own, the binding was just a pattern of etchings. Omar had assumed he had enough magic in his blood to make the magic work, but his black blood had only ever killed things. What he needed was a jinn. A jinn who could sink their magic into the runes.

The answer caught in Aisha's throat. She saw Omar reach for his knife. Saw impatience spark in his eyes as—

The door burst open, startling them both. Samar stood in the entryway, eyes round with panic. "Sayyidi." His voice was faint. "The palace is under attack."

Omar spun toward the window. Aisha, who had been standing with her back to the glass, turned to follow his gaze. She blinked in surprise when she saw the fire that had broken out in the courtyard. Tongues of flame devoured the grass while the air swelled with smoke.

"It seems the ifrit has returned." A faint smile touched Omar's lips. "It is about time." His attention flicked briefly toward Aisha and then away as he walked past her toward the doors. "Hold your position, Samar. I will be back soon to deal with Aisha."

He promptly vanished into the corridor, leaving Samar to watch them both.

Aisha searched the courtyard for any sign of Qadir. From what she could tell, more than one fire had been kindled in the area. But Qadir would not have been able to start a fire in multiple locations... right?

She supposed it did not matter who had started the fires. If she wanted to escape, she only had as long as it took them to put the flames out.

Aisha glowered at Samar as she reached for the key in her sleeve. She hoped he could not detect the movement behind her back. "Does Omar truly think he can take on a jinn king?"

Samar regarded her grimly. "Why not? He has already captured him once."

Aisha twisted her wrists until she had inserted the key in the lock. Her concentration cost her. When she did not respond, Samar stepped forward, eyes narrowed with suspicion.

Hakim shot to his feet, stealing Samar's attention away from her. "Your *king* thinks he knows everything. That has always been his greatest mistake."

Aisha smiled at Samar's confusion. "No," she said. "His greatest mistake has always been underestimating *me*." Another twist, and her shackles fell. Aisha lunged toward Samar as the Resurrectionist's magic flooded back into her body. She tackled him to the ground.

He threw her off, but not before Aisha grabbed a dagger from his belt and aimed a stab at his shoulder. He hissed as the knife sliced through his skin, then threw Aisha back with his blade. He whirled on Hakim as she stumbled back.

The mapmaker had already retreated to the window. Aisha yelled when he yanked it open, thinking he meant to throw himself outside. The warning caught in her throat when she saw the black lizard on the windowsill.

The creature was small enough Samar did not notice it at first. But when Qadir slid off the sill in his man shape, there could be no mistaking his identity. The moment Samar spotted the bodyguard, he stumbled back, face blanched with fear.

It had been so long since Aisha had seen Qadir in this form that she was briefly taken aback by the intimidating figure he cut. Even now, weakened and fatigued, he still loomed. Eyes and arms aglow with magic, he looked exactly like one of the nightmares humans believed jinn to be.

"I-ifrit." Samar held up his hands. "Mercy. I will not harm you."

Qadir raised a sharp brow. "You had no qualms watching your king torture me before."

"There was nothing I could do! I promise, I mean you no harm."

A sharp crashing sound drew everyone's attention to the window. The fire outside was spreading fast, blazing through the courtyard at an almost unnatural speed. It seemed the thieves hadn't yet extinguished it. Aisha looked at Qadir. "Did *you* set that fire?"

"No." His lips slanted into a not-quite smile. "That was Dahlia's doing."

Dahlia bint Adnan? Just how many contacts did the woman have?

Qadir turned to Hakim. "I appreciate you letting me in. I had anticipated breaking a window."

The mapmaker inclined his head. "I assumed you would find us when the fire broke out."

They both turned at the sound of retreating footsteps. Aisha cursed when she saw that Samar had fled, leaving the door open behind him. If he told Omar—

Qadir grabbed her by the shoulder. "Where is Omar's binding?" When Aisha darted another nervous glance at the door, he said, more forcefully, "When I was imprisoned, Omar told me he was working on one. Show it to me, bint Louas, and then you may go after him."

With a grumble, she did as commanded, leading them both to the hidden storage room. She pulled the door open, kicked over the rug, and gestured at the etchings on the floor.

She frowned at Qadir as he studied the magic. "What are you doing?"

"I am completing it."

"Completing it? But Omar—"

"Will not be the one using it." The ifrit called on the mapmaker to stand by the door and then glanced around the room. At first, Aisha did not know what he was looking for, but then his eyes fell on an object on the shelf: a shamshir with a gemstone on the hilt.

It seemed better suited for display than battle, but Qadir handled it carefully, like it was some priceless object. He turned the weapon over in his hands, observing it from various angles before he declared, "This is my blade."

Aisha recalled the shamshir Qadir had carried with him on their last journey. As far as she remembered, he'd used it only once, against Omar's thieves. Perhaps its value was sentimental. She was surprised, then, when he proffered it to her and said, "Use it to distract Omar."

Aisha took the blade with a frown. "Why? What are you doing?"

Qadir selected another knife from the shelves. With a look, he summoned bright blue fire to its edge. He spoke as he knelt beside the binding. "Dahlia said you both needed my help to reach your prince. This magic will take us to the jinn realm, to him and Loulie. I need only connect it to the right place."

Aisha bristled. "You're using me as a *decoy*?"

"The minute your sultan realizes I am not outside, he will return." He gave her a sharp look. "He cannot enter this room until I am done. You alone might be able to distract him."

The damned ifrit was right. With a curse, Aisha turned and rushed out the door. She put on a burst of speed as she made for the courtyard, where, finally, Omar's thieves had smothered the fire. But the moment they saw her, freed and unshackled, their directive changed.

Aisha stood her ground as they approached.

49

AISHA

I will not run.

It had been nine years since Aisha had made that promise to her once king. Nine years since she had vowed to face her adversaries head-on so that they could not stab her in the back first. The promise had kept her standing against terrible odds, had fueled her determination even when fear threatened to expunge it.

Now it was a curse, rooting her in place as the thieves descended on the courtyard like a murder of crows. Even so, she would not falter. She had not come this far to cave to fear.

As the thieves congregated—Aisha counted five of them in total, including Junaid and Samar—Omar slid past them with his hands clasped behind his back. Even now, he wore his smile like a weapon, a *dare*. "Obstinate until the very end, I see."

The thieves moved to flank him. Aisha's eyes flicked between them, assessing. Junaid's and Samar's abilities she had already witnessed, but she did not know what to make of the other three thieves. And then there was Omar, who had never needed magic to best her.

That was before. Amina's confidence was her own, burning through her veins like fire. *But you are stronger now. We are stronger.*

They were outnumbered, it was true, but the ifrit was right. All they had to do was keep the thieves occupied long enough for Qadir to finish the binding. And if Aisha managed to kill them in the process, then . . . well, it would be an unexpected boon.

Omar inclined his head. "Any last words, bint Louas?"

Aisha reached for Qadir's shamshir. She altered her stance, one foot in front of the other. The thieves tracked her movements—but they could not see Aisha reaching for the threads of magic running beneath them.

Omar had the audacity to chuckle. "Fine. Then let us speak to each other with our blades."

Aisha let the ifrit's amusement bleed into her expression, let it pull up the corners of her lips in a smile that was and was not her own. "I have a different idea."

By the time the thieves realized what she was doing, it was too late. They had been moving to deflect a blade, and none of them expected her assault to come from beneath their feet in the form of a wall of thorns. Under Aisha's influence, the garden that had been a graveyard transformed into a battlefield. Though only Aisha could hear the memories of the dead, the courtyard itself was screaming—the grass hissing, the branches snapping, the leaves crackling.

Aisha was gratified to see the smile slide from Omar's face as he hacked at the thorns. He charged toward her like a storm, with enough momentum to lop off her head.

Aisha knew better than to meet his strike head-on. She feinted, ducking behind a tree as Omar's blade cut through the air. His swing took off a branch, but Aisha had already seized a different strand of magic. She yanked, sending another branch whipping toward him. As Omar dodged, Aisha retreated. She made it only a few steps before another thief came for her.

Junaid. Aisha could not hope to match his speed, so she reached again for her magic, loosing a flurry of leaves through the air and obscuring the thief's vision as she swept around the tree to attack him from behind. The strike caught him in the shoulder, but he had already vanished before Aisha could land a second blow.

She stepped back—and immediately came up against another obstruction. A tree, she thought at first, until she felt large arms wrap around her. The air left her lungs in a pained gasp as Samar crushed her rib cage. He sounded distressed as he whispered, "Princess, I—"

"*Don't call me Princess.*" She flung herself back, bashing his face with her head. With a surprised grunt, he released her, affording her enough time to stagger away—into another thief.

"I never thought I would see *you* relying on magic, Aisha." Now it was Omar behind her, the tip of his blade pinned between her shoulder blades.

Aisha threw a vicious smirk—hers or Amina's?—over her shoulder and said, "Jealous?"

His eyes flashed as she slid away. Aisha felt the sting of his blade in her shoulder but quickly shoved the pain aside. Knowing she had neither the stamina nor the advantage to carry out a drawn-out fight, she pivoted to defense. As the thieves chased her, Aisha sank her mind back into the roots of the courtyard, reaching for the souls buried there.

One of the thieves planted himself in front of her. With a gesture, he shifted the ground beneath them, throwing her off balance and using the movement to pin her against a nearby hedge. Aisha gritted her teeth against the impact and reached for the nearest thread. She pulled—and sent one of the surrounding topiaries crashing down on him.

Relief surged through her at the sound of his crushed body.

One.

The courtyard became a blur as she shot through it, avoiding blades and magic. All the while, Omar circled her from the fringes of the fight, antagonizing her from a distance. Aisha had counted on him playing with her; it was the only reason she was alive now. But while *he* circled like a vulture, the rest of the thieves attacked with bloodlust in their eyes.

Before she managed to slice one thief's throat, he stabbed her in the leg.

Two.

The injury slowed her movement, which made it easier for the third thief to land a blow to her hip. Aisha yelled as she spun on him, deflecting his next strike and slashing the shamshir through his torso. He collapsed with a gasp, his weapon tumbling from his hands.

Three.

When Junaid appeared, his strikes came in quick succession, too fast for Aisha to dodge. Nicks, all of them, but she could no longer ignore the blood seeping from her injuries. Aisha reached for the roots beneath her feet, but the thief would not be caught off guard again. Before she knew it, her back was up against a tree, and she was shaking with exhaustion.

For as much good as it would do her, she held up her blade.

Junaid approached with a serpentine smile. "What a pathetic way to die, bint Louas."

He readied his blade, shifted on his feet—and then stumbled. Belatedly, Aisha saw the shadow behind him. Samar, holding a bloodied rock in his hand. His eyes shone with remorse as Junaid crashed to the ground, and then with panic as Aisha gaped at him.

"Go," he whispered. "Find answers—for both of us."

Shock coursed through her as she fled. That sorrow in Samar's eyes—how many times had she dismissed it as empty empathy? How long had he planned to turn on Omar and why?

Perhaps your king is not the puppeteer he fancies himself, Amina said.

Aisha had no time to wonder, because moments later, that so-called puppeteer stood before her. "Aisha," he said, and his voice was cold like steel. "Do you think yourself invincible?"

When he started to move toward her, she sidestepped in the opposite direction until the two of them were circling each other. Aisha felt as if she had become trapped in some obscene dance. Only, this was a dance of steel and magic, and the wrong move would lead to her death. As tense as the air had become, this was familiar to her. How many times had Omar tested her like this, judging her movements while she learned from his? Aisha had been waiting to outmaneuver him.

Never mind the binding. Never mind Omar's plans. All that mattered in that moment was that she bury her blade in his chest.

When she did not answer, he continued, "Do you know what you are?" She saw the subtle slide of his fingers across the blade, the slight shift of his feet. "*You* are an abomination, and that is the only reason you are alive now."

He shot forward like an arrow, his blade a flash of steel through the air. Even before he pivoted, Aisha saw the feint in his step and swerved out of the way of his slash. His second strike came right after, a stab she barely deflected. The force of it rattled her bones. Aisha tasted blood on her lips and realized she had bitten her tongue.

He was no longer playing; she could see that now. He had come in for the kill. It was, in a way, a relief. He was no longer toying with her, because he knew she would not bend her knee to him again.

Finally, he had recognized her as an enemy.

The triumph was quickly replaced with horror as he advanced on her. Though she had always known Omar as a hunter, she had never experienced him as a *killer*. This viciousness, trained entirely on her, was a tempest she had never weathered before.

Distract him, Amina said. The moment she said it, Aisha knew how she would turn this battle. Omar may have been a master of manipulation, but she knew how to wield her words as weapons too.

"You realize"—she ducked beneath his next strike—"that *you* are an abomination as well?" His eyes flashed, a sign that she had struck a nerve. She grinned, injecting more venom into her words as she said, "At least *I* am an abomination that can use magic. How terrible it must be, to have the blood of a monster in your veins but not be able to use it for anything."

His next strike rang against her blade so forcefully it made her knees buckle. "When I cut that relic from your neck, *you* will be nothing but a corpse," he snapped.

She gritted her teeth as she pushed him back. Her hands were trembling as she said, "You think yourself a king, but what king has to resort to stealing from others?"

The words struck him like a blow. In that beat of stunned silence, Aisha spotted movement in one of the open-air corridors. Hakim, come to call her back. Omar saw him too. His expression went flat, but Aisha could read the murderous intent in his eyes.

When he charged the mapmaker, Aisha gave chase. This time, she did not bother with her blades. She threw herself at him, reaching for the magic at the same time. The grass pulled at Omar's feet, slowing his footsteps, and it was enough for her to tackle him.

Their blades fell as they crashed to the ground. Aisha kicked Omar's sword away before he could reach it. But she ought to have known better, because in the next moment, he grabbed one of the black knives in his sleeve—how had she forgotten that he *always* carried extra knives?—and stabbed it through her shoulder.

Pain lanced through Aisha's body. Static filled her mind, her vision, and she did not realize she was screaming until the darkness cleared and she saw that Omar had pinned her beneath him. Whatever mercy had been in him had vanished, replaced with a blind wrath as he stabbed another knife through her hand.

Aisha's vision seared white with agony as she pulled the knife from her hand and aimed it at his heart. He deflected it with another dagger and then—

She felt a tearing in her chest. A pain so terrible it scorched through her veins.

Vaguely, she was aware of Omar's hands around her neck—around the *collar*. "How many chances did I give you, Aisha? How many?"

The Resurrectionist was screaming in her mind. Aisha felt the clasp of the collar unlock, felt the relic being pulled from her throat...

The pain was a current of agony, coursing through her veins and making the world go black. She didn't scream. She couldn't. Her throat was torn, and the last of her words had spilled onto the sand with her blood.

The sensation was both memory and reality. The blood, the tears, the agony, it was all in her mind, but it was all *real* because her body was shutting down, her borrowed life extinguishing. Even the eye the Resurrectionist had given her was failing.

Aisha was dying, again. She could feel the inevitable pressure crushing down on her limbs, her heart. The world flickered in and out.

To live is a matter of belief, Omar had once told her. All this time, she had believed.

And she would never *stop* believing. She had died for Omar before. Never again.

The moment he pried the collar from her neck, Omar's eyes became glassy and unseeing. It was hard to tell if he was trapped in his own mind or if the Resurrectionist had possessed him. Whatever the case, he must have thought Aisha dead. He did not see her reach for the shamshir.

And he did not see her blade as it came down on his hand, chopping it at the wrist.

In that moment, there was no shock. Just a terrible desperation as Aisha crawled toward the collar. She pried Omar's fingers from the relic and clasped it around her neck.

The world rushed back in a dizzying wave and with it, sensation. The coldness of her body, the immobility of her limbs, and Omar, screaming. It was a scream that rent the very air, a sound filled with so much agony she could not at first comprehend it was coming from Omar.

But then she saw his hand—bloodied, limp, *detached*—and she saw Omar on the ground, clutching the stump where it had once been, and her heart hitched with terror. She had done that. She had done *that*, and he would skin her alive for it.

Pain shuddered through her body as someone picked her up off the ground. At first, she thought it was Hakim. It was only when the stranger turned to take her away that she recognized the strength of his arms.

She craned her neck to look up at him. *"Samar?"*

The name came out hoarse and thin, like her throat *had* been torn. The thief said nothing as he rushed her through the halls. At least, not to her. But Aisha could hear him speaking to someone else—Hakim, who was running beside him.

Too late, Aisha realized she had not thought to retrieve Hakim's ring. She had neither the energy nor the voice to say this to him. She could barely feel her body.

Thief? Amina's voice echoed strangely in her mind, a distant whisper. *Hang in there.*

Eventually, she heard the click of a door opening. Inexplicably, Dahlia bint Adnan stood on the other side. When she saw Aisha, her face became ashen. "Bint Louas, are you—"

"She's not dead," Samar said. "But if you don't leave now, she will be."

Aisha's mind spun as the thief walked her forward. The room resolved around her as they moved, the binding coming into view. The magic was no longer faint. Now it was *burning* on the ground. Qadir stood on the other side of the etchings, brow furrowed.

"What will you do?" he asked. Aisha put together that he was talking to Samar.

Samar just smiled—that same pained smile he always wore. Now she realized that grief had never been for her. He had been carrying this betrayal with him for a long time, waiting for the opportune moment. And now he was staying behind to ... die? The thought infuriated her.

Perhaps Samar could read her mind. He gave a sharp, jerky shake of his head as the chamber door rattled on its hinges. Aisha could hear a voice on the other side. Junaid, demanding Samar turn Aisha over. But though Samar's expression was twisted with fear, he did not cave. "I have not been able to return to my country and my family for a long time," he said softly. "But *you* can. Find out the truth, bint Louas. Find out why my queen forsook us."

He paused in front of the binding and handed her over—like she was *dead weight*—to Qadir, along with the shamshir. And then he stepped back, putting himself in front of the door.

Dahlia stood beside him, smiling grimly. "Make sure you return with Loulie. Don't die."

Qadir nodded once as Hakim joined them on the other side of the binding.

The terrible sound of splintering wood came from the other room. Aisha heard more yells, more footfalls. Samar shot a panicked look over his shoulder.

"What are you waiting for?" Dahlia snapped. "*Go.*"

Qadir stepped into the binding. The moment his feet touched the burning magic, the etchings rose up around them into a labyrinth of fire. Aisha gasped, but the fire only licked harmlessly at their skin as Qadir faced Dahlia.

"Stay safe, Dahlia bint Adnan," he said.

Aisha never knew if Dahlia answered him, because in the next moment, the ground gave way beneath them. There was a roar as the flames surged.

And then there was no fire at all. No magic.

There was only darkness and the sensation of falling through nothing.

50

LOULIE

As the dark surface of the lake closed over her head, Loulie was struck by an eerie familiarity. The last time she had plunged into a body of water like this, she had been in the city of Ghiban with Qadir, looking for a relic.

The two of them had been fighting then—or rather, Loulie had been ignoring him—and she had dived into a lake to prove herself self-sufficient. Beneath the surface she had come face-to-face with a fish monster known as the dendan, a creature with milky white eyes and a terrible smile filled with rows of sharpened teeth.

Loulie would never forget that face. And she would never forget the sensations of the dive: the darkness that had felt like cold, invisible hands and the terrible, suffocating pressure in her ears. After that awful experience, she had vowed never to reenter marid-haunted waters.

Yet here she was again, sinking into a lake, and the same dreadful sensations overwhelmed her. The darkness, the chill, the pressure, and the terror all muddled together in her mind and screamed *danger*. This time, Qadir would not be here to pull her out.

But it did not matter, because this time, Loulie would save herself.

Her fingers tightened over the pearl tucked beneath her robes.

She drew in a deep, impossible breath. As Nabila had said, the ship was wound in an enchantment that kept the air in their lungs. Loulie wondered if it was the same magic that unfurled the sails.

Darkness stretched around them. When the anchor had fallen, Duha had been chained to it, but now neither the anchor nor the marid was visible. Given the speed at which the ship was descending, Loulie could tell it was being pulled. Whatever form Duha had taken, it was big enough to drag the ship under. When she squinted, she thought she could make out the flash of scales in the dark, along with razor-sharp teeth and fathomless, ink-black eyes.

I am what you humans would call a monster.

The memory of Duha's words echoed in her mind. Loulie had heard from Mazen the destruction Duha was capable of in this form, but she had never witnessed it herself. Now, thinking of the terrible dendan that had nearly devoured her, she wondered if it was better that way.

The ship sank for a long time. Long enough for the darkness to press on Loulie like a burial shroud. Long enough that she began to wonder if the depths had stolen her sight.

But then: light.

Loulie blinked rapidly against it until she could make out shapes. She nearly screamed at the sight of the skeletons hovering above her. Or at least, they looked like skeletons at first. But then she saw the unnatural way they writhed through the dark, and realized they were *creatures*. Some were thin and sinuous, others large and bulbous. At one point, Loulie saw a stream of what may have been luminescent jellyfish bobbing above her head, but she could not be sure. She had no name for any of these creatures; she wondered if any human did.

It was not just the creatures that glowed. As they descended, Loulie saw that light eclipsing the city as well. From above, the landscape had looked like a mess of roofs. But down here, the buildings rose around them like a maze built *upward*, walls and balconies filled with glowing algae. At first, Loulie struggled to comprehend what she was seeing. She had expected the city to be at the bottom of the lake bed, its roads flat on the soil. But then she realized the "pathways" in the marid city cut up toward the surface.

Unlike the human and jinn cities, the Eastern Marid City had not been constructed on the ground. Instead, layers of ruined floors rose *up* around them, punctured with enormous, gaping holes that served as entryways between the levels. The holes were big enough for their ship to pass through.

Perhaps Nabila could see the confusion on Loulie's face. She spoke from the prow of the ship. "The marid do not live as we do. There are no closed doors between them." Her voice echoed strangely in Loulie's ears, muffled by her invisible magic. "Still, even if no doors bar our path, it can be difficult to find one's destination if you do not know the ways between the buildings. That is why only the marid can navigate their city."

Loulie hesitated to put air to her words but forced herself to ask, "Where are we going?"

"If the binding is directly beneath the Audience Hall, then we must make our way to the throne room. It is in the same tower, but on the lowest floor."

"There's no way to go straight down from the surface building?"

"What use are stairs that go beneath the water? No, the pathways here never go straight down. Every floor of the building has its own entryway."

The deeper they dove, the more Loulie understood. The marid thought in levels, not buildings. Had Loulie been asked to locate anything in this city, even with the compass and the pearl, she would have been hopelessly lost. But she did not need to memorize the routes between constructions. All she needed to know was that the way to the surface was *up*.

Loulie glanced down at the compass, at the arrow pointing her toward the magic even now. For what reason had Khalilah led Loulie to these bindings? Into this conflict that did not involve her? Was this Khalilah's or Qadir's doing? Only Qadir would be able to tell her, and she did not know when he would return for her.

Wait for me, he had said. But the time for waiting was over. Qadir had told her before that he had always run from his mistakes—and now Loulie had no choice but to face them on his behalf.

Eventually, they arrived at the throne room entrance: a set of gargantuan doors thrown open into a shadowed corridor. Duha did not enter with them. Instead, Nabila disembarked from the ship and ushered Loulie after her into the building. The ifrit carved an air bubble around them but the magic moved with her, forcing Loulie into a run.

"Hurry," Nabila called ahead of her. "We do not have much time."

Loulie thought she was talking about the binding until she realized the ifrit's breathing was labored. The magic she was using was clearly draining her. What would happen if she ran out of it while they were down here? Loulie did not want to imagine.

She chased Nabila into the dark hall. At first, all she heard was their breathing. But then she discerned another sound: a faint but persistent moan. Loulie shuddered at the sound of it. She could not stop herself from glancing back into the darkness.

Her heart nearly beat out of her chest at the sight of the gigantic black eye blinking at them through the doorway. Loulie stumbled back into Nabila, a scream trapped in her throat. Her gaze remained pinned on the eye as it flashed past them. Again, she saw the glimmer of scales and teeth, and then the creature swept upward, taking the ship with it.

Duha, her mind pieced together belatedly. But if her eye had been that big even from a distance, she could not fathom how large the marid must be in her entirety. In this form, Duha would not have to snap Loulie between her teeth to kill her; she could simply swallow her whole.

She and Nabila watched the vanishing marid together. It occurred to Loulie only then to ask how they would return to the surface.

"Duha was meant to wait down here for us," Nabila said. She looked troubled. "She must sense some disturbance above."

Disturbance could mean an enemy, but it could also mean Mazen and Rijah—or Qadir. Loulie wished there were a way for her to know.

"Never mind. If need be, we will find our own way up." Nabila glanced at her sharply. "For now, we must focus. Or do you not want to see your bodyguard again?"

Loulie snapped to attention at the mention of Qadir. The ifrit was eyeing her warily. And there was something else in her gaze too—a cloudiness Loulie would not have noticed had Nabila still been incorporeal. Now she recognized the expression as concern. For Duha, she imagined. What had brought the marid back to the surface?

A tense quiet settled between them. They walked for a long time, the glass windows in the hall allowing them a glimpse into the skeleton of what Loulie was sure had once been a remarkable city. Now it was a hollow corpse. Not a dendan skeleton as the sailors had hypothesized, but the city had its bones.

Loulie could not help her curiosity. "Did this happen when the city sunk?"

"The city collapsed during the descent into the Sandsea. And then it was attacked."

"Attacked?"

"Many jinn resented the marid for remaining neutral during the war. They raided the city at its weakest moment." Nabila's lips twitched into a frown. "The jinn queen arrived after the battle, a scavenger. She called what happened here a just punishment."

Loulie flinched. So the marid had been punished for pacifism. She thought of Mazen, who had been abused for his kind heart, and of her tribe, who had perished simply for existing in the wrong place at the wrong time. It was as Mazen had said: it was always the people caught between greater powers that suffered.

Nabila continued, "Duha thinks half of the city fell because Ramiz's binding was incomplete. But she does not know for certain."

There was a lot they did not know about this ifrit, Loulie thought. His motives, his allegiances—but it was useless to ponder those questions here, where she would find no answers.

Eventually, the pathway led them into the large chamber Nabila claimed was the throne room. But all Loulie saw was a crater, the walls carved down, bowl-like, into a deep floor.

The two of them stared into the depths.

Nabila was the first to speak. "This is the bottom of the tower," she said. "And where the marid would have visited their queen."

The dread Loulie felt was uncannily familiar. She had felt this way when she stood on the cusp of the binding in al-Malath. But at least *that* binding had been in a visible place. Here, there was no indication of any magic at all.

"You must enter the binding alone," Nabila said.

Loulie's trepidation settled like frost across her skin. "How am I meant to reach it?"

"Have you forgotten? You alone are impervious to magic when you are inside." Her words were clipped with resentment.

Loulie took a deep breath and stepped forward. At first, when she stepped out of Nabila's bubble and felt the resistance of the water around her body, she was convinced the ifrit had lied to her. Instinctively, her fingers went to the pearl hidden beneath her robes. It was the silence of the magic that made her realize she was drawing air into her lungs without its assistance. Nabila was right; the binding *was* keeping her from drowning.

Loulie ventured deeper. Like Nabila's wind, the water had its own voice, but she could not pinpoint the source of the sound in the dark. Though she saw flashes of motion, the binding kept all living creatures out—which meant that anything floating around her would be dead.

Eventually, Loulie came to the bottom of the hole. A lone throne sat in the center of the space: an enormous pedestal made of sea glass. The slab was oddly shaped, chipped and pocked with holes. Seeing those strange indentions, Loulie thought of the story Nabila had told of the spear the Marid Queen had shaped for the Tide Bringer from that throne.

She forced her attention to the center of the binding: a circle of phantom fire that wrapped around the throne like an eddy. Loulie felt the heat of it beneath her body.

Carefully, she slid down the slope, dagger in hand.

The water was its own wall, pulling her up and away from the binding the deeper she went. But Loulie persevered, pushing her straining legs until she came to its center. This close, the ashfire glowed a strange, foggy white.

Unable to plant her feet on the soil, Loulie used the throne to anchor herself to the lake bed. The hiss of the water in her ears sounded like a condemnation. A threat. A warning.

But this was not *her* past, and Loulie would not be cowed.

With a deep breath, she plunged the dagger through the heart of the third binding.

51

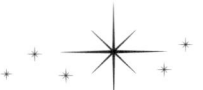

MAZEN

Two days after leaving Kharjem on a borrowed boat, the fearsome firebird of legend woke Mazen with a jovial trill. It was, Mazen thought, the sweetest wake-up call he had ever risen to. It was unfortunate its sweetness was tainted by an overwhelming sense of dread.

Azhar, for its part, did not seem aware that they were heading from one danger to the next. When it saw Mazen had risen from his pile of blankets, it chirped again, excitedly butting its head against the lantern until Mazen rose to open the glass door. He smiled sleepily as the bird flitted to his shoulder.

"Appalling," said a dispassionate voice from the edge of the ship. Rijah, who was standing by the rails, lazily gesturing the dhow across the Sandsea.

Mazen rubbed at his eyes. "What is?"

"You," Rijah sighed. "If your relationship with that bird was not a marvel, I would kill you for it." They gestured emphatically at the firebird, which sat blinking its hollow eyes at them. "That is a creature made from *legendary fire*, and you treat it like a domesticated animal!"

"It likes sitting on my shoulder," Mazen said defensively.

The firebird peeped in agreement.

Rijah turned back to the Sandsea with a grumble. They cut their hand aggressively through the air, turning the ship so sharply that Mazen had to grip one of the spars to keep from being thrown into it. The firebird dug its tiny claws into his shoulder until he had regained his footing. He frowned at Rijah's back but decided irritating them further was an unwise idea. It was because of the ifrit's magic that they were able to sail across the Sandsea right now.

He cast a glance around the deck, searching for their store of meager supplies. What little they had brought with them from Kharjem was below deck. All except for the lamp, which sat upon a pile of folded cloaks. It was hard to believe the small object contained not only Rijah's magic now, but the ashfire as well.

Mazen awkwardly cleared his throat. "Were you able to rest?"

"Rest? Ha! I do not need rest. This is the most awake I have been in a long time." Rijah flashed a grin at him and, as if they had read his mind, summoned a burst of ashfire to their fingertips. Mazen watched, awed, as the fire coated their knuckles.

With an excitable squawk, the firebird swooped toward Rijah's head. The ifrit laughed—*laughed*—in delight, and it was such a cheerful sound that Mazen forgot, briefly, the reason for their journey across the Sandsea.

But the joy faded as he glanced past the ifrit. The first time he had traveled across this ocean of sand, it had seemed infinite. Now, on the horizon, he saw the edges of the realm—the walls of sand crashing down, as well as the golden cracks illuminating the dark sky like suspended bolts of lightning. Even when the curfew fell, the fractures glowed ominously.

Mazen was still staring at that sky as Rijah began to navigate the archipelago of mountains hiding the marid city. "What will happen when Loulie breaks this last binding?"

"I do not know. But the magic holding this world afloat will have reached its limits by then. We will have to move fast."

Mazen swallowed. This was all his fault. If he had not trapped Azhar and unintentionally put out the ashfire, then perhaps the kingdom might have been better prepared for what was to come.

He caught Rijah frowning at him. "You are overthinking again," they remarked. It wasn't a question, but Mazen nodded anyway. The ifrit turned to the Sandsea with a sigh. "When will you learn, human? Confidence is key."

Mazen remembered when Rijah had first told him that upon their arrival in Dhahab. But it seemed that no matter what he did, he was destined always to be the fool, the man led astray by his emotions. He could never be the leader his father had wanted him to be.

When he told Rijah this, the ifrit looked as if they might strangle him. "Foolish human. You think a war is won without sacrifice? A crown earned without strife? A kingdom saved without *tenacity*? Your weakness is not your incompetence or your cowardice. It is your inability to forgive yourself. *I* have failed, time and again, but so long as I breathe, I will not falter.

"To live is to persevere. For the world, and in spite of it."

Mazen was at a loss for words. He had never thought of it that way before, had never considered life a chain of failures leading up to hard-earned victories. But Rijah was right; Mazen may not have been able to save Madinne, but he had helped save the populace of Kharjem. They still had time—he had not failed yet.

He came to stand beside Rijah with a smile. "They should start calling you the wisest of jinn, I think."

Rijah grunted in assent. "I *am* always right." When Azhar tweeted in agreement, Rijah beamed as if they'd received a compliment from their own king.

The ifrit quieted as they continued toward the city, their concentration focused on navigating the ship through the straits bracketed by looming cliffs. Mazen directed Azhar ahead of them to light the way. The ashfire was dim, barely brighter than a dying candle in the dark world, but together with Rijah's memory, it was enough to guide them.

As they approached what appeared to be an open gateway into a lake, Mazen could tell something was wrong. He felt it in the air, which had suddenly become bitter and cold, and in the water, which rippled strangely beneath their boat. As Mazen watched, those ripples became waves, and then the boat was *shaking*, juddering so wildly he had to grip the mast to keep his balance.

Even on water, he recognized the feeling of a quake. He shot an alarmed look at Rijah. "The binding?"

Rijah gave a terse nod. "The merchant must have broken it."

The statement was punctured by a sharp crash as the water lashed viciously at their boat. It was a storm, Mazen realized, though it appeared to be affecting only the lake. It was unnatural in the same way Nabila's magic was—was it a result of the broken binding?

He rushed to the front of the ship. The first thing he noticed as they passed through the lock was the large glass tower rising above the turbulent waves. Then he noticed the ships locked in combat. The boum on the left was Nabila's. And the one on the right...

Even from a distance, Mazen could make out Ziyad's purple coat on the prow. His presence was proof that their plan had worked. Mazen had called, and Ziyad had come.

But where was Loulie?

Rijah raised a palm to their eyes and squinted into the chaos. It was only then Mazen saw movement in the water. He had not noticed it at first, because the shape beneath the waves was... big. It was like a shadow cast by clouds, stretching so wide it looked less like a living thing and more a part of the landscape.

Mazen inhaled sharply. "Duha?"

The shadow surged forward, forming waves strong enough to send their dhow into the air. There was no time to prepare. One moment the water loomed. The next, it had crashed over their heads and sent Mazen tumbling head over heels beneath the surface. His chest burned as he tried and failed to push back up. But the lake was pulling him down, and the lamp—

The lamp.

He saw it floating underneath him, a gleam of copper. Mazen dove toward it.

He had just recovered the vessel when a long, writhing shadow cut through the water. Mazen swerved, panic slicing through his chest when he realized it had the twisting body of one of Ziyad's serpents. But before he could flee, the creature was beneath him. Pressure built in his ears as it...pushed him up toward the surface?

Mazen crashed through the waves with a choked gasp.

"PULL YOURSELF TOGETHER, HUMAN."

Mazen sat up with a wheeze, only for the serpent to curve abruptly beneath him. He floundered and instinctively moved to grasp something—anything—when his hands found purchase on a surface that felt like rock.

No, not rock. Scales?

His surroundings resolved in sudden, vivid detail. The thing he was grasping—it was indeed a ridge of scales resting above turquoise eyes.

"Rijah?"

The ifrit snapped their jaws, uprooting Mazen from his spot on their forehead. A rumble that sounded distressingly like a chuckle emanated from them as Mazen struggled to regain his balance. *"DO YOU HAVE THE LAMP? OR SHALL I THROW YOU BACK IN THE WATER TO RETRIEVE IT?"*

Mazen checked to make sure it was still tucked beneath his arm. "I—I have it."

The ifrit gave a sound of assent before swerving once more. This time, Mazen was prepared, bracing his feet on either side of their undulating body as they turned. He clenched his teeth to keep from screaming as Rijah picked up speed. The wind lashed at his clothing, his face.

He spoke through chattering teeth: "Wh-wh-where—"

The question died in his throat when he saw the gigantic creature charging after them. Mazen recognized the large fish, though her scales were marred with blood and her back was punctured with arrows—projectiles the sailors on Ziyad's ship were even now shooting at her. Despite their best efforts to aim for Duha, Mazen still felt arrows whistle past his body.

"Wait—" He gripped Rijah's scales. "Why is she coming after *us*?"

"*BECAUSE WE ARE A MOVING TARGET,*" Rijah said. "*YOU SAW HER STRATEGY IN AL-MALATH. WHEN SHE TAKES THAT FORM, WE ARE ALL THE SAME TO HER.*"

Thinking back on it, Duha *had* swallowed Ziyad's ship without any thought to who was on it. Mazen wondered if that cecity was the reason Ziyad preferred not to take that form at all.

Still, though he had called Ziyad here for contingency's sake, Mazen had never meant to hurt Duha. The plan had always been to help Loulie if things went wrong.

Mazen shook his head frantically. *Stop!* he wanted to scream, but Rijah charged ahead, heedless of his hyperventilating.

At the last moment, Rijah turned abruptly in the water, winding around the tower and causing Duha to crash into it. She released a terrible, piercing shriek. Mazen pressed his hands to his ears with a grimace. He forced his attention to the single building at the center of the lake. If Loulie was anywhere, it had to be there. When he told Rijah this, the ifrit obediently shifted, pushing toward one of the glass bridges on the water.

A friendly call greeted him from the sky as Rijah deposited him on the structure. Mazen looked up to see Azhar circling above the chaos. He sighed with relief as it flitted to his shoulder.

"*FIND THE MERCHANT,*" Rijah said.

Mazen did as commanded, leaving Rijah to handle Duha as he burst through the doors of the building. A binding, broken and fading, flickered weakly by his feet, but Loulie was nowhere to be seen. If she was not *here*, where could she possibly be?

As he ducked back outside, his eyes flew past the battle to the reflection on the water. No, not a reflection—there was a landscape of *ruins* stretched beneath him. The marid city.

Mazen's heart dropped to the soles of his feet.

He understood then where Loulie was.

52

LOULIE

At first, as Loulie floated in the depths, it was difficult for her to tell if she had succeeded in breaking the binding. But then water seeped into the circle, and her lungs started to burn. The ground beneath her quivered—an earthquake she could feel even on the lake bed.

The binding was unraveling, along with her protection against the elements.

Panic set in. She had just reached for the pearl when the air around her changed. Abruptly, she was no longer floating. Loulie looked up, puzzled, and realized the water around her had peeled away. Nabila stood before her, holding it back with one of her barriers.

"It is over," Nabila said. The declaration had the grave weight of a death sentence. "Soon these lands will rise, and we can finally return to the country that belongs to us."

Belongs to us.

Loulie smothered her nerves. "And after that?"

Nabila looked at her. Loulie had expected storm clouds in her eyes; she was unnerved by the placidness she saw there instead. "After that, I take it all back. Our cities, our lands, our *lives*...Everything that was stolen by you humans."

It was the response Loulie had feared, the one she had dreaded.

It was one thing to anticipate a war, another entirely to know it was an inevitability. "Were the stories true, then? About you wanting to destroy the surface?"

Nabila frowned at her. "It is you humans who have been defiling the land. You who have been painting it with *our* blood."

"If you start a war, even more innocent blood will be shed."

Rage flashed through Nabila's clear eyes like lightning. "So be it. It will be better than a massacre. At least in war, there can be retaliation. In war, there can be *justice*."

"And is that justice worth it when you must pay for it with others' lives?" The words, so reminiscent of Mazen's own speeches, were out of her mouth before she could stop them. Loulie knew the appeal of vengeance; she had spent her whole life chasing her family's murderers. But she would *never* seek it at the expense of harming others.

"What do you know of justice, human? Your meager existence is but a blink in time to us jinn. You are nothing. Your opinion is nothing." The ifrit's glare bore into her with an intensity that boiled the water outside of her barrier. "Why? Why would my king ever choose *you*? A child who knows nothing of the costs of war?"

Loulie bristled. "Qadir didn't choose me. He found me. But he—"

"He chose you over us, his loyal retainers!" Nabila's voice cracked with her frustration. "I did everything for him. I helped him construct his bindings. I tried to save him. And then he left me behind in a broken country and *found you*."

Loulie flinched back at the accusation in her words. "Why is it my fault he chose me? I did as you asked. I broke your damned bindings. We had a deal—"

"I do not honor deals with humans."

The ifrit spoke the words with such venom they made Loulie cringe. She hesitated, then drew in a short, tight breath. "What are you going to do with me?"

With a gesture, Nabila compressed the pocket of air around them. When Loulie tried to move, she found herself suddenly rooted in place by the ifrit's magic. Her chest tightened with panic. "You used me the same way Qadir used you! You are just like him."

"No." The word lashed against her heart like a whip. "We were comrades. *You* are a human. I never owed you a thing."

In that moment, Loulie hated that part of her had been holding out hope even now—hope that Duha's trust in Nabila might not be misplaced, that she might not have to make another enemy when they should have been on the *same side*. But how could they work together when Nabila wanted her dead?

When the ifrit turned away, Loulie knew they would never see eye to eye again. Nabila was not even going to bother fighting her; she was simply leaving her here to drown.

Rage surged through Loulie as she grabbed at the pearl hidden beneath her scarves. When the familiar looseness came into her limbs, it was enough to break the ifrit's hold on her.

Nabila had just raised her hand to destroy the air bubble when Loulie rushed her with the dagger. The movement caught Nabila off guard. She turned at the last minute, causing Loulie's strike to go wide.

Still, the attack grazed Nabila in the chest. Silver blood splattered to the ground as she stepped back, her fingers darting to the wound. Her lips curled into a vicious scowl as she retreated to the edge of her barrier. "This is the grave you deserve, human," she spat.

With a snap of her wrist, she broke the barrier. The moment she vanished, water surged into the binding. Panic clouded Loulie's mind as she reached frantically for the pearl.

On the surface, she had only ever used the magic to redirect the wind. Now she focused on the lightness the magic instilled in her body. Picturing Nabila's barrier in her mind, she swept the pearl in an arc, trying to craft the wind around her like a shield.

It was a flimsy attempt. Even now, the pressure of the water crushed down on her limbs. Knowing the magic would not keep the water out of her lungs for long, Loulie began to swim.

Her heart beat a frenzied crescendo as she shot between the buildings in search of paths that led *up*. She swam as she never had before, even as the magic began to drain from her body, leaving her limbs heavy and her lungs screaming for air.

Loulie saw the surface of the water above her, but the light had begun to smudge in her vision. She could feel herself choking. When she tried to push herself up, her limbs would not obey her.

A memory returned to her then. A memory of Qadir diving into the water to rescue her. But Qadir was not here. He had not made it in time after all.

The world faded as Loulie drifted. She was vaguely aware of a burning sensation in her throat and of a hollowed-out feeling in her chest. She felt simultaneously as if she were too hot and too cold, her senses fractured like glass.

Her lips had just parted when she felt arms beneath her. *Not Qadir.* The hands on her skin were too nimble, the body pressed against hers leaner.

The figure pulled her up and through the lake. Loulie gasped as they crashed through the surface. She tried to breathe, but there was water in her throat, and she kept choking. The waves were turbulent, throwing them back and forth. Loulie could barely keep her head above them.

A gentle voice spoke in her ear, pressed thin with breathlessness. "I have you. Hang on."

Loulie slumped against him as they struggled through the water. Once they were on flat land, she leaned over and heaved. Her whole body trembled with the effort, and she struggled to draw air into her lungs in between sobs. All the while, she felt a firm, comforting hand on the small of her back.

When she could finally breathe, she rose slowly to her knees and glanced blearily around her. She was on a glass bridge with a tower behind her, and in front of her—

"Mazen?" His name came out a hoarse whisper. "Where—"

He pressed a finger to his lips. "We're hiding." This close, she saw how harried he looked. His clothing was soaked, his shirt clinging to the contours of his chest. Droplets of water dripped from his hair, which hung loose and wild in front of his face.

The firebird sat on his shoulder, slowly blinking its hollow eyes at her. She imagined it must have taken to the air while Mazen was beneath the water.

Loulie slowly pieced together what he had said. "Hiding from what?"

"From that." He gestured to the water, where two ships floated on the turbulent waves.

One of the ships—Loulie recognized Nabila's dhow—was fleeing through the lock. From this distance, Loulie could make out neither the ifrit nor the marid on deck. The ship looked as if it had weathered a particularly harrowing assault, its hull punched through with holes and the sails torn.

The second ship floated by the tower. Even from a distance, it had an ominous, looming quality to it. Loulie did not recognize the vessel, but there was only one person—*marid*—who could be captaining it. "You were able to contact Ziyad," she said.

Mazen nodded. If the marid was here, it meant that their plan had succeeded. Mazen had called Ziyad to the marid city so that they would have a transport back to Dhahab if Nabila discarded her. And yet Loulie could not shake her sense of foreboding. They had called Ziyad out of desperation, but what was to stop him from punishing them?

After Loulie summarized the events beneath the water, Mazen recounted what had transpired above it. He told her about Duha and the skirmish that had broken out. The battle had lasted only as long as it had taken for Nabila to emerge from the depths of the city, at which point the injured ifrit had rescued Duha and immediately sailed away.

While Mazen had been looking for Loulie, Rijah had decided to chase after Nabila's ship to make certain she would not return for them. As for Ziyad . . .

Mazen cleared his throat. "He knows we're here, and he's waiting for us."

Loulie sank onto the bridge. Her eyes fluttered closed with her exhaustion. For one minute—for just *one* godsdamned minute—she wanted a break.

A few moments later, Mazen sat beside her. "Loulie?"

Azhar tweeted quizzically from his shoulder.

Loulie drew Qadir's dagger from her pocket. She searched the edge, but there was no sign of his eyes. No sign of *him*. He had told her he was coming for her––what would happen if she left this city before he arrived? Would he be able to find her without the compass?

Where are you, Qadir?

If they stayed here much longer, Ziyad would haul them onto his ship himself. But Loulie could not bring herself to move on yet, not when there might still be a chance Qadir would appear.

Her fingers curled over the hilt of the dagger. "He has five minutes," she muttered.

53

AISHA

Aisha did not know what she had expected falling between worlds to feel like, but it was not this: this mad plummet through darkness, with nothing to cocoon her body from an unbearable heat. Briefly, she considered that the binding Omar had crafted was a trap and that she was hurtling toward nothing but her own death.

But then, eventually, there came an end to the fall.

Aisha gasped as she collided with solid ground. Her body hummed with pain as she struggled to rise on her hands. There was a buzzing in her ears. The voices of the undead, she realized, encroaching on her thoughts even now. She shoved them to the back of her mind.

Her first thought was that she had woken in some underwater ruin. The walls were overrun with coral and moss, and reef balconies hindered her view of a domed ceiling. A ceiling that, like the walls, was constructed from a lustrous material that reminded her of sea glass.

She rose to her feet with a groan. Her body felt bruised, but—her injuries were *gone*. The pain had been replaced with a faint prickle beneath her skin. Magic, she realized. Magic the Resurrectionist must have drawn on to heal her body.

Aisha turned her mind inward, to Amina. *Where is this magic coming from?*

Do you not see, thief? The ifrit's voice quavered with excitement. *Magic is not a thing to be borrowed here. It simply* is. *Can you not feel it in the air, in the land?*

Much to Aisha's amazement, she could. The magic was neither greenery bled from jinn corpses nor purloined enchantments. It was a living thing. The more Aisha reached for it, the sharper her awareness of it became, until the acuity was a blade stabbing through her head.

By increments, she shuttered her mind against it to focus on her companions. She noticed Hakim first. He was still on his knees, staring around the space with a wide-eyed wonder she had never seen on his face before. In that moment, he looked so remarkably like Mazen that Aisha could have believed they were brothers in more than name.

"What *is* this place?" he pondered aloud.

"It is a part of the marid city."

The second voice, soft as a whisper, made Aisha jump. But then she realized she knew its timbre, weak as it had become. Sure enough, when she glanced at her shoulder, she saw Qadir perched there in his lizard shape.

Hakim swayed slowly to his feet. Unlike her, he still bore the injuries he had sustained in the palace, his arms riddled with the lacerations from Omar's torture. Aisha steadied him as he looked around. "The marid...you speak of the wish-granting jinn from the stories?"

No, Aisha thought. *Not wish granters.* The marid she—the Resurrectionist—knew were different creatures. In her mind she saw monstrous shadows swimming beneath water aglow with silver blood; black eyes in murky tunnels; a scaled queen with a mouth full of incisor-sharp teeth.

The marid she knew *were* powerful enough to grant wishes, but they were also selfish, isolated creatures with little reason to. They were the same creatures who, when begged for assistance during the war, had left them all to perish at the hands of humans.

The mapmaker looked at the ifrit, troubled. "Why did you bring us here?"

Qadir responded softly, "Because it is where Loulie is."

They both straightened at the mention of the merchant. "And my brother?" Hakim's hazel eyes shone with hope. "What of Mazen?"

"I know nothing of your brother's whereabouts," Qadir said. "I spoke only with Loulie. But I imagine the two of them must be traveling together still." He paused, and Aisha felt the prick of his nails as he shuffled on her shoulder. "The magic here feels...different. Weaker."

Before he could clarify, a tremor waylaid the conversation. Qadir inhaled sharply as Aisha frowned at the floor. When the tower shook again, it was because of a full-on quake.

Qadir dug his nails into her shoulder. "I understand now. The binding—it is broken."

The words meant nothing to Aisha, but the screeching walls and cracking windows did.

It sounded like the whole godsdamned world was breaking.

Qadir hissed in her ear, "*Run.*"

They did not need to be told twice. The mapmaker was already darting down the hall with a limp in his step, leaving Aisha to chase after him. As they ran, the space began to shift. The ruined walls cracked, bleeding streams of water onto the floor. The balconies rumbled and then shattered, the rock and coral spraying through the air like deadly rainfall.

So they ran—from one danger right into the next.

Outside, a storm awaited them. Waves crashed against the building, rocking it to its foundations. Aisha could barely make out glass bridges swaying atop a turbulent lake. One of those bridges stretched before them, leading to stable land. But it was not empty.

A figure stood before them on the shifting glass. The jinn—*marid*, the Resurrectionist corrected her when they saw his black eyes—blinked at them with mild surprise.

"I had rather hoped you were someone else," he said.

The bridge shattered.

Aisha woke to a gentle, almost hypnotic swaying. The last thing she remembered, she'd been sinking through water. But when her vision cleared, it was not the lake she saw beneath her, but a crosshatch of wooden planks. The scene resolved in its totality when she looked up and saw sailors striding across a deck.

She was on a ship.

Now that the waves had died down, there was a strange staleness to the air. Aisha glanced up at the sky. At first, she perceived the cracks above them as distorted beams of sunlight, but then she noticed that the jagged lines stretched for miles and that the pattern was too erratic and wide to be natural. It looked like the sky had been fractured.

This must be a result of the broken binding, the Resurrectionist said. *But who would be foolish enough to destroy it—to endanger this realm?*

Neither of them knew the answer to the question. Cautiously, Aisha tested her limbs. She felt a burning against her arms—*ropes*—and a beam pressing into her back—*mast.* She sensed a tug on the rope at her wrists and knew immediately she was not the only one bound to the beam. Hakim sat on the other side, breathing shallowly. Qadir was nowhere to be seen.

So, they had regressed into being prisoners once again.

It was not long before someone noticed them stirring and called for the captain. While she waited for him to appear, Aisha leaned back against the beam and whispered to Hakim. "Any idea where the lizard went?"

Hakim mumbled a soft "No" under his breath.

Aisha's attention snapped up and away at the sound of approaching footsteps. She fixed a glower on her face when she saw the marid approaching with an overbright smile. "What is the meaning of this?" she demanded.

The captain was unperturbed by her indignation. He stopped before her, brows raised into a look that managed to be both infuriatingly condescending and sincerely curious. "I am afraid I will have to reflect that question back at you. Who are you, and what are you doing here?"

Aisha considered her answer. Deception had never been her strong suit. Usually, when she was asked to lie, she said nothing at all. She did not have the patience to weave fictional tales like Mazen or to barter like Loulie.

She lifted her chin. "I am searching for an acquaintance. Someone who is *not* you."

"That much I could gather. But you have not answered my other question." He crouched in front of her. This close, Aisha could see the scales on his skin. "*Who* are you?"

It was Hakim who answered on the other side of the mast: "We are nothing more than humble travelers, ya sayyid. I promise we mean you no harm."

He grinned. "Come now, humans; you can lie better than that." He stood, sliding his hands into the pockets of his pristine coat. "Your *acquaintance* has a much more vivid imagination."

It *sounded* as if he was describing Mazen.

As always, Hakim was one step ahead of her when it came to his brother. "You know him, then, our friend? Do you know where he is?"

The marid tapped his chin. Aisha could tell by the gleam in his eyes that he was scheming. He *knew* where Mazen was, and would not tell them, not without receiving something in exchange. Aisha wished that she knew who he was. What *he* was doing here.

"We are waiting for the same person, you and I," he said after a moment. "Perhaps while we await his arrival, we can exchange information?" His eyes glittered as he caught Aisha's gaze. "I am most curious about the ifrit relic around your neck."

Aisha froze at the mention of the magic. Even the Resurrectionist was momentarily stunned. "You can sense it?"

"It is easy enough to recognize. The Resurrectionist always wore it, after all."

Aisha eyed the marid warily. She felt no spark of recognition from Amina, which meant he had either heard of the collar or met the ifrit centuries ago. Either way, the past did not matter to Aisha. "Tell me who you are, and I will tell you about the collar."

He obliged her. With a flourish, he introduced himself as Ziyad, the envoy of the jinn queen. Aisha felt a spark of surprise at the title. She recalled the haunted look in Samar's eyes when he had told Aisha about his queen's silence. And his plea: *Go. Find answers—for both of us.*

This was the perfect opportunity to gather information. "If you are the queen's envoy, then you must be the one in communication with my sultan."

Genuine surprise flickered across Ziyad's cool expression. He seemed to truly take her in then, his gaze sweeping over the blood on her clothing, her scars. His dark eyes lit with recognition. "You are one of Omar bin Malik's forty thieves."

So, he *did* know Omar.

Aisha felt Hakim tense behind her, but he said nothing as Ziyad continued, "Forgive my disbelief, ya sayyida, but you are... different than what I was expecting."

"Because I am not jinn?" She smiled at his surprise. "I assure you I am stronger than any of my comrades. Why else do you think my sultan would entrust me with this relic?" She was surprised by how easily the lie came to her; perhaps she had learned something from Loulie and Mazen after all.

Ziyad crossed his arms. "Then your sultan sent you here to find this *acquaintance?*"

"He is both an acquaintance and a criminal—a man who fled our world the same way your criminals flee yours. We wish to punish him the same way we punish the jinn."

"Hmm. So you are aware of the deal your sultan struck with Her Majesty. Interesting." He regarded her thoughtfully. "I am sorry to say this, ya sayyida, but he sent you here to die."

The fatal declaration made Aisha's blood run cold. "What do you mean?"

He clucked his tongue. "Your king must be desperate, to hide the full truth from you. Otherwise, he would have told you that Her Majesty has called off their deal." He must have mistaken Aisha's shock for horror, because his smile returned, making his black eyes glimmer. "My queen wanted ifrit relics. Your king wanted an army. But look around you—the ifrit magics the queen *does* possess have not saved this realm. Neither the spear in her throne room nor a living ifrit could fix the bindings. And so she has declared their deal done."

It was strange to hear Omar described as a pawn. Strange to know that there were jinn here who had manipulated *him*. Samar had confessed his fear that his queen had gone silent, and Ziyad had just given Aisha the reason for that silence.

Omar bin Malik had been working with a jinn—and she had betrayed him, in the end.

Aisha would have felt more vindictive had she not currently been at the mercy of said queen. She also had no idea who or what was destroying these bindings. She needed to find a way to escape this place and reunite with Mazen and Loulie—*then* she could assess this new threat.

Ziyad turned to the tower with a smile. "You will make an excellent hostage. You—"

A scream sliced through the air. Aisha straightened as one of the sailors came dashing up the steps, blabbering about a fire he could not put out. From here, Aisha could make out the smoke. Her nostrils flared at the smell of charred wood.

It's about damn time he shows up.

Qadir's fiery distractions may have been uninspired, but at least they were effective.

Ziyad rushed away with a curse as the blue-white fire began to spread on deck. Moments later, Aisha felt the ropes around her wrists loosen. A voice whispered in her ear, "I assume you were able to gather the information you needed?"

"It was enough." Aisha cracked her neck as she rose. Later, she would uncover this scheme between jinn and thieves. But before that, she had old companions to get out of trouble.

She faced the inferno with a smile.

54

LOULIE

Their escape plan was on fire.

From a distance, this was not immediately apparent. On the other side of the tower, Loulie had not heard the crackle of the inferno or the screaming. But then, as she and Mazen approached the ship that was meant to take them out of the city, she saw the flames.

Her heart leapt into her throat at the sight of the ashfire coating the deck.

Qadir?

She saw the same suspicion in Mazen's eyes as he stared at the ship. "It can't be Rijah if they haven't returned yet." Azhar, who remained on his shoulder, chirped in agreement.

Loulie rushed toward the dhow. She could hear Mazen chasing her, but whatever warnings he was yelling were incomprehensible.

Qadir was here. Qadir was *here*.

Adrenaline surged through her as she rushed up the gangplank, her vision narrowing to the inferno. Had it been a normal fire, it would have burned her. But this was ashfire, Qadir's magic, and it did not harm her—it never had.

Instead, the fire embraced her like an old friend, curling harmlessly against her body as if welcoming her into the mayhem. When the curtain of smoke parted, she was able to take in the chaos with greater clarity.

She saw the queen's soldiers, marked by their crimson uniforms, trying and failing to put out the fire, and she saw jinn fighting...each other? It was only when she saw the gaping wounds on their bodies that she understood: These soldiers were not alive. The battle raging on the ship was between the living and the dead.

She was still processing this revelation when one of the jinn spotted her in the smoke. Loulie brandished Qadir's dagger. Too late, she saw the soldier was coming at her with a two-headed spear, a weapon she could not possibly defend herself against.

She fell to her knees as he swept the spear through the air. The edge passed inches above her head, but before she could regain her balance, the jinn lunged again. This time, he caught her in the hip with the shaft.

Pain roared through her body as she crumpled to the ground with a gasp. Her vision went spotty, and it was all she could do to roll out of the way before she was impaled. She missed the spear by a hair's breadth.

She stumbled to her feet as he raised the spear, his eyes fiery with determination—and then he froze. Silver blood leaked between his clenched teeth and then from a rip in his chest as a blade tore through his lungs.

A red-eyed shadow stood behind the dying soldier. The figure held a familiar blade—a shamshir with a red gem on its guard. Loulie recognized the weapon immediately. And the shadow—she recognized it too. Between blinks, it resolved into a jinn she knew.

Loulie stared, stunned, at Qadir.

He was the same yet different. The planes of his face were chiseled by fatigue, and his body looked thinner beneath his torn clothing. Wounds marred his trembling arms, along with silver blood. And his eyes—they were glowing, burning with such naked hatred it made Loulie step back.

Then his gaze snagged on her, and his expression slackened. The fierce light in his eyes guttered out until he was blinking very brown, very human eyes at her.

"Qadir?" His name was a whisper on her lips.

How many times had he appeared in her dreams looking just like this? What if that was all this was—another dream? An illusion, constructed from some twisted magic?

But then Qadir stepped forward and drew her into his arms. There was no doubt then, as he embraced her. As he said, "I am sorry I kept you waiting."

It was the sound of his voice that fully convinced her. His voice, which had always kept her anchored, and his warmth, which no illusion could ever replicate.

Before Loulie knew what she was doing, she was returning his embrace, gripping him as tightly as she had ever gripped anyone in her life. She felt tears on her cheeks as she pressed her face to his chest. "It took you long enough."

She wanted to laugh. She wanted to scream. All she could manage were these damned tears, which rolled down her cheeks without her permission. But then, as the truth of him sank in, so did the rest of their situation.

Loulie pulled away abruptly, rubbing at her eyes as Qadir faced their next opponent, a jinn who wove illusions through the air. She had just braced herself for the attack when *another* figure lurched toward her in the smoke. With a scream, it threw itself at the jinn attacking Qadir.

Loulie recognized that scream. She stared, incredulous, at Aisha bint Louas. The thief had looped an enchanted rope around the jinn's neck and was pulling on it. The soldier struggled but Aisha's grip was unyielding. Triumph shone in her eyes as, slowly, the jinn grew limp beneath her. She did not release the rope until he had stopped moving.

"Midnight Merchant?"

Loulie spun, dagger raised. The man who had been approaching her quickly held up his hands in surrender. Loulie scrutinized him.

Like Qadir, he seemed to be in a fragile state, his skin blemished with painful-looking scratches. He was familiar. She recognized his hazel eyes, which had been downcast when he saw her and Mazen off in Madinne.

She gaped as the memory snapped into place. *"Prince Hakim?"* She shot a look at Qadir, but he seemed unsurprised by the prince's appearance.

Mazen's older brother lowered his hands. "I am glad to see you again, al-Nazari." He stepped toward her. "My brother—is he here with you?"

With a start, Loulie realized she had not stopped to check on Mazen in the chaos. When she searched for him in the maze of fire and smoke, she saw nothing. Had he followed her onto the ship beneath his shadow? Or had he stayed behind to wait for Rijah?

Aisha rose to her feet with a grumble. "I *told* you to steer clear of the battle, mapmaker." She turned to assess Loulie, gaze cutting from her damp clothing to the knife in her hand. "It's good to see you in one piece, merchant."

Loulie stared at them both. At these people who she knew, here in the jinn realm. How and why were they here? She glanced questioningly at Qadir, but the jinn had already rushed off to deal with another soldier. "I will explain later," he called over his shoulder.

Loulie had no choice but to turn her attention back to the battle. In the ensuing chaos, Hakim's question remained unanswered. As the skirmish scattered them across the deck, it was all Loulie could do to focus on dodging and deflecting. But all the while, the absence of something—*someone*—tugged at the back of her mind.

It was only when she had a moment to catch her breath that she remembered.

Ziyad.

Remembering Duha's ability to transform in the water, Loulie rushed to the rails of the ship, but she saw nothing below except for her own harried reflection.

"Looking for me, human?" She felt the kiss of a blade at her neck and froze. Any words she might have said died in her throat as Ziyad pulled her away from the water.

She swallowed against the knife's edge. "What are you—"

"I ought to have known this was your and Yousef's plan all along. He did not call me here for my assistance, did he? Your plan has always been to steal my ship."

What could she possibly say? That, in truth, she had meant to use him to get back to the city, but their plan had gone awry when Qadir appeared? She could not bluff her way out of this.

She felt the marid's sigh against the back of her neck. He yanked her backward, one arm secured tightly around her waist while he held the dagger to her throat. "Ifrit!" His voice boomed across the deck.

All at once, the fighting stopped. Loulie saw Qadir standing in the fire, staring at her with wide eyes. The moment he marched forward, Ziyad pressed the knife harder against her throat. "Watch your step. My blades are venomous."

Qadir froze, expression calm but for the tight press of his lips. Feet away, Aisha crouched beside an injured Hakim, glaring.

"Let me tell you how this will go," the marid said. "You all will lay down your weapons and surrender. You will be shackled and brought back to the city."

Loulie's panicked gaze skirted the deck, taking in the wreckage and the bodies, which Aisha had released from her magic. The soldiers approached silently in the stillness, pressing their advantage.

Ziyad had told them all to relinquish their weapons—but one of them was still missing.

He seemed to notice in the same moment. "Where is Yousef?"

The ashfire, which had moments ago been calm, suddenly *surged*. A shape erupted from the wall of flames. Loulie saw the wings first— the fiery feathers that spread so wide above their heads they ate up the sky. And then she saw the body, the beak. A bird, made of fire. The massive creature soared across the deck, sweeping the soldiers toward the rails with its fire.

She stared in shock. *Azhar?*

Mazen had told her before that the bird had been larger when it first appeared in Dhahab, but she had never anticipated it being *this* big. Even Ziyad floundered, his grip on her loosening as he stumbled back. Loulie saw her opening and took it, swinging an elbow into his stomach and scrambling out of his arms.

She made it only a few steps before he grabbed hold of her cloak. Loulie spun on him with the knife, but she was too slow.

In one deft motion, he backhanded her across the face. Loulie was so stunned she dropped the dagger. Ziyad kicked it out of reach before she could grab it, then put himself between her and the fire. Silhouetted in the garish light, his black eyes were wells of darkness.

Loulie reached for the pearl around her neck. *Please work.*

The feeble wind stirred as she yanked her hand to the side. It was nothing but a stray breeze, but it was enough to throw Ziyad into the rails. Unfortunately, the magic had unbalanced Loulie as well. She tripped over her own feet trying to escape.

A flutter of motion caught her eye as she fell. Loulie felt a steadying hand on her arm and then a gentle push as she was shoved away from the fight. She stumbled, turned—and saw the moment Qadir's dagger *vanished* off the ground. She heard rather than saw Mazen cross the deck, his footsteps quick and light on the floorboards.

There was a flash of steel in the air. Before Ziyad could recover, Mazen plunged the dagger into his shoulder. The marid screamed— a sound more shocked than anguished—as Mazen's shadow slipped from his body.

There was a moment when he and Ziyad locked eyes. The marid flashed a rictus that could have been a grin or a grimace. "I suppose," he said coldly, "this is a fitting comeuppance."

He yanked the dagger out with a pained grunt, throwing it to the floor as he shoved Mazen away.

As Loulie rushed to catch Mazen, the marid climbed onto the rails. One last time, he faced them. "I will see you in Dhahab before the end, I am sure." He fluttered a bloodied hand through the air in a weak, mocking wave—and then he fell.

By the time they had reached the rails, Ziyad had already disappeared. The only proof that he had fallen into the water was the silver blood clouding the surface. If what he had told Mazen about marid magic was true, then he had likely just transported himself back to the city.

Loulie turned slowly to face the gathered crowd. Azhar had vanished with the dimming ashfire, and everyone—ally and soldier alike—stood frozen, waiting to see what would happen next. What would they do with the jinn, now that their captain had left them behind?

The silence lingered. Loulie could not bring herself to speak in the sudden tension. But then a voice spoke peevishly into the quiet: "Is the battle over already?"

Loulie craned her neck to the skies. She saw a shadow in the sails. Rijah, returned from their pursuit and hanging from the ship's ratlines. Their gaze swept across the crowd. When they saw Qadir, they released their hold on the lines to land hard on the deck. The soldiers flinched back, but Rijah paid them no mind as they strode toward Qadir.

They knelt in front of him, head bowed in supplication. "Sayyidi. Welcome back."

Qadir looked at a loss for words. If it was a profoundly uncomfortable moment for him, then it was even more so for the assembled crowd, who stood watching him uncertainly.

At last, the ifrit raised their head and snapped, "What are you all waiting for? Ready the sails, set the course! We are returning to Dhahab."

The command was followed by a burst of bewildered outrage from the soldiers. When they reached for their weapons, Loulie feared the fight would start anew. Hakim cringed away as Aisha rose, blade at the ready. Mazen reached for Loulie's hand.

"Fools!" Rijah hissed. "Do you not realize who it is you insult?"

The bewilderment faded to confusion as, finally, the sailors took in the sight of the glowing magic on Qadir's arms, his burning eyes. "Ashfire King," they whispered, and there was both reverence and fear in their voices.

One by one, they surrendered.

Rijah oversaw their submission with the smugness of a war general. "That is right." They flashed a crooked, triumphant smile. "The Ashfire King has returned."

55

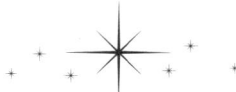

LOULIE

In the aftermath of the battle, the ship was filled with a flurry of activity. Fires were put out, damage was assessed, survivors were threatened—mostly by Aisha—and the vessel was made ready for sailing. For Loulie, the procedure felt bizarrely routine. She had voyaged many times with Nabila, after all. But it was no longer Nabila's crew who flitted about her.

Every time she looked away, Loulie expected her companions to disappear. But there was Mazen, standing with Rijah at the prow and helping them navigate the straits out of the city with the compass. And there was Aisha, interrogating the soldiers and waving a knife around to punctuate a point. As for Qadir—

Her bodyguard was below deck, tending to Hakim's injuries.

The Ashfire King has returned.

Loulie had heard the sailors echoing Rijah's declaration around the ship. Had noticed their eyes, round with fear, when they spotted Qadir.

It had been centuries since anyone in this realm had seen Qadir. Unlike her, they did not know how much the Bowels had diminished him, how weak and tired he had become. She was the only one who had felt his pain through the dagger. The only one who had felt the weight of his silence, an absence carved out by iron.

But he had kept his promise, despite everything. He had come back for her.

A strange dissonance swept through her as she moved about the ship. Over the hours, she had to keep reminding herself that she was no longer anyone's prisoner. Now she was returning to Dhahab of her *own* volition to break the final binding.

Sometime later, when Qadir had still not returned, Loulie sought out Mazen. She found him at the edge of the ship, conversing with Aisha. Loulie studied her from a distance. At first glance, the thief had not changed much. She still carried herself with the same intimidating pride and frowned at everyone as if they had personally inconvenienced her.

But then Loulie saw the way she was leaning back against the rails, and reflected that there was a softness in her that she had not witnessed before. It was in the relaxed line of Aisha's shoulders, in the gentle incline of her head. She looked as if she were interested in what Mazen had to say, rather than suffering through his conversation as she had before.

She's at ease, Loulie thought with some amazement.

Loulie caught the tail end of their conversation. "... came to me of its own volition," Mazen was saying. "I didn't *ensnare* it. I just gave it a name."

"You gave a dangerous flaming bird a name," Aisha repeated dryly, but the faint curve of her lips betrayed her amusement.

"It's only dangerous when it wants to be," Mazen objected.

"Were you trying to be clever when you came up with the name? *Azhar.*" She snorted. "How long did it take you to land on that?"

Loulie piped in: "It was one of the first names he came up with."

They both turned to face her. Mazen's consternation faded, replaced with a bright smile. It never failed to impress her, how easily he wore those smiles. She was relieved the incident with Ziyad had not shaken him as much as she had feared.

"Salaam, al-Nazari." Aisha arched a brow. "I hear you almost drowned."

Loulie shrugged. "Another day, another peril." She glanced at the collar around Aisha's neck. Another change: the relic the thief had once kept hidden beneath her cloak was now on full display around her neck. "How is the ifrit?"

"A nuisance as always," Aisha said, but her words lacked vitriol. "She is . . . grieving the state of this realm. It is a different place than in her memories."

The good mood dissipated as they took in their surroundings. In the chaos that had ensued after the binding breaking, Loulie had not had a chance to take in the degradation. Now she saw the unmistakable threads of magic spreading across the sky like a scar. The air was starting to fill with sand—Loulie could feel it settling in her clothes. The Sandsea had also grown turbulent. Though it was calm now, the waves lapped at their boat in a way they never had.

Mazen broke the somber quiet first. "What was it like before?"

For a few moments, Aisha was silent. When she did speak, her voice was filled with a wistfulness that confirmed she was no longer completely speaking for—or as—herself.

The ifrit said through her, "There were no islands, no Sandsea. The land was filled with magic—not the strange, wild energy in the air now, but a calming, steady presence." A faint smile touched her lips. "But you must have gathered all of that from Rijah's stories."

She cut a sharp glance over her shoulder. Loulie followed Aisha's gaze to a bird roosting on the crow's nest. *One of Nabila's spies?* Loulie reached for her knife before she could help it.

But then she saw the unmistakable blue shade of the bird's eyes and sighed, exasperated. The moment the Shapeshifter realized they had been spotted, they flitted away.

Loulie sheathed her knife. Though Rijah had reassured them that Nabila would not give chase—not when she was unaware of the final binding and focused on helping her injured first mate—Loulie could not help but be jumpy around birds.

Mazen stared after the ifrit, baffled. "Has Rijah been there this whole time?"

"They are avoiding us," Aisha said, pointing at herself. *Us.* Her and Amina. It was strange to hear her willingly use the plural. "I do not think they quite know what to make of our deal."

Mazen looked disconcerted by this epiphany, but Loulie immediately put it from her mind. The ifrit's business was their own; all she cared about was the immediate future. "What happens when the lands rise again?"

What would become of the country *she* knew? Would life return to the barren desert, or would what little nature they had be razed to the ground?

"That is up to you."

It was not Aisha who responded. Loulie turned to see Qadir approaching. He looked exhausted, beleaguered—and yet he was undeniably her Qadir.

Loulie's heart twisted at the sight of him. Ever since their reunion, things had been strange between them. It had never been difficult for Loulie to speak to Qadir before, and yet it seemed neither of them knew how to pick up where they had left off after the skirmish. There were too many secrets and too much history.

Loulie shuffled uneasily on her feet. "What do you mean?"

"What is it Dahlia always says about information-gathering?"

Loulie's heart eased some at the mention of the tavernkeeper. "That intel is power?"

Qadir nodded. "You all are the only ones who know the truth of both kingdoms. What you choose to do with that information is your decision."

Your decision. How could he say that after he had left her in this country—*his* country—alone? When her only "decision" had been to fix Qadir's mistake or turn away from it?

"I never wanted this." Her words came out cold, clipped.

She felt Mazen and Aisha glance at each other over her head. Some silent exchange must have passed between them, because moments later they were both drifting away. Aisha departed silently, Mazen after giving Loulie's shoulder a reassuring squeeze. He handed her the compass as he left. And then it was just her and Qadir, alone for the first time since his return.

His expression lost some of its edge in their absence. "I know," he said softly.

"And did you know that things would come to *this*?" She gestured to the black sky.

A muscle feathered in his jaw when he swallowed. "Never."

The two of them stood staring at each other. Loulie yearned to bridge the distance between them, but she did not know what she would do when she did. Her eyes wandered to the glimmer of steel at his side. The shamshir, which she had gifted him so long ago. She found herself saying, "You still have the blade?"

"Of course. It was a gift from you." He nodded at the dagger. "You kept my knife."

"It is a good thing. This country would have been doomed without it." She regretted the words immediately when she saw the flicker of shame on his face, and hurried to add, "You entrusted me with it. I would never lose your magic."

Her fingers curled around Khalilah's compass as she said the words. She could still remember the ache in her heart when she had misplaced it. Perhaps Qadir could read some of that guilt on her face. He reached out a hand for the relic.

Loulie relinquished it to him without complaint, but Qadir surprised her by grasping her hand in his. "This was always meant to be my burden to bear, Loulie. Not yours."

Something cracked in her at the words. She realized, then, that Qadir had always kept his secrets for the purpose of protecting her. Was that not what she had always done as well? Kept herself separate, apart, so that she would not have the chance to hurt or be hurt in turn?

What if all of this was just a part of the punishment Qadir had inflicted upon himself?

My burden to bear, he had said. But he was wrong.

She glowered at him. "After all these years, you still trust me so little? If you had told me about this before, I might have understood. It would have been nice to hear the truth of the Ashfire King from *you* first."

Qadir flinched at the title. The ashfire in the ship's lanterns rippled with the motion. Slowly, he withdrew his hand. Loulie feared he would push her away as he had before. She was relieved when, instead, he came to stand beside her. "You are right. This is a story long overdue."

He began to tell her his truth. It was the same story Nabila had shared, but spoken in Qadir's words. He admitted he had indeed been a wanderer before he was a king and that he had traveled a long time before settling. He had seen his throne as a duty and an honor, but he had never meant for it to be his only legacy.

That was why he had called upon the ifrit to help him rule: so that he could one day pass on the responsibilities of his crown to jinn who would uphold them with dedication. *Family*, he had called them, and Loulie felt a prickle of jealousy when he smiled at the memory.

But then the humans had appeared, ruining his plans.

"Why?" Loulie gestured at the sky, the fractured islands. "Why sink the world? You could have kept fighting. Nabila is convinced you would have won."

"Perhaps. But how many more sacrifices would it have taken? War is hell, Loulie."

She thought of the refugees on the island, then of her own tribe, cut down like stalks of wheat in a field. *Collateral damage*, Omar had called them. How many more casualties would there have been in a war? How many more would there be in the future?

"You said it would be our decision what happens next," Loulie said softly. "But, Qadir, I'm not..." She faltered. "I'm just a merchant."

Qadir raised a brow. "I never thought I would hear the Midnight Merchant speak so lowly of herself."

"I'm a magic-peddler, not a tactician! I don't have an army. I don't want one."

To Loulie, power had always seemed an overrated ambition. Her greatest aspiration had always been to live freely and comfortably, with no shackles.

Qadir smiled. A sad smile. "I had an army," he said. "And I had the magic to carve out an entire world. Even so, it was not enough to save it. Power is not always the answer."

"What else is there?"

He shook his head. "Perseverance. Ingenuity. Allies."

"Deception and connections, then."

He sighed. "You are as jaded as Dahlia."

Loulie laughed. "What did you expect? You both are bad influences." It was the first time she had laughed since the battle. And when she chanced a glance at Qadir, she saw that his expression was clearer too. It was not a smile, not exactly—but the corners of his lips had pulled into something resembling one.

"I have a proposition for you," Loulie said. "This business— we all tackle it together. No more running, Qadir. And no more secrets." She scrunched up her face in what she hoped was a threatening expression. "This time, we work as a team. All of us."

Qadir blinked at her. "*You* are suggesting teamwork?"

"Unlike you, I learn from my mistakes."

Qadir set a hand on the rail and smiled. "The student has become the teacher, I see."

The last of the awkwardness between them fell away as Loulie laced her fingers through his. "Mad queen, sultan, ifrit—it's all the same. We'll make them regret threatening us."

Qadir smiled. "They always do, in the end."

56

MAZEN

They had been on the Sandsea for a day when Mazen finally made it to Hakim's temporary study. Earlier, he'd been pacing the deck and nervously watching the horizon for Dhahab. He had seen firsthand the impact of the broken binding on Kharjem; the thought that such a magic might overtake Dhahab as well was unbearable.

At least, that was what Mazen had told Qadir when he'd asked. But the ifrit had not been fooled. "You are distracting yourself," he'd said. "But from what?"

"He's avoiding his brother," Loulie had said from the rails. "Gods know why."

She had been correct. Mazen had just been too embarrassed to admit it.

Now, as he stood before Hakim's room, fist hovering over the door, he realized it was shame he felt. His brother had not only journeyed through the desert to find him but broken into a prison and faced *Omar*. And what had Mazen done for him? Nothing.

He was still standing there when he heard footsteps. It was Aisha, striding down the corridor. Mazen was glad to see her until he noticed the scowl on her face. Before he could consider fleeing, she knocked on Hakim's door in his place.

"Mapmaker!" she called through the wood. "Your spineless brother is here to see you."

Mazen stepped back, aghast. "That's—that was the wrong knock."

She stared at him flatly. "What are you talking about, foolish man?"

"We have a knock," Mazen said weakly. "One only the two of us recognize—"

The door opened to reveal Hakim. Mazen did not realize how tense he had been until then, when he relaxed at the sight of him. His face was blanched with exhaustion, and he looked to be favoring a leg, but he was here, alive.

Hakim's brows rose when he saw them. "Bint Louas. Surely you did not drag my brother here yourself?"

"He dragged himself. But it seems he must have forgotten your *special knock*, because he was out here shaking his fist at the air."

Mazen resisted the urge to bury his face in his hands. He was grateful he did not, however, because he would have missed the smile on Hakim's face. If his brother could smile like that—at a brusque thief, no less—then perhaps he was not in as terrible of a state as Mazen had feared. The realization loosened something in his chest.

He managed a feeble smile of his own. "I'm sorry it took me so long to visit."

"As always, you apologize unnecessarily." Hakim glanced at Aisha. "I appreciate you reminding my brother how to knock."

Aisha merely shrugged before turning away. Hakim huffed with amusement as she strode away from them, not once glancing back. "That one shows affection in odd ways."

Mazen smiled after her. "She does."

He followed Hakim into the room and shut the door behind him. A quick glance told Mazen that this must have been Ziyad's cabin. There were sailing tools on the shelves and maps on the walls. Whatever mirrors had been in the space had been shattered; Mazen had earlier seen Aisha depositing the shards in the Sandsea.

Before Mazen could think how best to begin the conversation, Hakim pulled him into an embrace. For a few moments, Mazen stood frozen. And then the relief came, shuddering through him in a wave. Hakim had survived. His family was not broken after all.

There were tears in Mazen's eyes as he returned his brother's embrace. Wrapped in his arms, he felt like himself again. Not Yousef. Not a traitor. Not a criminal. Just Mazen bin Malik.

They spent the rest of the evening talking. After everything that had transpired, Mazen had worried Hakim would harbor some resentment toward him, but their talk flowed as easily as it always had. In fact, it flowed *better*. Before, Hakim had always let Mazen do most of the talking. Now he was more engaged. His posture was less rigid, and his expressions were softer around the edges, as if he no longer felt it necessary to wear them like armor.

To Mazen it did not seem as if Hakim had changed so much as he had finally been allowed to become himself. *This* Hakim was more like the boy Mazen had grown up with. He supposed he owed Aisha for that. She had not only kept Hakim alive but... befriended him? Or so he assumed. Mazen doubted Aisha would ever use the word herself.

Hakim looked thoughtful after they had finished recounting their journeys. "Everything that's happened to us—it sounds like one of your stories."

Mazen smiled. How many times had he come into Hakim's room with a new tale to share, and how many times had Hakim patiently listened while he rattled on about things the two of them had only ever dreamed of seeing? The story he was living right now was not nearly as heroic as those stories, but he had survived it, hadn't he?

Overcome by the sudden urge to prove it was all real, Mazen reached for the lamp in his satchel. The object gleamed a dull copper in the light of the ashfire.

Hakim tilted his head. "So, this is the lamp that started this mess."

Mazen rubbed at the vessel. "You can come out if you want."

One moment the lantern at the center of the table was filled with ashfire. The next, it was Azhar's new home. The firebird swiveled its small head and trilled sweetly when it saw them.

Hakim's lips parted in awe as he peered at the bird through the glass. "How did you manage to capture it in the lamp?"

"Do you remember the stories Father used to share? The ones that call the lamp a prison that can contain anything?" Mazen tapped the vessel. "Those stories are true."

Hakim assessed the bird quietly, hands steepled. When Azhar tweeted at him, the sound was so melodious it brought a smile to his face. "It seemed a lot more fearsome earlier."

"It *can* be fearsome. Ashfire is immortal fire, and anything Azhar sets aflame is difficult to put out. That is why I keep it in a lantern most of the time. It doesn't seem to mind."

Hakim's brows shot up as the bird headbutted the glass. "And how did you catch it?"

"It came to me." There was more to it than that, of course. He remembered what Duha had said about him shaping the ashfire with his words and will. But Mazen still struggled to believe he could possibly *create* the firebird.

Perhaps Hakim sensed his disbelief. There was a knowing glint in his eyes as he looked at the bird. "You have a knack for attracting unusual magics, akhi."

Mazen shook his head. "I'm not like Loulie. I don't find them myself."

"Since when is taking earning? Do not let Omar's way of thinking taint your mind. You have these magics because you were entrusted with them. That is a far greater honor."

Mazen's heart eased at the reassurance. Hakim had always been adept at quashing his fears. He may have been a man of few words, but he had always known how best to use them.

Mazen glanced at his brother's hand, thinking of the magic Hakim had been entrusted with. Of the ten rings he was accustomed to seeing, only nine were accounted for. It was strange to think that one of those rings had always been different, special.

Hakim saw him looking and smiled ruefully. "Omar may think he can use the ring now that he possesses it, but Jubayr chose me. It will take him some time to glean the magic's rules."

"We'll get it back before that happens."

They had stolen Omar's earring from him—they would find a way to take the ring too.

Hakim's smile softened as he nodded. "While we are on the subject of heirlooms..." He made his way to the corner desk, where he had deposited his satchel. Mazen watched him rummage through the bag until he pulled out a piece of rolled-up fabric.

His mouth fell open at the sight of his mother's shawl.

All those months ago, when Mazen had left Madinne, he'd given it to Hakim. "You kept it safe," he said softly. With everything that had happened since, he had assumed the shawl had been left behind or destroyed.

"Of course. I knew how much it meant to you."

Mazen took the shawl from Hakim. He was seized by sudden emotion when he ran his fingers over the embroidered silk. The garment no longer reminded him just of his mother, but of his lost life. How simple things had been before, when he was just a child prince.

He swallowed a knot in his throat. "I wonder what Shafia would have thought of all this."

"I think she would have thought it a remarkable story." Hakim inclined his head, a curious look on his face. "Have you ever given any thought to finding her tribe?"

The question startled Mazen. *Her* tribe meant *his* tribe, but he had never experienced anything beyond a distant yearning for that side of his family. Wherever his mother's tribe was, they had never deigned to come to Madinne. Perhaps they resented the sultan for stealing Shafia away, or perhaps they had settled in a different country entirely. Meeting them had never been anything more than a fleeting dream to Mazen, trapped in the palace as he'd been.

"You could find them," Hakim said. "Just as I found my tribe."

The possibility filled Mazen with a strange lightness. When he had seen his face on a wanted poster, he had thought his life over. But what if there was another life out there for him, with a different family? He couldn't think about it now. But perhaps, if he survived this, it would be a journey for the future.

Mazen draped the shawl over his shoulders. "I think I'd like to try. After this is all over."

Hakim smiled. He looked like he might say something else, when a knock sounded on the door. It was a mere courtesy; Loulie al-Nazari popped her head into the room before giving them a chance to answer. "Meeting upstairs," she announced.

Mazen saw the look on her face and said, "Are we scheming?"

She smirked at him. "Always."

—◊◊—

It would have been easier to scheme with more intel. What little information they had to go on had been given to them by Ziyad's sailors, and it was vague at best. Dhahab had been in a dire state since the ashfire had vanished, the sailors said, and riots had broken out in the curfew darkness as the queen turned her efforts to evacuation. But it was anyone's guess what had happened since.

At moments like this, it would have been nice to have access to Nabila's spies.

"Good riddance," Loulie said when Mazen brought up the disappearance of the birds.

Azhar seemed to take personal offense to this and squawked from its lantern to convey its displeasure. In response, Loulie shot a glare at Qadir, who had been quietly watching them squabble over their plans. He met Loulie's frown with a questioning brow.

"Can't you make it act less birdlike?" she asked him.

The brow rose higher. "It is not my bird."

"It's made of *your* magic."

"You should know by now that the ashfire has taken on a life of its own." Qadir glanced at Mazen when he said this, gaze assessing. "I assume it has taken this shape because of you."

Mazen shifted beneath the group's scrutiny. "It reacted to a story I told in Dhahab about a bird made of fire. Nabila's first mate told me it was shaped by my will?"

Rijah snorted from where they leaned against the mast, but

Qadir looked thoughtful. "Fire is as much an element as iron or stone; you just shaped it with words rather than a chisel."

Loulie scowled. "Why doesn't your fire listen to me?" When Qadir looked flatly at the dagger she held in her hands, she objected, "An enchanted blade is not the same as a living bird."

"I thought you did not like birds?"

Aisha, who had been studying a map of Dhahab, stopped to glower at them. "Are you done discussing magic birds? We have a city to breach." She pinned the parchment with a finger, waiting until she once again had their full attention before reviewing their plan.

There were two things standing in the way of them saving this realm. First: the queen. After what they had done to Ziyad and his crew, and given the effects their "meddling" had already had on this realm, Mazen doubted she would be happy to see them in her city. Second: the binding itself, which they would be able to track once they made it inside.

"The magic will be in the sky," Qadir said. "I drew it above the city."

After all the strange magics they had witnessed here, a binding in the sky should not have shocked Mazen. But he could not puzzle out the technicalities. "How will you get to it?"

Loulie looked unbothered. "I'll track its location. Qadir will unseal it. Simple."

Mazen felt a faint stab of jealousy, though he knew it was foolish. The magic was Qadir's; it made sense she would choose him to accompany her.

He returned his attention to the map. "I'll light the city, then. If the curfew is causing riots, then the ashfire might quiet the upheaval." Mazen had been the one to put out the fire—it was his responsibility to bring it back.

Rijah declared they would go with him, insisting the task would go faster with the two of them. But when Hakim also volunteered, Mazen objected. "The streets will be dangerous."

"Everywhere is dangerous, akhi. I made you a map for your

journey once. Now I would guide you myself." He raised a brow. "I may be magicless, but the least I can do is read a map."

Mazen faltered. He did not want to put Hakim at risk, but how could he possibly turn his brother away when he had followed him into another realm to make sure *Mazen* was safe? "We'll go together, then." He flashed a grateful smile before glancing at Aisha. "What will you do?"

"*I* will head to the palace." Aisha frowned at their quizzical looks. "What? I can't use ashfire, and I'll be dead weight at your binding."

Loulie eyed her, suspicious. "What will you be doing there?"

"Stealing, of course." She smirked at Loulie's surprise. "The queen's envoy mentioned magic belonging to one of the ifrit in her throne room. If we are bringing these cities back to the surface, I want to seize that magic before either the queen *or* Omar can use it for war."

Loulie had mentioned the possibility of the Tide Bringer's spear being in the throne room as well. Given how little they all knew about the former alliance between the queen and Omar, it would not be a bad idea to recover it. But still, Mazen was concerned. "How are you going to get into the palace? You've never even set foot in the city before."

In answer, Aisha tapped her temple. "I have memories, remember?"

Not her memories, Mazen realized, but the Resurrectionist's. He did not know if he was more surprised that Aisha had just insinuated that she would willingly work together with the ifrit, or that she was offering a solution that would avoid violence.

With their planning concluded, everyone left to make their preparations. Mazen must have been staring at Loulie and Qadir as they headed for the cabin, because when Aisha came to join him by the water, the first thing she said was "Your lovesickness is showing, sayyidi."

He frowned at the formal title. "I am no longer a prince."

"*That's* what you say to me after I travel the whole godsdamned desert to find you?"

"The way my brother tells it, you were already heading to Madinne?"

She shrugged. "I promised to kill a man."

That promise was yet unfulfilled, but at the very least, Aisha had escaped. Mazen was glad for it. "Shukran. For keeping Hakim safe. For reuniting us."

She pulled away from the rails with a grumble. "I do not think I could be rid of your family even if I tried. You and your brothers are a curse on my existence. Besides that, I had to make sure you were alive with my own two eyes."

The words made him smile despite the circumstances. "You sound suspiciously like you care. Did you miss being my bodyguard?"

Her eyes flashed at the memory, a ghost of a smile touching her lips as she shook her head. "Hmph. I suppose I can be convinced to suffer through the job one last time."

One last time. He settled his arms on the rails and stared into the horizon.

For all their sakes, he hoped this *was* the last time.

57

LOULIE

The first time Loulie had seen Dhahab on the horizon, it had appeared as a brilliant haze of gold. Now, as they approached the city under a shroud of unnatural darkness, it had transformed into a landscape of shifting shadows.

The lightless city was a disquieting sight. Loulie only grew more unsettled when she saw the line of ships floating on the Sandsea in front of it. At first, she feared an ambush, but when Rijah returned as a bird to report on the scene, they explained the ships were for evacuees.

"The city is sinking," Rijah said miserably. "Her Majesty has been trying to evacuate the citizens, but there are not enough ships. Also..." They gestured past the boats to the sunken city wall. "The gate is gone."

Aisha scowled into the darkness. "What do you mean *gone*?"

"There is one gate in and out of the city, and it is no longer accessible," Qadir said from where he stood at the prow. Standing erect with his hands clasped behind his back, he could have been a figurehead at the front of their ship.

Loulie squinted past the line of bobbing ships to the city wall. Sure enough, the gateway they had once used to cross into Dhahab was simply . . . gone. Sunken beneath the Sandsea.

Was the city really breaking apart *that* fast?

"What about the barrier?" She eyed the translucent magic rising above the walls. Even Nabila had not been able to surmount it before, but the magic seemed to be flickering now. If the foundations of the city were cracking, then perhaps its barrier was weakening as well.

"It is damaged but still intact," Rijah confirmed.

Loulie glanced at the compass. The instrument was still pointing them through the wall, which meant they had to find a way to break in. She could feel Mazen watching the instrument over her shoulder. "How are we going to get inside?" he asked.

"It would take considerable force to break down the barrier," Qadir said.

Rijah cracked their knuckles. "I could destroy it in my rukh shape."

"No." Qadir regarded them sternly. "You would break your body against that magic. We would need something much bigger to shatter it. And heavier."

Loulie studied the barrier as the others thought aloud. Rijah asked if there was a way to burrow beneath the city through the Sandsea. Mazen hesitantly suggested burning a way through the barrier with ashfire. Aisha proposed finding a weak spot in the magic they could exploit. But it was Hakim's suggestion that gave Loulie pause.

"Is there a way to go over it?" the mapmaker asked.

The question unearthed a possibility in her mind. It was a brash and dangerous plan, but if they gained enough momentum, it could work. No, she would *make* it work.

"I have an idea." She grinned at their wary looks. "We may not be strong enough to break the barrier above the wall, but this hunk of rotting wood is."

They all gaped at her with varying levels of concern. None of them were comforted when she told them she had a magic pearl that would make the ship fly.

Qadir released a long-suffering sigh. "I see your plans are as reckless as ever."

Loulie winked at him. "You can admit you missed them."

In absence of a better strategy, they had no choice but to settle on Loulie's. She breathed a shaky sigh as she wrapped the necklace around her fingers. She had only ever used the pearl to shoot *herself* through the air. If she intended to pull this off, she would need to blanket the entire ship with the magic, which was easier said than done. But this was her plan—she had to make sure it succeeded.

Loulie gripped the ship's rails as it sped across the Sandsea. She closed her eyes, trying to recall the feeling of weightlessness that had overcome her when she lifted herself onto Ziyad's ship. She remembered the looseness of her limbs, the sensation of the ground giving way.

"*Hurry*," Rijah snapped from the prow. They had drawn close enough to the city that the wall was looming.

Loulie's fingers tightened over the pearl. While her own body felt lighter, the ship was still very solid beneath her feet. She was vaguely aware of Mazen inching toward her. He leaned close enough to yell over the wind. "You told me that Nabila was able to move her own ship—do you remember what the magic felt like?"

Loulie did. How could she forget the sentient winds pulling at her sleeves? The breathing of the planks beneath her feet? Under Nabila's influence, the ship had been not just a vessel, but an extension of the ifrit herself.

"Al-Nazari!" Aisha yelled in warning.

Holding the memory of Nabila's ship in her mind, Loulie raised the pearl above her head.

The air caught in her lungs as the dhow *jumped*, the Sandsea abruptly falling away as the sails snapped to catch a magical wind. Loulie heard screams, curses—but she had never felt more weightless. The sensation was terrifying. And it was *exhilarating*. When the ship crashed through the flickering barrier and into the city, Loulie bit back a hysterical laugh.

"Loulie!" Qadir called from the prow of the ship. "Release the magic slowly."

She obeyed. Or at least, she tried to. But it was difficult to judge what *slow* was when the magic was propelling them forward so fast.

Loulie lowered the pearl—gradually, she thought—but the change in the air was immediate. Suddenly, they were not drifting, but falling.

"Hold on!" Qadir roared.

His voice was the last thing Loulie heard before the ship struck the water on the other side of the gate. She gasped, clinging to the mast as the dhow plunged through the surface. They were falling, falling—and then the ship reemerged.

Loulie slumped to the deck with a wet cough. She glanced around blearily. From what she could tell, they were all soaked but in one piece. When she searched her hand for Firas's surveillance magic, she saw nothing—no eyes, no markings. Perhaps his magic too had weakened in the chaos.

As her eyes adjusted to the dimness, she noticed the gathered crowd on the docks. Evacuees, most likely, based on the overfilled wagons behind them. Two soldiers stood before the group, staring at them in shock. Seeing the water sizzling off their fiery skin, Loulie assumed they had been caught in the landing splash.

Before any of them could react, Aisha threw herself over the edge of the ship and darted toward the soldiers. The first, she knocked out with a hard punch. The second, she caught in a headlock before he could call for help, though his silence mattered little when the citizens scattered, yelling about some mad human.

By the time the rest of their group had made it onto the docks, both jinn were incapacitated. The sailors, wisely, scattered before they could be threatened.

Loulie sighed. "Well, that was a dramatic entrance."

The thief's eyes narrowed. "If you wanted to avoid showy entrances, then we should not have crashed into the city on a *flying ship*." She threw a look at the two brothers, who were frowning at her with mirrored disgruntlement. "What?" she snapped. "I left them alive, didn't I?"

At the very least, Aisha had given them time to regroup. Hakim took out one of Ziyad's city maps, Mazen summoned the firebird, and Loulie retrieved her compass. Qadir had already shifted into his lizard form so that he could sit on her shoulder and preserve his energy. Much to Loulie's surprise, he entrusted his shamshir to Aisha, claiming she would find better use for it. The three of them would be traveling together to the palace until they split up—her and Qadir to unseal the binding from the highest rooftop in the city, and Aisha to the throne room.

When their preparations were done, Loulie faced the group. "I'll see you all when this is over." She had never been one for moving speeches. Instead, she spoke the words like a threat. She did not want anyone—especially Mazen—thinking she would condone sacrifice.

Mazen lingered after Rijah and Hakim had turned away. His eyes cut between her and Aisha, hesitant, before he said, "You remember our promise? I'll see you on the surface."

He left before she could say anything, rushing after Hakim with the firebird on his shoulder. Loulie watched his back as he left. She committed his wobbly smile to memory, then turned to follow the compass into the city.

—⚅—

Even though Qadir had chosen to take his lizard shape, Loulie was grateful for his presence. For as competent of a warrior as Aisha bint Louas was, her stringent demeanor did little to calm Loulie's nerves as they wandered the shadowed, empty alleyways of the darkened city. Her focus seemed turned inward; perhaps she was communicating with the ifrit in her mind. Loulie was glad, at least, for her familiar banter with Qadir.

"I never thought *you* would worry for one of the sultan's sons," Qadir was saying.

"Only this one," Loulie muttered as they passed through another alley. The shadows on the wall recoiled as she held up the ashfire-lit dagger. This area, like the last, was empty.

"He grows on you like desert moss."

Loulie startled at the sound of Aisha's voice. She turned to see the thief watching her, brow cocked. Loulie's cheeks flushed when she realized she must have been listening in on their conversation after all. "Was that meant to be a compliment?"

"Just the truth. You admitted it yourself." The thief passed her with a shrug, but Loulie did not miss the smirk on her face. She was torn between mortification and vindication. When Qadir chuckled in her ear, she flicked his tail with a grumble.

The three of them had just arrived in the city's royal quarter when Qadir called a sudden warning in her ear. Loulie backed away from a crater she had nearly missed in the dark. Though they had run into many broken roads, this chasm was especially large. Aisha, of course, had already circumvented the gap. She frowned at Loulie from the other side.

"Let us go around," Qadir said.

Loulie nodded. She managed only a few steps, however, before the ground lurched, throwing her off balance. *Earthquake,* her frazzled mind supplied, but there was no time to process the revelation. The chasm in front of her was crumbling inward, yawning wider as it swallowed the cobbled streets. Loulie turned on her heel and ran.

Somewhere in the distance, she heard a portentous crack, along with the terrible sigh of crumbling stone. It sounded like a falling building, though it was difficult to tell where it was.

Afterward, when the shaking stopped, Loulie glanced across the chasm. Aisha, who had been feet apart from her, was now yards away. She looked disgruntled but otherwise safe.

Given the destruction of the streets, it would take more time for them to regroup than to find their own way to the palace. When Loulie recommended Aisha go on ahead of them, the thief was more than happy to comply. She called one last warning before departing.

Loulie was grateful, at least, that she still had Qadir with her as she backtracked into another square. Based on the stalls and wagons, she suspected this place must be a souk. But the shops now lay abandoned, and the few jinn remaining in the area were on their way out. Loulie saw mothers ushering crying children from broken homes, saw families dragging their belongings behind them. More evacuees, Loulie assumed, heading to higher ground.

When another quake rolled through the area, they steadfastly carried on, pausing only long enough to eye the shadows of the quivering buildings. None of the jinn paid Loulie any mind; they had more tangible fears to face.

Loulie kept moving. The more she saw of the city, the more nervous she became. What if they reached the binding too late? What if she wasn't moving fast enough?

"Loulie." Qadir pressed his nails into her shoulder. Not hard enough to break skin, but firmly enough to reassure her of his presence. "Remember: you are not alone."

She breathed out a shaky sigh. They would all make it out of here alive—they were too close to fail now. Still, she wished Qadir had been able to guide her, to *walk* beside her.

"You'd be more useful in your man shape, you know," she said as she followed the compass into another clearing. The area was completely empty, the only motion coming from water bubbling in a center fountain. "What good are you in a fight when you're a lizard?"

Qadir sighed in his familiar long-suffering way. "I already told you that my magic is diminished..." He paused. "Loulie, to your right."

It was strange, how she knew who it was before she even turned to face him. Perhaps she had been expecting him after his threat on the ship, or maybe she had caught the glimmer of his sharp teeth in the dark.

"Kayfa haluki, merchant?"

Ziyad emerged from the shadows. Dressed in his rich coat and sporting his usual smile, he could have been out for a casual stroll. He looked illogical in the crumbling city, like a puzzle piece that had made it into the wrong picture.

Loulie's grip tightened on the dagger. "What are you doing here?"

"What do you think? When we heard the reports of your arrival in the city, Her Majesty sent me to capture you."

The queen had scores of soldiers; why had she sent her envoy?

Ziyad's grin widened as he stepped forward. The water in the fountain shuddered with his steps. "Perhaps it is more accurate to say I *volunteered* to go after you. I am still rather insulted by that stunt you pulled on my ship."

Loulie raised her knife as the fountain water rose, the liquid sharpening into an angular head. Her heart seized when the watery bust swiveled toward her. She stumbled back, putting as much distance between herself and the creature as she could.

"Tell me, Layla." The marid's black eyes glittered with mirth. "Can you outrun water?"

Qadir's nails dug into her shoulder. *"Loulie."*

The serpent shot forward. This time, when Qadir yelled in her ear, Loulie ran.

58

MAZEN

Dhahab was falling.

The manors Mazen had once passed with Loulie were in ruins, shattered by the quakes that had rocked the city in their absence. Craters littered the broken streets, filled with debris and dust. More than once, Mazen nearly tripped into a patch of Sandsea.

Azhar, at least, kept the curfew illusions at bay. The bird burned bright, lighting the streets as it swept ahead of him and Hakim. The creature was a shocking sight to the jinn they encountered. Most of them appeared dazed when they saw Azhar lighting the lanterns and braziers. Whenever Mazen could, he flashed them a smile or offered a comforting word. Perhaps they did not trust *him*, but they were at least calmed by the light of the ashfire.

Still, the city was a tomb with no escape. The evacuees Mazen spoke to were heading to higher ground in the hope that their queen would find a way to save them. Their fear fueled Mazen's own. He found himself measuring the intervals between aftershocks and wondering what it meant that they were getting shorter. How fast was Dhahab sinking? How much time did they have left?

What if, by the time we finish lighting this city, the ashfire illuminates nothing but ruins?

A tremor shook Mazen from his musing. He struggled to keep

on his feet as it rolled through the ground beneath him. He could immediately tell that the quake was more severe when the buildings around them began to groan. Mazen nearly stepped right into a hole, trying to avoid the withering shadows, before Hakim yanked him back.

Somewhere in the dark, Mazen heard a sharp snap. He looked up just in time to see a building at the end of the block crack. As he watched, the fractures spread like a web across the granite, shooting up from the structure's foundation like ruptured roots. And then, between blinks, the building collapsed as easily as if it were sand.

The avalanche shook the street, debris plummeting through the air like deadly rain. A cloud of dust followed, and suddenly, there was sand everywhere—in Mazen's clothes, his skin, his eyes. When he blinked, he felt as if there were shards of glass behind his lashes. He wrapped his mother's shawl around his face but too late. His senses had all but been obliterated by the destruction.

Hakim looked similarly discombobulated, though he had moved faster to cover his face. His hazel eyes were clearer than Mazen's as they both took in the orange haze where the building had moments ago stood.

Gradually, as the dust parted and Azhar's light brightened, Mazen could make out jinn fleeing the destruction. He gathered from their panicked conversations that the building had been a refuge during curfew-fall. That it had housed entire families.

Mazen's feet guided him toward the collapse before he could stop himself. He paused only when Hakim grabbed urgently at his arm. "Akhi, what are you doing?"

"Seeing if we can help." He nodded toward Azhar, who circled restlessly above their heads. "If there are any survivors, we may be able to spot them in the light."

Hakim hesitated, but he must have known Mazen would not be deterred, because he ultimately relented, guiding Mazen through the crowds. When they came into the clearing where the building had collapsed, Mazen's attention went to the pile of rubble before them. The building's innards lay crushed, entire walls turned to dust in mere moments. Small objects lay amidst the clutter—mundane things like shattered cups and torn tapestries.

And then Mazen saw the silver blood staining the ground, and he saw the bodies it had come from.

Most of the corpses were nothing but limbs. A bloodied hand reaching through layers of broken glass, a torso barely visible in a sea of silver-drenched tile. Mazen's stomach roiled at the sight of a face staring blankly at him from between pieces of cracked wood.

Hakim clamped a steadying hand on Mazen's shoulder, but he could not help his trembling. Had these jinn all been in the building, or had they been fleeing when the quake hit, their screams lost beneath the avalanche?

"Mazen," Hakim murmured. "Help has already arrived."

He was right. Mazen saw soldiers sifting through the wreckage in search of survivors. It didn't look as if any of them had noticed him and Hakim.

"We can help!" Mazen called as he made his way through the debris. Azhar followed him from the sky, blanketing the fallen rock in a gentle light.

The soldiers startled at his approach. One of them whirled, a weapon already in hand. His movements were jerky, his glassy and panicked eyes on Mazen. He looked as if he were seeing...something else. Perhaps it was the influence of the curfew on his mind.

With a yelp, Mazen threw himself out of the soldier's path. His blade arced sluggishly through the air above Mazen's head, clipping Azhar's wing. The bird shrieked in agitation. Its body surged with fire as it shot toward their assailant.

"Wait, Azhar!" Mazen held up a hand. "*Stop!*"

The bird halted inches from the soldier's face. The jinn staggered away from its fiery wings with a cry, his gaze clearing with every blink.

Before Mazen could call Azhar off, he felt the tip of a dagger at his back. He gasped as an arm came around his stomach. He could tell from his assailant's grip that they were shorter than him. And then he heard her voice, and he knew her scathing tone immediately.

"Call your *spy* back," Hayat hissed.

"Hayat?" Her name came out a stunned whisper.

Still, the jinn must have heard him, because she immediately released him. She blinked her catlike eyes at him as Hakim came to stand beside him. Mazen looked her over for injuries, but the blood and grime he saw on her seemed to have permeated no deeper than her clothing.

"Human?" She took a cautious step forward. "*Yousef?* Is that really you?" She kept rubbing at her eyes as if she expected him to disappear.

"Yes. It's me. And the man beside me is my brother." When she frowned at him, clearly suspicious, he pointed to Azhar. "You remember the firebird we saw during the summit? It isn't Nabila's spy. It's been helping me light the torches."

Her expression slackened with shock. "*You're* the one lighting the streets with ashfire?"

He nodded. "Me and Rijah."

An irritated squawk punctuated the statement. Mazen looked up, but it was not Azhar that had cried out. Another bird glided above them, its eyes the blazing blue of ashfire. Rijah shifted shape midflight to land easily on their feet. Mazen stepped back at their sudden appearance.

Rijah smirked. "You summoned me?"

Mazen reached instinctively for the lamp in his satchel. *Had* he summoned them?

Hayat looked as if she were holding back tears. "Welcome back, *traitor*." She shoved their shoulder, and it had all the impact of a child throwing herself at a rock. "You told Her Majesty you were going to help us protect this city! You said—"

"I know what I said." Rijah raised a sharp brow. "Why do you think I am back?"

Her confidence all but deflated at their words. She suddenly looked small, uncertain. Mazen took in her full appearance then, looking past the blood on her clothes to see that her smoky cloak was in tatters, her curly hair knotted and singed. Though Mazen had never been able to pin down her age, this was the youngest and most helpless she had ever looked to him.

"Hayat." Mazen tried to keep his voice soft, calm. "What's happened?"

The jinn threw out a hand toward the soldiers pulling bodies out of the rubble behind them. "This." She swept her hand across the buildings draped in shadow. "And this." Her eyes glimmered with wariness as she regarded them. "You . . . are not here on Nabila's orders to destroy Dhahab?"

Mazen shook his head. "It's like Rijah said; we're here to help."

The jinn glanced between the three of them—the ifrit, the map-maker, and the storyteller—before she relented. "Her Majesty has locked herself away. Tensions reached a breaking point when the city started sinking. Then the gate vanished, and the evacuations had to stop. Now there is a crowd at the palace, demanding blood. But you—you can help the queen?"

Mazen flinched at the hope in her eyes. They had certainly not come to this city with the intention of protecting the queen who had tried to kill them, but how could Mazen deny Hayat?

He glanced past her toward the palace. He had told Loulie he hoped to break up the riots with the ashfire. If the crowds had congregated at the palace gates, then perhaps this was better accomplished by lighting the torches across the palace walls and courtyard.

Hakim, who had always known him best, was the first to pick up on his change of mood. "What are you thinking, akhi?"

Haltingly, Mazen told them all about his plan to make the palace a beacon. Afterward, he expected resistance, protests. But even though Hakim was quiet, no one reprimanded him. Rijah, in fact, looked relieved.

They waved a dismissive hand. "Go, human. I do not need your help lighting the city."

Hayat bristled. "*We.* I will assist as well."

Mazen glanced between the two of them. "Are you certain?"

Rijah sighed. "Do you remember what I said before? That I had failed? These earthquakes—they are caused by *our* failing magic.

This is not your problem to fix." They pointed at the palace. "But if you can light the ashfire on the palace walls, it will help us all see."

He wavered. Before, when he had left Rijah in the palace diwan, he had feared he would never see them again. Now he wondered if he ought to stay and—

"Mazen." The sound of his name on Rijah's tongue was such a shock it pulled him from his stupor. The ifrit had never called him anything other than *human* before. Even Hayat startled, though Mazen assumed her confusion was for the foreign name rather than the sentiment.

Rijah raised their hand, calling ashfire to their fingers with a flick of their wrist. With the other, they pointed at the lamp in his hands. "If you have need of me, all you must do is call me through the lamp."

Not summon. Not command. Call, like a friend.

"Shukran," Mazen said, voice tight. He looked at Hakim. "You will help Rijah?"

"Only because I cannot sneak in with you. But promise me one thing." His brow furrowed. "If something goes wrong, you will put yourself first and flee."

It occurred to Mazen that his brother was asking this of him because of Loulie. Mazen had told him of the injuries he sustained trying to save her. But he had promised Loulie too—that they would all make it out of here alive.

He clamped a hand on Hakim's shoulder. "I promise."

With a whistle, he called Azhar down to his shoulder. He turned toward the looming palace, lamp in hand. From this distance, he could see the towers standing sentinel before the moat. If there was any way for him to access the wall, it would be through those towers.

"Ready to light it all up, Azhar?"

The bird gave an affirmative chirp as they made their way to the palace.

59

AISHA

It was surprisingly easy to sneak into the palace.

The crowds pouring in through the gates were dense enough Aisha could lose herself in them. She had expected more of a fight, but the rioters were too busy riling each other up to notice a cloaked figure skirting the crowd. Even the soldiers were overwhelmed, shouting to be heard over the protests as they held the masses back from a barred palace door. As Aisha had expected, she would not be using the front entrance.

I know a hidden passageway, Amina said. *I will guide you to it.*

Aisha was following the ifrit's directions when a sudden motion on the palace walls caught her eye. She looked up, half expecting Loulie al-Nazari to be making another one of her showy entrances. Instead, she was greeted by the sudden appearance of ashfire. One of the braziers, moments ago empty, had erupted with a startlingly bright blue-white fire.

Others had noticed it as well. A sudden hush enveloped the crowd as they pointed at the fire. And then there were more cries of surprise as a second brazier and then a third and a fourth were lit. From this distance, all anyone could see was the flaming creature darting between the torches. Azhar. Mazen must have decided to light the palace braziers as well.

Perhaps some of the jinn here had witnessed him lighting torches in the city, for she could hear his alias being whispered in the crowd. *Yousef the Storyteller.* She heard other names too, the Shapeshifter and the Ashfire King among them, but the rumor of the storyteller and his firebird must have been the most alluring, because it was that tale that now spread like wildfire.

Aisha smirked beneath her hood. *Not bad, Prince.*

Later, she would have to tell him about the rumors. For now, she would put his distraction to use. Quietly, Aisha slid through the stunned crowd to the back of the palace. It was easier to take in the golden domes and towers outside of the chaos. The sight filled her with a strange, misplaced longing.

Home, she thought as she took in the courtyard. How many times had she—Amina—walked these gardens, consoling families who had lost their loved ones? This palace had been her—*Amina's*—home once, the place where she would rest at the end of a long day.

Aisha made her way to the hidden passageway. At first, the old servants' entrance was hidden from even Aisha's sight—the rusted gateway was patched over with such intricate illusion work that her mind at first refused to perceive it. But then, as she swept her hands across the surface, she felt the latch of the gate. With a few forceful yanks, it gave. Inside, the palace halls were dark enough Aisha had to navigate by Amina's memory.

Memory, and magic.

Distantly, she was aware of the voices of the dead. Aisha followed the unsettling susurration down the corridors to a set of elaborate doors. The throne room. The moment Aisha opened the doors, the voices crashed down on her like a wave, rocking her on her feet.

"Fuck," she whispered.

Bint Louas. The Resurrectionist spoke sharply in her mind. *Look at the walls.*

Aisha forced her heavy head up. Perhaps to most, the objects on the walls would have looked like mere weapons. But Aisha recognized them as relics. Their memories filled her mind like a poisonous fog. And there was something else too—a layer of magic that stretched across the relics like a heavy gloss. When Aisha drew nearer, she could feel that magic hum dangerously beneath her fingers. It was both familiar and strange.

These relics are protected by the queen's magic, Amina said. *It will steal a thief's life.*

"But not ours?"

Amina scoffed. *My magic* is *death. You need not worry. Just look for the spear.*

Aisha braced her hand against the wall as, slowly but surely, she eased the channel in her mind closed. She carefully surveyed the weapons as she wandered the hall, but saw no spear made of sea glass. However, there was another sensation building at the cusp of her mind.

Aisha did not understand the feeling until she came to the end of the hall and realized she was not alone. Before her sat a golden throne, and reclining atop it was a lone figure. A jinn, tall and gaunt, watched her with unnerving intentness. In the shadow of the alcove, her features were sharpened to severe points. Aisha was struck by her dark eyes—so black they were like pits. The jinn seemed oddly faded, the pallor of her skin almost sickly.

Aisha saw the crown on her head and knew immediately she must be the queen.

The two of them stared at each other for a long time, sizing each other up. And then something flashed in the queen's eyes. She rose from her throne. *"Amina."*

Aisha froze at the name. The queen had spoken it aloud with a vehement recognition. She sifted through the ifrit's memories and felt a faint flicker of remembrance.

I know her. Shock slivered through the ifrit's voice. *She was a soldier charged with speaking to the dead. Basira, her name was. She would join me sometimes on my patrols.*

In Amina's faded memories, Basira was…different. Warmer, vibrant, not the cold creature that strode toward them now. As she moved, the weapons on the wall began to rattle. But something else had caught Aisha's eye. A thread, hovering around the queen. Where it led, Aisha did not know, but she was shocked by its presence. Did the queen have it because they possessed similar magics?

Aisha reached for her blade. "Amina is not my name. Can you say 'Aisha'?"

"You lie through your teeth." The jinn's colorless lips pulled back in a snarl. "I know your magic, ifrit." She jutted a finger at the relic around Aisha's neck. "I know your *relic.*"

Basira was fast approaching, and Aisha could see now what she had not before—that she wore a terrifying number of weapons. Was it for show? Surely it was impossible for anyone to have mastered so many blades.

Be cautious, thief, Amina warned. *You are facing an opponent who is centuries old.*

Aisha would not let herself be cowed. She lifted her head in challenge. "Of course you would recognize a relic. After all, you struck a deal with a human to collect them."

The jinn froze at the accusation. "You know the human traitor?"

Traitor?

Aisha recovered quickly. "That traitor was my king before I discovered the deal you had struck with him. You gave him thieves—to murder, to pillage—all so you could obtain relics? Your soldiers did everything on your orders, and still you turned your back on them?"

The queen slid a blade from a scabbard at her hip. "How dare you twist the story to make *me* the villain?" She lunged, moving with such speed Aisha barely caught the brunt of her strike against Qadir's shamshir. Basira was fast; she followed the first strike with a quick second and a third, never giving Aisha the chance to do more than defend.

Aisha swerved, dodging the jinn's next stab but taking a punch to the gut. The sword fell from her hands as her vision flared white. Before she could recover, the queen kicked the blade away and rushed her again. Aisha was quick enough to dodge the slash to her stomach but caught the strike in her arm instead.

She stumbled away with a hiss. The queen watched her, nose

wrinkled with disgust when she saw the blood on Aisha's arm. "You still bleed red?"

"The ifrit and I made a *deal*," Aisha snapped. "She has not taken my body."

"How shameful."

When Basira lunged again, Aisha reached blindly toward the walls. The moment her fingers curled over the hilt of one of the swords, she felt the brief, stabbing pain of the queen's magic in her chest, followed by a surge of voices in her mind. Screams, cries, pleas.

The owner's memories poured through Aisha's mind as she pulled it off the wall. She saw a battlefield, blood, corpses... all felled by the owner's hands.

Dive deeper, bint Louas, the Resurrectionist urged. *Before death, there is always life.*

Aisha dove. As memories flashed through her mind, she remembered not just the shape of the sword master's life, but the extent of his skill. She readjusted her hand on the hilt to match his memory of the blade and sprang toward the queen.

She and Basira collided at the center of the throne room. The queen startled, no doubt surprised Aisha's technique had suddenly changed. But then her dark eyes flashed with comprehension. Their magics were similar, after all. To understand death was to understand life.

Suddenly, Aisha knew why the queen kept all these weapons. She was not using them as tools. With her magic, she could become the master of each blade. This, Aisha thought, was the ultimate theft. A theft of life and all its memories.

Their battle became a storm of blades. When one weapon was rendered obsolete, Aisha reached for another. The two of them fought, steel against steel, human against jinn, but Aisha's body had its limitations, and she was becoming more and more aware of them as the queen pushed her.

Then Aisha saw an opening. Basira had reached for a sword. When she shifted, her shoulder rose, and for a moment, Aisha saw the path to her heart exposed. She did not hesitate. She charged, throwing her weight into her blade as she plunged it through the queen's chest. Basira gasped as the sword slid through bones, muscles, and heart.

It should have been a killing blow.

But there was too little resistance and no...blood? When Basira began to laugh—*laugh*—her lungs were clear. There should have been blood in her throat, should have been gore oozing from the wound. Aisha's mind whirred helplessly as she tried to comprehend the absence of it.

The queen grinned as she yanked Aisha's blade out of her body. The terrible gash Aisha had ripped into the queen's chest should have been fatal. But it was not. Because, Aisha realized with horror, Basira was not alive.

She was fighting a corpse.

"How?" The question was both hers and Amina's. Neither of them had ever heard of a corpse that could animate *itself.* She gaped as the queen resumed her stance.

"How do you think I have kept my throne for so long?" Basira said. "I have persisted where others have failed because I *cannot* be defeated." She flashed a vicious smile. "I will not lose to you. I will not lose to anyone."

With frightening nonchalance, she selected a new blade from the wall and faced Aisha. She curled her fingers in a beckoning gesture. A taunt.

"Come, *Aisha.* Let us see who the true master of death is."

60

LOULIE

The water serpent shot after Loulie like a torrent with icy teeth, lapping up water from the city's canals as it gave chase. It was so fearsome a force it did not charge past the buildings so much as crash through them. It shattered glass and splintered walls in its mad dash, and Loulie was left fleeing through the falling debris with nothing but Qadir's dagger for protection.

The blade burned brighter than it ever had before, bright enough to throw white shadows across the cityscape. In that light, Loulie could see jinn peering at her behind windows and through open doorways. She could see their expressions, twisted with fear.

Loulie made it as far as the city's uppermost tier before the serpent caught up with her. When she saw its shadow rising above her, she did the first thing she could think of—she hid, throwing herself behind a broken wall just as the creature rounded the corner.

"Merchant!" Ziyad's voice rose above the rushing water. "Will you not surrender?"

No. Loulie clenched the word between her teeth as she darted a glance past the wall. The serpent had paused, looking for her. Loulie was horrified when, before her eyes, its body split into *two* writhing forms. She pressed herself back against the wall with a muttered curse.

Qadir still clung to her shoulder, nails pressed into her skin. "We will have to sneak around the serpent to get to the palace."

"Can't you do something? Evaporate the water with your fire?"

"And what then? He will just draw it from another source."

Loulie was about to retort that *any* evaporated water would be an advantage, when the serpent's shadow loomed over the wall. She nearly stopped breathing when she saw its eyes—*Ziyad's* black eyes—boring into her.

"Found you," the creature said with his voice.

It threw itself against the ruin, splintering rock and loosing a wall of dirt on her. Loulie coughed sand from her throat as she stumbled to her feet. Tears blurred across her vision as she fled, searching for an escape. Her eyes darted across the skyline and—

The palace walls.

She recalled the city as she and Mazen had seen it from the flying carpet. The two of them had entered the palace through a golden bridge, but they had seen a wall running around the courtyard as well, accessible through the sentinel towers. If Loulie could get to one of those towers, then maybe she would be able to lose Ziyad on the wall.

She tracked the nearest tower to the west. "Cover me," she said to Qadir.

The ifrit obeyed, watching her back and calling warnings in her ear as they navigated the city. To spare the populace, Loulie kept to the alleys. It was an unwise decision. She had little experience roaming the streets, and even Qadir, with all his memories, had trouble recognizing the city, which had changed so much in his absence.

It was inevitable they would hit a dead end.

When Loulie turned, she saw one of the serpents was already blocking their way out. Qadir hissed a warning in her ear. Loulie could tell from his faintly glowing body that he was about to use his magic.

"Hold your position," he said.

Loulie's heart trembled. Her arms quivered. But she did not flinch.

As the serpent crashed toward them, the ashfire in the dagger brightened to a blistering arc. The fire licked at Loulie's arms, her face. Even now, it was a comfort. She wasn't alone—she never had been, with Qadir's ashfire guiding her and Mazen's paths.

Loulie screamed as she rent the serpent with her blade. Where steel met water, steam filled the air, dense enough to cloud her vision. By the time the mist parted and the serpent lay liquefied at her feet, Ziyad had caught up to them. Much to Loulie's annoyance, he was clapping.

"An incredible magic trick, merchant!" As he walked, the water on the ground shuddered and rose, re-forming once more into a serpent. "I had not realized you could command a *king*."

Loulie faltered at his approach. With the only exit blocked, she searched behind her for anything she might have missed. Her attention caught on a flash of color in one of the windows—a single pair of burning eyes, watching her through a slit in the curtains.

The moment their gazes locked, the jinn snapped the drapes closed. But though the home's inhabitant had vanished, an idea had occurred to Loulie. If the alley did not have any exits, then she had no choice but to make her own.

Apologizing in her mind for what she was about to do, Loulie wrapped her fingers around the pearl and launched herself up on a faint current of wind. She grabbed the window ledge just as the serpent slammed into the opposite wall. Then, before she could second-guess herself, she threw her body through the window.

The glass gave, shattering as she crashed to the floor on the other side. She was only vaguely aware of the screaming occupants as she darted through the apartment in search of an exit. When she heard the roar of the serpent behind her, she cursed. How could *water* be so damned tenacious?

At the front door, she fumbled with the locks, turning them in her hands until she could escape outside. The moment she slammed the door shut, the wood creaked and buckled as the serpent collided with it on the other side. Loulie turned and ran before it could follow.

The detour had bought her some time. Ziyad, who must have

thought she was heading for the palace bridge, had backtracked toward another path. Loulie used the opportunity to cut through the alleys toward the westernmost sentinel tower.

Perhaps because of the *other* unspoken horrors haunting the night, only a few guards patrolled the area. When they saw her darting through the clearing with a flaming knife, they hesitated. Loulie took advantage of the confusion to rush past them, scattering the jinn with frantic sweeps of her blade as she made for the doorway.

By the time she had thrown it open, one of the damned serpents had found her. Loulie glanced frantically around in search of stairs. She spat a foul curse when she saw only a rickety rope ladder in front of her. *Of course* this was the only way up.

"What are you waiting for?" Qadir hissed in her ear. "*MOVE.*"

Loulie threw herself at the ladder as the serpent swept into the tower. While the stunned guards on the ground floor circled the beast, the ones on the scaffolding watched her ascent with alarm. When one of them leaned forward to cut the ropes, she yelled in despair.

Thankfully, Qadir moved faster than her. He scrambled up her arm toward the jinn, his body regressing into a blur as he shifted into his human shape. In mere seconds, he had smashed one soldier into the wall and pushed the other off entirely. The soldier could do little but scream as he fell into the jaws of the snapping serpent.

Loulie forced herself not to look down as Qadir held out a hand and helped her up. The moment she was back on her feet, the ifrit had already reverted to his lizard shape. "Faster, Loulie," he whispered in her ear. "You must move *faster.*"

Loulie pushed through the door and stepped onto the wall. She was briefly overcome by vertigo when she saw that the ground was now miles below her. Sweat rolled down her back as she dizzily swept her gaze across the courtyard, searching for a way off the wall. But if there were staircases that led down, she could not see them.

Her eyes fell on the buildings. She recognized this place—it was the guest quarters where she and Mazen had stayed. From above, she could make out the rooftops pressed close together. If she could jump onto one of those roofs and climb down onto a balcony . . .

The serpent roared as it swept up behind her. Loulie staggered to the edge of the wall. For a few moments she was off balance, her arms pinwheeling as the ground loomed beneath her. When Qadir yelled at her to jump, Loulie had no choice. She leapt onto the nearest roof. The impact sent a shock wave of pain through her body. She slid, the rooftop tiles scraping into her hands and feet. By the time she had regained her balance, her palms were bloody.

When she saw the serpent rising above her, she fled, darting off one rooftop and onto another. Moments later, the beast had crashed into the tile behind her. It ghosted her footsteps.

"Loulie!"

She looked up at the sound of her name, shock briefly eclipsing her terror when she saw Mazen bin Malik standing at the edge of one of the balconies. The firebird sat on his shoulder, chirping urgently. Loulie had no time to process why they were here. Her attention focused on the distance between them. The balcony was nearly level with the rooftop she was running across, but it was far.

Would she be able to reach it—reach him—at this distance?

Mazen held out his hand as she approached. *Trust me*, his pleading gaze said. She realized then that he was asking her to leap. That he was asking her to trust him to catch her.

Loulie put on one last burst of speed. The wind tore at her lungs as she sprinted down the sloped roof. It pulled at her robes and hissed a warning in her ear. Loulie ignored it.

She trained her eyes on Mazen, who stood on the balcony waiting to catch her.

And she jumped from the rooftop.

61

MAZEN

The world narrowed to Loulie al-Nazari and the void that separated them.

At first, Mazen feared she would not jump. Terror blanched her expression as she wavered on the spot, eyes cutting between him and the watery beast rushing after her. But then she turned determinedly toward the balcony and launched herself off the roof.

Mazen leaned over the rail, hand outstretched toward her.

There was a moment of suspension as Loulie jumped. She was a streak of glowing white in the darkness. A falling star in her white-dusted robes.

Mazen grabbed her hand. Loulie scrambled to latch on to him as he slid toward the edge. There was a moment—a terrible, terrifying moment—when Loulie was too heavy, and he was too weak. Mazen's arms trembled as he tried to pull her up. She struggled to hold on, palms slick with blood.

But he wasn't strong enough. They were sliding, falling—

And then Mazen saw the lizard.

The red-eyed reptile scrambled up Loulie's arm, past her and Mazen's linked hands, and onto the balcony. Between blinks it shifted shape, transforming into a familiar umber-skinned man who moved quickly to stand beside Mazen.

He grabbed Loulie's other hand, and together, they pulled her onto the balcony.

Even when Loulie was safely over the ledge, the three of them sat collapsed on the terrace, panting with exertion. Qadir rubbed at the ash on his forehead while Mazen steadied his breathing. Loulie lay prostrated between them, gulping in air.

Mazen glanced past them both to the magic that had been chasing Loulie across the rooftops. He immediately recognized Ziyad's water serpent with its gaping eyes and icy teeth. Behind the creature, Mazen saw a figure silhouetted in the ashfire glowing on the walls.

"Ziyad," Loulie said between gasps. She cast a nervous look over her shoulder.

Mazen tensed as the marid raised a hand. He drew closer to Loulie, ready to pull her in through the balcony doors. But when he looked up, he saw that the serpent was ... retreating? Mazen watched, baffled, as Ziyad cut a hand through the air in a wave. Was he giving up?

Loulie slumped against the balustrade with a weary sigh. "He said the queen sent him."

The three of them watched the marid until he disappeared over the edge of the wall, taking the serpent with him. Mazen frowned at his vanishing figure. If the queen had sent Ziyad to capture them, then why was he retreating now, when he'd had them cornered?

Mazen turned back to Loulie. "Are you..." He saw the blood seeping between her fingers and swallowed. "Okay?"

"I've been better." She sighed. "Shukran. I may have underestimated that leap."

Qadir reached expectantly for her hands. Loulie obligingly offered them. She flinched only slightly when Qadir cut his skin and began to heal her injured palms with his own blood. While he worked, the ifrit answered Mazen's questions—explaining how they had separated from Aisha in the city and how they had come to be here in such a bedraggled fashion.

Afterward, Loulie caught Mazen's anxious gaze and frowned. "What are *you* doing here? Weren't you supposed to be in the city with Hakim and Rijah?"

"They have everything under control. I came here to light the palace. I thought it could serve as a beacon."

Loulie glanced around, startled. Based on her reaction, she seemed to have just now noticed the ashfire dotting the courtyard. She shot him an appraising look. "Not a bad idea."

"It should help calm things for now," Qadir agreed as he set her now-healed palms in her lap. "We should focus on the binding."

Mazen glanced between the two of them. "Where are you going?"

Loulie pointed to the palace. "If the binding is in the sky, then one of those towers should bring us closest to the magic."

She hesitated as she looked at Qadir. Though the ifrit was the one urging them forward, there was no mistaking his exhaustion. Mazen had overheard him tell Loulie that he was taking his lizard shape to conserve his energy.

Qadir must have noticed their concern. He straightened with a sigh. "Do not worry about me. I am feeling the strain of the binding, nothing more." He glanced at Mazen, then at Azhar, who was still roosting on his shoulder. There was a subtle shift in his expression as he took in the bird—a flicker of a frown across his lips.

Mazen was immediately nervous about that look. "Is something wrong?"

The bodyguard considered him with a dour expression. "My magic is tied to the binding. When it vanishes, so too will the ashfire in Dhahab."

At first, Mazen did not understand why this was a bad thing. If the country rose when the ashfire went out, then there would be no need for it anymore. But then, with a start, he remembered that the bird on his shoulder was a creature of ashfire.

He reached protectively for Azhar before he could stop himself. The firebird tweeted, a soft quizzical sound that made his stomach churn. "But you said the fire had a life of its own." He hated how his voice cracked. Hated how Loulie looked at him with pity in her eyes.

Qadir shook his head. "All magic has its source, regardless of the life it takes on."

It was exactly what Rijah had told them on al-Malath: the ash-fire that had for so long lit this realm was just an extension of the binding. Mazen's story may have shaped the ashfire, but it could do nothing to save it.

He wanted to object, insist that there was some other way. But when the balcony began to sway with the effects of another quake, the protest died on his lips. Down below, Mazen heard the panic of the jinn gathered at the palace doors. There was no time for hesitation.

"All right." His voice came out thin, pinched. He had begun to scratch soothingly at Azhar's head, but there was no fooling anyone about whom he was trying to comfort.

Loulie glanced between him and the bird. Her expression was somber when she said, "To the palace, then?"

Qadir nodded. "To the palace."

—ɯ—

It was much easier to navigate the palace with the ashfire. Though Mazen could command Azhar to light individual torches, Qadir's mere presence was enough to light the braziers as they walked the corridors. The moment the ifrit stepped in through the hidden entrance, the sconces relit, the halls filled with a gentle blue-white light, and the few jinn hurrying to vacate the area paused to stare at them.

When they saw Qadir, eyes alight with ashfire, they fled. Qadir seemed unbothered.

When Loulie saw Mazen staring, she snorted. "Don't worry about it. Qadir is used to being intimidating," she said.

Qadir cast a look over his shoulder. "Speak for yourself."

The three of them passed dusty doors and walls Mazen had never seen before. The longer they walked, the more aware he became of the palace's depth, its *size*. Even Qadir looked disgruntled. At first, Mazen assumed it was because he had forgotten the palace's layout. But then, suddenly, the ifrit whirled on them.

When Qadir's fiery gaze landed on Mazen, he backed away, suddenly alarmed. The ifrit's eyes narrowed. "It would behoove you to show yourself."

Mazen and Loulie exchanged bewildered glances. Before either of them could ask, the shadow beneath Mazen *shifted*. He scrambled away as it rose up from the ground, looking, for all the world, as if it were rising from sleep. It was only when Mazen saw the slivers of blue on its face that he realized he was looking at the shadow attendant that had once tended to them.

He gaped at her. "How long have you been following us?"

Despite her shadowed features, Mazen had the impression the attendant was raising her brows at him. "For a human that possesses shadow magic, you are awfully unobservant of the darkness."

Loulie had already pulled her dagger from its sheath. "If you get in our way—"

"Her Majesty sent me to observe you," the attendant said. "Nothing more."

Loulie glowered. "She hasn't sent you to finish Ziyad's job?"

Though nothing about the attendant's expression changed, Mazen could tell from the silent way she watched them that she was thinking. Finally, she said, "Her Majesty did not send Ziyad after you. If he pursued you, it was for his own purposes."

Again, he and Loulie exchanged glances. She looked equally confused, the dagger raised in front of her as if she expected the attendant to charge after them. But Mazen could sense no hostility from the jinn. Did that mean the queen *didn't* mean them harm?

"If you wish to observe us, do so from afar," Qadir said. "Stop hiding in his shadow."

The attendant seemed to find this permissible. She nodded, and as they began to ascend the staircase to one of the tower roofs, she remained watching them on the bottom floor. Loulie looked reluctant to turn her back on the attendant, but Qadir had already pushed ahead.

By the time they had finally come to the rooftop, Qadir was breathing heavily. The markings on his arms flickered, and a muscle fluttered in his neck as he turned his gaze to the city beneath them. From here, they could make out the entirety of Dhahab. Though the ashfire still burned in defiance, that light seemed faded from a distance, lost beneath a curtain of thick sand. The air had worsened since they'd come inside; Mazen was grateful for Shafia's shawl.

Loulie already had the compass in hand. Her head was tilted to the sky, to a band of faint lights hovering above them that flickered like the magic on Qadir's arms. The binding, Mazen assumed, though it was so high up he could not discern its shape.

Loulie turned toward them both. Her eyes fell on Qadir. "Are you sure you're okay?"

Mazen contemplated the binding as the two of them spoke in soft whispers. Qadir had said he could break it—but what if there was another way to reach it with the dagger? "I have an idea," he said. "A way to reach the binding without you needing to exhaust yourself." He reached into his satchel and withdrew the lamp.

Loulie must have realized his intention; her eyes lit up as she glanced at Qadir. "Let us handle the binding. I've done it three times already; what's a fourth?"

Qadir gave his assent with a reluctant nod. After he had shifted into his lizard shape and taken his spot on Loulie's shoulder, Mazen turned his attention to the lamp. He cut his palm with Loulie's knife, then set his bloodied hand upon the surface. "Rijah, can you hear me?"

At first, nothing happened. The only sign that he had interacted with the lamp at all was that it subtly warmed beneath his fingers. But the third time he called their name, Rijah answered.

They swept onto the roof in the form of a blue-eyed hawk, huffing belligerently. "I heard you the first time, human."

Mazen rushed toward them. "Rijah," he said. "We need—"

"Yes, yes. You need my help." They lifted their beak. The gesture was imperious even in bird form. "I only came because I knew you would be helpless without me."

Mazen pointed to the sky. "We need to get to the binding."

For a moment, Rijah said nothing, just scrutinized the sky above them in thought. And then, with a flap of their wings, they transformed. Their feathers lengthened, their wings expanded, and suddenly they stood before them in a much bigger avian shape.

Mazen hurried after Loulie as she strode toward the ifrit. When she turned to object, he said, "I'm coming with you." He spoke the words decisively so that she could not argue.

Thankfully, Loulie said nothing else as she climbed onto the rukh's back. While she was hauling herself up, Mazen addressed Rijah. "I'm sorry to have taken you away from the city." He hesitated. "My brother, is he—"

"Your brother is with Hayat." They inclined their feathered head at him, a sharp, birdlike motion. "I have made certain they are both out of harm's way."

Mazen swallowed around a sudden knot in his throat. But before he could thank them, Loulie was calling to him from Rijah's back, urging him upward. The ifrit clucked at him impatiently. "What are you waiting for, bin Malik? Do not waste my time."

Mazen needed no further prompting. Loulie shifted as he pulled himself up. When he wrapped his arms around her from behind, she stiffened only briefly before Rijah took to the air. The moment they were airborne, she fell back into him, her breathing a nervous rasp. Mazen could feel her trembling.

Remembering the last time they had flown—the last time he had *convinced* Loulie to fly—he smiled and said, "Are you scared, Loulie?"

She cast a sharp look back at him. Just as they had been then, her eyes were filled with defiance. She gave him the same answer.

"Never."

62

AISHA

Aisha had bested a slew of opponents over the years, but she had never fought anyone like the queen, who could absorb her strikes without consequence. Attacking her was like stabbing needles into a pincushion. Short of severing her limbs, Aisha could think of no way to defeat her, and the jinn moved too quickly for her to make the attempt.

She had always considered herself resourceful, but what could she possibly do against an undead opponent she could not control?

Survive, Amina urged her.

But even that seemed an impossible feat given Basira's speed. She was relentless, driving Aisha back at every opportunity. And, unlike Aisha, she did not tire.

"Are you jealous, ifrit? Jealous that I still have my body while you do not?" The queen slammed her blade into Aisha's hard enough to drive her into a wall. Aisha grunted, gritting her teeth against the shock of the impact.

The queen smiled. Though her body bore the marks of Aisha's assault, her torn skin was unmarred by gore. Aisha did not think she was breathing. Did not think she *needed* to breathe in that body, untouched by exhaustion as it was.

The queen leaned forward, close enough Aisha could see the

perfect circles of silver around her pupils. "Your body must have been in a terrible state for you to discard it."

Memories flashed before Aisha's eyes. Men looming above her—above Amina—with blades. She remembered the agony that had torn through her as they dismembered her. But worse still had been her terror as her beloved Munaqid was tortured beside her. They had done more than obliterate her body; when they had killed him, they had destroyed her soul.

"The body is just a vessel," Aisha managed through her grimace. "Death opens many doors. But I—we—chose the best option."

With a grunt, she threw off the queen's blade, rolling away just as Basira's strike cracked the wall. Plaster rained down as Aisha rose shakily to her feet.

The queen must have seen her fatigue. Her movements were unguarded, casual even, as she faced Aisha. "Perhaps. But you are still bound to an object." Her gaze cut to the collar around Aisha's neck. "This whole time, I wondered what form your relic might take."

Aisha could not stop her gaze from straying to the weapons on the wall. She remembered what Ziyad had said about the queen gathering magic. "The deal you made with my king—you gave him your soldiers in exchange for ifrit relics?"

"They are my best hunters," Basira confirmed. "And our deal was twofold. Soldiers to take a city for magic that could save mine."

"And what of the jinn they hunt? Omar said they were criminals."

"They *are* criminals. A force loyal to Nabila. I could not allow them to gather on the surface."

Aisha considered the jinn she had slain over the years. While some of them had doubtless been warriors, many had been innocents. She remembered a small jinn child one of her fellow thieves, Tawil, had chased through the Ghiban streets. Surely, he had not been a threat.

"You commanded them to kill *children*?" she asked.

The queen looked momentarily taken aback. "I would never condone such a thing." Her eyes narrowed with suspicion. "You are trying to confuse me, just like your wicked king did."

The jinn could have been lying. Her bewilderment could have been a mask, meant to conceal her true goals. But what did she have to gain from lying to Aisha? Samar had said they lost communication with the queen's messenger—but what if it was Ziyad who was lying? What if it had not been the queen who turned away from Omar but the other way around?

What if Omar had conflated his mission to kill jinn with the queen's? What if he had tricked her soldiers into carrying out *his* will?

Aisha's thoughts scattered as the ground beneath them lurched. While Basira steadied herself with her blade, Aisha had no such strength. She fell against the wall with a curse, trembling as the room stabilized. But the tremor—Aisha could still feel it beneath her feet.

They were running out of time.

Basira must have realized it too. She turned on Aisha, eyes narrowed. "I no longer have time to entertain your human toy, Amina. Let us put an end to this charade."

She shot forward, faster than an arrow. Expecting a fatal blow to her upper body, Aisha feinted right. But she had miscalculated the arc of the queen's blade. Basira's blow swept low, toward Aisha's legs. The flat of the sword smashed into Aisha's knee with a sickening crack.

Her world splintered with agony. Some raw, animal sound left Aisha's throat as her legs gave way beneath her. The pain was an obliterating force, sweeping through her in nauseating waves. It was all she could do to heave air in through her lungs.

Thief! Amina's voice was urgent. *Get up! We cannot fall here.*

When she tried to rise, the bone shifted like knives beneath her skin, making each motion torture. She was vaguely aware of Amina's magic working against the current of pain, but Aisha did not know if she could mend bone the same way she did skin.

Basira was already coming at her again, blade raised above her head. Aisha thought she saw pity on her face as she said, "It is over, ifrit."

A loud boom echoed through the throne room like thunder. It was only when Basira shot a look over her shoulder that Aisha realized the sound had been the doors.

A thin, strangely transparent jinn stood in the doorway, his body more smoke than flesh. Based on the rich fabric of his robes, Aisha assumed he was some high-ranking official. It was not his appearance that caught her attention, however, but the golden thread hovering around his body. The thread stretched across the throne room to Basira.

He staggered forward. "Your Majesty, the mob in front of the palace is demanding to see the Ashfire King."

Basira stared at him. *"Who?"*

He wrung his hands. "There are rumors that he has been spotted in the city..."

His voice faded to a murmur in Aisha's ears, lost beneath another wave of pain as she attempted to stand. The moment she had seen the thread, she had realized something. It was an epiphany that might be able to save her, if she could get her damned body to move.

A cold magic snapped through her veins. The Resurrectionist, seizing control of Aisha's limbs. *If you will it, I can push your body past its breaking point,* she said.

The jinn were still arguing. Neither of them was paying attention to her, dead weight that she had become. Aisha clenched her teeth. Her heart spiked with fear—and then resolve.

So be it. When she reached for Amina's magic, it was like taking an outstretched hand.

And then the ifrit was yanking her *up*. Aisha's limbs locked with anguish—and then loosened, forcibly. The ifrit tore through the defenses of her body like a virus, forcing her to move beyond the debilitating pain in her knee.

Basira yelled in surprise as she shot toward the doors. Aisha's limbs protested every moment. Her vision wavered erratically. She was vaguely aware of the scream leaving her throat, a sound so piercing it made her target flinch back. The golden thread rippled with the motion. Aisha focused on that magic as the queen gained on her.

The only sounds she could hear over her agony were the voices of the relics. The pressure of the magic made Aisha's head ring. But then she realized she could *use* that rage.

The ifrit and she were of one mind in that moment. When Aisha reached toward the weapons, the Resurrectionist was there to unspool the thread that connected her to each one. The golden threads hung around Aisha like a spiderweb, frayed and torn.

Aisha uttered a single command: "*Shatter.*"

The blades, which had been rattling against the wall, shot forward. The air became a maelstrom of metal and sharp edges, a cacophony of violence aimed directly at the queen. The jinn screamed, but Aisha paid her no mind. Her eyes were on the stranger in rich robes, the jinn who was backing away toward the doors. But he was too slow. By the time the relics had all clattered to the floor, Aisha stood behind him with a blade to his throat.

The world tilted beneath her feet. One more step and she would faint. It was only the Resurrectionist's control over her body that kept her standing.

Basira approached slowly. A knife had found purchase in her shoulder—she yanked it out with a growl. "Coward! Leave my wazir be."

Ah, so he was her wazir.

Aisha tipped the blade closer to his throat. Basira paused as silver blood dribbled down his neck. "If you dare touch him—"

But Aisha had already moved. One swift stab into the wazir's stomach. He screamed, louder than any of the relics in the room, and when Basira keeled forward with an agonized moan, Aisha knew her suspicions had been correct. The jinn may have been undead, but her body was still bound. Not to a relic, but to her *wazir*. The golden thread proved their connection.

"You will give me what I want," Aisha said. "And then I will release him."

The wazir trembled in her grasp. She could feel his blood on her hands, dripping between her fingers. She swallowed her revulsion as the queen rose to her feet. The jinn had a hand pressed to her stomach in the same place Aisha had wounded her wazir. "How..." Her voice was faint. "How did you know of our connection?"

This time, it was Amina who responded through Aisha: "I can see it."

The floor roiled again, sending a shock wave through Aisha's body. She did not have the time for this. "Your envoy told me you have an ifrit's magic here. A spear. Give it to me."

Confusion rippled across Basira's expression. "Ziyad told you this?"

Aisha held the dagger to the wazir's throat. "The magic for his life. For *your* life."

For the first time since they had fought, Aisha saw a vulnerable emotion on Basira's face: terror. The jinn whirled, scouring the field of weapons for the spear. She found it lodged in the cracked floor not too far away. From a distance, it was nearly transparent; it was no wonder Aisha had not spotted it on the wall.

Basira threw the spear at Aisha's feet. Slowly, biting back a groan of pain, Aisha reached down to grab it. The object did have a voice... but it was the voice of waves, of winds. She could not determine the nature of its enchantment. Was this truly ifrit magic?

"Now, let him go." Basira's voice was pressed thin with panic. "Release Firas."

Aisha considered. If she did as commanded, Basira would destroy her. But if she didn't—

"The wise thing would be to kill him."

Aisha startled at the voice. It was neither Basira's nor Firas's. Basira looked up at the sound as well, her eyes widening when she saw the figure that had appeared behind Aisha.

Ziyad smiled at them pleasantly from the entryway. "I had wondered what dark secret you were hiding, Your Majesty. Tell me..." His smile sharpened at the look of shock on her face. "How does it feel to be upstaged?"

63

LOULIE

The first time Loulie had flown on a rukh, she had been falling into the jinn realm.

Now the ifrit who had taken them beneath the Sandsea shot them up toward the stars. Or at least, Qadir's binding *looked* like a constellation, glimmering too high in the sky for any mortal to reach. Loulie was reminded of the constellations Rijah had crafted in the palace courtyard, the same stars she and Mazen had observed from atop a floating carpet.

Rijah flew them high—high enough that Loulie's lungs strained for air. High enough that the wind became a frigid chill and she could not stop her teeth from chattering.

"HUMANS." Rijah had to yell to be heard over the wind. *"WHERE ARE WE GOING?"*

Loulie hesitated. Now that they were approaching the binding, she realized she did not know how to find its center. It was Qadir who suggested they fly higher for a better vantage point.

As they rose, Loulie's ears began to pop with the pressure. When she chanced a look at the city and saw that it had shrunk to a miniature stage, she nearly succumbed to vertigo. The feeling swept through her with a sudden violence, unsteadying her on Rijah's back.

It was then she felt Mazen's arms come around her, holding her stable as he grasped her hands. His palms were cold—she could feel him shivering—but she felt secure in his hold.

"Almost there," he whispered.

Loulie's eyes stung with tears as Rijah pushed upward. They were high enough above the binding that Loulie could see it spread beneath them in its entirety. Qadir had been correct. From here, she could make out its center—a tangle of knotted lines that wavered like a flag.

The firebird had followed them in the air. It flitted beside them with a melodious trill, unaware of its impending doom. Loulie saw the grief on Mazen's face and felt, again, that pang of sympathy for him.

He forced a smile when he saw her expression. "Ready?"

"Ready for this to be over," she muttered back.

She asked Rijah to dive lower. The ifrit obeyed, drifting until Loulie could make out the pattern directly beneath them. Even up here, the ashfire was a comforting presence.

Soon. They were almost there. Almost *there*.

But this high up, the effects of the weakened binding were more apparent. It was not just the darkness that had grown thicker, but the sandstorm. Loulie was focusing on the binding when a powerful gust hit Rijah, strong enough to throw them off balance.

She pressed closer to Rijah's back. "The center," she yelled. "Fly to the center!"

Rijah obeyed, circling until they were hovering above the middle. Loulie clutched the dagger in her hand. Terror had closed a fist over her heart, but she forced herself to focus on the binding directly beneath her. She considered her strategy. Was it possible to break the center of the magic without putting Rijah in the path of the ashfire?

While she pondered, Azhar circled the center like a bull's-eye. Loulie faltered as she stared down at it. She knew the bird would vanish when the binding broke. And yet, foolishly, she still worried that unsealing the magic would harm it.

She glanced at Mazen, who was trying to call the bird back to him. He shifted behind her, hand outstretched toward the creature.

It was at that moment another gust of wind crashed into them.

The impact was hard enough to make Rijah tumble through the air. Loulie screamed as the sky and ground shifted position beneath her. A terrifying weightlessness took hold of her as her feet fell away from Rijah's feathers.

But then, amazingly, the ifrit straightened.

Loulie looked up. She noticed immediately that something was amiss. The weight of Mazen's arms around her was gone. The storyteller was no longer behind her.

Loulie peered over the bird's wing to see him falling through the sky.

No.

With Rijah still dazed, Loulie did not think. She reached beneath her scarves for the pearl necklace and wrapped it around her fingers. With her other hand, she gripped Qadir's knife.

And then, without waiting for Rijah's assent, she threw herself off their back.

One last time.

The binding rushed up to meet her, its gentle light folding around her like an embrace. The nexus of the burning constellation beat like a heart.

One last time.

With a scream, Loulie stabbed Qadir's dagger through the final binding.

64

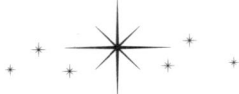

MAZEN

Mazen fell, and it was like falling into the sun.

The sky, which had for so long been shaded by that impenetrable darkness, was burning the same white blue as the binding. And then, before Mazen's eyes, that brightness began to spread, the cracks growing until they had overtaken the expanse entirely.

In that stark whiteness, Mazen could see nothing. Not Azhar. Not Loulie. Not Rijah.

He fell, flailing uselessly as he tried to reach for something—*anything*—that could stop his plummet through the air. As the ground rushed up to meet him, Mazen thought with startling clarity, *This is the end*. For so long, that fear had haunted him.

When Omar had killed the sultan, he had assumed it was the end. When he had seen his face on a wanted poster, he had assumed it was the end. When he had stepped in front of Loulie on Ziyad's ship, he had assumed it was the end. How many endings had he faced?

But he had been living past the end this whole time. Persevering, as Rijah had said. It was only now that Mazen realized with a start he did not *want* the end to come. And so he struggled. Even though he possessed no magic that would save him, even though the wind was stealing the breath from his lungs, he still reached up—

Toward a shape darting through the ashes.

Loulie al-Nazari shot toward him, hand outstretched. She was falling fast—fast enough she could grab hold of his arm before he hit the ground. She said something he could not hear over the wind but that he could make out on the shape of her lips.

Hold on.

Mazen held on. The wind entangled their bodies, and they fell through the sky together. As Loulie's hold on him tightened, Mazen felt a change in the air. The pull of the wind softened, then became a strange lightness. Belatedly, he saw the pearl wrapped around Loulie's knuckles.

Mazen was seized by a peculiar feeling of weightlessness as they landed on the tower roof. His gaze darted back to the sky—just in time to see the binding *explode*. Sand crashed through the broken magic, so thick it painted the world the suffocating black of a sandstorm.

The ground beneath them had begun to rumble, but now they were not sinking, but *rising*, the broken constellation looming closer and closer—

Until they were through it. As Dhahab surged back toward the surface, the binding fell away like a shattered rooftop, the ashy whiteness peeling away to reveal a vivid blue sky untouched by magic.

They had done it. They had returned the cities to the surface.

At some point, Mazen had folded Loulie into his arms. Now they both stood stunned, arms wrapped around each other as light— natural, godsblessed *light*—eclipsed the city for the first time in centuries. For a few moments, they were too shocked to do anything but stare. Even though the rumbling had stopped, Mazen could feel the memory of the tremor beneath his feet. He blinked, dazed, at the sandy but *real* daylit sky.

Loulie bunched her fingers in his shirt, threw back her head, and *laughed*. It was the most startling, most joyous sound he had ever heard from her, and it made him smile.

"We did it," she breathed. "That damned binding—it's gone." She pointed triumphantly to the sky, to the clouds—*real* clouds— dotting the bright expanse.

No one could have wiped the grin off Mazen's face in that moment. How long had he taken this sky for granted? He would never do so again.

He must have laughed then, or else made some other sound that drew Loulie's attention, because when he glanced down, he saw that she was looking at him. He was taken aback by the intentness of her expression. She examined his face as if it were a puzzle she was trying to solve.

Mazen resisted the urge to smooth the dent between her brows. He had the strange impression that she had drawn closer, that her face was nearer than it had been moments ago. But then Qadir made a grumbling sound on her shoulder, and she hurried to step away.

A large shadow drifted above them. When Mazen looked up, he saw Rijah soaring through the sky in their rukh form.

With a sweep of their wing, they shifted shape, feathers melting back into skin as they dropped gracefully to the rooftop. They assessed Mazen with an unimpressed frown. "I am glad to see you in one piece, bin Malik."

Mazen managed a feeble smile as he echoed the sentiment back at Rijah. Now that the world had stabilized, he was once again aware of his surroundings—and of the lack of ashfire. As Qadir had said, the pinpricks of magic in the city had disappeared. Which meant...

Azhar is gone.

Mazen felt the absence of the bird acutely. He had known this would happen. And yet he had still foolishly tried to save it. Even though it had amounted to nothing in the end.

Rijah frowned at him. "Take out the lamp, bin Malik, and speak its name." At Mazen's quizzical look, they sighed. "You know who I am referring to. Try it."

Mazen's heart twisted with hope. He pulled the lamp from his satchel, set his injured hand upon its surface, and whispered, "Azhar?"

There was a flash of light, ash in the air—and then fire. *Ashfire,* drifting down toward him on feathery wings. Mazen cried out in relief as the firebird settled on his shoulder. It preened when he stroked its feathers, chirping in the familiar way.

Mazen whirled toward Rijah, uncomprehending. "How did you...?"

"Did you forget? You trapped the bird in the lamp, which means it is now as much my magic as it is yours."

Loulie seemed mildly impressed as she looked at the flaming bird. "I suppose this means I need to actually befriend a bird now." She smiled. "I'm glad for you."

Mazen was glad too. So glad he could have cried. But as he took in the sight of the sky and the cheering crowds below them, something occurred to him. "Rijah, have you seen Aisha?"

They raised a brow. "The thief? I have not seen her since we broke into the city. Why?"

Mazen cast a glance at Loulie, who was talking to Qadir on her shoulder. She muttered some response before glancing at Mazen. "Qadir says he senses the Resurrectionist's magic below. But..." She hesitated. "Something's wrong."

The words filled Mazen with dread. "We need to find her."

65

LOULIE

Though the city was alive with celebration, the palace halls were silent as a crypt.

Loulie's gaze darted suspiciously around the corridors as they walked. Now that Dhahab had returned to the surface, natural sunlight filled the halls in place of ashfire. But though the shadows were gone, the weight of the unnatural silence was just as foreboding.

Where in nine hells is *everyone?* Loulie wondered.

The queen had been notably absent during their run of the city—was it because she had apprehended Aisha in the throne room? And, if the queen was still inside, where were her soldiers? As the compass led them to the throne room—to Aisha—not a single soldier or servant barred their path. Even the shadow attendant appeared to have fled.

Mazen looked just as nervous as she was. The firebird huddled close to his neck, perhaps in an effort to comfort him. With Rijah gone to check on the state of the risen city, only Qadir and the bird remained with them.

Qadir spoke as they arrived at the throne room doors. "I can sense magic barricading the doors on the other side," he said. Even after the binding had faded, he sounded tired, but he'd brushed off Loulie's concern, telling her it would take time for him to regain his energy.

Mazen faced the entrance with a frown. "Let me try something."

He commanded Azhar into the air. Ashfire spread from its wings as it swept across the entrance. Loulie stepped away, alarmed, before she realized the bird was trying to melt away whatever obstruction lay on the other side.

She knew it had succeeded when the wood gave beneath her hands. "Be on your guard," she warned.

The doors opened into a battlefield. The floor was slick with blood and water, and blades jutted between the tiles like gravestones. On the walls where the queen's weapons had been, there was now a strange coating of glass. The material was warped and murky and looked like a darker version of the sea glass they had seen in the marid city. It twisted, branch-like, across the walls and ceiling, and even through the windows.

The glass must have been blocking the entrance as well; Loulie could see the remains Azhar had burned at her feet. She wondered if that glass had coated the doors outside, and if it was keeping the soldiers out.

Loulie spotted Aisha by one of the far columns, crouched over an unconscious figure. *Firas*, she realized with shock.

When the thief noticed them, she gestured sharply toward the throne at the end of the hall. Two figures stood by the seat. One was the queen, though she looked more disheveled than Loulie had ever seen her, her clothing torn and her weapons strewn about her. The other was Ziyad. Inexplicably, he had the tip of a spear at the queen's throat. A water serpent circled idly by his feet, but the moment Loulie stepped forward, its gaze snapped toward her. Ziyad barely spared them a glance before commanding the serpent after them.

Not again.

Loulie yelled as she threw herself out of the creature's path, barely missing its icy teeth as they clamped down on air. By the time she had regained her balance, the serpent had split itself in two. One chased after Mazen, who had fled in the opposite direction. Loulie cursed as the other doubled back to go after her.

As she ran, the ashfire on her dagger flared bright with Qadir's magic. "Avoid the teeth," he hissed. "And ambush it from behind."

Loulie's attention snapped to the columns. In this cramped space, they were the only obstacles she could use.

She turned a hard left. The creature's watery body tangled as she wove between the pillars, twisting in on itself. Then, as Qadir had suggested, she charged the serpent from behind, cleaving its body with the ashfire. When it collapsed in two halves on either side of her, she used the temporary defeat to double back toward Aisha.

She was nonplussed when she saw the thief *still* hadn't moved. A biting remark sat on Loulie's tongue before she saw how injured she was. Aisha was not kneeling in front of Firas; she was collapsed beside him. Loulie's stomach roiled at the sight of her knee, bent at an odd angle and swollen with blood. Before she could ask what had happened, Mazen spontaneously materialized beside them, surprising them both when he threw off his shadow.

The moment he saw Aisha's knee, he paled. "What happened?"

Aisha glowered at him, but her usual ire was dimmed by pain. "What does it look like? I came in here to steal the Tide Bringer's spear, but it was a trap. The weapon is marid magic—the queen's envoy just needed someone to steal it for him and to reveal the queen's weakness." She nodded toward the battle unfolding around the throne, then briefly explained the twisted connection between the queen and Firas.

Mazen cast a nervous glance at Azhar, who was frantically circling above the re-forming serpents. "We need to get you out of here."

Aisha's eyes flashed with indignation. "That *snake* tricked me. You think I will run from him?" She made to rise but quickly collapsed with a muffled cry.

Loulie frowned at her. "We don't have time for your bravado." She glanced between the serpents and Ziyad, then looked at Mazen. "Can you get them out of here? I'll buy you time."

Aisha hissed a frustrated breath between clenched teeth as she attempted once more to stand. "I can..." She shuddered. "The Resurrectionist can walk me through the pain."

There was little time for them to question the thief's capabilities.

When Loulie saw the serpents moving toward them again, she grabbed Mazen's arm. "I'm trusting you to escape."

He blinked at her, dazed, before his expression hardened with resolve. He nodded, briefly setting his hand atop hers before moving toward the fallen wazir.

Loulie faced the serpents. This time, she rushed forward with the goal of drawing them *away* from the storyteller. She whispered to the lizard on her shoulder, "Help me?"

Ashfire surged up her dagger in response. Loulie waved the blade in the air, drawing the creatures to her with the light. Thankfully, because the beasts did not have the cunning mind of their master, they followed her thoughtlessly.

But mindless as they were, they were still ferocious. When one of the creatures snapped at her ankles, Loulie yelped and stumbled. Her footsteps became confused, panicked, and then she was falling to her knees. Qadir's nails dug into her shoulders. *"LOULIE."*

As the serpent crashed down on her like a tidal wave, it was all Loulie could do to hold up the dagger like a shield. She squeezed her eyes shut as the creature bore down on her.

But the attack never came.

When Loulie blinked her eyes open, she found herself surrounded by a wall of fire. A shadowed figure stood before her, arms aglow with magic. His shoulders were stooped, his breathing labored—but Qadir stood firm as the flames died away, leaving no trace of the serpents.

He had saved her.

Before she could thank him, he slumped to the ground. Loulie yelled his name as she scrambled toward him. His arms were trembling, and drops of ash rolled down his skin. The markings on his arms flickered erratically, like a dying flame. Even now, she could tell he was pushing himself.

"Qadir." Loulie set a hand on his shoulder. "Are you all right?"

He nodded, a faint dip of his head, but before he could say anything, they both froze at the sound of footsteps behind them. Loulie turned to see Ziyad approaching. He twirled the spear in his hand.

The motion was casual, graceful; he handled the weapon as if it were an extension of his body.

When Loulie searched for the queen, she found the ruler pinned to the wall behind the throne. Not with a weapon, but with a sheet of that strange glass Ziyad must have crafted with the spear.

The marid flashed his knife-sharp smile at her. "We meet again, merchant. Your dedication to thwarting my plans would be admirable if it were not so annoying."

Loulie remembered, then, what the shadow attendant had told them about Ziyad. She had wondered why the marid would chase her so incessantly only to turn his back on her. Now she assumed he had been driving her away from the palace, playing with her only for as long as it took Aisha to recover the spear for him.

Her lips curled back in a snarl. "I don't appreciate being used as a pawn."

Ziyad laughed as if her vitriol was a joke to him. "No," he agreed. "It is an awful feeling, is it not? Being blackmailed into carrying out the agenda of a ruler who has stolen from you, who would hurt those you love..." His eyes flashed. "You understand the feeling."

Loulie remembered what Duha had said about the destruction of the marid kingdom. Neither she nor Nabila had known why Ziyad was working for a queen who had condoned that violence. Now she realized his loyalty must have been bought with this spear—this single remnant of his ruler's magic.

"It is in your best interest not to interfere," Ziyad said. He gestured to the entrance—to doors that had once more closed over with glass. Much to Loulie's relief, Mazen had already disappeared with Firas and Aisha.

Ziyad tapped his spear idly on the ground. "Tell me: What reason do you have to protect a queen who condemned you?"

Loulie faltered. It was true the queen had once tried to kill her. But that had been when she assumed Loulie was working with Nabila. When Loulie had first come to this city, she and the queen had made a deal. This world's safety for a means to destroy Omar. Loulie did not have an army—but the queen *did*.

Loulie squared her shoulders. "I made a deal with her, and I take my bargains very seriously." She glared at him. "Take your spear and leave. I won't interfere in your business if you don't interfere with mine."

The marid's good humor vanished with the comment. "If you would stand in the way of my revenge, then I am afraid you are a nuisance." He swept the spear through the air. Loulie was shocked when it rippled and *changed*, the sea glass sharpening into a wicked-looking sword.

He gave her no time to process the magic before he lunged.

66

LOULIE

Possibly, Loulie had made a mistake.

If Ziyad had been playing with her before, he was now actively trying to kill her. The marid came at her with a surprising speed, striking relentlessly with his shifting weapon. Loulie was no warrior; when he came at her with his blade, the only thing that kept her alive was the ferocity of the ashfire blazing on Qadir's knife.

Ziyad must have picked up on her lack of skill. The moment she hesitated, he changed tactics, transforming his sword into a hook with a glimmering chain. Loulie goggled at the weapon; she had never seen anything like it before.

When Ziyad threw the hook, she barely managed to dodge in time, and she stumbled into Qadir, who was finally back on his feet. Ashfire blazed in his eyes as he turned her toward the doors. "Go. Let me handle this."

The wise thing would have been to obey. But the last time Loulie had turned her back on Qadir, he had disappeared. She would not leave him again, especially not when he was injured. She shook her head, adamant.

His eyes flashed at her disobedience, but before he could say anything, Ziyad had thrown the hook again. Loulie gasped as the weapon crashed by her feet. Where it landed, the tile shattered, and

Loulie felt shards dig into the soles of her shoes as she stepped back. The pain was sudden and sharp and brought Loulie to her knees. She hissed in agitation.

Qadir was glaring at her. *"Loulie—"*

"Iskut!" she snapped. "You remember what I said before? I'm not letting you do this alone." This was *her* bad decision. She would see it through to the end.

Murder was not their goal here. All she had to do was find a way to knock Ziyad out, and then they could let the queen do with him what she wanted. Already down on the ground, she aimed for his feet.

Ziyad easily sidestepped. He scraped his spear across the tile as he moved, and where it touched the ground, that strange sea glass sprang up like moss. Loulie gasped as the glass coated her hands. Qadir crushed it underfoot before it could spread farther, allowing Loulie to yank her fingers out. By the time she had recovered, the marid and Qadir were locked in combat.

An ancient king and a marid who refused to take his true shape should not have been evenly matched. And yet the longer Loulie watched, the more aware she became of Qadir's sluggish movements. Ziyad was quickly gaining the upper hand.

The marid's smile was vicious as he laughed. "Is this truly the full strength of the legendary Ashfire King? The king who sunk this world? Who *destroyed* it?"

Qadir did not respond except to reach for one of the fallen swords by the throne. A flick of his wrist, and the edge of the blade flickered with faint fire. He lunged at Ziyad with the blade. The marid easily parried his blow. When Qadir came at him again, he shifted the spear into a shield, causing Qadir's blade to bounce off it ineffectively.

Qadir stepped away, eyes narrowed. "You have stolen Ramiz's magic—"

"This is my *queen's* magic," Ziyad snapped. "She gifted it to him, despite my advice. I told her the jinn are not to be trusted. And look at what happened—he betrayed us in the end. Helped *you* draw a binding across our city so that he could break it in two."

Qadir flinched. "The bindings were meant to protect this world, not break it."

"You think your *intentions* matter to me, King?"

When Ziyad lunged, the glass beneath his feet surged up with him. Qadir fell back, but the glass had already cemented his feet. Loulie, still on the ground, knew she would not be fast enough to protect him. Desperate, she reached for the pearl around her neck.

"Come on," she whispered. "Yalla, *yalla*."

The wind responded immediately when she swung the pearl sideways. Qadir, who was rooted in place by the glass, did not move. But the wind unbalanced Ziyad, throwing him back against the throne. As he struggled to regain his balance, Loulie rushed to Qadir's side to cut at the glass around his feet.

This time, when the marid came at them, they fought together— a wall of wind and fire against a torrent of water and glass. Loulie fought close, dealing a flurry of smaller blows in between Qadir's wider sweeps. But while the two of them were more coordinated than they had ever been before, Ziyad had an entire arsenal at his disposal and they could not break his guard.

What had she been thinking, picking this fight? Mazen had escaped, but what would happen when Ziyad went looking for Firas? Would he destroy the city, searching for the queen's single weakness? Had Loulie made things worse by denying him his revenge?

She fell back, winded. Beside her, Qadir was barely keeping to his feet. Loulie had done this to him. Perhaps, if they stepped aside, if they let Ziyad go on his rampage—

Fire streaked through the air. Loulie looked up, expecting Qadir's magic, but it was a different fire that arced above them. She immediately recognized Azhar, circling in the air. She turned to see Mazen standing at the entrance, returned with a group of soldiers.

Loulie had never been more relieved to see him.

The moment Ziyad noticed the soldiers, he swept his spear across the ground. The black glass shifted off the surrounding walls with the motion, coalescing before him like a dam. The glass was not the only thing that shimmered around him. When Loulie squinted, she could make out a large puddle of water beneath his feet. It seemed the spear was capable of creating both.

Too late, she realized what was going to happen. She remembered Ziyad falling through the enchanted waters in the marid city and vanishing. He would do the same thing now—fall through the water and escape.

Above them, the firebird had begun to attack the thick wall of glass, but it re-formed faster than the bird could chip away at it. Loulie saw Mazen rushing forward with the soldiers, yelling Ziyad's name.

She considered throwing herself at the glass. Considered burning a hole through the barrier to get at the marid. But she hesitated. Was this really her battle? Her life to take?

She slowly stepped forward.

And the world went still.

On the other side of the wall, Ziyad had frozen. He stared, uncomprehending, at the shaft protruding through his chest. Even Loulie did not know where it had come from—not until she saw the jinn behind him.

Somehow, despite the many impossible injuries her body bore, the queen was still standing. Most likely, she had fallen from the wall when Ziyad reshaped the glass. Her body, little more than a hollowed-out husk, gripped the spear driven through Ziyad's chest.

The marid opened his mouth. It appeared, for a few moments, like he might laugh. Perhaps the terrible wheezing sound that left his throat *was* laughter. Blood seeped between his lips as he collapsed to the floor. The glass around him shattered with the motion, clattering to the floor.

When Ziyad finally managed to speak, his words came out garbled with blood. "How pathetic, to die a pawn. A..." His words collapsed into a gasp as the queen withdrew the weapon from his body. Without flinching, she stabbed him again—and again, and again—until he was punctured through with enough holes to drown in his own blood.

After it was over, she stood staring down at his corpse blankly.

And yet there was an undeniable tremor in her voice when she whispered, "You could have been more, had you trusted me as I trusted you."

With a gesture of her torn hand, she commanded the soldiers to her. Loulie watched with a strange numbness as they moved the corpse. It seemed inconceivable that the marid who had chased them for so long could be dead, killed by his queen's own hand.

When Mazen reached for Loulie's hand, she did not draw away. He might have been the only one in the throne room who understood how she felt.

Qadir and Mazen stood protectively on either side of Loulie as the queen approached. Loulie was shocked when she held out Ziyad's sea glass spear. "An expression of my gratitude," she said, though her voice lacked any warmth.

Loulie eyed the spear warily. "And our deal?"

"I am true to my word. But we will speak of this later." She turned back to the corpse of her envoy. In death, Ziyad's face had taken on an ashy quality. His skin had grown gray, and the scales that had once glimmered on his skin were now dull and loose.

Loulie wondered what Duha would say when she found out her ever-tenacious brother had finally met his end. The thought that she might blame Loulie for his demise made her heart twist. Nabila may have betrayed her, but Loulie had never wanted to hurt Duha.

The queen stopped in front of the corpse. Loulie understood what it was she meant to do only when her eyes turned pitch black—the same color Aisha's were when she used her magic.

"*Rise*," the queen said.

When Ziyad's body sat up, its eyes were blank, and the smile was gone from its lips. The sight was so wrong, so obscene, that it made Loulie waver. She let Mazen and Qadir guide her out of the throne room as the queen commanded Ziyad to relay his deceits from beyond the grave.

67

AISHA

Where homecomings were concerned, Aisha's stay in Dhahab was the strangest she'd ever experienced. It was uncanny to feel nostalgic for a city she had never visited, and odder still to think of it as a place that had once been home. It did not matter that the sentiment was Amina's; ever since Aisha had opened her mind, the lines between their memories had blurred.

We are one and the same, Amina had said. Now Aisha understood her meaning.

She had not had the time to reflect on the feeling after the battle. According to Mazen, she had passed out for two days after their run-in with Ziyad. All Aisha remembered from that restless slumber was darkness and nightmares. When she had woken, it was to the news that the queen had begrudgingly called a truce and that Aisha's injured knee was mended—to a point.

Whatever fracture she'd suffered had been severe. A dull pain still shot through her leg when she turned it the wrong way. When she walked, it manifested as a limp, altering her sense of balance. The knee had not yet healed—but that did not stop Aisha from venturing into the city.

In the days following the resurfacing, she explored Dhahab. Each time, it was apparent to her that though she had helped save the city, the jinn did not know what to make of her. Aisha may not have had to worry about using her magic here—not when Dhahab's own godsdamned *queen* was undead—but she was still a human with an ifrit's abilities.

An abomination. Even now, Omar's words haunted her.

Aisha forced the thought away as she walked. Though she had been called to put on some magic display for the visiting zuama'a, Aisha intended to take her time returning to the palace. She took in the city as she wandered: expansive, broken, and filled with so much dust it looked as if the whole thing had just emerged from the sand—which, she supposed, it had.

Days later, jinn still swept up debris and mended cracks and breaks with simple magics. In the sky, laborers worked to fix the landscape, repairing everything from shattered windows and rooftops to more complicated infrastructure. Rather than ropes, the builders relied on floating carpets for elevation, using them to travel through the air.

In Aisha's eyes, the city looked more a ruin than a haven. And yet everywhere she turned, she saw smiles as the denizens turned their eyes toward the night sky—to the black expanse glittering with stars rather than glowing magic.

When Aisha allowed her own focus to stray, she saw *beyond* the present. The Resurrectionist's memories shrouded the city like a mirage. Between blinks, the ruined plaza vanished, the walls replaced with tall trees and garlands of flowers that stretched across the branches like a ceiling. Glittering fruit drooped from low-hanging branches. When Aisha brushed her fingers against one of the apples, she realized they were made of glass.

In the center of the orchard stood a beautiful jinn with gentle brown eyes and a mane of black hair that fell in a thick curtain past her waist. The phantom turned with the apple in her hands. Her eyes sparkled with mischief as she said, "Amina, *watch.*"

She crushed the fruit between her hands. Juice dribbled between her closed fingers, but when she spread her hands, the glass had reshaped itself into a butterfly with wings that flashed a kaleidoscope of colors. The illusion—the *memory* of the illusion—flitted through the air above Aisha's head. When she reached for it, the insect passed through her fingers.

Nostalgia speared through her as the Mystic spun through the orchard, weaving her illusions. Her magic spread like sunshine, soaking into its surroundings so naturally it was as if it had been there all along. Aisha saw flowers sprout from windows, saw whole trees rise from the ground. But the true spectacle was not the illusion. It was Aliyah herself, whose gown shifted in the light, one moment made of molten gold, the next stitched with leaves and flowers.

The ifrit was smiling, *laughing*. "What do you think? Impressive enough to be real?"

Neither Aisha nor Amina could smile at the memory, not when they knew the truth of what had become of Aliyah. She had been so carefree back then, so full of affection—and in the end, it had been that hopeful love for jinn and humans that had been her demise. Now she was trapped in a relic, and the only illusions she wove were nightmares for her son.

Aisha wondered how Omar might have turned out had his mother been spared the sultan's wrath.

With a sigh, she passed through the memory. The sensations of the illusion lingered like dew on her skin. Aisha mindlessly rubbed at her arms as she came into another plaza.

Here, she saw another familiar face. The memory of Jubayr, the Wanderer, sat on a bench. He paid no mind to the jinn passing through the area, his attention fixed entirely on the scroll in his lap. He did not seem to notice the flowers blooming beneath his feet, nor the leaves that fell on occasion from his hair. He raised a hand in greeting without ever looking up.

On the way through the royal quarter, Aisha became aware of a phantom breeze nipping at her heels. She allowed the wind to pull her attention up to one of the low rooftops, where a vibrantly dressed figure watched her with a mischievous grin. The coins on her headdress twinkled as she inclined her head, revealing a pearl necklace around her neck.

"Amina," said the memory of Nabila. "Do you ever tire of your duty?"

No, Amina said in Aisha's mind. *It is an honor to serve the king. To serve the dead.*

"What use is honor anyway?" The memory of Nabila craned her face to the sky and held out a hand, smiling as a phantom bird came to rest on her palm. "Honor is a shackle. A ball and chain. I would much rather live unbound and free."

The memory of the ifrit smiled at Aisha's back as she walked past. *Is it more freeing to chase revenge, then?* Aisha wondered, and she thought of her own feelings toward Omar, the king she had once dutifully served and now the target of her revenge.

Perhaps she and Nabila were not so different.

No, Amina said. *Your past may have defined you, but it has not shackled you.*

Aisha did not know if that was true. She certainly did not *feel* whole in this body that was only a hair's breadth away from death. But it was true things had...changed recently. Once, all she had thought about was revenge. Now she wondered about absolution.

She raised her gaze as she approached the golden bridge leading into the palace. Again, the past and present overlapped. She saw the edifice as it was now: cracked and worn thin with age. And then she saw it as it had been before: bright and shining and swarming with visitors. A jinn wreathed in scaled armor stood in the moving crowds, watching her.

The Tide Bringer bowed when she passed. "Sayyidati."

Aisha raised a brow. "It is blasphemous to bow to anyone but our king."

"Even His Majesty knows only a fool would not respect death."

Death. It was strange to be called that, but not unwelcome. Death had broken Aisha, but it had also been her weapon. In the end, death had even saved her. In a way, they were old friends.

Amina chuckled. *I never thought you would admit to us being friends.*

"I was not talking to you," Aisha mumbled, but the deflection was halfhearted. She glanced down at her arms—at both her scars and the henna that overlaid them.

When Umm Jaber had first painted them, Aisha had hoped the intricate patterns would cover the now-dead color of her scars. She had been in denial, then, of what the Resurrectionist's magic had done to her body. Now, as she traced the poetry the matriarch had drawn across her skin, she reflected that the moment of weakness had been unlike her.

Aisha *had* changed—but that did not mean she was weaker for it.

She felt lighter as she came into the palace courtyard, where jinn servants and guards scrambled across the garden to tend the visiting zuama'a. In the days that had followed the skirmish, the jinn leaders had made clear whether they were allied with the queen or Nabila. It did not bode well, Aisha thought, that there were so few of them visiting the capital city.

The last person she was expecting to see in the rabble was Rijah. The ifrit seemed to be in the middle of a conversation with a younger jinn, a soldier wearing a smoking cloak.

Memory or reality?

She received her answer when the Shapeshifter looked up. Aisha knew from the way Rijah's eyes cut into her—*her* and not Amina—that she was in the present.

"Bint Louas." They greeted her stiffly.

"Shapeshifter," she responded. She glanced past them to the jinn in the cloak, who looked annoyed to have been interrupted. At Aisha's look of scrutiny, she puffed out her chest and straightened her shoulders. Based on the way she was squinting at Aisha, she knew she was more than a human. Perhaps she had heard the rumors around the palace.

Aisha let the Resurrectionist's smile touch her lips. "You look awfully young for a soldier."

"I can't be much younger than *you*. And besides that, what does it matter if I can serve?"

Rijah set a hand on her head, and the jinn was so surprised she stopped talking. "Hayat helped me light the city," they said. "She is one of the bravest soldiers I know."

With that single compliment, they averted Hayat's stormy mood. She smiled smugly. *"And* I can shapeshift. True shapeshifting, not like what you are doing now, pretending to be a human in that vessel."

Even spoken by a child, the words made Aisha flinch. How many times had she wondered if she was no longer human now that her life was tied to the collar around her neck?

Abomination. Omar's voice echoed in her head again, taunting.

She was surprised when Rijah said, "Death is its own realm, unknown to us. It would be unwise to make such assumptions."

Hayat's only response was an irritated shrug. Aisha was amused despite herself. Hayat had a sharp tongue, but for all her moxie, she still acted like a temperamental child.

Aisha glanced at Rijah. "Were you summoned here too?"

Rijah nodded. "My king called, and I came. But I had time to spare and so spent it advising Hayat." They cast a glance at the young shapeshifter, who straightened to attention. "Think on what I have said. When next I see you, I expect you to be in the new shape."

The jinn nodded, but Aisha did not miss the look of consternation on her face. "Of all the shapes you would have me practice... why a bird?"

"Know the enemy to best the enemy." They patted her shoulder. "You will thank me for the wings."

Hayat mumbled her consent as she walked off, her gaze tilted toward the sky. At first, Aisha thought she might be looking for birds, but then she realized her gaze was on the stars. The jinn was smiling—a smile so full of hope it made Aisha's chest ache.

Rijah openly wore their heartache as they watched Hayat walk off. "She is following in her brother's footsteps," they said. "Apparently, he was one of the queen's best hunters, but he died during a skirmish with Nabila's forces."

Hearing that story, Aisha better understood Hayat's adamance. After all, she had barely been more than a child herself when Omar taught her to use a blade. The cruel reality of their world was that violence did not discriminate.

When she turned away, Rijah fell into step beside her. "I have a question for you."

"For me?"

When she saw the quiet frown on their face, she knew they were asking to speak to the Resurrectionist. Aisha begrudgingly made space for the ifrit in her mind as Rijah said, "How is it that you came to trust humans?"

Amina's amusement sparked in Aisha like a flame. "The same way you did," she said to the Shapeshifter. "One human at a time."

She turned her back on the bewildered ifrit and headed for the palace.

68

MAZEN

His whole life, Mazen had assumed he knew his fate.

He was the sultan's third son, destined to live in splendor but never with power. He was a storyteller who would only ever live his adventures through his tales. *There are not many stories to tell of a prince locked in a palace*, he had once told Loulie, and he had believed it.

But that had been before.

Before he had set off on a quest to find a magic lamp with Loulie, Aisha, and Qadir. Before he had discovered Omar's treachery. Before he had fallen into another *realm* and learned the truth behind a centuries-old war.

Now, seated in the queen's diwan and telling a story, Mazen realized his destiny had never been more than a lie. Worse still, it had been a lie he told himself.

What if? he asked himself. What if, instead of sneaking away from his responsibilities, he had faced them? What if, instead of caving to his father's demands, he had fought against them? Mazen would never know. The past was the past, a story already told, and though he could certainly weave it into a different tale, it would not change the reality.

And right now, the reality was this: Dhahab had returned to the surface, as had the other jinn cities. For the first time in centuries, the desert was whole. But it would not remain at peace for long. And that was where he, Prince Mazen bin Malik, came in.

The queen—Basira, Mazen had overheard Aisha spitefully call her—reclined on a mound of pillows in front of him, her face foggy behind the thick smoke coming from her shisha pipe. Relaxed as she appeared, Mazen could see the signs of fatigue on her body. The queen may have been deathless, but whatever injury Aisha had inflicted on Firas had clearly impacted her as well. Mazen could not help noticing the absent way her hand kept wandering to her stomach as if in memory of some phantom pain.

It was disconcerting to bear witness to that vulnerability. And after everything that had transpired, it was surreal to be seated before her in peace. A truce, she had declared it.

Only for as long as it's convenient, Loulie had muttered to him.

Mazen returned his attention to the present as he finished telling his story. Unlike the first history he had told the queen, *this* was the full truth of the circumstances that had brought them to Dhahab. He told her about Omar's capture of the city and of his attempt to master bindings and steal ifrit relics.

She sighed after he had finished, breathing out another cloud of smoke that fogged the air between them. "What happens next, then?"

He hesitated. Not long after the cities had risen, many of the zuama'a had gone missing. No longer able to rely on Ziyad's magic to reach them, the queen had resorted to scouts, who had returned with disquieting news: many of the leaders had fled to an island spotted on the ocean. It was familiar, filled with birds and protected by a barrier of wind. Nabila, it seemed, had finally had the opportunity to start gathering her forces.

There was also the news of human sightings. Mazen could only imagine the reaction the resurfaced cities must be garnering from travelers. Before his venture into this realm, *he* would have had a heart attack seeing such a megalopolis suddenly appear where there had once been sinking sand.

How long would it be before a human attempted to enter the city? Mazen had no doubt the jinn hunters would come soon after, goaded on by his own brother.

Omar. As always, it was his brother who was the problem.

Mazen cleared his throat. "You were working with my...with the sultan before. Do you really think he would turn on you so quickly?"

Basira scowled. "He has already cut off communication with me and tricked my own soldiers. I have no doubt he will attempt to move them against me."

Mazen flinched. That sounded like Omar. Perfect, conniving, charismatic Omar. When he did not charm people, he pressured them into submission. That had always been Omar's way. In that, he was very much like their father had been.

The queen leaned forward. It was easier to see her frown between the parted clouds of smoke. "Now that Ziyad is gone, I cannot hope to reach the zuama'a as I did before. And even then, your half-blooded sultan remains on the throne. I am in no position to back away from a fight. If he or Nabila provokes me, I will reciprocate in kind. So I ask again, Mazen bin Malik..." Her eyes locked onto his, expectant. "What happens next?"

As his father's son, he knew his way forward was clear. He had a duty to retake the throne and the city he had been meant to rule. It was his responsibility to step into his father's shoes and to guide the country down a more peaceful path, one where no one—neither humans nor jinn—would fear a war. And yet the task felt impossible. How could he possibly manage such a thing from a throne? If ruling transformed people into pieces, how could he possibly save them all?

He should have said, *I will take back my throne and ensure there is peace.*

Instead, what he said was "We will stop the war before it starts."

The queen raised a brow but did not press him. If she thought him a coward, she did not say so. Mazen was glad when the door to her diwan opened, revealing the shadow attendant. She bowed when Basira's eyes fell on her. "Your Majesty. The wazir is awake."

Basira's face cleared as she stood. With one curt, decisive motion, she waved the smoke away to the edges of the room. For the first time since he had been summoned, Mazen beheld her appearance unhindered. As she had been upon their first meeting, she was dressed mostly in weapons. And then he saw the markings on her skin. He had never noticed them, faded as they were against the pallid shade of her flesh, but they bore a striking resemblance to the bindings on Rijah's arms. He ought to have realized sooner what they revealed about her.

Dead, he thought with amazement. The queen was as dead as the ghouls Aisha had controlled in the desert, and yet she spoke and acted as if she were alive. He did not want to think about how she had bound such a magic to herself through the wazir. Did not want to think what it would be like to tie your life to someone else's in such a way.

Basira must have noticed him staring at the scars; she quietly pulled down her sleeves. "I have not forgotten the deal I made with you and Loulie. A kingdom for a life. When you find out what your sultan's plan is, I will help you defeat him."

She dismissed him after that, freeing Mazen from both her company and the smoky chamber. He exited the room feeling heavier than when he'd entered. That was, until he beheld the person waiting outside for him. His heart eased at the sight of Hakim studying some scroll.

When he saw Mazen, he rolled up the piece of parchment and tucked it beneath his arm. "How did the negotiations go?"

Mazen stifled a sigh. "It was less a negotiation than an admission. I do not have a plan."

"Yet." Hakim lifted a brow. "You give yourself too little credit."

As always, Mazen was grateful for his brother's unwavering faith in him. Calm, patient, and compassionate, Hakim had always been reliable in times of strife. It was a shame that Hakim had not been the sultan's true son. Perhaps if the two of them had been related by blood, the sultan would have realized Hakim possessed the leadership qualities Mazen did not.

The thought startled Mazen. He shoved it guiltily to the back of his mind as he cleared his throat. "What about you? Any luck gathering information in the archive?"

"I have yet to find anything that will help us uncover Omar's plot, but..." His eyes glittered. "Have you seen how many *maps* Jubayr has drawn? He charted whole countries!"

Hakim's enthusiasm was infectious. Mazen felt himself relax as Hakim detailed his discoveries. In the week they had been here, his brother had practically lived in the archive, dedicating his time to searching for living documents that might help them devise their own plans.

Hakim tapped the scroll beneath his arm. "Do you know what this is? An old map of the marid routes. It reveals the ocean paths they used to travel between cities..."

Mazen's mind drifted to Ziyad as Hakim spoke. It was strange, to know the marid who had so long haunted their footsteps was gone, dead with vengeance still in his heart. Mazen would not soon forget the sight of his dead eyes staring into him as the queen interrogated his corpse.

Hakim must have noted from Mazen's silence that his mind was adrift. "Let us continue this conversation some other time. When you want to talk, you know where to find me."

By the time the two of them exchanged farewells, Hakim already had his map open and was scrutinizing it on his way back to the archive. Mazen smiled at his back before letting his gaze wander up to the sky. Some of his dread fell away when he saw the constellations—the *real* constellations hanging above him. The sight reminded him of the night he had ridden on a floating carpet with Loulie.

He remembered the wonder on her face, the unbridled joy as they floated amidst Rijah's magic. Suddenly, more than anything, Mazen wanted to see her. Wanted to see those beautiful eyes of hers, crinkled in a secret smile meant just for him.

For a moment, Mazen forgot his duties. He forgot his destiny. As he went searching for Loulie al-Nazari, he thought only of the merchant's smile, and of the promise he had made her.

Their survival was a miracle—and they would not waste it.

69

LOULIE

Amazingly, there were stars in the sky.

Loulie half expected the sight to vanish every time she looked away, but the jinn-made illusion had vanished, as had the threads of binding magic. In their place, familiar constellations illuminated a sprawling desert landscape.

It was the most beautiful thing she had ever seen.

"I thought I might find you up here."

She turned to see Mazen bin Malik ascending the final steps to the rooftop of their shared apartment, a lantern in hand. The ash-fire inside chirped cheerfully when it saw her. Azhar's trill made her grin. "The bird is as vocal as ever, I see."

Mazen smiled. It was a tired smile, but sincere. He settled the lantern on the roof as he sat beside her. The moment he unlatched the glass door, the firebird flitted excitedly to his shoulder. "I think Azhar likes the stars too."

She turned to look at them—the storyteller and his bird.

The first time she had met Mazen, he had introduced himself with a different name. *Yousef*, the starry-eyed scribe who spent his free time searching the souk for a storyteller. And then, when they had traveled together, he had worn his brother's face and called him-self Omar.

Perhaps that was why, for the longest time, Loulie had assumed he was a liar like the rest of his family. It was only when he'd shared his stories that she had realized the truth of him: even when he was in disguise, Mazen bin Malik always wore his heart on his sleeve. Before, she might have thought that a weakness.

Now she saw the smile on his face and felt a soft warmth kindle in her chest. She was unprepared when he flashed that smile at *her*, and that warmth burned to a deeper heat that made her heart flip.

She was the first to break eye contact. Her gaze skidded past him to the courtyard beneath them, where a circle of jinn stood. Before Mazen had arrived, she had been eavesdropping on them. Or, more specifically, eavesdropping on Qadir, who had been roped into the conversation.

Currently, he was weathering the questions of the few zuama'a who had pledged themselves to the queen with a long-suffering look on his face. Rijah and Aisha stood among the rabble, the former wearing an attentive grin as they nodded along with everything Qadir said and the latter looking exceptionally despondent. Loulie, who was not engaged in the conversation at all, was just as tired of watching.

Qadir must have felt her eyes on him. He looked up, saw her on the roof, and raised a sharp brow. When she palmed her forehead and let out a dramatic sigh, the brow only inched higher. The zuama'a must have caught the movement as well. They looked up, and when they saw her on the rooftop, they huffed and moved the discussion farther into the courtyard. Aisha's lips tilted in what may have been a smirk as she followed.

Loulie sighed. "Politicians are the same everywhere, aren't they? Vultures."

Mazen blinked at her. "Does that include me?"

"That depends. Do you consider yourself a politician?"

Mazen looked thoughtful at the question. He gazed into the distance, eyes roaming beyond Dhahab's broken walls and toward the rolling dunes. But Loulie knew he was looking farther into the distance, to a city neither of them could see.

Madinne. *Home.*

Aisha had already recounted the intel she had gathered from the queen. They knew about her broken deal with Omar—ifrit relics in exchange for soldiers—and they knew about Omar's attempts to craft a binding with Qadir's magic.

Every time Loulie thought of him torturing Qadir for that information, her skin crawled. It was because of *her* Omar had found out about the bindings at all. But what could she have done? Qadir had already chided her for apologizing.

There was also the matter of the missing ifrit relic—the ring Omar now wore on his finger. They would need to get it back before he used it for anything nefarious.

"I think..." Mazen sighed. "I don't know yet."

"Whether you're a scheming law appointer?"

"Whether I want the throne." The confession seemed to deflate him. When he looked away in shame, Loulie was almost offended.

"You don't think I would judge you, do you?" She frowned. "Look at what happened to Qadir. He became king and sunk an entire country." At Mazen's wide-eyed look, she waved a dismissive hand and said, "I doubt you could do anything so drastic on a throne, but my point stands. A throne is just a symbol. There are other kinds of power."

They both looked at the firebird, the most "drastic" show of power Mazen had ever flaunted. Loulie imagined that if Mazen wanted to, he *could* shape the ashfire into a dangerous magic, maybe even one he could use to take back Madinne. But she could not imagine him leading such a destructive conquest when, in his hands, the fire had always been a guiding light.

Mazen gently pet the bird on its head. The briefest of smiles touched his face when it released one of its melodious trills, but faded in the next moment. "I was born for the throne. My father *died* because he planned to bequeath it to me. My wants mean nothing."

"I don't care if you're born into magic *or* power. I believe we make our own destiny. And how many times do I have to remind you that your father was murdered?" She rested her elbows on her knees with a sigh. "If you want the throne, we'll take it back. If you don't..." She shrugged. "Then we find someone else. Or we let the vultures do it."

Mazen stared at her. "You would help me take back a city?"

"You followed me down into another *world*." Because she could already see him preparing an objection, she held up a hand and said, "You did have a choice. You could have stayed and given up. And when you came down here, you could have easily locked yourself away in your room and never come out. Instead, you..."

You chased after me on the Sandsea. You followed me through haunted ruins and into the dark. You risked your life to save me, time and again.

She swallowed. "You helped me. Let me help you."

Loulie had hoped for the words to bring a smile to his face and was not disappointed. That smile of his—the *genuine* smile that brightened his golden eyes and made him laugh—was one of the things she admired most about him. Even when he was suffering, he wore that smile sincerely. Not a shield, not a deflection, but the truth of him.

Perhaps that was why she felt so drawn to it—to *him*. Most of the men she had known preferred to cloak themselves in secrets. But there were no such barriers between her and Mazen. She knew who he was and whom he yearned to be. And he knew both sides of her as well—the merchant and the wanderer. It was a relief, to be known.

To be known by *him*.

There was that feeling again, that frenzied flutter in her stomach. It was a dizzying sensation, all the more so because she could not escape it. It was trapped inside her, a flurry of moths. It made her antsy, made her bold.

Before she realized what she was doing, Loulie had reached out to touch his cheek. When she turned his face toward her, his smile froze, wavered. This close, she could see how blown wide his eyes were, how intent his gaze on her had become. His cheek was warm beneath her fingertips, and she could feel the pounding of his heart—or was it hers?—against her skin.

"Loulie?" He spoke her name, softer than a whisper, but their faces were close enough she could feel it as a sigh on her own lips. She heard the question in his voice.

She did not know how to answer. There was just that feeling, that anticipation, building and building inside of her as his gaze latched on to her mouth, as he tilted her face and ran a finger across her lips, parting them with a light press of his thumb as he leaned in—

—and she pulled away, skin burning where he had touched her, breath rattling out of her in a stunned gasp. She had the peculiar feeling of resurfacing from beneath water, of drawing air into lungs that had moments ago been starved. Belatedly, she became aware of the distance between them, of the space *she* had rushed to carve out before their lips brushed.

Mazen was still staring at her, a dazed look on his face. His eyes were cloudy, consumed. Moments ago, the full intensity of that look had been pinned on *her*. The thought made Loulie tremble, though with want or panic she was not entirely certain. Slowly, Mazen drew away. As always, his expression was raw, a mixture of confusion and concern.

"I'm sorry," she blurted. Her mind had begun to whir, replaying what had just happened. She had wanted—she had *always* wanted—to trust someone like this. But distance had kept her safe. Distance had kept her *heart* safe. She had been lying to herself after all; there was still this—this one barrier she had always been too afraid to cross.

When his expression dampened, she shook her head, panicked. The last thing she wanted was to hurt him. But how could she explain this to him in a way that he wouldn't take personally? Words built in her chest, but before she could fumble through them, a motion in the trees caught her scrambled attention. A bird—a myna—sat watching them. It could have been a normal bird, but this one had a trained focus to its gaze.

Nabila.

How long had her spy been watching them? Or had it been watching the zuama'a?

She and Mazen rose at the same time. The firebird squawked, looking as though it might give chase if Mazen commanded. But then something strange happened: the ashfire flickered.

It was strange for two reasons. First, because every lit torch and lantern in the courtyard wavered in unison, as if disturbed by some strong breeze. Second, because the magic had been stable since Qadir had rekindled it on the surface. What could possibly upset it now?

The disruption came again. This time, the ashfire burned not low but *high*, shuddering so violently that even the jinn shrank away from the torches, suddenly alert. But it was the reaction of one jinn in particular that caught Loulie's attention.

Qadir stood rigid amidst the surging fire, shoulders tight, hands clenched at his sides. And as if *that* reaction was not alarming enough, Loulie had noticed that the ashfire was not the only magic that had been disturbed. The markings on Qadir's arms had begun to glow.

But no, that was impossible. They had unsealed all the bindings, had swept away any lingering traces of Qadir's magic from this world—

Except for the one in the Madinne palace. The one binding Qadir had finished to find her.

Loulie reached for Nabila's pearl before she could think. It warmed in her palm as she threw herself off the balcony. The wind caught her as she fell, softening her landing to a dull thud as she rushed toward Qadir.

At this point the ifrit had collapsed to his knees. A pang of terror ran through Loulie at the sight of him keeled over. She had never seen such naked terror on his face, never seen him look so small, so confused.

She reached out to touch his shoulder as she knelt, only to pull away when the markings on his skin *burned* her. "Qadir? What's happening?"

One by one, the ashfire-lit torches around them went out. The light in Qadir's eyes seemed to gutter with it. When he looked at

Loulie, the warm brown of his eyes was enshrouded in smoke. "I made a mistake," he managed.

Loulie was dimly aware of Aisha standing beside her. And then, moments later, Mazen had emerged from their apartment and was on her other side. The firebird made a nervous, warbling sound on his shoulder.

Aisha's expression was grim, her lips pressed into a thin line as she gave a rough shake of her head. "Only the binding in Madinne remains, but it is no longer connected to anything. Besides that, nothing can activate it except for Qadir's magic."

The thief said what Loulie already understood but with an uncertainty that made her heart shudder with fear. She turned back to Qadir, struggling to make sense of what she was seeing. The binding was connected to Qadir. Only *he* should have been able to use his magic. And yet...

"You said my brother carved marks into his own skin." It was Mazen who spoke. Mazen whose expression lit with sudden understanding as he looked at Qadir.

Aisha frowned, nodded. "Yes, but he still does not have magic in his blood."

Nothing but poison, Loulie thought. And yet a terrible understanding was beginning to dawn on her. They had assumed Omar was trying to anchor a binding to himself, but she remembered what Rijah had said about the magic needing a source of energy. And she remembered what Aisha had told them about the queen—about *her* connection to another living, breathing jinn.

As the last of the ashfire in the courtyard vanished, Loulie realized Omar had not been trying to imitate Qadir's magic at all; he had bound himself to it. He had bound himself to *Qadir*.

They had assumed their enemy's goal was to steal ifrit magics. But he had gone one step further by stealing the magic of a king.

Omar bin Malik had bound himself to the Ashfire King.

ACKNOWLEDGMENTS

After many drafts, much strife, and a startling number of real-life plot twists, it feels unreal to have reached the part of this sequel where I can reflect on the journey. *The Ashfire King* was a marathon, and I am incredibly grateful to the people who cheered me on to the finish line.

First, to my agent, Jennifer Azantian: Navigating this industry can sometimes feel like stumbling through the dark; I am incredibly thankful to have you as my guide. Thank you for always being there when I need the support and for being this series's fiercest advocate.

To my US and UK editors, Brit Hvide and Emily Byron: I am so grateful to you for reading the many drafts of this sequel and for providing the feedback that led me to this—the truest and best version of *The Ashfire King*. Finding this sequel's heart was like searching for a perfect pearl in the ocean; thank you for exploring the depths of the Sandsea Trilogy with me.

Thank you to Mike Heath for another gorgeous cover illustration and to Lisa Marie Pompilio for the design direction—Azhar has never looked more majestic! And to Tim Paul: I am so thrilled to see this world once again brought to life in one of your beautiful maps.

A huge shoutout to everyone on the US and UK Orbit teams for helping me transform this manuscript into a beautiful book, and for helping to get it into readers' hands. To my US team—Nick Burnham, Lauren Panepinto, Ellen Wright, Bryn A. McDonald, Stephanie A. Hess, Natassja Haught, Jo Wyckoff, Alexia E. Pereira—and to my UK team—Aimee Kitson, Maddy Hall, Nazia Khatun, Joanna Kramer, and Serena Savini—I couldn't have done this without you!

To Kamilah Cole: I promised you a paragraph in the acknowledgments if you were right about that one thing (you were), so here it is. But seriously, it's been such a joy to share the sequel journey with you. Thank you for reading *all* those drafts—complete and not!

To Gina Orlando: Thank you for bringing some much-needed levity to my brainstorming. I value all your suggestions...even when I can't, unfortunately, find a way to work in a random dance competition that will magically solve all my characters' problems. (If only!)

To Rochelle Hassan: Thank you for the sequel chats and for all your amazing comments and memes—especially the ones about the brothers.

To Monica Bee and Morgan Paine: I so appreciate your insightful notes and comments. Also, our chats about architecture, horses, and miscellaneous book things. Never a dull moment!

To the East Coast writing group: Maddie Martinez, Ysabelle Suarez, and Melissa Karibian. Whether we're all writing (commiserating) at a coffee shop or chatting over text, I am always thankful for the cheer and inspiration I find in your company.

To the immensely talented Sarah Mohand-Saïd: I will always be grateful to you for drawing this cast with so much love and care, and for all your incredible attention to detail in my preorder campaign art and beyond. Here's to more chaotic collaborations in the future!

To Will Bottoms: Thanks for listening to me talk in circles for *hours* about my worldbuilding and for helping me unknot plot threads. I always look forward to our bookish conversations.

To everyone who helped me brainstorm or provided feedback on specific parts of the outlines or drafts—Angeline Morris, Ben Baxter, Jasmine Peake, Arianna Emery, Gates Palissery, E. M. Anderson, Sara Schonfeld—thanks so much for your thoughts!

The lion's share of my gratitude goes to my family, whose unwavering belief in me has kept me afloat during the most difficult parts of this process. To my sister, Neesa: Thanks for all the sibling mischief and shenanigans, and for always encouraging me to take breaks. To Dad: Thank you for sharing the stories and histories that are a source of inspiration for this trilogy, and for all the map chats. To Mom: You are the best cheerleader a writer (and daughter) could ask for; I am so grateful to have celebrated every step of my publication journey with you. To Ichi, the sweetest of cats: Thanks for seventeen years of emotional support and joy. I miss you, buddy.

Last, I want to thank you, reader, for continuing with this series. The Sandsea Trilogy is near and dear to my heart, and it means so much to me that it's found a home on other bookshelves. Thank you for following these characters on their latest quest. I hope to see you at journey's end.

About the Author

Chelsea Abdullah is the award-winning author of the Sandsea Trilogy, an epic fantasy series that begins with *The Stardust Thief*. An American-Kuwaiti writer born and raised in Kuwait, she grew up listening to stories about mysterious desert creatures and wily (only sometimes likable) heroes. Consumed by wanderlust, she has put down roots in various states. After earning her MA in English at Duquesne University, she moved to the East Coast, where she currently lives. When not immersed in her own fictional worlds, she spends her free time playing video games, doodling characters and hoarding books she doesn't have the shelf space for.

Find out more about Chelsea Abdullah and other Orbit authors by registering for the free monthly newsletter at orbit-books.co.uk.